Praise for Catherine Kirwan

'Catherine Kirwan's deviously plotte[...]
vivid characters, distinctive dialogue and a detail[...]
loving portrait of the "real capital of Ireland" is captivating'
Irish Independent

'*Cruel Deeds* has a vividly drawn sense of place, an amused
eye for character, class and all manner of Corkishness
and, above all, in Finn a winning, vital lead character;
her vibrant energy and good humour animates and drives
the action at break-neck pace. Hugely enjoyable'
Irish Times

'Agatha Christie vibes with the added atmosphere and
intrigue of the murder occurring in a university. A great read'
Patrica Gibney

'A propulsive mystery that feels both fresh and assured'
Catherine Ryan Howard

'A clever twisty tale that feels completely
authentic; Catherine Kirwan is on to another
winner with *Cruel Deeds*. I loved it'
Jane Casey

'The believability of the characters is
undeniable. Powerful writing'
Woman

Pacy, gripping and atmospheric . . . a cracking read!'
Andrea Carter

'Twisty and ingeniously plotted . . . a real page-turner'
T.M. Logan

'Chock full of secrets and with a compelling
plot . . . will keep you glued to the pages!'
Lesley Kara

Catherine Kirwan grew up in the parish of Fews, County Waterford. She studied law at University College Cork and lives in Cork City where she works as a solicitor. She is the author of three previous legal thrillers featuring Cork solicitor Finn Fitzpatrick. *The Seventh Body* is her fourth book.

ALSO BY CATHERINE KIRWAN

A Lesson in Malice
Cruel Deeds
Darkest Truth

THE SEVENTH BODY

CATHERINE KIRWAN

HACHETTE
BOOKS
IRELAND

Copyright © 2025 Catherine Kirwan

The right of Catherine Kirwan to be identified as the Author of
the Work has been asserted by her in accordance with the
Copyright, Designs and Patents Act 1988.

First published in Ireland in 2025 by
HACHETTE BOOKS IRELAND

1

All rights reserved. No part of this publication may be reproduced, stored in
a retrieval system, or transmitted, in any form or by any means without the
prior written permission of the publisher, nor be otherwise circulated in any
form of binding or cover other than that in which it is published and without
a similar condition being imposed on the subsequent purchaser.

All characters in this publication are fictitious and any resemblance
to real persons, living or dead, is purely coincidental.

Cataloguing in Publication Data is available from the British Library

ISBN 9781399729536

Typeset in Bembo Book MT Std by Palimpsest Book Production Ltd,
Falkirk, Stirlingshire

Printed and bound in Great Britain by
Clays Ltd, Elcograf S.p.A.

Hachette Books Ireland policy is to use papers that are natural, renewable
and recyclable products and made from wood grown in sustainable
forests. The logging and manufacturing processes are expected to conform
to the environmental regulations of the country of origin.

Hachette Books Ireland
8 Castlecourt Centre
Castleknock
Dublin 15, Ireland

A division of Hachette UK Ltd
Carmelite House, 50 Victoria Embankment, London EC4Y 0DZ

www.hachettebooksireland.ie

For Rob and Nicola

ONE

Her blood.

Everywhere.

Inescapable.

The spray.

The seep.

But we dug and covered.

Bleach-cleaned till we nearly bled.

Made no difference.

Because the better part of us was buried with her and that's the truth.

Or maybe it isn't.

Maybe we were bad all along.

1

COMING UP TO MIDDAY, THE DOOR BURSTS IN.
Detective Sergeant Sadie O'Riordan. Her hair in a messy pony-
tail as usual, but she has on a black suit jacket, a white T-shirt
tucked into black trousers, and black Asics trainers. Normally
in the station, she wears a grey hoodie and brown leather
Birkenstocks with thick socks.

She narrows her eyes. 'What are you doing? Are you hiding
or something?'

'No?' It comes out like a question.

She makes a point of looking around. At the grimy disused
interview room. The slowly collapsing mountain of bloated
document boxes in one of the corners. The dim October
morning filtering queasily through windows not cleaned in a
decade or three.

Looking at me straight again, she says, 'There's no one else
here so it's just you and me. Get your butt out of that chair.
Unless you're welded to it. Are you?'

I press my fingernails hard into my palms and stand up.

'Apparently not,' she says.

Snapping my laptop shut, I stuff the loose pages I've been
working on into a file cover and follow her out through the

general office – quiet but far from empty, I notice – down the hall and stairs to the back door. She's taller than I am, with a longer stride, so it's an effort to keep up. Full disclosure, I haven't exactly been beating a path to the gym lately.

I've spent half the morning slogging through the statements for the burglary of a semi-detached house in Deerpark. Parsing the statements line by line. Listening to the recording of the complaint call that I requested specially and saved to a folder marked 'VARIOUS' on my computer. Doing all this – over-doing it – even though the case is as low level as it gets. Even though there used to be a time when an investigation like this wouldn't have cost me a thought.

Yeah, well, it does now. It's not just this one either. These days, I agonise over everything, second-guessing myself so often that I feel like someone permanently going the wrong way on an escalator.

I've ended up as lead detective on the Deerpark burglary because Fintan Deeley, the original lead, has gone up in the world. Because, in an ironic twist, he's been granted a dream transfer to the Garda National Bureau of Criminal Investigation – the GNBCI – in Dublin.

To the place I used to work, in other words, and I can't say it doesn't sting a little, or even a lot. Apart from anything else, Deeley's younger than me. Yet he's risen, while I'm lucky to be clinging on here by my fingernails.

In the car park I say, 'You told me there was no one else here.'

'You've got to get back on the horse sometime, Alice,' Sadie says. She throws the keys at me. I feel a foolish sense of achievement that I manage to catch them without fumbling. She says, 'You might get lucky. It actually could be a horse. I read somewhere that they used to bury horses' heads beneath the floors of houses for luck, I don't know, to keep the devil or the fairies away. Might be one of those. But whatever it is, it's no longer alive. You up for that?'

I feel the wind go out of me but manage to ask, 'Where are we headed?'

'The big building site around the middle of Barrack Street.'

'On the right going towards town?'

'That's the one.'

After starting the engine, I roll down the driver's-side window but traffic is heavy. We climb at crawling pace along the crammed, potholed streets, moving from riverside to higher ground, and the fresh cool air I need never comes. By the time we get to where we're going, my hands are leaving sweat marks on the steering wheel and I know that my face is as red as ketchup even though I don't dare look in the mirror to check.

Two high-vis-vested uniformed members shift the barrier erected at the four-way junction with Noonan's Road and Green Street, allowing our unmarked vehicle to pass. When we get through, on Sadie's 'Here's fine,' I swing the car into a tidy spot in front of Broderick's chemist at the top of the street. Behind us, on Bandon Road, is the Gallows pub.

Sadie pulls the elastic band from her hair – it's shoulder length – and gives it a quick comb through with her fingers, retying it more securely in a tight bun at the nape of her neck. I reach into the back seat for my GARDA-emblazoned rain jacket, a handy reminder of who I'm supposed to be.

We get out. She flips open the boot, hands me a white suit and a pack of shoe covers. 'You'll be fine,' she says, and my face gets even hotter as I realise she's noticed my discomfort.

But the short stroll downhill through the drizzle does me some good. We're walking on what used to be the main access route into the city from the west, a narrow road more suited to horse and foot traffic than motorised transport. The majority of the buildings along here are two or three storeys high, most at least a hundred years old, many older. Every door and window on the street and the skinny side alleys off it used to hold a shop or pub or other business, not all of them legal. If we had the time, and listened closely enough, maybe we could hear the ghosts.

'I told you you'd be fine,' she says, as we reach the site. 'Now, breathe, take notes and as many photos as you can. Keep a log. That's why you're here. Nothing you haven't done a million times before. It's like riding a bike.'

'No probs, skipper,' I say, double-blinking like a faulty wind-screen wiper.

Immediately inside the site perimeter, we suit up, don hard hats and bend to put on our shoe covers. She finishes faster, presumably because her hands aren't shaking. Pulling a notebook and pen from the inside pocket that also contains my phone, I go after her.

2

BEHIND PROTECTIVE HOARDINGS THAT PROMISE forty-six new apartments, the building site is extensive. What used to be here has been demolished, but nothing has been erected to replace it yet. It feels bleak and eerily quiet, the giant yellow and black machines stalled and empty.

I find Sadie in front of a Portakabin, surrounded by construction workers, silent and serious-looking. I stand beside her and listen. The first thing I find out is that the man facing her isn't a builder. Unshaven and slightly hunched, he has longish grey hair and looks about sixty.

'Yeah, right,' he says. 'We've been kind of expecting something like this. Watching for it. We're less than five hundred metres from the old gallows field up in Greenmount and there were numerous battles fought around here over the centuries too. It could be Viking, possibly, though it's not deep enough, I think, on my initial assessment. After that, take your pick. The Nine Years War, maybe? The Williamite War? We can't say with certainty yet, but . . .'

'You reckon it's probably old,' Sadie says. She turns to me, 'Detective Garda Alice McCann, this is Dr Tim Hanna, the resident . . . Em, what are you? What's your title?'

THE SEVENTH BODY

'I'm the director of excavations,' he says, 'because we're in a historic part of the city. I'm here under one of the planning conditions.' He grins like it's Christmas Day and Santa Claus has been extra generous.

I take down his name and contact details. Sadie nods her approval. As I write, I breathe more easily with every word. Old is nothing to worry about. Old is as okay as it gets.

'Tell us what happened, Tim,' Sadie says.

'It was shortly after eleven and the lad here, Johnny Mac,' he gestures to the man standing behind him, 'was digging out to the rear of what used to be Bertie Allen's pub.'

'Digging out how? By hand?' she asks.

'He was using a digger. We take the site down in layers. What's below is normally older than what's above. Archaeologists call it the rule of superposition. It's based on geological . . . Yeah, I guess you don't need to know that. When we find something that looks interesting, it's then we dig by hand. I was observing the works when I noticed a change in the soil conditions that led me to suspect an event.'

'An event?' Sadie asks.

'A change in colour. A cut into the level of the earth that might indicate something, a burial or . . . Anyway, I waved at Johnny Mac and told him to stop the machine. I then entered the area myself and, after some further excavation, I uncovered a section of what appear to be human skeletal remains. Given the depth, it's a possible criminal-law issue. I called for a halt to work and, as per protocol, I alerted An Garda Síochána and the city archaeologist. Uniformed gardaí arrived within about fifteen minutes and they set up an exclusion zone.'

'And the coroner's been notified too, obviously,' Sadie says. 'Come on, let's have a look.'

She and Dr Hanna set off at a diagonal across the open rutted ground. I hang back to take the name and contact details of the JCB driver: Johnny McDonagh from Galway, age thirty-four and as sulky as a teenager. That bleached, rangy west of Ireland look about him and eyes of the palest blue. Working via a construction agency. Here a few weeks. Specialist archaeological digger and mini-digger driver.

'Not intending on staying around long,' he says. 'Soon as the job's done, I'm off.'

I make a note for myself to double-check his home address with our guys up his way. He's a link in the potential chain of evidence so we have to be able to track him down if need be. Although, with an attitude like that, you'd hope to God he'd never have to give evidence.

Another man introduces himself. 'Artur Lewandowski. Site foreman. You need anything, you ask me. No one else.' A bear of a man with a delicate pink-skinned face, he says, 'The body is this way.'

3

YOU DON'T SEE IT COMING, THE THING THAT derails you. That's what I told other people, my family, my work friends, before they stopped calling. Truth is, back of it all, I've always known there's a flaw in me, that if something's going well, no matter how long it takes, I'll wreck it. I did my best to hide it, my flaw, worked so hard, but there was no escaping it.

Inside the inner cordon, there's a big tarpaulin erected on steel poles over the dig area and, beneath the makeshift tent, a lamp lights the scene.

I ask, 'Who erected the tent?'

Dr Hanna replies, 'We did. To protect the area. After we saw that.' He points to the indistinct line of earth that indicates the grave site. 'That's the fill there,' he says, 'where the earth was replaced on top of the body.'

It doesn't look like much – less of a different colour than a marginally different grade of the same colour – but he's the expert. I take notes and more photographs than we'll ever need with my phone. I'm not the official photographer but I'm using my phone to keep a record of initial impressions of the scene. It's essential work because, if this does end up being declared a crime scene, every stage of the process must be noted. You can't predict what defence counsel will seize on. As I know to my cost.

Sadie will make an assessment, based on what we discover, and report back to the superintendent. He's the one who designates it as a crime scene or not. For now, we're acting as if it is, because a case is always live until it isn't.

Dr Hanna gets down on his knees, steadying himself on one of the thick planks of scaffolding wood edging the digging area. He's wearing milky latex gloves, his large bony hands like monstrous chicken feet. Leaning carefully over the dig area, he points to the item that caused him to alert the authorities. It looks like a dark brown stick.

'It's too big to be anything but a femur, a thigh bone,' Hanna says, straightening up again. 'Now that you're here, can I continue?'

Sadie says, 'Given what you've said about the likely age of the find, I don't see why not. But you'll need to wear one of these outfits just in case.' She unzips and digs out the car keys. 'Detective McCann will sort you out.' She hands me the keys. 'Fast as you can. Bring a few. And extra masks, shoe covers and gloves.'

The crowd of builders has moved from the Portakabin to the edge of the inner cordon around the tented area by the time I return. I pass a suit, gloves, mask and shoe covers to Dr Hanna.

I say to him, 'You'll need new gloves, and you should put up the hood. Your hair.'

'Do you not like it?' he asks.

'I just mean . . .'

He laughs. 'It's not my first rodeo.'

Sadie addresses the builders like their hearing-aid batteries are running low. 'Move away, lads.' She turns to me then and, not quietly enough for my liking, says, 'Keep them back. Remember why you're here. Make yourself useful.'

She's treating me like a raw recruit but my anger morphs into shame as I recall that, in the months since I've moved here, I've given her no reason to think she can rely on me.

After Hanna lowers himself into the trench – hip height and the size of two jagged double beds – I side step to a spot beside the lamp so that my photographs will be well-lit.

'Here goes,' Hanna says, but he doesn't move straight away. He stands and surveys the area afresh, his head bent, arms hanging loosely by his sides. He holds a small trowel in his right hand and a tiny scraping tool in the other.

He kneels and, painstakingly slowly, centimetre by centi-metre, removes the soil to the left of the original excavation area. As he works, I monitor the smell: reassuringly musty. In time, he exposes a second, third and fourth bone, all smaller than the first.

He looks up. 'This is part of the ribcage,' he says, 'not where I'd expect to find it.'

I hear myself ask, 'What does it mean?' My voice sounds strange to me.

He replies, 'I'll tell you as soon as I know.'

The minutes slow and the buzz of the city quietens. The only thing that matters is happening down in the trench in front of me. Hanna moves back to the line of the first bone and concentrates on the area above it, using the tools and his gloved fingers gently to prise the earth free. All of a sudden, he stops and angles his head backwards so that he can look up at Sadie. He pulls down his mask, smiles.

'More ribs, DS O'Riordan,' he says. 'I think there are two of them.'

4

HE'S WRONG. THERE ARE FOUR SKELETONS IN THAT grave, all of them tea-stained the colour of the rich earth in which they're buried. The bodies lie head to toe, face up in a terrible rictus, their arms and hands stretched behind their backs, as if they've been bound, knees bent, their feet likely to have been bound too, though nothing remains of the bindings or of any clothing.

Hanna says, 'The way they're buried appears hurried and disrespectful. Careless.'

A few days later, a double burial is discovered, upper bodies only, both lower skeletons missing, perhaps as a result of previous building work or another post-mortem disturbance, any alternative explanation being too terrible to contemplate. Six bodies in total in less than a week.

A shock to see them, the skeletons, I'm not going to say otherwise, but the shock fades. None of them is my fault or my responsibility. They're dead a long time – a few hundred years at least, according to Dr Hanna's estimate, though the full set of scientific tests will take time – which means that the chances of a garda inquiry are zero.

But the word is out that bones have been discovered and half the town wants to drop in for a gawk. Quickly, the policing emphasis switches to management, and to health and safety. Inside the excavation area, the archaeologists are running the show. Uniformed mules from the Bridewell are in charge of securing the site overall and ensuring only authorised persons have access, but the exclusion zone is now limited to the site itself and the footpath just outside it. For days, I've been the only detective on the street. I've had little to do and a lot of time to think.

Like how it is that a person who died hundreds of years ago matters less than someone who died more recently, and why. The quick answer? Because there's no one left behind to miss them, and no one alive to blame.

Which brings me to another question. What am *I* still doing here? The others don't need or want me. I'm like a lonely kid at Halloween, wandering aimlessly in my white crime-scene costume day after day, taking a photo or note every so often.

That said, I'm glad of the mask. Wish I could wear it the whole time.

'You're performing an important role for us,' Sadie had lied, as she shook the dust off and returned to base – metaphorically, because there's no actual dust. As more rain falls and more boffins arrive to examine the finds, the boggier it becomes, wellies a prerequisite for navigating the puddles and the clinging, sucking, Glastonbury-worthy mud.

I think back to something else Sadie said, in her office at Coughlan's Quay a few days before all this. 'Just a chat,' she'd said, 'about how things are going for you.' She was smiley. Warm, encouraging, leaning back in the chair, all casual like.

She'd beckoned me in as I was passing on my way back from

the photocopier. Pulled out a seat for me and shut the door so fast I didn't realise what was happening. Hadn't a chance to escape. Felt jolted backwards at first, but I gathered myself. 'I'm doing great. Good. Really feel like I'm starting to fit in.'

'Glad to hear it,' she said, after a pause that felt longer than it was, 'but remember you've plenty of other options, both within and outside the force. No shame in any of those choices either. You made detective however many years ago, but it's not a life sentence. What d'you reckon? Any thoughts?'

'One or two, maybe.'

'Right,' Sadie said, and then, her tone just as casual, 'because there's no room for passengers here at Coughlan's Quay.'

'I get that, of course.'

'And there *is* the formal date with the Cig. Which is out of my hands, obviously. Four weeks, to be precise, actually, that meeting.'

She meant my upcoming performance review with Inspector Feeney. Which is make or break for me. If I don't pass muster, I'm out. Back in uniform at best. Trouble is, Feeney's an old-school hard man. Less carrot, more stick.

'Shape up or ship out, McCann,' he says to me, every time I pass him in the hall.

I said to Sadie, 'I haven't forgotten about the review.'

'I didn't think you had.' Another smile. Less convincing, this one. 'And remember, my door's always open. Unless it's shut, of course. Might be doing my nails, or something.'

I laughed slightly more than the joke deserved.

'You don't do enough of that, you know,' Sadie said. 'Go on, get to it.'

After the 'just a chat', I'd scuttled back to sit at what should have been my desk. Thirty seconds I lasted before retreating again to what had become my semi-official lair, the aforementioned grubby interview room, rarely used by anyone except yours truly, knowing that when Sadie passed by later she'd be annoyed or disappointed not to see me in my rightful place.

A feeling of drenching uselessness then, even though Sadie and I aren't far apart in age, and could easily be the same rank by now. Not just the same. Me outranking her wouldn't have been beyond the bounds of possibility at one stage. Now the chances of that are as remote as an undiscovered moon in a faraway galaxy.

Funny thing is, I used to see it as my superpower on the job. My flaw, I mean. I thought it gave me X-ray vision. Used to think, if inside I'm a mess, I can see other people.

Suspects, I mean, scrabbling to come up with the right story, the one that'll get them out of trouble. I'd probe and I'd poke till they'd crack open like a Kinder Egg. Till they'd spill their spangly guts for me, signing confessions like stage-door autographs.

Whenever it happened, I never thought it was because I was good at my job. I thought it was because I'd got lucky that one day.

That it was only a matter of time before I was found out.

Fallen.
   Faded.
   Factories closed.
   Think Detroit.
   Think Cork too.
   Nothing left but the tunes.
   The beats.
   Deep and low and slow.
   Smog overhanging the city.
   Keeping the music in.

5

I'VE TAKEN TO CALLING ON ARTUR LEWANDOWSKI, the foreman, in his Portakabin, when I hit the site in the mornings. A tad later as we enter week two, but not indecently so: my ins and outs are being faithfully recorded by whatever hapless junior is staffing the access point.

'How's tricks?' he asks, with a rising cadence, the Kraków accent nearly vanquished by a decade and a half on Leeside. My own native tones are returning too, growing stronger as the months pass.

'Ah, sure you know yourself, like,' I say.

'This fucking shit,' he says. 'My completion schedule is gone out the window. All I want to do is build my fucking apartments. Why such a big delay?'

'Don't ask me,' I say. 'It's different from what I'm used to as well.'

Which brings me back to why I'm still here.

Out of harm's way is the conclusion I've come to. Out of sight, out of Sadie's mind. And Inspector Feeney's. An attempt to buy me time before the review. Or maybe she thinks the fresh air will help to shake me out of my paralysis.

If that's her reason, despite the constant rain, she's not wrong.

The space she's given has led me into considering things. These last few nights at home, and during the endless days on the site, however vaguely, I've started turning over what the other options she mentioned in her office might be. I haven't got much beyond surmising that a jump is better than a push, that honest labour somewhere else has to be an improvement on the hiding and worrying I've been doing. That a complete change of scene might be what I need. Somewhere far away from the reminders. Away from humans in general, maybe.

'Fucksake,' Artur says, 'you want coffee?'

'Just had one, thanks.' His coffee is stuck-together mouse-coloured powder and comes out of a jar. 'What's going on anyway?'

'Moving inside the back wall of the pub today, at fucking last,' he says, 'where it used to be. I had to bring back a couple of guys to help lift the floor. Fucking archaeologists, destroying my fucking life. You too, huh?'

'Chalk it down,' I say, an expression I haven't used since I don't know when. It's all coming back to me. Whether I want it to or not.

Like the job I used to do. Not the whole job, part of it. Something I got diverted into because I got results. Interviewing sex offenders. Nasty men. The nastier the better.

They liked me. Said things to me they wouldn't say to anyone else. Because I was nice to them. I smiled. Made them consoling cups of sweet tea.

I was thinner back then. Smaller. They liked that too.

6

I LEAVE ARTUR AND CIRCLE AROUND THE BACK of the site, approaching the excavation from the rear. Easier to move than yesterday. Someone has laid a path of hardcore, rough but serviceable, and a big improvement on what was here.

The former Bertie Allen's pub looks like it's been bombed from the air. The roof is gone, but for a few horizontal laths, like bony fingers, stretching across the gap. The front and one of the side walls are all that remain of the structure, two sides of a right-angled triangle, steel girders holding them in place.

Everything is gone from inside too, no bar counter or shelving or tables or benches. The marks left by removed ceilings, the rectangles in the peeling paint where pictures once hung and windows blocked with rotting plywood give the only clues to what was here before.

Artur's men have already lifted some of the flagstones from the floor and stacked them by the side wall. They're rectangular, in good condition, and look like high-quality stone, the kind of thing you'd find in a salvage yard. I figure that an enterprising member of the building crew – Artur himself maybe – will ensure that that's exactly where they'll end up.

I take up a position beside one of the lamps. There are three today, and the extra two are needed: with the heavy cloud cover, and despite the missing roof, the walls cast more shadows and steal more light than you'd expect. It's presumably for that reason that, although the archaeology team have put up the tent poles, they've held off raising the tarpaulin. Plus, by now, it's several days since anything's been found.

And yet I sense an air of anticipation, but it's not about what might be lying beneath the floor. It's because this is the last plot to be explored. After this, the builders will be able to start and the archaeologists will move on to their next dig, or to writing up this one. I'll be going too, back to Coughlan's Quay station and the decision I have to make. Before it's made for me.

As the morning passes, the work goes on with an almost pleasant hum. The floor is being excavated in strips. As each length is removed, the mini-digger, operated by Johnny McDonagh, moves in. I'm watching closely but I'm wearing ear protectors and the effect is almost hypnotic. The flagstones lining up. The careful digging and scraping and shifting of earth. Mission accomplished, or near enough.

But in the early afternoon, as everything feels like it's winding down for the day, the director of excavations, Dr Hanna, starts to wave frantically. Surprised, I yank back my right ear protector. He's shouting, 'Stop the machine. Stop it now.'

I step forward. 'What is it?'

Hanna points to an area near where the rear corner of the pub would have been, by the still-standing side wall. 'There, close to what was a fireplace, do you see the line of the chimney running up along? The change in soil colour alongside? It's another event.'

'Is it a burial?'

'No way of telling this early. Could be utilities. Pipes or cables often show up where they're not supposed to be.'

'What's next? Take up the rest of the flagstones?'

'Not yet. We need to move more slowly. We'll trowel back by hand to clean up the loose soil beneath the edge of the stone floor to get a better look at the shape of the cut.'

I note the time and Hanna's words, and take a couple of photographs. He observes and carries on a running commentary while two of the other archaeologists – Lorcan and Eileen, both hand-knit-jumper folkie types in their late twenties to early thirties – do the close work. Eileen – Dr O'Hara – is a forensic archaeologist, one of the specialists who descended after the first find.

'The curve is broader and flatter than I'd expect with utilities,' Hanna says.

'Shovel marks,' Eileen says. 'Not at all like what we've seen on this excavation up to now. They look more . . .'

'More what?' Hanna asks, but before she has a chance to answer there's a shout from Lorcan.

'Something here. And it's not a water pipe. Give us a second.'

He and Eileen work on for what feels like an hour but is only nine minutes because I've noted the time of Lorcan's water-pipe shout.

When it comes to what they ultimately find, there are no words from Lorcan and Eileen. Silently, they move back and get up from where they've been kneeling. At last, we can see what they've seen. The mini-digger driver. Hanna and the three other archaeologists who've left what they've been doing else-where and come to watch. Artur's two men who lifted the flagstones. Artur himself who, by some instinct, has emerged from his Portakabin in time. We can all see that this is different.

A jolt of electricity courses through me. Immediately, I get out my phone and call Sadie. With adrenaline pumping, muscle memory kicks in and my voice doesn't wobble. Like riding a bike, Sadie had said, and I'm determined not to fall off this time.

'You need to get here. We have a crime scene. A body that isn't ancient history.'

'How do you know?'

I say, 'It's the shoes.'

7

THE SHOES ARE PLATFORM TRAINERS, LIKE THE SPICE
Girls used to wear. For that reason, even though assuming
anything at a crime scene is a cardinal sin, the assumption I
make from the start is that the body is female. From the start,
I think of her as 'she'.

For a long time, they're all I can see of her, those shoes, their
thick blue synthetic soles, and what look like the bones from
one of her legs. I study the scene, take photographs.

A while after, Sadie and the rest of the team arrive. She comes
to stand beside me at the edge of the dig area, as the buzzing
swirl and chatter of the crime scene assembles around us, and
the white tent and the plastic tape go up, and the step pads go
down.

She asks, 'What do you think?'

'Based on the angle of the shoes, the soles, the body was
buried in a face-down position. Female and young, probably,
but not a small child. The shoes look too big.'

Sadie doesn't disagree. 'Size five or six?'

'Yeah,' I say.

'Remind me, when were they a thing? Those trainers?
Nineties?'

'Mid to late. The Spice Girls' "Wannabe" was 1996 so I'm guessing after that.'

'And I'm guessing you didn't need to google that date,' Sadie says.

I smile. 'You guess correctly. I was totally obsessed.'

'So our girl could be in the ground twenty-six, twenty-seven, twenty-eight years?'

'Maybe she was into vintage. The shoes may not be all that helpful in dating her.'

'Except they do tell us that she's late twentieth century at the earliest. That she's different from the others.'

I reply too fast and too sharply: 'Stating the *very* obvious, yes, they *do* tell us that.'

Sadie darts a look at me. 'Are you okay? Do you need to take a break?'

I know that she wouldn't have asked anyone else that, though I take the question at face value, reckon it's kindly meant. But it also confirms how fragile she thinks I am. Or second rate. Not up to the job any more.

She could be right. The harder I worked at my old job, the better my results, the worse I felt, and I kept driving on, not wanting the wheels to come off, not willing to stop and check if they might.

And the problem might have been a confession too hastily obtained, the wrong statutory warnings given, say. But that wasn't it. It was simpler. So basic you won't believe it.

Taking a breath, I say, 'No break necessary. I really am fine.' After a while, I add, 'As she's face down, that could mean speed. Or that whoever did it didn't want to look at her afterwards. Too ashamed, maybe. Or too sad. Might have been close to her.'

Sadie makes no reply and I don't know what to think about that but I shelve my concern because I'm concentrating on what's happening in front of me. The official garda photographer is crouching on the edge of the pit and Noel Tobin is in it. He's a SOCO, a crime-scene specialist.

Tobin says, 'The body is lying prone,' confirming my initial impression.

'What's the burial depth?' Sadie asks.

'About one and a half metres. Less than five feet.'

She looks at me, expecting me to say something. It's like she's testing, reminding, ensuring I keep focused. I can't think of anything incisive so I make a stab at a general comment.

'That's closer to the surface than the other bodies,' I say, 'not that I'm suggesting they're related though at this point we can't rule anything in or out.' I add, 'The bones look paler than the first six. Lighter brown. Why is that?'

Dr Eileen O'Hara replies, 'This one hasn't been in the ground as long as the others.'

Sadie asks, 'Is that skin? The white?'

Eileen O'Hara says, 'No skin left. The white substance around where the buttocks would have been is adipose tissue. Body fat.'

Noel Tobin says, 'There are some fragments of clothing adhering, too. The colour and fabric aren't identifiable in these conditions. Could be underwear. There may be more to see on the other side after we turn her.'

A northern-accented whine behind us says, 'I see ye started the party without me.'

I jump. It's a voice I haven't heard since my GNBCI days. It belongs to Professor Barney Friel, the state pathologist, a Derry man. He's nearing retirement but still tall and straight. In his youth, he was much thinner than he is now, hence the nickname 'Boney'. He's a familiar figure to anyone who's ever watched the news on television or attended a murder trial. He's based in Dublin, and more often than not the local assistant state patholo-gist would work a case in the Cork area. I wonder how he's got down here so fast, and why.

Without anyone asking, he says, 'I was giving a guest lecture in the university when I heard. A good excuse to nip away speedily afterwards. If the other option is small-talk and plonk, give me a decent set of bones any day.'

Sadie greets him and says, 'You know Alice McCann?'

'Of course,' he says, without meeting my eyes. 'We've run across each other before when Alice, ah, worked in Dublin.'

He lowers himself into the pit with a grunt and starts muttering observations into a handheld digital recorder. He confers quietly with Noel Tobin and takes a few steps back. Tobin bends over the body again.

We lapse into silence because they've exposed her hair. It looks like a cheap plastic wig, shoulder length. Bleached blonde – there are dark roots – and loose because there's no scalp remaining. The hair is sitting oddly. It reminds me of something. As Noel Tobin teases it from the skull, vertebrae and shoulder-blades, I feel a shiver up the back of my neck.

'Wait,' I say, 'is there a hair tie? Are there two?'

I'm remembering a nineties hairstyle, a small bunch, or pigtail, each side of the head, the rest of the hair left loose.

'Looks like there's something here,' Noel Tobin says. 'We'll do a comb through in the lab. If there are any threads or traces, we'll find them.'

He bags the hair. He's efficient. You can get good at anything with practice.

Boney Friel moves in over the body again. Every so often, he asks the officers to angle the lamps to illuminate his areas of interest. As time goes on, I realise how dark the twilight has become. Night is almost full when he stands back and says, 'Ready?'

Three of the SOCOs slip a waterproof mat beneath the body and roll it as gently as they can, exposing the front. The ribcage. The white adipose powdery substance marking her breasts. The place her face used to be. And the damage done to it.

8

THE REASON BONEY FRIEL WON'T LOOK ME IN the eye? The thing I did to end up working down here instead of being still in Dublin at the GNBCI?

It was a faulty search warrant. Unintentional, but my fault and no one else's. Because I was rushing. Wanting to get the job done faster, better, sooner. Before the perpetrator could do it again.

A young white Irish woman walking to the corner shop to buy milk at eleven o'clock in the morning. Emma Nicholls. She waived her anonymity afterwards.

A stranger rapist with a knife. No need to burden you with his name.

The kind of crime that leads to lurid tabloid headlines, brings baying crowds and steel barriers to courthouse steps.

It was the wrong paperwork. No big deal, you might think, nothing fatal, but it pulled the thread of the case, and the whole carefully built edifice came tumbling down.

Mistrial declared.

We walk away from the dig area with Boney Friel.

'What do you reckon?' Sadie asks him.

He says, 'I'll stay in Cork tonight so that I can do a full examination in the morning. And, no, before you ask, I don't know how long the body's been buried. The most I can do for now is confirm what you know already. That it looks like a young female with blunt force trauma to the skull.'

I ask, 'Were the injuries inflicted before or after? Were they the cause of death?'

'I've said all I can for now. Anything else would be speculation and that's not my job last time I checked.'

He looks past me as he adds, 'A wee reminder, Alice, that if any bones have become dislodged in the course of moving her and placing her in the body bag, I want each item bagged and labelled separately and added into the main body bag.'

I squirm as he goes on, 'What I'm saying is, and I'm sure I don't need to,' meaning he absolutely *does* feel the need, 'but do bear in mind, Alice, please, that not every fragment may belong to her.' He raises his eyes to the darkening sky and makes as if to say something else but instead shakes his head and stays silent. He takes off his mask and gloves and rubs his face, damp from the rain, as if he's scrubbing it clean.

As he walks away, I say, 'I should've left my dunce's cap at home this morning.'

Sadie says, 'Aren't we lucky to have Boney around to mansplain things to us?'

'Em, I think he was just talking to me.'

'Whatever. He didn't need to say it but that never stopped him. And looking up to the heavens for guidance? He's always been a pain, full of his own importance.'

'Thanks,' I say.

She gives me a look that tells me there's only one way to thank her and that's by doing my job. Doing it right.

❖

There had to be a full retrial of the Emma Nicholls case.

The expense of it. The extra risk of an acquittal, the prosecution case weaker than the first time around. The added trauma for Emma of having to give evidence a second time. All of it my fault. Even when the accused was convicted ultimately by majority verdict.

Afterwards, Emma talked to the media, told her story, named and blamed me, my incompetence, my negligence.

Emma only told the truth. She said nothing about me that I didn't already know.

9

AFTER BONEY FRIEL LEAVES, THE CRIME-SCENE
manager makes the decision to shut the site down until 8.30
a.m., fifteen minutes after sunrise, the sun being very much a
theoretical proposition, given the incessant drizzle. On television, when a body is found, the police work on in the dark,
with tiny pin-light torches. Here, it's hard enough to see during
daylight hours with three lamps.

Also, there's the thorny issue that, even though the flagstones
were lifted in strips, no record was kept of their specific location,
which means that no one can say for sure yet under which of
them the body was found, and no one appears to have noticed
if there was anything different about how the relevant stones
were set before they were removed. The labourers will have to
be spoken to individually and each and every one of the flagstones examined and, where necessary, bagged up, taken away
for lab analysis, and any person who's touched them swabbed
for elimination purposes. For now, they're left where they've
been stacked.

We check for alternative access routes and ensure that a
uniformed garda is stationed at every possible ingress point. The
merry band of rubberneckers with phones, as well as genuine

journalists, is back, clambering over each other like puppies to get as close as they can to the action. But the street is closed off again. This time it will be shut for longer.

Sadie calls us together. 'Go home, everyone,' she says. 'I'll see ye at seven a.m. We'll have a run-through first thing and allocate duties. The most important thing is to keep an open mind. The investigation is at a preliminary stage. All we know for certain is that a body has been found. Remember that it hasn't yet been formally confirmed if it's male or female and that we don't know when it went in there.'

A few minutes later, I see her standing at the traffic barrier in the glare of the camera lights, beside Detective Inspector Shane Feeney – the future judge, jury and executioner in my upcoming performance review – as he delivers more or less the same speech to the waiting press. Feeney is about six foot, black hair turning grey, mid-fifties, weekend cyclist. He does a passable impression of a genial man of the people, with an unthreatening generic culchie garda accent that I can't quite pin down to a specific county. In reality, he's a shark – seriously good at his job with a nose for the politics of it – and he allowed me to transfer down here when no one else would take me. I should be grateful to him. Except part of me figures he only gave me the chance so that he could be the one to experience the pleasure of firing me.

The hands in the air and the neverendingness.
  Like we were caught in the middle of a tornado.
  In a good way.
  You see, for a long time, it was nothing but good.
  Love everywhere. No shortage.
  Ours to share.
  All of us equal. Everybody the same.
  No barriers. No prejudice.
  So much love.
  None of us remembering the thin line.

10

INSTEAD OF GOING HOME, I HEAD TO THE STATION
at Coughlan's Quay, to my own spot in the general office for
the first time in weeks. My desk is set facing a blank wall,
slightly apart from the rest, with a row of filing cabinets for
company and no distractions, which should be good. Except
that the others at the desks behind can see me, but I can't see
them, so I never know who's watching, or if anyone is. It makes
me uneasy. It's one of the reasons I retreated to the interview
room.

Adjusting the seat so that it's comfortable and the right height,
I anchor my feet on the floor and place my palms flat on the
desk for a long moment. I grab a Kleenex from a small packet
in the top drawer and give the surface a wipe, and the keyboard.
I crumple the dusty tissue into a ball and dump it in the bin.

I walk to the disused interview room. Stand breathing in the
dust when I get there. It was a terrible thing that I did. The
mess I'd caused. Unforgivable.

Bad enough by itself, but the ripple effect on other people's
careers.

And because I'd been trusted, because other people had relied
on me, it became their fault as much as mine.

Because the buck stopped with them, the bell tolled for them too.

I shove my laptop and files under my arm. Slam the door behind me.

On the way back to the general office, I stop off in the kitchen, another place I've been avoiding. I stick a teabag into a white mug, badly stained with tannin but clean, and snap on the kettle. In the fridge, I find a multi-pack of full-sized Twixes – I don't know who they belong to but they're replaceable. I take one and, after smelling the milk, stick with black.

Returning to the general office, I fire up my desktop and start checking the missing-persons database. Date of birth. Date missing. Location. Last seen wearing.

More than nine thousand people go missing in Ireland every year. Many want to disappear and many are found quickly, alive or dead. Then there are the others.

I don't know enough for an effective search so any scrolling I do now is a waste of time. I do it anyway. Apart from anything else, it will remind me of what we don't know yet and what we need to find out. We don't have an age. We don't know for certain that she's female. We don't know her height or her exact shoe size. We don't know if she's Irish or if she's come from another jurisdiction. We don't know how long she's been buried, if she was killed where she was found or moved there from somewhere else. The post-mortem and lab tests will provide some answers but that means waiting, and waiting can be the hardest part of an investigation. I feel the old impatience in my stomach, the desire to get on with it. After all this time, it comes as a relief. But it shouldn't. I need to watch it. It's what makes me careless.

As if on cue, as if I *am* being watched, the text message pings: *Tough day?*

A second message ninety seconds later. Nine hugging hearts. One more emoji than last time. No way to know if the number difference is deliberate. Probably is.

Might not be.

Shouldn't matter.

But it does. Messes with my head.

Quiet for four minutes – longer break than normal – until the third message: *Mind yourself.*

I wait, but that's it. No follow-up tonight. Three messages, not four, though the fourth could come at any time. When I'm going to bed. When I turn off my light.

A pounding in my head. In out, in out with the breath. Faster first, then slower.

And, after that, the usual.

Delete. Delete. Delete.

Forget. Forget. Forget.

Try to.

11

THE PUBLIC-OFFICE DOOR SWINGS OPEN AND OLLY
Fogarty ambles in.

'Well, look who's here,' he says.

He comes and stands over my desk. He's another one out of Garda Central Casting. A big soft country boy, amiable, and a lot cleverer than he looks. I catch a whiff of alcohol from him. A few after-work pints that I haven't been invited to join in although, even if I had been, I'd have said no. Better, in a way, not to be asked.

'What are you doing here so late? You heard the boss. We're in at seven.'

'I could ask you the same question.'

'I left something here, a prescription I collected this morning for the missus, some woman's thing. I could tell you but then I'd have to kill you. Didn't want to go home without it, especially as one pint turned into three. Fuck. And now I've to take a taxi. Unless?'

'Sorry. I'd give you a lift, of course, only I didn't bring a car this morning. From my place, with all the one-ways, it's easier to walk across town to Barrack Street than drive.'

'Stroll away, so.'

'I will in a while. I just wanted to do something or feel like I was doing it. I was there when she was found. I knew immediately she was different from the others.'

'That's some shitty detail the skipper's had you on for the last couple of weeks. She should've rotated you. And there's a few who might say you shouldn't have been there at all, that there was no need for detective cover, but in retrospect she was right. Sadly, she always is. She's going to be even more insufferable now.'

I laugh. He and Sadie have been the best of work buddies for years.

'I was fine with the job,' I say. 'No need to feel sorry for me.'

'Ah, now,' he says, and I can tell that's exactly how he feels, about this and in general. I'm surprisingly okay with well-meaning pity, though. It beats most of the alternatives.

'Go home,' Fogarty says. 'That's where I'm going, to my lovely partner Mia and the screaming changeling the teething fairies have substituted for my beautiful baby daughter.'

It's no secret that Mia's pregnancy had come as a shock to him, in what he'd considered a casual relationship, and that she wasn't the only woman he'd had on the go at the time. But they seem to be making it work.

'You poor guy. Will you get any sleep at all?'

'I'm so tired I'd sleep on a rock so, you never know, I might. You're going?'

'Yeah,' I say.

After he's gone, I take the cup back to the kitchen, rinse it out and leave it upside down on the draining-board, making a mental note to bring in a washing-up sponge at some mythical point in the future.

I walk home through town, passing empty fast-food places and closed-down shops, like broken teeth. It's apocalyptically quiet. The in-between time. The work and the after-work crowd gone, the only activity the silent queue for the evening soup kitchen beneath the canopy of what used to be the Savoy night-club and shopping arcade; before that a grand cinema where women in furs and men in dinner suits posed for old-style flashbulb cameras.

I pause for a while on the eastern footpath at the centre of Patrick's Bridge, where the city opens to the moonless night sky. I think about the ocean, miles away at the edge of the harbour, forever waiting on the river. I think about the girl and the decades she's been waiting.

12

SENIOR MEMBERS OF THE FORCE HAVING TO apologise, take part in endless Garda Ombudsman – the dreaded GSOC – inquiries, deal with press scrutiny. Forget about Emma Nicholls and what she had to go through, what about nearly bringing my superiors down? Exposing their delicate posteriors to cool winds? It turned out *that* was the truly unforgivable sin.

Especially when one of the superiors affected was my long-term boyfriend, Detective Inspector Calum Pierce. The man I loved. Shared my life with. Had a joint savings account with. Had bought a two-bedroomed apartment in Phibsboro with. Was expecting to marry. Which didn't happen.

Because he dumped me faster than you can say 'Suspended with full pay pending investigation.'

I live halfway up the right-hand side of Wellington Road, where it gets steep, in one of the unpainted dark plaster mansions, with an unkempt terraced garden at the front falling down to Summerhill. I enter via the back door. There's a spongy grey carpet on the wide period staircase, its carved beauties cloaked in centuries of white gloss paint, and it's an easy hop up to my flat. First floor and everything magnolia, but it's got a spectacular view – the rooftops, the water, the lights and, when it's clear, the green hills edging the city.

Even without the view, it would be in high demand. There's nowhere for rent in Cork. It's only available to me at all, and at a semi-affordable price, because my parents are friends with the owners, a cute-as-a-fox 1980s teacher and nurse couple: bought low, when these houses were dirt cheap, did much of the work themselves, lived in one of the flats for a few years, paid off loans early and, crucially, didn't go mad during the Celtic Tiger boom years.

When I moved back first, I tried living with Mum and Dad. I've always been their most troublesome – troubling – child, and each of them, in their way, has tried taking care of me. With her it's 'Are you making friends?' and 'Say yes to every invitation' whereas he's a 'Leave her be, there's no rush' and an 'All in good time' man.

I couldn't rest. I'm too old to live at home. I felt like a burden, like I was putting a stop to their gallop, and I was. They used to work as teachers and retired a few years ago after a gigantic joint retirement bash in the Metropole Hotel. Both of them are in better health than I am, and they've always wanted to travel, take advantage of tour bargains and off-season golden-years discounts.

With me back, they had to stay put until I was, quote unquote, settled. Their plan was that I'd be buying somewhere of my own in the city, or one of the surrounding commuter towns, and once I did, the globetrotting would resume.

I'm not sure if I want to buy a place again. Or if I want to stay in Cork. Or if it'll be an option after my upcoming review with Feeney. I read the *Irish Examiner* property supplement every Saturday but that's as far as I've got. I haven't viewed a single house.

I've got most of the money for a deposit because Calum bought out my equity in the apartment in Phibsboro. For way less than it was worth. Around the time I heard he was seeing someone else. Younger than me. Blonder. And that wasn't the reason I caved, really it wasn't, but it was the last straw.

Long story short, against legal advice I agreed to Calum's pathetic offer. I wanted to draw a line. Get the whole miserable shit-show over with. I had no idea then that it was only getting started.

Anyway, when this flat came up, I leaped at it. My parents were pleased too. One of the advantages of Wellington Road is that it's five or ten minutes by car from their place so they feel they can keep an eye on me. Plus I can water plants, turn on lights and open windows while they're away. They left again four days ago on a last-minute cancellation cruise of the Norwegian fjords ('A steal,' Dad said), but I was up at theirs yesterday, so I have the night off.

'You should come with us sometime, love,' my mother said, as they were going.

'Cruises aren't really my thing,' I said.

What I nearly said was 'I'd rather cut off my foot,' because living at home for a few months turned me back into a teenager. I'm doing my best to grow up again. Cooking my own dinner – even if it's only scrambled eggs – is part of the process.

The toast pops, a thick slice of proper crunchy sourdough. I scrape on too much butter, dump the eggs and an extra grind of black pepper on top, and sit in the armchair by the window looking out. It's a soothing sight if you don't over-think it, which I have an unfortunate tendency to do. I see lights, I think shadows. I see main street, I think alley. I've been spending too much time alone but, after everything that's happened, alone is where I feel safest.

I eat the eggs directly off the toast, without fork and knife, holding the plate under my chin as I bite. I think about the bottle of Rioja in the press – an impulse purchase a few days ago from the delicatessen in St Luke's when I was in there buying bread. I think about having a glass, but it's nearly ten and I need a good night's sleep. Wine only wakes me up. Also, I'm not allowed alcohol with the tablets I'm on. I don't miss it – it was never the problem – but when something is forbidden, it always becomes more attractive.

I check my phone for messages. There's nothing apart from several updates in the family WhatsApp group. I dot a few hearts and thumbs-ups around the comments. It's necessary maintenance because if I say nothing I'll have my parents and each of my siblings phoning me individually to check if I'm okay. Or my brother Billy, who lives nearest except for my parents, will be instructed to do a drive-by. They all know that I'm working on my first murder case in a long time and they're even more worried about me than they usually are.

It takes me ages to do the washing-up. I used the wrong saucepan for the eggs, and whatever the opposite of non-stick is, this is it. As I scrub, I think again about the girl. About how I'm going to give her back her name. How I'm going to find the person who killed her.

Afterwards I sit at the kitchen table and make detailed notes of my thoughts in an A4 hardcover notebook that will never see the inside of the station or be disclosed to the defence. I transfer the highlights – a cryptic list of reminders – to my black garda-issue fliptop notebook and put it in my inside jacket pocket, on a peg on the back of the door, ready for the day ahead. In the bedroom, I hang tomorrow's clothes, underwear and socks included, at the front of the wardrobe. I take a shower and, after checking my phone for messages again, I go to bed.

In bed, the memories come, the ones I run from during the day.

No door policy.
   No Neat Dress Essential.
   No microphone for the DJ.
   No Top of the Pops *intros.*
   No strangers.
   Only friends.

13

IT'S EARLY, BUT IT'S MORNING AND, IN A NICE
surprise, I realise I've slept for a few hours. Around me, the
house creaks. Pipes bang and clank at varying decibels and
irritatingly irregular intervals. Upstairs, someone is having a
shower. I imagine myself going out for a run and coming back
and doing some free weights, like I used to have to do in my
Calum days. I stay in bed. Baby steps.

Eventually, the alarm goes off. It's still dark. I dress quickly
and leave the house after necking a pint glass of tap water. My
car's down the street, looks to be intact, no broken wipers or
smashed mirrors – not guaranteed around here. I drive to work.
A Renault Clio. Four years old. More trouble than it's worth
bringing it through town most days but it's a quick spin today
– only a few people out and about yet – and, you never know,
it might come in handy.

I park in the station car park and nip across the road to the
Centra. I buy a large milky coffee, two Twixes and a sausage
roll from the glum but reliable Hassan, a low-sized guy who
always wears perfectly ironed business shirts, mostly blue, occasionally pink. He does the early shift, even though he's told me
loads of times that he's not a morning person.

'More rain today,' he says. 'We're sick of it now.'

I make it into the office by six forty-five. In the kitchen, I put one Twix in the fridge, paying off the loan I took last night, and keep the other in my bag for later.

Sadie's door is open. I stand on the threshold. She's sitting at her desk. Tidy, like the rest of the room, but not freakily clean. She's wearing her office hoodie and a scarf. It looks like she's been in for a while.

'Is that sausage roll for me?' she asks.

'Em, yes, skipper. If you want me to starve, like.'

'Joking. Jeez. Anyway, how are you getting on? First murder case in how long?'

'A while,' I say.

Meaning not since I was in my old job. As Sadie knows. Because I haven't been allowed within a mile of a murder since I came here. Haven't wanted to be till now.

'So how *is* it going?' It's the second time she's asked. She isn't giving up.

'Actually, I'm okay. Way better than I thought I'd be.'

She takes in what I've said. I reckon she believes me.

She sucks in a breath and says, 'I want you on site this morning. You know the run of the place and a lot of the workers.'

I wait a beat before replying. Being on site means I won't be in the autopsy room when Professor Friel is carrying out his examination. I feel a pang, but keep it to myself. 'Suits me,' I say. 'I really am fine, you know.'

'Good. Any ideas about the case so far?'

'No . . . Except we need to find out how long ago the pub closed, how long it's been vacant, if it's ever been used for anything else. If there was anyone living upstairs, before and after it shut.

Officially or squatting. We need to talk to neighbours, even though that won't be all that easy because there's a high population turnover in that area. We'll have to find and talk to current and previous owners. Get tenancy records. Rent books. Check the Land Registry and the City Council rates department. We'll need to dovetail that information with our likely time of death. If we're lucky, we'll get a year or a short span of years during which the murder could have occurred from the bone analysis. Maybe even DNA. If not, we'll have to broaden . . .'

I stop when I realise how fast I'm talking.

'You have no ideas at all, so.'

'Not many, no. I've been keeping an open mind, like you said.'

She laughs, gets up from her desk. 'Come on. Party time.' She must think I'm confused because she adds, 'The morning briefing. Incident room. It's nearly seven a.m.'

'Of course,' I say, with unnecessary acidity and, from the glance she gives me, I know she's filed it away as evidence that I'm not as well as I'm letting on.

'Sorry,' I say. 'Look, I understand why I'm on site, but I *would* like to see her.'

'You can't be at the post-mortem. His eminence, Professor Boney Friel, has a bee in his bonnet about you. Spoke to Inspector Feeney on the phone last night. Wondered about the wisdom of having you on the case.'

'What did the Cig say?'

'He told me to keep you away from the post-mortem today.'

'Shit. Does he agree with Boney Friel? Does he want me off the case?'

'Shane Feeney is his own man. If you're off the case, it'll be his decision, not Boney's. But we need things to go smoothly this morning. That means you're on site. And, if you think about it, it's where you can add most value to the investigation. The body might be — is — gone but the site excavation continues today. Keep your eyes and ears open and your head in the right place. If you do that, you should be okay.'

'It's going to follow me forever, isn't it?'

She stands in front of me, purses her lips, lets out a breath, then says, 'Yeah. Yes. It is. You know that. Until your story changes, that's the one they're going to tell. It's up to you to give them something else to talk about. Something better. As of now, you're on the case. How could you not be? You were there when they found the body. No one expected anything to show up except possibly one or two more historic bodies, least of all Shane Feeney, or he'd never have risked you. But you *were* there so . . . Anyway, don't give him — or anyone else, including me — an excuse. This is your chance to come back. Take it.'

I want to say something to reassure her. And me. But she's gone already.

It's not easy to say it, but I had a nervous breakdown. They don't call it that any more. What I'm trying to get across to you is that it wasn't a pretty Instagram hashtag mental-health-hacks situation.

I'll spare you the details, but it was ugly. Major meltdown first. Then I couldn't get out of bed, couldn't function. Had to go into hospital and stay there. And take antidepressant medication. Effexor. Which I'm a fan of. It helped when nothing else did. Still does. Though I'm on a gradually reducing dose now. I don't plan on being on it forever.

14

THE NAME 'INCIDENT ROOM' SOUNDS IMPRESSIVE
but the Coughlan's Quay reality isn't much bigger than an
average sitting room, crammed with plastic chairs set out in a
few short rows and eight small tables that can be assembled into
a single big one for case conferences. I slip into a seat at the
back beside Olly Fogarty. His eyes are ringed with black.

'No sleep so?'

He shakes his head. I break the sausage roll in two and offer
half to him on a paper napkin. He wolfs it in two or three bites
while I force myself to nibble at my share, despite the sick
feeling I now have in my stomach. I sip my coffee. Wish I'd
chosen black. I do my best to listen. To look like I'm listening,
even though there's nothing to it. Duties are being allocated,
and people are being told where they're needed, but I already
know where I'm going. As it turns out, I'm with Fogarty for
the day.

Which gives me an idea.

15

I MAKE SURE WE'RE FIRST OUT OF THE INCIDENT
room. Tell him I want to drive my own car to the site.

After we clear the gates, I say, 'We're mad early. Realistically,
nothing's going to be happening till nearly nine o'clock. You
could have a kip there in the passenger seat for a while if you
like.'

He looks at me. First, doubtful. Then, grateful. So I tell him
what I want in return.

I bully my way past the uniformed garda on the autopsy-room
door, flashing my ID too fast for him to check it and palm him
a piece of paper with a phone number on it. 'Detective Garda
Olly Fogarty from Coughlan's Quay Regional Detective Unit
is outside. He wants you to call him urgently.'

I push open the door before he has a chance to say or do
anything else.

And it's nearly better this way, being on my own with her.
Not completely because I make sure that the mortuary attendant
– Padraig Murphy, an older seen-it-all guy, in his sixties with

a bad smoker's cough – stays in the room at all times and I video everything with my phone so that no one can say I touched her or contaminated evidence. I know I'm stretching things by being here this morning. I justify my presence by telling myself I'm not banned from *seeing* her, just from the post-mortem. Yeah, I'm not convincing myself either.

She's on a steel table, no need for refrigeration in this case. Padraig's uncovered the body already, in preparation for when Boney Friel and the APT – the anatomical pathology technician – and whoever's attending from Forensics arrive later on, so there's no real harm.

I take a moment, close my eyes, pay my respects to her. But there's no time for niceties. I proceed.

I'm wearing a mask and gloves and my hair is tied back, and I've brought a torch with me, a strong one. I angle it, moving slowly down the length of her. She's unclothed, which could mean that what she was wearing – natural fibres such as cotton, linen or wool – rotted during the time she's been buried. Or that she was naked when she went into the ground.

I bring the light closer, to the area of adipose tissue over her ribcage. I think I see a wire. It could be part of a bra. And, at her pelvic area, the light reveals what might be underwear remnants and what look like lengths of thread, presumably synthetic. All of the fragments will be collected by the technician and, where appropriate, sent for analysis by Forensic Science Ireland. I'll find out the results later but that takes such a long time. Too long for me.

I examine her head, the front of the skull cracked and fractured. Considerable force would have been required. It doesn't look like an accident. It looks deliberate. Brutal. But I'm not a pathologist. Appearances can deceive. We don't yet know when the injuries occurred.

Her mouth is open. I angle the torch to examine her teeth. I spot at least one filling. Dental records will be sought but there's no central register so it's a needle in a haystack. Works best as confirmation when you know who you're matching to and we're way off that here.

I come to the shoes. The soles are intact, because they're made entirely from synthetic material. The uppers are only partial: the leather has rotted but there's stitching left, what looks like some of the lining, both heel mouldings, and a small rectangular label that's no longer legible on each upper. I don't need a microscope to tell me what it says. They're Buffalo boots. The real thing, not imitation. Would've been expensive.

My phone alarm goes off. It's 8.15 a.m. We have fifteen minutes to get to the crime scene before it reopens officially. We should be there now, eager to start, but it'll be chaos this morning. Hopefully no one will notice if we're late.

'I have to go, Padraig,' I say. 'I can't thank you enough. Are we good? We are?'

'You're grand, girl. If Detective Fogarty says you're okay, that's fine by me.'

He knows Fogarty well from previous cases. Promised him he'd keep quiet about my visit. Only time will tell if he does. But I can't help thinking of something my grandmother used to say. Three can keep a secret if two of them are dead.

16

FOGARTY'S SNOOZING WHEN I GET BACK TO THE
car. I start the engine, decide to let him wake up by himself.
I'd be glad of the extra time to think, but he stretches and blinks
awake straight away, yawning. 'How's Padraig doing?'

'He was very nice to me. He's a big fan of yours.'

'One of many, girl. I sorted the mule on the door for you as
well. C'mere, you've a touch of the necrophiliac about you,
have you?'

'Not really. Just wanted to see her one last time. Had to.
Can't explain it.'

'We all have our little foibles, I s'pose. Wouldn't be my kind
of thing. Speaking of, is there anything left in that?' He gestures
at the coffee in the cupholder.

'Yeah, but it's stone cold. Iced coffee without the ice.'

He takes a slug. 'Fuck, it's rotten.' He finishes it. 'Jesus.'

'I'm dying for a wee,' I say, 'but I'll have to try to hold it.
The Portaloos are foul.'

'Did you see anything? When you were in there?'

I tell him. It doesn't take long.

'Nothing so,' he says.

'Nothing much, no.'

I think about that. How we've reduced her life to nothing much. I wonder if that's how it always was for her.

❖

We get snarled in traffic on the way out of the hospital car park maze, then stuck in a logjam on the Wilton roundabout. When we finally arrive at the scene, I'm left with no choice but to chance the smelly toilets while Fogarty goes on ahead to the excavation area. Afterwards, I bump into Dr Eileen O'Hara, the forensic archaeologist.

'What's the plan?' I ask, as we walk.

'We'll be expanding the zone of interest beyond the immediate grave site, and we'll be digging deeper in situ, to see if any artefacts were placed with the body concurrent with the burial. Some items may have become dislodged as the flesh rotted – jewellery, piercings. There might be some clothing. A coat or a jumper, perhaps, a purse or handbag. In the wider area, we'll be checking to see if there's any evidence of the spill being scattered across a more extensive part of the site.'

'The spill?'

'What comes out of the hole to make room for the body. It has to go somewhere.'

'Would there have been much?'

'Quite a bit.'

'Are we talking a wheelie bin full? A few supermarket bags? Or black sacks? More than that?'

'I can't say yet. We need to see how deep the cut is. But it's something to keep in mind. How did the killer get rid of the spill? And earth is heavy. It would take effort to move it off-site. Did the killer use a wheelbarrow? A car?'

'It's something I've thought about,' I say. 'Not the spill so much as the time. In a busy pub, open every day, when do you get enough time to kill someone, lift flagstones, dig a hole, replace the floor and, afterwards, put everything back where it's supposed to be, all of that without everyone noticing?'

'My head's melting even thinking about it,' Eileen says.

We've reached the excavation. Noel Tobin, the SOCO, is standing beside Olly Fogarty, waiting for Eileen.

She says, 'We'll see what we can do to help them, Tobin, won't we?'

'We will,' he replies. 'Sure the poor little lambs would be lost without us.'

'I think ye're losing the run of yerselves,' Fogarty says, 'but, yeah, go on. Find us an oul' credit card with a name on it or a student ID and we can all go home.'

17

THE SILVER LINING OF BEING SERIOUSLY MENTAL IS
that they called off the dogs, left me alone to lick my wounds
and recover.

Had to, legally. Probably thought I'd leave the job eventually,
under my own steam after raking in maximum sick pay.

Didn't happen. Because another thing that helped was time.
And group therapy. Learning that my self-destructive thought
loops were more common than I'd realised. Especially among
women.

Until, gradually, as slowly as joining the wrong supermarket
checkout queue, a notion began to form in me that I might be
able to do this job again.

That I might even be okay at it.

At the end of the day, we huddle near the forensics van. No
ID cards have been found but some large loose coins – pre-euro
Irish currency – were. The coins are heavily crusted with soil,
which means that if they were in a purse, a bag or a pocket it
was made of a natural fibre and rotted a long time ago.

Alternatively, someone placed the coins in the grave. They'll have to be cleaned off in the lab to enable the dates to be read, and the soil will have to be analysed to see if it holds traces of any other substance. But even without the exact dates, they narrow my focus.

I say, 'Euro coins were introduced in Ireland in January 2002. I reckon we take 2002 as one end of the time span, the *approximate* span, and – relying on the boots, and the Spice Girls' first hit tune – 1996 as the other end. That means we're looking at six years max. And if the coins and the boots reveal more, we might be able to zoom in on an even shorter time frame.'

'You're the one giving the evidence about the Spice Girls,' Fogarty says, 'if we ever get that far. And don't you think you're jumping the gun having '02 as the cut-off point? Nothing to say she didn't have the coins later than that.'

'You're right,' I say.

'Yeah, well, it is *some*thing, I'm not saying it isn't.' He turns to Noel Tobin. 'That jewellery you found earlier. Will you be able to get anything off it?'

Tobin replies, 'So far, we've discovered a small ring, possibly a nose-ring, and two bigger hoops made of what looks like plastic with metal inserts. My gut feeling is that we won't get much from them. But it won't be for the want of trying, I can tell you that for nothing.'

I have to turn away when he says that. His openness has caught me off-guard, the realisation that someone else cares as much as I do. But the truth is, we've all been affected by finding her things, these pathetic relics of a life cut short, including Olly Fogarty, though he'd die before he'd admit it. I clear my throat and turn back.

'The jacket might be our best hope,' Noel Tobin says. 'It's deteriorated because of where it was, directly underneath the decomposing body, all those fluids and so on. As of now, I can't say what colour it was, let alone the brand or any details of manufacture. On the upside, the fact that it's still here means it's composed entirely of man-made fibres so we might get something from it. And don't forget the boots. They're distinctive. If the jacket's the same, who knows what someone might remember?'

'What about the rest of her clothes? I think there's . . . What I mean to say is, there might be some underwear traces.'

'Any synthetic remnants will have been collected at the postmortem.'

'You've heard nothing from them so?'

'I've been a small bit busy,' Tobin says.

'Sorry, yeah.' I look at Fogarty. 'Can you think of anything we need to ask?'

'No, because I'm exhausted. I entered a vegetative state around four o'clock. I'm surprised ye didn't notice. Are we done?'

'Nearly,' I say. 'Eileen, Dr O'Hara, remember what you were talking about this morning, the spill? Did you find any sign of it being dispersed over the rest of the site?'

'No, but I've had a close look at the flagstones. I'm nearly sure that I've identified the ones that were lifted to enable the burial to take place. Six or seven at most. A different material was used to seal around them than for the rest of the floor. Not as solid.'

'Needs analysis,' Tobin says, 'but it could be tile grout or Polyfilla. A sign of non-specialist intervention. The rest were laid with lime mortar. All subject to analysis too. Remember, there's a health warning on everything we've said here. Don't take it as gospel.'

Eileen adds, 'We'll continue examining the rest of the scene tomorrow. But the immediate area around the cut where the body was found has probably yielded up everything it's going to. It wasn't as deep as a normal grave. It was a case of get in, lift the floor, dig, get out, roll in the body, cover her, replace the floor. All of it as fast as possible, I think.'

Fogarty says, 'You said "roll in the body" there. Is that what you think happened? Is that why she was found face down?'

'Either that, or she was lifted in.'

I ask, 'Could one person have done it?'

Tobin says, 'Depends on height and weight. We'll get the exact height from the post-mortem. We'll be able to size the jacket, get an idea of weight from that. Should have a better idea then.'

I say, 'One last thing. When you were excavating earlier, Eileen, you said something about shovel marks. Have you anything to add to that? Any observations?'

'The shovel marks were made by modern implements, not historic ones.'

'You used the plural. Are you saying there was more than one shovel in use? Two different kinds, maybe?'

She grimaced. 'No. It's the same shovel, a gardening spade. To be clear, it's the same *type*, at least. No distinguishing marks, no ridges. New or very lightly used before the event. But some of the cuts around the edge are stronger and more, for want of a better word, certain. Some are weaker.'

I ask, 'Are we talking two people using two shovels of the same type?'

'Or could it be two people using the same spade alternately?' Fogarty asks. 'One gets tired, the other takes over?'

Eileen replies, 'You're putting me on the spot here, but in theory both of those scenarios are possible. The other scenario is that it's just one person all the way through. He's stronger at the start, and weaker later on, suffering from fatigue. It's imposs-ible to be sure. There could be one, two, more, involved in the dig. Your guess is as good as mine at this point.'

I return to the car with Fogarty, my head spinning with possibilities.

If you weren't there, you can't know what it was like.
For a brief shining time, we were at the centre of the world.
And the world was a happy place. Made of pure joy.
Most people never have what we had.
We were lucky. Felt it too.
It was perfect and we knew it.
Seems laughable now that we thought it would last forever.
We were innocent, you see, before we were guilty.

18

ON THE TELLY, POLICE STATIONS ARE OFTEN depicted as high-tech palaces made of glass. We have no glass here, unless you count windows that rattle when it's windy, and we have mice in the attic, who, I'm told, occasionally venture forth to say hello, though I've been lucky not to see any yet.

We also have solid walls and doors, which means I can't tell if Sadie's in her room or not. I think about knocking, press my ear to the wood. Decide against when I hear her on the phone, though I can't make out what she's saying.

About ten minutes later, she stops by my desk. She has her coat on. 'Olly gone?'

'A few minutes ago.'

'Anything to tell me?'

I update her on the day's finds. She listens in silence, her expression grave. It occurs to me that she might have found out about my excursion to the morgue.

When I've finished, she says, 'Is there anything else?'

I stand to face her. 'There is. I saw the body this morning. Early. I . . .'

'I heard,' she says. 'Luckily Boney Friel didn't. But Feeney did. And he's fucking apoplectic about you interfering with evidence. He says it's gross misconduct.'

My stomach on the floor, my mouth like the Sahara, I say, 'I'm sorry but I didn't touch her, I swear, and I have a video on my phone that proves it.'

I play it for her. She takes it from me. Plays it again.

She throws the phone onto the desk and looks at me venomously. 'Send me that video. I'll tell the Cig I inadvertently allowed you to view her. That I wasn't clear in my instructions. But that's the last time I'm doing *anything* like that for you. Do you hear?'

'I do. I appreciate everything you've—' I puff out a breath. 'Did you . . . Is there any news from the post-mortem? Any findings?'

'There is,' she says, 'quite a bit. Professor Friel is giving everyone a briefing in the morning at eight before he goes back to Dublin. You'll hear it all then.'

She leaves without saying anything else and I slump into my chair. I figure I'm on my ninth life. I'd better make it count.

Even after I'd made up my mind to go back to work, I thought about it some more. Finally, when I told them I was ready, it felt right. I put in for a transfer at the same time.

And here I am in Coughlan's Quay. And it's been tough. Giving up would be easier. And then the girl comes along, and reminds me why I wanted to do the job in the first place. And I know I'll do everything I can to solve this case.

For her. For both of us.

19

THE NEXT MORNING, I TAKE WHAT'S BECOMING my regular spot at the back of the incident room beside Olly Fogarty. I love the routine, the feeling of being part of the gang again, for however long it lasts. Olly looks brighter today.

I ask, 'Better last night?'

He stretches out his arms and looks up to the ceiling. 'My angel hath returned. Aided by a lorry load of Calpol.'

I let out a guffaw, press my hand over my mouth to stifle it, but there's no need. It's lost in the rumble. The place is packed. Up front, Feeney is banging on the desk.

'Shut up, would ye, and listen. Professor Friel has a train to catch.'

'I'm driving, actually,' Boney Friel says, from his seat in the front row, 'but the point is well made indeed.'

Feeney's nostrils flare with irritation. He doesn't like Boney either. Then Olly drops his head and I see his shoulders, his whole body, shaking. We shouldn't be laughing but he sets me off again.

'Right,' Feeney says. 'The full report will take time. I don't need to tell you that there will be further tests but Professor Friel is going to take us through his findings now.'

'My preliminary findings,' Boney Friel says.

'Exactly.' Feeney retreats and leans against the side wall.

Professor Friel gets to his feet and turns to face the group. 'Good morning, everyone. I'll deal with the remains first, and Deborah, who was with me during my examination, will deal with the collection aspect.'

Deborah Winters works for Forensic Science Ireland. I know her from my time in Dublin. We used to get on well – I still have her mobile number in my phone – but, for obvious reasons, I haven't been in contact with her in a long time.

By the 'collection aspect', Boney Friel means samples taken or evidence recovered by Deborah during the post-mortem. The fact that he's made reference to it, and that she's at the briefing, gives me hope that they may have found something important. I'm recalling, too, what Sadie said last night. That Boney had found 'quite a bit' during the post-mortem. I feel my heart-rate quicken.

Boney reads from notes in a ring binder, brown-framed reading glasses perched at the end of his nose. His Derry twang is nasal, with a hint of what comes across as sarcasm. It's just the way he talks, but it doesn't endear him to people.

'The remains *appear* to be those of a young female. Following preliminary dental analysis and radiological examination, I found most of the epiphyses fused with the exception of the clavicle. *Therefore* I believe the deceased female to have been between the ages of eighteen and twenty-one years at the time of death. Indications are that she was Caucasian.

'I found no historic healed fractures to the skeleton,' he glances up over his glasses towards Sadie, who's standing by the window, 'which suggests that the chances of medical records proving a fruitful aid to identification of the deceased are low.' He continues, 'My initial observations are that the deceased had undergone an extraction of one of her adult teeth, and that she had two fillings. Nothing remarkable about the fillings, nothing to indicate that she was, for example, Eastern European or from any further afield. Other than the extraction and the fillings, there was no further dental intervention, even though the deceased would have benefited from braces for the upper mandible.'

He puts down his folder, takes off his glasses and proceeds to polish them with his tie. 'Far be it from me to draw any over-hasty conclusions at this stage. Nevertheless, it appears to me that the deceased's dentition is *not* indicative of a higher socio-economic class.'

Replacing his glasses, he says, 'Moving on now to the skull area . . .' He turns a page. Clears his throat. After a lengthy pause, he says, 'Yes, the skull. You will have seen photographs, and some of you will have seen for yourselves. I found significant blunt-force trauma to the front left of the skull, the left eye socket and the left *side* of the skull. Of particular significance is the depressed fracture of the frontal bones – the forehead – and the further trauma, less obvious to the naked eye, to the side. Both injuries are likely to have caused intracranial haemorrhage, in other words bleeding inside the skull. The side injury may have impacted the middle meningeal artery, which would have led to major internal bleeding and, I might add, considerable surface bleeding too. The skull injuries would have been quite sufficient to cause death.'

He looks up from his notes. 'The level of injury is too severe to have been caused by a punch or a slap, or any number of same. It is my current hypothesis that death occurred as a result of the deceased's head being brought into contact with a hard surface. The simplest solution is often the most likely. Accordingly, if we take the location into account, we might consider that the head may have been slammed repeatedly against a flagstone floor.'

He removes his glasses again, and speaks jauntily: 'Ladies and gentlemen, it is my belief that what we are dealing with here is a particularly savage murder. Any questions?'

20

THERE'S A PAUSE AFTER THAT, A WEIGHTED SILENCE,
heavy with disgust at what we've heard. But there are no pearl-
clutchers here. This kind of case is why most of us signed up.
So, along with the horror, there's anticipation, tingles of excite-
ment, people shifting in chairs, keen to get moving, to *do*
something.

Not me. Not yet. I want to get moving but, first, I want to
soak up as much information as I can. In fairness, it's been a
while, but from what I recall, headless chickens rarely solve
murders.

Feeney is first to speak. 'Thank you, Professor Friel, and I
hope ye heard all that. What the prof said and what he *didn't*
say, including that, for the moment, we still have little to no
idea how long she's been in the ground.'

Boney responds, 'That's right. At this time I can only say
with some certainty that it's years rather than months.'

'And to save any know-alls the bother of googling on their
phones and pestering me afterwards when I've better things to
be doing, what about carbon-dating? Would that help?'

'Not in the slightest,' Boney says. 'As we discussed last night, it's not accurate enough. There is the option of isotope testing but that takes time and it's budget-dependent.'

'No decision made on that yet,' Feeney says, 'other more economical avenues to be exhausted first.'

Boney says, 'And on that point, needless to say, I've taken bone, hair and tooth samples for mitochondrial DNA extraction purposes, which, as you know, also takes time. I don't need to tell you that cellular analysis – nuclear DNA – is not an option here given that the remains are skeletal only. But remember, the deceased was young and female. The chances of finding her on a DNA database are slim, I would have thought.'

Deborah Winters stands. She wears large round gold-rimmed glasses. She says, 'There *are* a few things that *will* help with dates, I hope.'

'The boots are important, I'd say, are they?' Fogarty asks, giving me a nudge.

And something about the smarmy way he asks the question makes me reckon that Fogarty is the one who told Sadie about my visit to the mortuary. That he's been tasked by her with keeping an eye on me. I feel something inside me fall away, but I steel myself again. It's nothing I didn't expect. And he won't be getting any more sausage rolls from me.

Deborah Winters replies, 'I believe so. We should be able to get manufacturing dates from the boots. Pretty quickly, I hope. A few days will tell a lot. And we haven't mentioned the nails yet.' She looks at Friel.

He pages through his notes. 'No evidence of scraping or digging with the fingernails. Accordingly, my hypothesis is that the deceased did not recover consciousness following the infliction of the injuries and that she was deceased at the time of burial.'

Winters says, 'Something to be thankful for, I suppose. And from our point of view, the nail varnish – green in colour. Fashion changes from year to year. Shades vary. Outside chance that may help us with dates.'

Sadie says, 'Is there any more news on the coins found with the body?'

Winters says, 'Not yet. Just to say, the absence of euros may or may not be significant in terms of dating the remains.'

DI Feeney asks, 'What about the jacket? What kind is it? Any hope of DNA?'

'No news yet but I must warn you that any DNA recovered from the jacket is most likely to be the deceased's.'

Feeney says, 'So I think we're done.'

As no one else has asked the question, I have to risk it. I put up my hand.

'Deborah, hi,' I say, 'one more thing, if that's okay?'

She glances at DI Feeney. He looks as if he'd like to throttle me.

'Sure,' she says.

'What about underwear?'

She nods. 'I should have said. Based on the synthetic threads we found, we believe she was clothed in a natural fibre such as cotton when buried. We found remnants of underwear but—' She breaks off as Boney taps his watch.

Boney says, 'But further analysis is needed. And before anyone asks, we have no way of knowing whether she was sexually assaulted prior to death. Now if Miss McCann has *quite* finished, I think we really are done. At any rate, *I* certainly am.'

'We won't keep you any longer,' Feeney says, 'though the rest of ye are going nowhere. DS O'Riordan will take ye through what's next. Apart from you, McCann.'

He steps forward to shake Professor Friel's hand and, afterwards, points at me. 'My office. Now.'

21

FEENEY'S ROOM IS BIGGER THAN SADIE'S, WITH a pleasant view of the river. On the wall, there's a photograph of him, his wife and three small kids in full active-wear on a snowy mountain peak. They look like future winning contestants on *Ireland's Fittest Family*.

Feeney stands in front of his desk, doesn't offer me a seat. His expression is neutral. When he speaks, his tone is quiet and conversational, which has the paradoxical effect of making what he says feel more menacing. 'I want you to know that you didn't get away with it.'

He could be talking about anything but it's probably the visit to the mortuary. And he's probably going to suspend me. With dogged resentment, I clamp my mouth shut.

'Your skipper did her best to cover for you, but I want *you* to know that I wasn't convinced. What do you have to say for yourself?'

No point in denials or excuses. I look him in the eyes. 'It won't happen again.'

He assesses me, his face giving nothing away. Time passes and I start to hope, praying that the phone video and Sadie putting her neck on the line might have saved me.

Eventually he says, 'You can be right sure it won't happen again, and nothing like it either. Because I'm watching you like a fuckin' hawk. Now go and find your sergeant. She has a nice job for you that'll keep you busy.'

Nice isn't the word I'd use. Tedious would fit better. But it beats being suspended and it's important work, essential for the investigation, and I'm happy to do it. Happy, too, that I'm tasked with doing it on my own.

The day is dry, but cool and cloudy. Walking along the south channel past the airy elegance of Holy Trinity Church, I make a call. I'm put on hold, the Muzak vying with the sound of the gulls, squawking and swooping above the water.

Arriving at the door of the newer glass part of City Hall, I show my ID at the security desk and ask for directions. At the hatch in the rates department, I ask to see Minnie Purcell, the council official I conversed with on the phone minutes earlier.

The desk attendant eyes me with curiosity. 'Take a seat there and she'll be out.'

I do as instructed and flick through my notebook. Sometime later, Minnie Purcell emerges, harried-looking and younger than her name had led me to imagine. 'Sorry for the delay,' she says.

'No need to apologise,' I say. 'I'm the one interrupting your day.'

I follow her behind the partition and she shows me to a desk, piled high with lever arch folders and hard-covered ledgers the size of a wallpaper sample book. 'If you tell me what you want from more recent years, I can do you a printout, no bother.

Everything's held on the system now. But you said you're looking for older records as well so I got these down for you. Hard copy is your best bet for the historic ones.'

I say, 'Let's start with the printout.'

Reading property records sounds boring and, no matter how you dress it up, it is. But it's the sort of donkey work that might lead somewhere. The information gleaned should allow me to compile a list of possible background witnesses. People who might become suspects.

Working through lunch, I leave City Hall after 2 p.m. I bolt down a pre-prepared tuna sandwich and a bottle of sparkling water at the School of Music café, while sitting at a table in the floor-to-ceiling window, overlooking Union Quay. The School is one of the few ambitious contemporary buildings in the city, the angled stone mirroring the turn the river takes in front of it. I like the feel of the place. Reckon it's got to do with the fifty-two baby-grand Steinways in the building. The vibrations or something.

My mum is a music teacher. She taught all of us piano. The others went as far as grade eight. I stopped at grade four. It's one of my regrets that I didn't keep it up. Yet another.

Coming on for 3 p.m, I arrive at the courthouse on Washington Street, a place I've been only rarely in recent years because criminal business has transferred to Anglesea Street, though it wasn't always so. In centuries past, this was where the assizes were held and all of the trials, large and small. The old cells have been converted for administration purposes now.

Entering at basement level, underneath the portico and the stone steps, I seek out the District Court Licensing Office, due to close to members of the public at 4 p.m.

I show my ID and tell the clerk I'm there to do an intoxicating-liquor licence search on Bertie Allen's pub. I ask if she can help.

She says, 'Sure, but like, you *do* know that all licensing applications have to go through the Superintendent's Office for the area. The records should be on your own system.'

I say, 'I just have a hunch there might be more information on the court files. I think it's worth a try. It's related to the—'

'I can *kinda* guess what it's related to,' she says. 'We'll see what we can do.'

Bleary-eyed, I get back to Coughlan's Quay at 5.30 p.m. In the kitchen, I make a cup of tea and borrow back the Twix I replaced yesterday. I have one final thing to do before I collate my notes and start preparing my report. I head down the hall.

You wouldn't believe it if you saw us back then.

Everything slouched. T-shirt. Tracksuit bottoms.

Everything practical.

Nothing tight. Nothing restrictive.

Because it was all about the music.

Because what we did during the week was irrelevant.

Bricklayer or medical student or shelf-stacker or architect.

The only thing that mattered was the weekend.

Being part of something bigger.

Crossing town on a wet Tuesday. Seeing someone else who went to the club. Exchanging a look. Both feeling like we were in on the secret.

My hair was a giveaway, for anyone really looking.

A frizz. Impossible to get the tangles out.

Later on, she sorted it for me. Gave me a special comb.

Ran it through my curls after a shower. No more tears, she said.

But she was wrong about that.

22

I HANG ON FOR A COUPLE OF HOURS, WAITING
for the text message, wanting to get it here instead of at home,
but it doesn't come. That's how it goes. Two, three nights in a
row, then nothing for days. Weeks, sometimes. Breadcrumbing,
it's called, I think, and I'm so tired of it. There's a solution but,
unless I change my number – which I don't want to do, because
why should I? – it's only temporary, which is why I haven't
bothered recently. But tonight's the night. Opening settings, I
block the latest number, and the buzzing in my head quietens
for now.

There's no one else from the Barrack Street murder-
investigation team around. We're exclusively a detective
outfit, except for uniformed members in the public office,
and some civilian support in various areas throughout the
station. We keep to days mostly, unless overtime is sanctioned.
In a case like this, with a long-dead victim and endless
cutbacks, that won't happen. Still, I'm mildly surprised to be
the only person staying late. Less so, after I've thought about
it for a while. I guess the rest of them don't have as much to
prove as I do.

I drive by the crime scene on my way home. I think about

stopping and asking the cold-looking guard on perimeter duty if he has any news, but I keep going. I'll find out at the 8 a.m. briefing. Besides, I have to check my parents' place.

They still live in the home where I grew up, a hilltop dormer bungalow in Ballyvolane, near the shopping centre, with a long back garden, like many of the older houses around here, where I spent a lot of time standing in goals between two piles of rolled-up jumpers while my older siblings scored penalty after penalty. Hilarious, apparently, as they seldom fail to remind me. I'm the youngest of four after a five-year gap, and even if my sister Marian hadn't told me when I was eight that I was *definitely* an accident, I'd have figured it out.

We're close, me and Marian and our two brothers, despite the confusing years of alternate torture and spoiling they subjected me to. I try phoning Marian from the car but get her voicemail. I leave a message: 'Just me. All good.'

I spend ten or fifteen minutes in the house, most of it in the utility room, rummaging through the chest freezer for something I can defrost for dinner, ultimately locating a promising Tupperware box marked 'Irish stew'. I snap a selfie with the plastic container and WhatsApp it to Mum. She'll be happy I'm feeding myself properly.

After that, I wet the plants with a minuscule quantity of cool boiled water from the kettle – I've killed several in the past – switch off the light in the sitting room downstairs, and switch on the one on the upstairs landing, which has skylights opening to both sides. By the way, I'm not convinced that any of this helps to deter burglars but it sets the parents' mind at ease and, if you've ever seen *Crimecall*, you'll know it's what we recommend. Also, it might assist with an insurance claim if the worst comes to the worst.

Home in Wellington Road by 9 p.m., and with the stew container spinning in the microwave, I flick on the RTÉ news.

And find out where everyone's been hiding. Our murder is the second item on the headlines because there was a press conference earlier, attended by the entire investigation team. Except me. Because I wasn't told about it.

Stunned, as the southern correspondent delivers a live piece to camera from directly outside the building-site hoarding on Barrack Street, I check my phone messages.

I've missed nothing. It's no accident. No error on my part. I've been deliberately sidelined. Excluded.

I turn off the microwave, replace the lid on the still partly frozen stew, and leave it on the countertop. I sit on the sofa and rewind the bulletin so that I can watch it again.

It's nothing I don't know already. Official confirmation that the gardaí are now dealing with a murder inquiry. An appeal to the public for assistance in relation to the death of a young female in her late teens to early twenties. A confidential helpline number. Shots of a few senior gardaí in uniform; Feeney seated at a table, doing the talking; knots of serious-looking plain-clothes officers from Coughlan's Quay standing around; all of them my work colleagues.

The press conference clearly took place this evening, late afternoon by the look of the light in the recorded segment of the report, about the time I got back to the station from the courthouse; in one of the big rooms at Divisional HQ in

Anglesea Street; in good time for the 6 p.m. bulletin; convenient to the RTÉ studio on Father Mathew Quay.

I've never cared about the publicity side of police work, especially after what I did to end up down here. But I've spent the day working my guts out and I was starting to feel like I was making a contribution. Cross my heart, I couldn't give a rat's ass about not being at the press conference. What matters is that someone, maybe all of them, didn't want me there.

And that hurts.

23

I TAKE THE BOTTLE OF RIOJA OUT OF THE PRESS and hold it by the neck. I think about opening it, but the truth is I don't want to drink it: I want to smash it. I put it back in the press, then sit on the floor, lower back to the wall, head between my knees, both arms clasped around my shins. Ages later, I scrape myself up and make my way to bed.

During the night – or sometime this morning, because I wasn't looking at the clock – I decide that if the entire force wants me to leave, the best revenge is to stay. To be seen to stay. If I leave, it's going to be when I want to, and it's going to be on my terms, and it's going to be when I think of a job I want to do more than this. Meanwhile, let them do their worst.

Making the decision doesn't help me rest but I catch an hour or two of broken sleep before the alarm.

I pick up a large Americano and a multi-pack of Twixes from Hassan in Centra. I make myself visible around the station, and I make sure I'm last into the incident room, but dead on time. There's always space in the front row so that's where I make for, an A4 pad, with some loose sheets tucked into it, under my arm. Out of the corner of my eye, I glimpse Fogarty at the back, and the vacant seat beside him.

Sadie comes in at 8.05 a.m., followed by DI Feeney. He pretends not to see me and takes up his regular position by the side wall.

But Sadie says, 'Good morning, Alice,' in a friendly way, superficially at least, and loudly enough for everyone to hear, forcing me to reply.

'Morning.'

She starts the meeting by asking Fogarty to provide an update on the state of the excavation. He starts to mutter a response. He's clever, great with the punters, a classic good cop, but public speaking isn't his thing, even among people he knows. He's better hugger-muggering in corridors, making friends and having quiet words, waiting behind after everyone's gone to reveal whatever juicy morsel he's uncovered.

'Stand up,' she says, 'so that everyone can hear you.'

'I'll come up the front, if you like,' he says.

Everyone laughs, including Sadie. But I don't. Neither does Feeney.

'Get on with the story, Fogarty,' Sadie says.

'Um, it's short. Nothing else has been found in the pub area or in what was the rear yard. The grave was dug, and the body was buried and there's no evidence that the spare earth was stored or dispersed anywhere on the site. There are and were numerous pubs in the area apart from Bertie Allen's. Several changed their names over the years,' he reads from a list, 'only a few are still open. Ye know which ones, some of ye a little too well, I imagine.'

He pauses for a laugh but none comes. He moistens his lips and goes on.

'Okay. Anyway, Bertie Allen's used to be part of a strip of four pubs: Nancy Spain's was at one end of the strip, siding onto an alley, and Bertie Allen's was at the other, siding onto another alley.

All were demolished to make way for the apartment development. Bertie's was the smallest of the pubs. There was a backyard and, of course, no space out the front because, like all the rest, the front door opens onto the street. The killer or killers must've got rid of the earth around the time of the murder or, maybe, stored it in the flat overhead, if the killer had access to it.'

He goes on, 'The other option is that the extra earth was taken out the side door onto the alley. You'd have to wonder why the murderer didn't take the body out that way too.'

Sadie asks, 'What about the site itself, anything else found?'

Fogarty says, 'The archaeologists are saying that our victim, the seventh body is what they're calling her, is most likely the last, and that there's no sign of any others. They brought in equipment yesterday, ground penetrating radar. They say they're as sure as they can be.'

Sadie says, 'DI Feeney?'

He replies, 'Yes. Final housekeeping this morning, and I'll be talking to the superintendent but, all going well, I expect the crime scene to be released some time today.'

'Hear that? Hasn't happened yet, though. Let's see how it goes.' She shuffles through a bundle of papers on the table in front and holds up an A3 sheet lengthways, her left hand gripping it at the top. It's a black-and-white printed photograph.

'The currency.' She holds up a second sheet with her right hand, A4, a colour printout. 'Silver glitter. Found on some of the coins. Could be eye-shadow, they say. Transferred from her fingers, possibly . . .'

She doesn't add that they're going to do further analysis. She lets the picture she's drawn for us sink in. A young girl getting dressed to go out. And never coming home.

At the beginning we were doing it straight. More or less. Pints of cider. Beamish, often, because it was cheaper. Dancing like dervishes on creamy pints of stout. You couldn't make it up.

Then we copped on.

E. Ecstasy. Called Yokes in Cork.

More or less pure MDMA at the start, though we didn't know that then.

Twenty-five quid each.

Straight from Amsterdam, people said.

Just take half, people said.

First the tingle, then the rush.

Pills in short supply to begin with. Got cheaper. More plentiful.

And did we go mad for them?

Some of us more than others.

Though we were careful.

Drank water. Buckets of it.

Sweated it out.

And if someone came up too fast or too much, we'd mind them.

Settle them. Hug it better.

Loads of stories about the dangers of dehydration.

And if it had been that, or a dodgy E, or too many of them, if that's what had happened . . .

But it was nothing to do with the drugs at all.

Old-fashioned, the way it went. A story as old as time.

24

SADIE PINS BOTH PRINTOUTS TO THE BOARD BEHIND
her, then works her way through the room.

Siobhan O'Sullivan is second last to speak. She's a sporty-
looking uniformed rookie drafted in to help with the
door-to-door canvass. She says, 'It seems like it was a very
unpopular pub. No one I talked to can remember being there.
It's closed ages as well. No one seems to know how long.'

Sadie rubs at her brow. 'Okay, Siobhan,' she says, 'sit down.'
She addresses Fogarty. 'Talk to me after this, Olly. We need to
get a handle, especially anyone who's been living in the area a
long time.' She turns to me. 'Alice, what have you got for us?
Stand up.'

At the start, my voice isn't as steady as I'd like but it gets better
as I go along. 'I spent yesterday in the council rates office, as
instructed. The pub was rated partly residential but that doesn't
mean someone was living there, just that they could. Then I
paid a visit to the licensing office in the courthouse. The pub
last held a licence in 2009, but it had lapsed for a couple of years
before then, possibly because the tenants renting the premises
didn't have tax clearance – apparently that wasn't unusual.

'Then, in 2009, the licence was revived before being sold on separately to a seemingly unconnected supermarket up in Dublin for use in a new off-licence. The pub itself wasn't sold at that time. It remained vacant and the owner was paying half rates for a few years, which seems to be a fairly common arrangement with the city council.

'Even so, the rates fell into arrears. The previous owner had died – natural causes, colon cancer, his widow provided the death cert. There's legal correspondence on the file from her solicitor, offering to pay the arrears when the property was sold. It sits there idle for another few years until, in 2011, it's bought by the developer who's building the apartments.

'Interestingly, though, in relation to what Garda O'Sullivan was saying about it being unpopular and no one going there, there's a record of a prosecution in December 1996 of nine people illegally found on the premises during prohibited hours. The only person convicted was the owner and pub licensee at the time, Maurice Bolger. The charges against the others were struck out on Bolger's guilty plea. I've got the list of nine, their names, DoBs and the addresses they gave. Some look false. There's a Robert Marley, for example. Bob for short, I imagine. Still, we should look into it.'

Feeney steps forward and stretches out his hand. I give him one copy of the list and a second to Sadie. She glances at it and then up at me. 'Great work,' she says.

'I would've told you when I got back from the courthouse yesterday. I was here for nearly three hours but there was no one around. For *some* unknown reason.'

It's petty and silly and, as soon as I've said it, I want to take it back.

Sadie says nothing aloud in response. Her expression conveys mild contempt, something along the lines of 'Grow up, you big child.'

Feeney scratches his chin, as if he hasn't heard me, as if he's ruminating on something, then says, 'I think this part of the investigation is best *not* dealt with by McCann.' He pauses. 'Fogarty, I want you to talk to the former owner's widow, as well as taking the lead on the information from the door-to-door. Interesting work on that, by the way, Garda O'Sullivan, ah, Siobhan, isn't it? Keep going like that and you wouldn't know where you'd end up. All right, we're done.'

The meeting breaks up in muffled laughter, Siobhan O'Sullivan's beaming smile fading fast as Feeney's meaning sinks in, the realisation that he wasn't complimenting her.

As the room clears, Feeney stays in place, watching. Not a single person talks to me. No one wants to be tainted by association.

In my mind, it's always summer, and it's always dry. Us queuing outside to get in. Crowds all the way down South Main Street. In front of the Beamish brewery. On the South Gate bridge. The road jammers with people and no cars bothering us and no guards either and St Fin Barre's Cathedral pointy grey against an impossibly pink flamingo sky. Bellies churning in case this is the week we don't get in. Not wanting to be one of the eejits left to listen outside.

And in my mind we're all in it together, fully formed as a group. Ready.

It wasn't like that. In real life, it rained and there were guards on duty and there was traffic and people straggled, arrived in different states of readiness.

But in my mind, we're all there together. Coming up together.

And the door opens. And there's a roar. And we're in.

Pay at the booth on the left.

Up the stairs, painted black with a white edge. Health and safety so no one trips. What a laugh.

Loads of girls, rucksacks packed with changes of clothes down to their bras and knickers. Just imagine.

Stash a gear bag with spare T-shirt, jeans and jacket in the room behind the DJ box for the party afterwards.

And, as the last of the sun dips in the west, it's Saturday night at last.

Sweat by name and sweat by nature.

Even the black walls dripping wet.

Main dance-floor, covered with some kind of gunk you could never wash out.

Sir Henry's nightclub.

Legendary.

Hey, did you know Nirvana played here in '91?

Still, it's somewhere you might find in any town or city. A Hard Rock Café on the cheap. A biker bar without the bikers.

But there's something about it. A special accidental acoustic aided by the Nexo sound system. Imported at huge expense from France, they say, if you're into that kind of detail.

And the DJs. Go Deep in the main room, Stevie G in the back bar, and famous visitors like Garnier and Kerri and Boo.

And the two-day Weekenders. Six rooms, a magic roundabout labyrinth spilling into the courtyard outside. People swarming on the place from everywhere.

All the incomers saying the exact same thing. That this is a great *club.*

They're wrong. Because it's the best *club.*

Dancing in circles. Arms waving. Feet jumping. Roof lifting.

And the bass. Always the bass. Pumping. Thumping.

Us pulsing inside one giant throbbing heart.

But hearts stop.

25

FEENEY SNATCHED THE JOB I HAD, BUT HE HASN'T
said I'm off the case. Not in so many words. I return to my
desk and stare at the screen. Feel the eyes of the room on me.
They've all heard the stories. Tough luck. No show today.

I'm half surprised by how stoic I feel. Numb to the same-old
same-old, maybe. And the jibes were dirtier up in the big bad
capital city. There's a reserve down here, a reluctance to plunge
the knife too deeply. Small town, when it comes to it. You
never know where you're talking. Half the population connects
to the other half one way or the other.

I click into my email. There's a message from court files at
Divisional HQ, asking for the Deerpark burglary statements.
The case I was struggling with in the disused interview room
on the day they found the first body. It feels like a lifetime ago.

But I have to finish it, and the sooner the better so that I can
focus on the murder case. With the plea-or-date court coming
up – when the accused has to apply formally for a full hearing
of his case if he's contesting the charges – it has to be sent to
Divisional HQ in Anglesea Street for onward delivery to the
defence solicitor. I write the email, but something stops me. A
niggle I still can't budge. I hold off pressing send, leave it in my

drafts. I go through the rest of my emails, reply to a few of the easy ones.

After a while, the attention of the room shifts from me and I stroll as casually as I can to the bathroom. I go into a stall and lock the door. I breathe in and out, reminding myself that I've done nothing wrong. Not this time. That I just need to hold my nerve. I sit on the loo and have a wee. When I come out of the stall, Sadie's waiting by the hand dryer.

She says, 'We need to talk, but not here. I assume you have other stuff that needs doing? Nothing to do with Barrack Street?'

'Yeah,' I say. 'There's a burglary I'd like to follow up on before I send the statements to the court files office. I'd need to head out, though. Wasn't sure if I should.'

'Do it. Go. I'll catch you later.'

She's either throwing me a lifeline, or pushing me further into the quicksand. There's only one way to find out which.

I grab the burglary file from my desk and leave the station without a word.

26

THE STATION BIKE POOL IS ONE OF FEENEY'S
budget initiatives, part of his plan to move up the ladder by
showing he has an eye on the permanently cash-strapped big
picture. Regular bikes, not electric. Cheap and climate-friendly
in theory but, in practice, after the first flush of enthusiasm,
rarely used. I sign one out of the station lock-up along with
an only slightly stained safety helmet and a hi-vis vest. I turn
the vest inside out to hide the GARDA label and take off
gingerly, exiting the car park via the pedestrian gate. Lots of
people cycle in Cork but, as it's a city of steep hills, except
on the flat island in the centre, it's a masochistic pursuit, in
my opinion.

Nevertheless, there are times when a bike is a useful prop.
Less threatening than a garda car, a cop on a bike gives off a
community-guard vibe. A cop on a bike says, 'Relax, you're
probably not getting arrested today.' Also, a helmeted cyclist
travelling at a steady pace and looking like they know where
they're going might pass most eyes unnoticed.

There's training and evidence and so on, but often this work is about instinct. Something felt off about the story we'd been fed about the Deerpark case. It shouldn't have bothered me, but it did, and now that I look at it again, it still does.

And, by the way, earlier on, when I called the case low level, that was a compliment. Like a lot of burglaries, and contrary to popular belief, it was a broad-daylight job. Guy enters through the unlocked rear sliding patio door of a 1990s red-brick semi-detached in Deerpark presumably expecting premises to be unoccupied (no sign of life, no car in the driveway). What he doesn't know is that the house owner is upstairs trying to get some shut eye after working late the night before. And the reason there's no car is because it's in for a service.

Anyway, said house owner – one Martin Campbell, recently divorced, two kids who live with their mother most of the time – is alerted to the presence of a master criminal in his sitting room by loud snoring. Campbell phones the guards. Us, in fact, at the Regional Detective Unit in Coughlan's Quay directly, rather than his local station or 999. Doesn't explain why he does that – at least not to me – but he's clearly prosperous, works in IT for a US company. Maybe a regular cop wouldn't be good enough for him. Whatever the reason, we deal with it, Fintan Deeley and me.

We arrive at Campbell's place – recently decorated in more shades of beige than I knew existed – to find the dozy perpetrator still asleep on the cream-of-chicken-soup-coloured but admittedly very comfy-looking sofa. We have to shake him awake to arrest him, and when Fintan searches him, he finds Campbell's iPad – name stencilled on the cover so the suspect doesn't attempt to argue – zipped inside the suspect's hoodie, along with a bank card, his own, and a Public Services Card. The photo on the Public Services Card confirms identity. The man is still saying nothing.

We also find a small plastic baggie containing a minute, barely visible, quantity of heroin. Or a substance resembling heroin that the suspect fails to confirm is the aforementioned opiate, meaning that we – I – have to bag it up and send it to Forensic Science Ireland.

Back at Coughlan's Quay, I check the suspect's record: Garry McCarthy. Fifty-two years old. He nods his confirmation to no fixed abode still being his address, though he looks and smells clean and appears well nourished. He may have sheltered accommodation somewhere or a bed in a hostel but he's not saying. He's a long-time addict with a string of convictions. Couple of years since his most recent conviction, though, and I wonder if he's been clean for a time and if this is a relapse. He doesn't say. Doesn't say anything when we charge him, or at any time during his detention. The only communication he makes is with the member-in-charge: he nods and shakes his head in answer to questions as to his welfare. All of which I found slightly weird at the time. On the other hand, if there's one thing this job teaches you it's that people are weird.

Also, even though he could only have been caught more red-handed if he'd dipped both paws in a tin of appropriately coloured paint, the accused indicated, via his solicitor at the first District Court appearance, that he'd be contesting the case. Every previous time he'd been prosecuted, he'd pleaded guilty so there was a good chance he'd change his mind later after his solicitor got the statements from us and advised him on his chances.

His solicitor gave the accused's address as 'care of Anderson's Quay', meaning the homeless shelter there. As he had a good record of showing up for court dates, we didn't object to bail and adjourned for preparation of statements.

On my own with the file after Fintan Deeley had left for the big job in Dublin, I went full OCD, worrying at it like a nettle sting for no good reason I could think of except the dire way things had been going for me over the last while.

I should've just scratched the itch and gone back to the scene. If I had, I would've found out a lot sooner that I was wasting my time. And that I'd been right all along.

27

CAMPBELL IGNORES THE BELL FOR THE FIRST couple of rings but his car's here – a 3-series BMW, two years old – and I reckon he's at home so I switch to rapping sharply on the glass panel. I'm about to call his mobile when he finally opens up. He does a fake double-take, as if he doesn't recognise me and then, all of a sudden, does. Bet you a tenner he's been watching from inside, hoping I'll get discouraged. The obvious question is 'why', but I'm not going to ask it.

'Oh, it's *you*,' he says, moving his mouth in a lopsided attempt at a smile.

I stay serious. 'One or two things I need to check with you, Mr Campbell.'

When there's no reply, I ask, 'Could I come in?'

This time the answer comes immediately. 'Absolutely. Tea or coffee? I have to warn you that the teabags are probably past their sell-by I so rarely use them. If I were you, I'd go for coffee. It's good – Badger and Dodo freshly ground, my one little indulgence.'

He rabbits on like that and leads me into the kitchen, avoiding the sitting room where Garry McCarthy was snoozing when Fintan Deeley and I were last here. There's a counter near the door with a perfectly good set of high stools but he takes me on further into a rear extension, past a circular dining table with four chairs, to an area by the patio doors with a two-seater sofa, an armchair and a ring-stained dark-wood rectangular coffee-table that doesn't go with any of the rest of the furniture. There's an iPad on the table.

I pick it up. 'Another?'

'What?'

'The stolen property. What the perpetrator had inside his hoodie? It was an iPad. Yours. We haven't given it back to you yet, I think?'

'Oh,' Campbell says, wearing the same mirthless halfway grin he greeted me with, 'it's new. With the kids, it's handy to have. Can't do without their screens for five minutes. We don't, my ex and I, allow them to have phones yet, they're both still in primary school, but the iPad doesn't count, right?'

I smile. 'You'll get back the other one when it's no longer needed in evidence. That's sort of why I'm here, actually.' I pause, clear my throat. 'Sorry, just thirsty. I think I *will* have that coffee. Small drop of milk, no sugar. Thanks.'

I settle myself on the sofa. 'Comfy. I wonder why Garry didn't sit here after he came in, why he went so far into the house when he could've just snuggled on this. What do you reckon? Though I suppose his version of the story will come out in the witness box if he gives evidence. Did you know he's contesting the burglary charge? So he says anyway. I'm not sure if we told you. And, actually, it'd be handy to have the receipt for the new iPad. Could you give me that, when you get a chance? It'll help the judge with the valuation for the other one.'

Campbell blanches. 'Milk, no sugar,' he says. 'Two ticks.'

'Do you mind if I take a look outside? At the access point?'

'Not at all. I'll come with you.'

He moves fast and makes it to the patio door before I do, sliding it open.

'Unlocked again,' I say.

'Well, I'm in the house.'

'Like last time.'

'Except I'm not upstairs in bed.'

'Fair point,' I say, 'but an easy thing to forget if you're going out in a rush.'

'I have no intention of forgetting,' he says.

We're in the garden. Narrow area paved with square concrete slabs near the house, the rest in rough grass, too short for meadow, too long for lawn. Not much space. The extension has gobbled most of it.

'I want to take a look at the side gate.'

'Don't let me stop you,' Campbell says, unmistakably tetchy now.

It's the same as it was at the time of the offence: flimsy, wooden, unlocked.

I look back at him. 'This isn't great,' I say, 'wouldn't keep anyone out.'

'It's on my to-do list,' Campbell says, 'but the divorce and the move, it's been one thing after another. And about the burglary,' he gazes mistily into the middle distance, 'I've been thinking, that man, the burglar, I don't want it to go any further. I want to drop the charges.'

'Why?'

'I don't want it on my conscience. I can't send him to prison for something so minor. He didn't harm anyone and, like you said, I'll get the iPad back and I should've had the door locked.'

'If that happens, if he's convicted, it wouldn't be you sending him to prison. It would be the judge's job to do that.'

'That's not how I see it.'

'And if your kids had been here, I'm sure they'd have been scared.'

'But they weren't. Anyway, the truth is I can't be bothered. I want it over. I don't like the idea of going to court, having to hang around for nothing except punishing a man for having a disease, you know what I'm saying? If there's anything I have to sign to withdraw my statement, I'll call into the station, no problem. Anytime. Let me know when it suits. Text or phone me. And, sorry, I just remembered, I've got an online meeting now so I don't have time for coffee. Can you let yourself out the side?'

He turns and goes back through the patio door. This time he locks it.

28

IF A COMPLAINANT WITHDRAWS HIS STATEMENT, the state can still pursue the prosecution, can rely on other evidence, can even issue a subpoena to force the reluctant witness into the box. In practice, when the complainant ceases to cooperate, the case dies. That's what will happen here as soon as I process it. But for now it remains alive on the system and I can back-burner it for a while to see what else might turn up to explain what went on in the house in Deerpark that day.

Which is looking less and less like a straightforward burglary and more and more like something else. Whatever happened, Campbell doesn't want the accused Garry McCarthy going into the witness box, either because, according to Campbell, he doesn't want to send a man to jail or because he doesn't want to waste time in court.

Cycling out of Deerpark, past the green area edged with mature trees and the red sandstone community centre on the corner, onto Pouladuff Road, I decide I prefer the third possibility, the one he didn't mention.

That Campbell is hiding something.

The Hacienda. Cream. Ministry of Sound. Just because it was abroad didn't mean it was better. Sir Henry's, the birthplace of house music in Ireland, was as good as any of them. We all said it and everyone knew it was true. In theory.

And yet, deep down, we had the usual Cork superiority-inferiority complex.

Deep down, we wondered.

Only one way to find out the truth. Field trip required.

Especially as, around that time, cracks had developed in the Henry's scene.

People were moving on. The casuals and the party crowd. Drifting away to other clubs. So much else happening around town back then. Cork was buzzing.

Henry's was still full every weekend but most of them were fresh-faced newbies and shirt-off madsers. Our crew was stripped back to the core.

Us.

Because first and foremost we were there for the music.

And, by the way, just in case there's any doubt, the music was as good as ever.

Better, maybe. Sublime.

Changes with us, though. Commitments. Not able to go every single Saturday any more.

And the unspoken understanding that we'd be among the drifters sooner or later.

That our day was passing. Was already gone.

The quality of the drugs had deteriorated too. All kinds of crap getting mixed in.

Anyway, Ibiza. We shouldn't have gone. Simple as.

If we hadn't gone, we'd never have met her.

And if we hadn't met her, she wouldn't be dead.

29

CONFIDENCE IS A FUNNY THING. A STRIKER FAILS to score four matches in a row and he or she thinks they're finished. But one goal, skilful or not, important or not, and they're back in the game.

It's like that with me. I've been torturing myself. Then I meet Martin Campbell and realise my instincts are spot on. There *is* something fishy about the Deerpark case. I need to track down Garry McCarthy and get him to talk to me.

Not yet. I stop the bike opposite Greenmount School. The triangle of cottages beside me is built on the old place of execution where the gibbet stood.

I send a short text message and, when the response comes, I take off, crossing through the junction, speeding downhill on Noonan's Road and Gregg Road, past the flats. The lights are in my favour and I swing right on Gilabbey Street, past St Fin Barre's cathedral, the route narrowing along Dean Street and even narrower Fort Street, locking my bike to a lamppost on the corner of Barrack Street, across from Murphy's coal yard and the dizzyingly high stone walls of Elizabeth Fort.

I keep my helmet on and my head down until I'm inside: the

crime scene is up the street but I've gone the long way around to get here and there's no point drawing unnecessary heat. As far as I'm concerned, I'm doing nothing wrong but Inspector Feeney would undoubtedly find an excuse to disagree.

I'm in Alchemy Café where it's always pleasantly dusk. Furnished with vintage pieces, it does a lively trade. I take a seat at a vacant table down the back.

'You missed me?' Artur Lewandowski says when he arrives.

'It's not you. It's your horrible instant-coffee powder. You were nice to me. Just wanted to buy you something decent to show my appreciation. And to show you the difference.'

'Like I told you before, the difference is money. I probably get twenty cups of *my* caffeine for the same price as one of yours. But, hey, why aren't you at the site? Is it true you're not working on the case any more?'

'Oh, I am,' I say, wondering who told him I'm not, figuring it's better not to ask, in case it leads to more questions, 'just not at the scene. We're nearly wrapped up there anyway. You must be happy.'

'Happy? Happier if there was no seventh body, if it was just the six old guys. It's a big distraction. And it's not nice to think about her. Sad, that girl, lying there for so many years. We'll go on with the build like a normal job, but unless there's something wrong with you, you're going to be thinking about her. She's going to be in your head. In *my* head, I mean.'

'Mine too.' I sip my Americano and take a beat. Think again about how she's still 'the girl' or 'Jane Doe'. How she doesn't have a name. How there must be someone who knows who she is. Someone who went looking for her after she disappeared. I say, 'I've been working on who occupied the building before it was knocked. You've been around since the start of the works?'

'Before. I was here before anything was demolished.'

'So you were in Bertie Allen's when it was still a pub? Still looked like one?'

'Yeah, it was closed but the same. The pub, all the tables and bar stools were still there. Pictures on the walls. Some beer left in the taps. I didn't drink it. No vodka or whiskey, though, nothing like that. Them maybe I would've tried but not the beer.'

'The corner where the body was found, do you remember it?'

'There was a long bench seat by the wall. Made of wood, I think.'

'Do you think the bench might have been put in after the murder to hide the burial? Where the flagstones had been lifted? Did it look newer?'

'From what I remember, it looked normal. Old, like everything else in the pub. Maybe not so old, I don't know. I didn't look closely. I think it was screwed to the wall.'

'How do you know? Did you move it?'

He laughs. 'Me? No. A JCB bucket moved everything. Or nearly everything.' He laughs again. 'Maybe some things went on eBay,' he holds up his hands, 'I don't know.'

'What about overhead? Did you go upstairs?'

'Of course. Health and safety. We have to check for hazards like gas cylinders and electrics. A museum up there. Someone's home but not for many years. Everything brown. Worse than the pub. Old clothes in the wardrobes. Nothing worth saving. Looked like the person who lived there died or went to a nursing home and no one lived there after.'

'So not rented out?'

'Don't think so, no.'

'What about the owner, the developer?'

'Ray Grant. Good guy.'

'I'd like to talk to him. Could you give me his mobile number?'

Lightning fast, he says, 'Mr Grant had nothing to do with the dead girl.'

I think about asking why Artur's being so protective but decide that it's better not to risk alienating him. I say, 'I'm not suggesting anything. The planning process must have taken years. If he knew she was there, he could have moved her.'

'Exactly. And some of your guys already talked to him. I don't know who but the boss said they acted like he was a suspect. He's angry about this. The building delays too.'

'All the more reason for me to talk to him. Explain that he's *not* a suspect.'

'Yeah? Okay. Nice idea. Maybe you can put him in a good mood.'

He pings the number to me and gets to his feet.

Shaking my hand, he says, 'Thanks for the coffee. See you, huh? You want to buy me another coffee sometime, you know where I am for the next three years, maybe—'

His phone rings. He answers. Listens. 'Two minutes.' Ends the call. 'At last, we can get moving,' he says. 'It's finally happening.'

'Yes, the crime scene is being released,' I say, because I want him thinking I'm more centrally involved in the investigation than I am, even though the precise timing is as much news to me as to him, 'but can I ask you for one last favour?'

After Artur leaves, I order another coffee, and a spinach and feta pastry. I check my phone and, finding no message from Sadie, start to wonder if doing as she suggested and disappearing from Coughlan's Quay for an open-ended amount of time is only going to make my situation worse.

But thinking about it isn't going to provide an answer. I scribble a few notes and finish up as fast as I can. There's no point in wasting the bike.

Ibiza was good, though. Anyone you'd ask would say it was brilliant.

Perfect climate for it too.

Sunset to sunrise.

The peak followed by the chill-out.

Hedonism fully organised.

Lookit, all that said, to be honest, it didn't particularly suit us.

Three amigos from Cork, cash burning our way through the nights, sun burning our way through the days.

Realising that the music in Henry's was actually better.

Less treble. More bass. More niche too.

And then we got talking to her one morning on the beach as the dawn crept over the horizon, uncertain at first, blinding orange as per usual after about two minutes.

Yet another bright new day after yet another long wild night.

But her.

Like a cool drink of water she was, and I don't mean that she was cool. What I'm saying is, she was pure. Like an angel. A pixie. Blonde hair in plaits. Manchester Irish. A gruff Coronation-Street-meets-Liam-Gallagher *accent that had us in stitches.*

All three of us thunderbolt in love with her from the second we saw her.

Even though she was too young for us.

Only eighteen and a half.

With less than a year left to live.

30

I SPIN DOWN DOUGLAS STREET AND, BEFORE I know it, I'm over the south channel and on the other side of the island, near the tip where the branches of the river reconnect and continue on to the sea. It feels more exposed down here, wider roads and rougher waters. I take off my cycle helmet and a biting breeze whips my hair across my eyes. I'm outside Cork Simon emergency shelter, a substantial corner structure, twenty-five or thirty years old, three storeys, limestone at ground level, brick on the upper floors, windows and doors a patriotic green as if to say, 'Remember, we're Irish too, with the same rights as the rest of ye.'

Inside, I place the helmet on the counter, say who I am and show the receptionist my garda ID. I tell her I'm looking for a man called Garry McCarthy. I describe him.

She answers quickly: 'Not one of our current residents.'

'He gave Anderson's Quay as his address. When was the last time you saw him? It's not bad news, by the way. It's good, actually. It'd be a help if I knew when he was last here.'

A shrug. 'Give me a sec.'

She returns. 'I don't know Mr McCarthy and I've been working here nearly a year. No one I've asked inside has seen him lately. Are you sure you have the right place? You could try St Vincent's?'

I hand her my card. 'If he shows up, please ask him to contact me.'

She laughs. 'Good news, is it? I'm sure he'll be on to you the very minute he hears you're looking for him.'

It's a straight run along the quays to the Bridewell, the garda station McCarthy selected for his weekly bail sign-on. I pick one of the civilian staff, figuring on a more cooperative response. He tells me McCarthy's been compliant so far but hasn't signed on for this week yet.

He says, 'I could have met him. I don't remember, like. It's a busy place and I only work daytimes. He's allowed to sign between nine a.m. and nine p.m. so if he signed outside my office hours I wouldn't see him.'

Again, I leave a message for McCarthy but messages left in garda stations are rarely delivered. Also, even if anyone remembers to tell McCarthy I'm looking for him, the woman down at the Simon was right: he's never going to contact me voluntarily. The only reliable way of getting in touch with him is via his solicitor and the only legitimate reason for contacting *him* is to say that the charges against his client are being dropped.

But I'm not ready to do that. Besides, I haven't done the paperwork or obtained the necessary approval. Disconsolately, I put on my helmet again and head for the door.

Then, for what feels like the first time in ages, my luck changes. As I'm leaving, a person is coming up the steps. He looks preoccupied and shows no sign of recognising me but it's Garry McCarthy, the man I've been looking for. I think about waiting by the entrance for him to come out, then following him, seeing where he ends up, but decide I don't have time. Instead, I turn my hi-vis vest the right way around with the GARDA insignia facing outwards and head back into the Bridewell to grab McCarthy for a little chat.

31

SIGNING DONE, HE'S TURNING AWAY FROM THE window in the public office when I get inside. We're a few metres apart, me by the door, him one elbow still on the counter. Whatever about earlier, he recognises me now. I've taken off my helmet and I'm giving him the stare.

'A word,' I say.

'Talk to my solicitor,' McCarthy says.

Because he stayed silent at the scene and after the arrest, it's the first time I've heard his voice. The tone is plummy Cork middle class. Not what I'd expected from his record. Even though addiction knows no barriers, the bald socio-economic truth is that most heroin addicts don't hail from leafy Blackrock. The general rule is that they come from places with fewer financial or educational cushions and less hope.

Looking at McCarthy, if you didn't know his story, you wouldn't pick him out in a crowd. An unremarkable middle-aged man in a khaki anorak, blue jeans and brown walking boots. Something off about the eyes, maybe, a hint of the pain he must have endured, and a few extra furrows in the brow, when you examine him closely.

He says, 'What do you want from me? I'm in a programme.

I'm clean. You have no business bothering me. I have better things to do than—'

'You're on bail, and you gave a false address. You said you were living at Cork Simon on Anderson's Quay but they say not.'

'I didn't mention the Simon specifically,' he says. 'There are other places on Anderson's Quay.'

'Where? Do you mean the Leonardo Hotel?'

'My solicitor can give my current address to the court if it's a problem but as far as I know I'm all straight with my bail conditions and I'm not under any obligation to stay in Anderson's Quay or anywhere else. The only thing I have to do is sign on here once a week and show up for my trial. We don't live in a police state quite yet but this conversation is starting to feel like garda harassment. I might have to think about complaining to GSOC, something I'm sure you're familiar with if this is how you behave. Hassling citizens who—'

'Steady on,' I say, 'and smile for the CCTV camera. If there's harassment going on here, it's not coming from me. With your record, McCarthy, I'd be a lot more polite. As for your address, you're on bail. Bail can be revoked, if necessary. But I'm in a *very* good mood so I'll go easy on you. Tell your solicitor to send me your current address within the next forty-eight hours.'

'Is that it?'

'That's it.' I step aside and gesture for him to leave. He walks slowly past me, out the door and down the steps. He picks up the pace as he crosses the street and ducks through the archway and down the alley by the side of Dennehy's pub. He turns his head to the right a couple of times, and snatches it back again, as if he wants to check if I'm still watching, but won't allow himself to. Then a stray thought flashes behind my eyes. About the baggage all of us carry. And whether it's me McCarthy's looking out for or somebody else.

32

THE CONVERSATION WITH MCCARTHY IS
unsettling but I box it off in my mind for the present. As I walk
the bike along Cornmarket Street, I return to thinking about
the girl and, on impulse, make a call to Deborah Winters from
Forensics. Nothing unusual when I worked in Dublin at
GNBCI. Now it feels risky. To my surprise, she answers. What
she says is even more surprising.

'If you only knew how many times I've been meaning to
contact you.'

But it's the *way* she says it – the unexpected warmth – that
strikes me dumb.

'You still there?'

'Sorry, yeah, Deborah. I'm here. How have you been?'

We chit-chat about the weather up there today versus how
it is in Cork for a minute, but we were never friends outside
the job. She knows I'm calling for information.

She asks, 'What can I do for you?'

'I'll take anything you've got – literally anything – but you
did say you expected something on the shoes soon.'

'We've got more to do on it but the first thing is that Buffalo
didn't have a shop in Ireland until the noughties. Before that,

if people wanted the shoes they usually picked them up in London or elsewhere in England. What I *can* confirm is that this particular style of boot was first manufactured in 1996 and that it was a regular feature of the range until 2003. I don't have the numbers but a hell of a lot of these boots were sold so chasing down purchase records or retail outlets stocking them is probably a waste of time unless we potentially have someone specific we're looking to connect them to. For ID purposes, I mean.'

'And the second thing?'

'They were too big for her. She was a five and the boots were a six.'

'What are you thinking?'

'That she didn't buy them new. Maybe she got them second-hand.'

I say, 'Or stole them?'

'Yeah, that could be it,' Deborah replies, 'and it'd explain the wrong size.'

I take that in. Feel something click in me. Like *now* I'm getting to know the girl.

'Any more info on what she was wearing?'

'We think that she was clothed when she went into the earth, like I said at the briefing. Based on the synthetic-thread traces remaining and the positioning of them, she was wearing a cotton or other natural material mini-dress coming to mid-thigh and now we know that she had cotton underwear, shorts type, underneath it, Primark brand – we were able to magnify the remnants of the label – and a white under-wired balcony lace bra with synthetic padding.'

'Do you know the colour of the dress?'

'White nylon thread so it could have been something like a white T-shirt dress but we can't say for sure. It could've been a light colour, maybe pastel, or Breton-striped, maybe blue and white, or red and white.'

I think about her blood soaking into the cotton dress. 'What about her hair?'

'Mostly down, but we found traces of white synthetic material in it. She probably had two small high bunches – one at each side of her head – and the rest loose.'

Just as I'd thought when I saw it the evening she was found.

I wait a beat, then ask, 'Her jacket? Is there any news on that?'

'Yes,' Deborah says, and I can almost hear her smile. 'The jacket that was lying beneath her. We think it was probably thrown into the grave first. That she wasn't wearing it at the time of the murder. And we found coal dust on it so we reckon fireside tongs were used to place it in the grave rather than someone's hand so the chances of DNA on it, other than the deceased's obviously, are slim. The jacket itself is a white Adidas zip-up, high collar, blue lettering, blue trim, to match the Buffalo boots. It's the kind of cover-up tennis players and other sports people wore in the seventies.'

I ask, 'So it's a replica?'

'No, it's the real thing. Vintage. Popular with dance-music fans in the nineties. I'm putting the details in my report but I was thinking maybe our dead girl was a raver?'

And again, the shiver of recognition. As if I'm getting to know her.

As if, somehow, I've always known her.

She was in Ibiza for the whole season, handing out club flyers and hanging around. Living in a tiny flat with a load of cockroaches and three flatmates. All recruited in Manchester.

Long hours. Hard grind.

Others came and went. She stuck it out.

And, when it came to heading home near the end of the holiday, we swore we'd keep in touch with her.

Empty promises in the time before iPhones and WhatsApp, and Facebook not yet a glimmer in Zuckerberg's brain. Way harder to stay in contact before the world shrank.

But the more we talked, the more we learned about her. That she'd grown up in care and had nothing to go back to Manchester for. And that she was nearly sure her old granny, who died when she was only five, was from Cork.

And before you know it, a plan was hatched. That she'd come home with us. Not straight away, but at summer's end she'd fly back to Manchester on her return ticket and we'd road-trip over on the ferry to collect her and her stuff. A pipedream, except it came true.

No trace of her entering Ireland, thanks to the common travel area and good old Irish Ferries.

Which is why no one ever looked for her here. No one looked for her there either.

When you're over eighteen, you can go wherever you want.

So she came to Cork. Moved into our gaff. Till she found her feet was the idea.

She liked the scene here. Wanted to stay.

Got a job. Said she was looking for a place of her own.

She never did get around to moving. No need, we said. Plenty of space.

The three of us and her so close by then.

Getting to know her better and better.

Caring about her more and more.

Four of us in the gang now, not three.

But four splits so easily into two twos.

Three knights in shining armour vying for the heart of a maiden fair.

If it sounds like a competition with her as the prize, that's because it was.

Never out in the open, never admitted, but always there.

Bubbling under.

On and on until one spring day she was gone again.

Afterwards, if ever anyone asked about her, we used to say, 'She went back.'

Only a few ever asked us where.

And when they did, like we'd agreed, we said, 'Maybe England.'

We said, 'Maybe Ibiza.'

'She was talking about going to Thailand,' we said.

In truth, we were the only ones who truly cared.

And we knew exactly where she was.

And sooner than you'd have imagined in your wildest dreams, she was forgotten.

As if she never was.

Never here at all.

Never anywhere.

33

TALKING TO DEBORAH HAS MADE ME REALISE HOW little I know about Cork in the nineties. The world is a different place when you're eight or nine, watching *The Den* on RTÉ after school and going for sleepovers, from when you're eighteen or nineteen.

Although one of the few things that *everyone* knows about Cork back then is that there was a famous nightclub called Sir Henry's on South Main Street. If our murder victim *was* a raver, like Deborah from Forensics suggested, she might have gone to Henry's. I need to find out about the scene. The internet is the obvious place to start, but it was still in its infancy in the nineties. The newspaper archive for the two locally based newspapers – the *Examiner* and the *Echo* – is more likely to have contemporaneous hard information. I think about going to the City Library, then stop. That research can wait.

What I need to do most right now is to start the process for the withdrawal of charges in the Deerpark burglary. It doesn't mean I can't still keep half an eye on Martin Campbell, who, my gut tells me, is all kinds of dodgy, but meeting Garry McCarthy has given me pause. Whatever he was doing in Campbell's house that day, and whatever his record, he's doing a convincing impression of someone who's trying to get his life back on track. It's not for me to deny him the chance of putting his demons behind him.

Plus, I have zero justification for keeping the offence hanging over him after Campbell's told me he's dropping the complaint. If it came out later that I hadn't finalised the case when I should've, it'd be another black mark on my record. The official garda motto might be 'Keeping People Safe' but written below it in invisible ink are the letters CYOAF: cover your own arse first. It's something I don't remember enough, but it's never too late to start.

Back at Coughlan's Quay, I return the bike and take the back stairs one flight up to the general office. Making it to my desk without having to engage with anyone, I burn through the necessary statements, print them and head for Sadie's door. Although she isn't the final decision-maker on the prosecution, I want to run my proposed withdrawal of charges against Garry McCarthy by her. And I want to find out why she encouraged me to disappear this morning.

Standing outside, I hear no other voices. I knock and poke my head around the door. Sadie is behind her desk with Olly Fogarty and Bugsy McKeown, a recent transfer from the West Cork Division, seated facing her. They look like they've been poring silently over a document, which is why I didn't hear them speak.

I don't think I've had a conversation longer than two words with Bugsy since he moved to Coughlan's Quay. He's in his late twenties with wet-look gelled hair and polished tan shoes, as if he's permanently on the look-out for a wedding to crash.

'Sorry,' I say. 'Didn't know you were busy. Just about that burglary. Deeley was the lead on it and . . .'

'Is it urgent?' Sadie asks.

'Not really,' I say. 'Not at all.'

'Is that what you've been working on all day?'

'More or less. I spoke to the complainant again and tracked down the accused. He'd given a false, a misleading, address.'

'You've got a lot of catching up to do,' Sadie says.

She picks up a document from her desk and holds it out to me. 'Read that at home overnight. Tell me what you think in the morning.'

'Will do, skipper,' I say. Stepping into the room, I take the document from her. Olly Fogarty and Bugsy exchange looks, then Olly raises his eyebrows to me in greeting, tipping his chin in a slightly upward motion. His expression is neutral to friendly. Bugsy looks at me as if I'm a creature from another planet, which isn't far off how I feel at times around here.

Backing out, I glance down at the front page of the document. My heart leaps. It's the preliminary post-mortem report, the written version of the incident-room talk Boney gave us a couple of mornings ago. There's unlikely to be anything in it I don't yet know. It's what it means that counts. It means I'm still on the case.

34

MY ELATION IS SHORT-LIVED. WHEN I ANALYSE what Sadie said, I conclude that she doesn't want to talk to me until the morning. That she wants me gone from the station again. She told me to read the report overnight at home. Out back, in the quiet of my car, I mull over why that might be and if I've misunderstood. To distract myself from over-thinking it, I google 'Sir Henry's nightclub Cork' on my phone and find a whole pile of nothing much.

Then my phone pings. It's a text from Artur Lewandowski: *Here. 10 mins. If you want to meet the boss.*

It's what I'd asked of him earlier in Alchemy Café, if he'd make contact with the developer Ray Grant for me. I didn't expect the meeting to happen so quickly but I'm not going to turn down the chance. Throwing the phone onto the passenger seat, I exit the car park.

There's a space in front of Tom Barry's, neat as a pin and painted royal blue with flower-boxes above the hand-lettered sign. The pub has long been a beacon amid the dereliction. Before getting out of the car, I double-check but it's as I expected. The street is a garda-free zone. No loiterers or gawkers either. The crime-scene circus has left. I cross to the entrance, texting Artur that I've arrived.

The reply comes: *He is in my office. Be nice* 😊

I text back a thumbs-up, push in the site door and enter. It's deserted. It's past 5 p.m. and still daylight, an hour left till sunset, but I've spent so much time here recently I could find my way around in the dark. Soon the construction will start and the place where the dead girl probably spent her final hours will be obliterated. I have to find out as much as I can before that happens.

Ray Grant is alone in the Portakabin. His face is familiar to me from numerous ribbon-cutting newspaper and television reports over the years. He's a self-made multi-millionaire, son of a widowed mother, a boy from a council estate who started out with a pick and shovel. He must be over seventy because he's been on the go since the 1980s yet somehow he managed to come out the other side of the economic crash seemingly unscathed. His hair is white and plentiful. He's wearing Hunter wellies and a Barbour jacket over a V-neck wool jumper, a check shirt with a green knitted tie and needlecord fawn trousers. He's standing by a filing cabinet, leafing through what appears to be a folder of delivery dockets.

He says, 'In my game, you never stop looking after the pennies, Garda McCann. When you do, that's when the trouble starts.'

'Call me Alice,' I say.

'Call me Mr Grant,' he says. 'I'm joking. Ray is what everyone calls me.'

I smile. 'Ray, as Artur probably told you, I'm interested in the history of the site here. What you can tell me about Bertie Allen's pub especially.'

'Did Artur also tell you that I've been made to feel like a criminal for buying a property where a body was found that had nothing to do with me?'

'He did, and I was sorry to hear it. Who interviewed you?'

'Detective Sergeant Sadie O'Riordan.' He pauses. 'You look surprised.'

'I am. I don't recall her mentioning your name as a possible suspect.'

He nods. 'Right. I'm willing to admit I might have overreacted . . . and I see I've surprised you again. A little recommendation, Alice. Don't take up poker whatever you do.'

'Sorry, Ray, I'm flummoxed here. It's just so rare to hear, em, well, let's face it, *any* man admit that he might have made a mistake.'

Grant laughs and points to a pair of chairs he's set up facing each other, away from Artur's desk. 'Take a seat. Let's see if we can help each other. The sooner this murder is solved, the sooner normality returns and we can get on with building forty-six new homes, *beautiful* new homes, if I do say so myself.'

As I wait for him to shuffle through some more papers, shut the filing cabinet with a screech, check his phone and eventually sit, I take a second to check how I'm feeling. An important interview like this would've had me in a lather of sweat a few weeks ago. Not now. It's a change, a welcome one, but I'd prefer not to dwell on the reason for it. Which is her.

35

I PITCH GRANT A SOFT OPENER. 'YOU'RE NOT UNDER caution, Ray, and as you know, I'm interviewing you purely as background.'

'First of all, is there any news on the identity of the dead girl?'

'Not yet,' I say, moving on before we get into a discussion on the details of the case. 'We're still looking at all angles. Can you tell me how you came to buy Bertie Allen's?'

'I'd started putting the land parcels together a good while before. Bertie's was the last bit of the jigsaw and one I never expected to get, but the owner, Maurice Bolger, got sick and his wife came to me after he died and asked me to make her an offer. Maurice was the original Bertie Allen's grandson and he would never have sold. Wanted the fourth generation to take over. *They* didn't. Ah, sure, the good is gone out of the trade. When was the last time you spent a night downing pints in a pub?'

He doesn't wait for an answer. 'It's all home drinking now or wine lists and cocktails and food, pizza ovens and burritos and whatever you're having yourself. Traditional old-man spit-and-sawdust hostelries like Bertie Allen's are a thing of the past.'

'When did you buy Bertie's?'

'As I'm sure you're well aware, my company RGP purchased it in 2011.'

'You got it for a song.'

'We got it for whatever the purchase deed says we got it for. We would've got it a lot cheaper if we'd waited until 2013 or 2014. You couldn't buy or sell a square inch in the entire country after the IMF took over in 2012. The banks wouldn't lend you so much as a shilling. That's why nothing happened with this site for years. That, and planning. Wheels move slowly in City Hall. And when we could finally get going, well, you know the story.'

'I'm sorry I have to ask this, but do *you* have any information that might lead to the identification of the deceased female whose remains were found on your property?'

'None whatsoever and, like I told your sergeant, if I'd had any idea she was there, I wouldn't have touched Bertie Allen's with a bargepole. Truth be told, I only bought the site to oblige Maurice Bolger's widow. I didn't need it. Yes, it allowed me to shoehorn in a few extra units but what no one seems to realise is that every day the build is delayed is costing me money. It's tight margins. In a site like this, you have to put up with the archaeologists. It's all part of the job. I expected a few bits of broken pottery or a bit of an oul' wall, maybe. Never in my worst nightmares did I expect six dead men and a girl. And people will forget about the men fast enough, but they're not going to forget about her. Not for a while.'

I say, 'Not ever, if I have anything to do with it.'

'Fair enough,' Grant says, 'you have a job to do.' His phone pings. 'We'll have to draw this to a close. My son is outside.'

He gets to his feet, starts to fasten his jacket. 'Any idea when she died?'

'Not really, other than that it's some years ago, obviously.'

He looks at me again. 'They were still serving drink in here up to 2007, you know. A tenant took over for a year or two after Maurice got sick. It was a busy place, when it was operating. No one could have killed and buried someone while it was up and running. But it was closed for a long time. It must have happened then. After 2007. Before I took over in 2011 and secured the site properly. That's four years when anyone could have got in, dug the hole and buried her. He wouldn't have expected her to be found. Probably reckoned the pub would reopen and Bob's your uncle. Carry on as before except there's a body no one knows about underneath.'

I ask, 'If that's true, why pick Bertie Allen's, though? Any thoughts on that?'

'The murderer was probably living in a flat around here. Long gone, no doubt. I don't know how you'd live with yourself. A thing like that would take a toll on most people, but there's others who'd view it differently. A psychopath, maybe, a serial killer going from town to town or country to country. An American, like your man Ted Bundy.'

It's always interesting when a witness talks too much and offers his own theories but we're running out of time so I say the main thing I've come here to say. 'Thanks so much, Ray. You've been generous. Very helpful indeed. Just before you dash off, I'm wondering if you have photos of the pub as it was before.'

His response is instantaneous. 'I don't.'

'Your engineer or your surveyor must. At drawings stage.

Pre-demolition. They'd almost certainly have walked the site. I'm sure they'd have taken pictures.'

He takes a while to reply. 'I'll look into it and get back to you.'

I hand him my card. He takes it.

Out on the street, he locks the access door, made of the same plywood as the partition blocking off the site, and padlocks it. His son pulls up in front, driving a burgundy Range Rover.

'Here's Conor,' Grant says.

Grant's son waves and leans across the passenger seat to open the door but I don't get a good look at him. Grant shakes my hand and gets into the car. Once inside, he rolls down the window and sticks his head out, suddenly cheerful. 'Always happy to help the boys in blue. And the girls.'

The car takes off down the hill. I assume Grant's heading home. I should've met him there, or at his office. On site, the interview was entirely on his terms. By responding to his summons, I've learned less than I could have about him. And I can't quite pin it down but I have the feeling that somewhere along the way I've made a mistake.

36

THE DOOR TO TOM BARRY'S BEER GARDEN IS OPEN.
I stare longingly under the arch, drawn by the greenery and the
old stone and warm lights and the buzz of conversation and
laughter. Recalling Ray Grant's question, 'When was the last
time you spent a night downing pints in a pub?' the answer is
'I can't remember.' That careless fun feels impossible, unreach-
able. Caught in a reverie, I don't notice Dr Eileen O'Hara until
she's in front of me.

'We've been shouting and waving at you for ages,' she says.
She points to one of the big picnic benches inside. There's a
heater overhead.

'Archaeologists with their woolly jumpers off,' I say. 'Looks
like fun.'

'Just a few drinks. We've ordered pizza. Join us?'

'I'd love to but I can't,' I say, 'I'll come in and say hello for
a minute, though.'

At the table, I spot Lorcan and Dr Hanna and a few more faces
whose names aren't relevant to the case and, as a result, are already
fading from memory. 'Celebrating the end of the excavation?'

Dr Hanna says, 'The beginning. The real work starts now.
Testing. Writing.'

'Yeah,' Lorcan says, 'the dig's the fun part. Oops, sorry, didn't mean . . .'

'Don't worry,' I say, 'you should hear the way guards talk when there's no one around to hear.'

'Sit down,' Dr Hanna says, 'come on.'

'Give me a minute,' I say, gesturing towards the bathrooms. Afterwards, on the way out, I bump into Johnny McDonagh, the digger driver, coming from the direction of the front bar. He's holding two pints of lager. 'You're not gone back to Galway yet? Are you here with the archaeologists?'

'I know them from other excavations. And it looks like I'm going to be down here another while. RGP have asked me to stay on. They're stuck for someone at the moment so they're paying me an extra few quid an hour and giving me a free room in a house. It's handy enough for a while and sure it's costing me nothing. I'm too old for the shared house, though.'

He laughs and I wonder how many pints he's had because he seems to have had a personality transplant. I like this version of him better. 'You might get fond of Leeside,' I say.

'Outside chance, I s'pose.' He grins. 'Can I buy you a drink? After I've got rid of these two, I mean.'

'I've the car with me,' I say, 'but thanks.'

'Another time so,' he says. 'You could give me the local's guide to Cork?'

I hear myself saying, 'Sure,' and not, 'No. You're a witness in a murder case.'

At the table outside, after another few minutes, I manage to extricate myself from the archaeologists' party. In the car, on the way up to my parents' house for plant-watering and light-switching duties, I find myself thinking about Johnny

McDonagh's drink invitation. I remember his pale blue eyes. His blond lashes too, something I've always had a weakness for.

But being caught fraternising with a witness would be the icing on the cake for Feeney, the final nail in my coffin. It's never going to happen.

37

ON THE WAY BACK FROM MY PARENTS', AT ST LUKE'S
— named for the former church at the crossroads, now an atmospheric live music venue — I turn left up the Middle Glanmire
Road, instead of right onto Wellington Road towards my flat.
I climb again past the Montenotte Hotel to where the road
splits. They say there are seven hills in Rome. Must be at least
that number in Cork. Admittedly, the resemblance ends there.

I take the right fork and drive steeply downhill on the charm-
ingly named Lover's Walk, one of the city's most exclusive
addresses, though it was originally called Leper's Walk, which
the residents tend to mention less often. Where my brother lives
is along a stretch with high walls and entrance buzzers. His
gates are usually open. He's too impatient to sit waiting for the
electronic jerk and the painfully slow mechanical swing. Also,
the road's so narrow here it makes sense to get off it as soon as
you can.

Something I may have forgotten to mention is that my siblings
are enormous over-achievers. My parents had run out of energy
when it came to me. Didn't object as much as they might have
when I said I didn't want to go to university, undoubtedly
because they expected me to change my mind eventually. They'd

already snagged the Cork parental ambition trifecta: doctor, accountant, lawyer. My sister's a consultant dermatologist; my other brother's a tax partner in one of the big firms on South Mall.

My Lover's Walk brother, the eldest McCann, is a barrister, a senior counsel who does defence personal injury and medical negligence. He works like a dog and drinks rarely but he had a hectic social life back in the day. He's the right age to know about Cork in the nineties.

The house is off-the-telly stunning, taking full advantage of a south-facing hillside position. Billy and his wife Justine, a barrister specialising in property and trusts, bought a nondescript 1970s bungalow for the location, then swiftly demolished and replaced it with cantilevered glass and concrete, like something out of Laurel Canyon. It shouldn't work in this grey rainy landscape but it does. Surrounded by trees and shrubbery at the back, it's open to the south, east and west so it catches whatever light is going.

Billy's study is in a garden room, off the main house, with a separate entrance, a wood-burning stove, wool rugs and a sleek hardwood desk with shelves to match. Week nights, if he's not at court in Dublin, he's here till eleven or twelve. It's October, and the High Court is sitting in Cork, so he's bound to be still working. I walk in without knocking. As the door opens, he swivels around in his padded leather chair, grumpy at first. His face breaks into a broad smile when he sees it's me. 'I thought you were one of the kids,' he says, 'looking for money again.

That's the only reason they bother their arses talking to me these days.'

I give him a hug and perch on the side of the desk.

'I'm glad you called in,' he says. 'I've been meaning to ask you. Number one daughter is in this speech-and-drama thing up at the Helix in Dublin. Granny and Granddad were supposed to be coming but now they're on that cruise so do you want to come instead? Here, I'll text you the details.'

My phone pings. I open the message. 'Looks great and I'd love to but you know I've too much going on with the Barrack Street investigation. I'm really sorry.'

'Ah, no worries. It's going to be horrendous. Packed with vicious stage parents. You're better off, believe me. What's up anyway? I assume your visit has a purpose?'

I get straight into it. 'Do you know anything about the rave scene in Cork in the nineties?'

'Nah, sis,' he says. 'I was a City Limits Comedy Club guy and I always stuck to the pints. No dance music and disco biscuits for me.'

'Even if you weren't involved, do you know anything at all about the scene?'

'A bit. If you lived in Cork at the time, you couldn't *but* know. The crowds, for one thing. Masses of people. Loads of scare stories in the press and from city councillors about violence but it was blown out of all proportion. As far as I know, the trouble came mainly from people who were barred and didn't get in. Public order issues more than anything else.'

'You're talking about Sir Henry's?'

'Where else would I be talking about?'

'You tell me. I was a child at the time. I was never there.'

'When was Henry's demolished? That site seems to have been derelict forever.'

'I googled it earlier on before I left the station. It was 2003. There's not much online about the club, apart from a bit about Nirvana playing there a few days before "Smells Like Teen Spirit" came out. There's a photo of Kurt Cobain but very few photos otherwise.'

'I assume this is about your murder case. Why do you think there's a Henry's connection?'

'I don't *think* there's a Henry's connection. I don't know. I'm just trying to find out as much as I can about Cork in the old days.'

'Jeez, thanks. The dim and distant past. Well, I guess you could be on the right track with Henry's. The location, for one thing. Bertie Allen's pub, where the body was found, is only up the hill, five minutes from where the club was. Sir Henry's was famous, you know. There used to be special buses travelling there from other towns and cities. They used to have these Weekender things. Guest DJs. Big names too. You'd see the posters everywhere. No social media in those days. The Weekenders were Saturdays and Sundays. The bank-holiday weekend gigs were massively popular, I think.'

'What about Easter weekend?'

'Saturday and Sunday maybe. Not Good Friday, obviously. Remember, it's only in the last ten years the pubs were allowed to open then. Before that, as you know, because you're not *that* young, Alice, Holy Thursday was one of the biggest drinking nights of the year. Queues in every off-licence. Loads of house parties going on into the next day. Pubs and clubs had to close before midnight. No exemptions permitted. You *do* remember that, do you?'

'I do. Holy Thursday would be a good night for a lock-in so, would it?'

'A small one maybe. You're the cop. It was heavily policed, I'd imagine. There used to be a garda station on Barrack Street. Closed, what, about ten years? If you're talking about Bertie Allen's, you wouldn't be able to have much of a lock-in on the same street as a garda station, would you?'

'The Barrack Street station closed in 2013. As for lock-ins, there was actually at least one in Bertie's because there's a record of a prosecution. And there was even a murder in a different pub on Barrack Street in 1995. The man was out in the front hall taking a phone call at the time. The case is still open and unsolved.'

'Any connection to this murder?'

'I can't see there would be. Different MO and, for reasons I can't go into, we're pretty sure this murder happened *after* 1995. Treat that as legal professional privilege, by the way. All of this is. We're not releasing any possible dates as yet.'

He rolls out his chair from the desk, looks up at me properly.

After a beat, he says, 'You seem different. More energised than I've seen you in a while. I hope you're not overdoing it.'

'I'm fine. I'm really well.'

'Have you heard anything from that fucker Calum Pierce?'

'I don't *want* to hear from him,' I say, and it's not a lie.

'You'd think he'd have reached out to you, the bastard. He must know that you're the one who found the body, that it might be . . .'

'I don't *want* to talk about Calum. I want to talk about Sir Henry's.'

Two more non-lies. The truth, but not the whole truth.

'Okay, okay. Well, you presumably know that the other thing Sir Henry's was famous for was the drugs. You could check Ecstasy – MDMA – possessions. Might be a way to track down a few ex-Henry's regulars.'

'That's actually a good idea.'

Billy says, 'It's why they pay me the big bucks.'

I kiss his forehead and head up the slope to my car, my feet heavier than they were on the way down because now Calum's in my head again.

Although it's not like he ever left, is it?

Because, despite what I said to Billy, I *have* heard from Calum. He's the one who's been texting me. It started after I got back to work from sick leave and transferred to Coughlan's Quay. A veritable flurry of sleazy, *How u doing?*, *What's the story?*, *Hope u ok?*, *You know you can call me anytime* messages.

Which I didn't respond to and deleted immediately. After more of the same, I blocked him. In my book, that was the end of it.

Except Calum kept doing it. Using other people's phones, even burners, possibly. I don't know because I never replied to any of his messages. I contained the problem.

But I noticed that the texts changed over time.

Less *Hope you ok?* and more *Thinking about you.*

Less concerned friend. More something else.

More dangerous.

I deleted them all.

And now Billy goes and mentions him. Releases him from the container in my brain. And the swirling sick feeling in my stomach is back. Reliving the years I wasted. How, when I needed him most, he abandoned me. Dropped me into the bin like a used tissue.

Before my mistake with the warrant, we'd both been haunting property websites, searching for a house instead of the apartment. Planning our forever family home. Our shared future.

Better you found out what he was like before than after the wedding, as my dad said.

You were wasted on him and at least you hadn't bought the dress, as my mum said.

He was never good enough for you, as my sister said.

Fuck him, sis, as my two brothers said.

Yes, to all of the above.

But.

When I get home to the flat, I take a long shower, almost hot enough to burn, and go straight to bed.

She comes to me at night. A whisper in my ear and I wake up wringing wet.

Always the one word.

Why?

Lately, she's coming to me during the day too.

A giggle.

A wisp of hair.

A blurry glimpse.

He was the first to kiss her.

I was the one she loved.

And I loved her.

So much.

But star-crossed lovers were we.

Slow learners too.

Deluded into thinking he'd ever accept us.

And what's done is done.

There's no bringing her back.

Too late now to protect her.

Too late to change anything.

Time to draw a line.

Time to end it.

38

SIX FORTY-FIVE, THE NEXT MORNING, THE DOORBELL buzzes, louder than a hundred bees. My first thought is that it's Calum, because I've spent the whole night awake, with him going around and around in my head. His voice in my ear, as if he was in the bed beside me. His face, right there in front of me, every time I closed my eyes. Maybe the lower dose of Effexor isn't such a good idea.

Anyway, it's not him. It's Sadie. Which is a different kind of unpleasant surprise, especially as I'm still in my pyjamas and only thinking about getting up.

She waits in the kitchen for me to get dressed. I fling on yesterday's clothes. In the bathroom, I scrape toothpaste over my front teeth and slather on concealer and too much foundation in an attempt to hide my puffy eyes.

When I emerge, the kettle is boiled and Sadie's opening and shutting press doors. She gives me an odd look. I wipe my hand across my face.

'Where are the teabags?' she says, which is better than 'Are you okay?' It's a question I'm heartily sick of.

'Red canister. Countertop. Or do you want coffee? Blue canister. I'll make it.'

'Coffee so.' She sits at the table. 'Did you read the PM report?'

'Shit, sorry, didn't get a chance. I was going to do it over breakfast.'

I'm faced away from her so I can't see her reaction.

She says, 'There's nothing new in it. Nothing the prof hadn't told us already. No DNA results yet. The bone extraction tests take longer, as you know. And no hair toxicology yet either, needless to say. I'm not expecting anything earth-shattering from those tests anyway.'

I make a cafetière of coffee and put it on the table with mugs and a milk jug. 'Do you want toast?' I ask.

'I don't. Are you going to sit down? You're unnerving me.'

Which, funnily enough, is exactly how I feel. I take a seat silently at the far end of the table. We're not talking board room: it's a six-seater pine rectangle.

'I wanted to have this chat outside work,' Sadie says, 'didn't want to make a big deal of it. I know things have been hard. And you've been on the defensive, attitude wise.'

'Right,' I say, my heart doing a Michael Flatley in my chest.

'Look, you know how I said the other day that I wasn't going to stick up for you any more.'

'I remember.'

'I probably shouldn't have said that.'

'I didn't take offence. I deserved it.'

'You shouldn't have gone to the morgue, you know that, but you should've been at the post-mortem and if I'd had my way, you would've been. And I know you're not Inspector Feeney's biggest fan, but he agreed with me. Initially. Then he changed his mind.'

'After Professor Friel . . .'

'He can't stand Boney. He'd have been delighted to annoy him. No, it was an intervention by someone else.'

'Who?'

'Your ex has been phoning. A lot. He's worried, he says, in case you end up locked-up in St Pat's again. That's why Feeney has been, the way he sees it, shielding you from the more pressurised public aspects of the case. So he claims anyway.'

'Like the press conference. And interviewing potentially important witnesses.'

'Yes.'

'Feeney doesn't trust me, does he? He thinks I'll fold. That I *will* crack.'

Sadie shrugs. 'I can't confirm or deny that. But if that *is* what he thinks, it's up to you to prove him wrong.'

I nod. Take a breath, then spit it out. 'Calum's been texting me too. I've blocked him. I'm none of his business any more. His choice.'

She takes in what I've said. 'It's guilt, I assume. Or it could be about control.' She pauses, leans towards me. 'Controlling behaviour isn't unknown with some of the lads in our trade. Is it a thing you're, ah, familiar with yourself?'

I dodge the question. 'Or maybe the relationship with his new woman has broken up and he's thinking any port in a storm.'

She's noticed my evasion but lets it go. 'Last I heard he's still with her. I did hear it mightn't be going all that well, but I don't know how true that is.'

'I'm going to kill him.'

'There's no need. Feeney got fed up of him calling. Told him to fuck off.'

'Oh.'

'He talked to me first. Asked my opinion. I told him I thought you had the potential to be one of the best officers in the division.'

My eyes well. I cover them with my hands. 'Sorry.'

'And now I hear you didn't even read the report I gave you. I'm hoping I haven't made a mistake.'

I wipe my eyes. 'You haven't. I promise.'

'Good. You're not out of the woods with me. Or Feeney. You'll have to do way more than you're doing if you're to get through your performance review with him. You've stepped up but you have to keep stepping up.'

'I'm on it,' I say, 'stepping up, down, sideways, whatever's needed.'

She laughs. 'Think I will have a slice of toast actually.'

'Can I ask you a question?'

'You can ask. I may or may not be able to answer it.'

'Why did you leave me at the excavation? After the first six bodies were found to be historic, there was no need for detective cover, was there?'

'No need at all. But I'm your sergeant. You're my responsibility and you weren't performing. If things went on the way they were, you wouldn't have lasted. You were on a one-way ticket to checking expired gun licences in Ballygobackwards.' She pauses. 'Or worse. I'd tried everything to get you out of that room you were holed up in all the time. When the first call came, I thought I'd bring you along. I expected it to be an animal bone. That's what it is most of the time. I left you there as a kind of exposure therapy. I thought being outside might be good for you.' She laughs. 'I was right, but not how I expected.'

Over breakfast, I tell her what I've been doing on the Deerpark burglary. She doesn't go overboard with her response.

'Write it up,' she says, 'and I agree with you. Process it, get Feeney to okay it, close the file and move on.' She stands. 'I'll see you inside. Incident room, nine a.m. briefing. You need to have another go at your makeup. It's a bit . . .'

'Like I've had an argument with a load of Ready Mix?'

'Yeah, that's not a bad description.'

Forty-five minutes later, as I cross the city centre, I feel the strength coming back into my limbs, the air flowing deeper into my lungs. I stop at Dealz on Daunt Square to pick up a packet of washing-up sponges and a sharing bag of mini Mars Bars for the kitchen.

I drop the papers for the Garry McCarthy prosecution on Feeney's desk while he's out of his room. After what Sadie said, I'm more confident but not enough to deal with him first thing.

And I hang back going into the incident room, taking an edge seat near the door because I'm not ready for being desk pals with Olly Fogarty again. Might never be.

The briefing has barely started when Dean Hennessy, one of the civilian support staff based in the public office, sticks his head in. He looks serious as he gestures for Sadie and Feeney to follow him outside.

Minutes later, Sadie returns to the incident room alone. Looking straight at me, she delivers the news. It hits me like a shotgun blast.

TWO

Patricia

In Cork, they shorten everything, but I'm known by my full name. Not Pat or Patsy or Patti or Tricia or Trish, and when I set up the shop first, I considered calling it 'Patricia's', but it doesn't tell a story, does it? I called it 'Wilde', a nod to Oscar.

In Cork, everyone adds an apostrophe *s* to everything too. People started calling it 'Wilde's'. After a while I stopped correcting them. I like to get things right, but I lost that particular battle.

It was a second-hand shop, what everyone calls vintage now, which has a much nicer ring. I started it the year I turned forty, 1991. Back then, there was a stigma to the trade. Not in Dublin or London, but down here there was. It's a small town. The segment of the market I was aiming for – high quality, designer – the ladies were terrified that someone might recognise the outfit, even see them crossing the threshold. That's why I branched into the teashop on the side, china cups and lemon drizzles and strawberries and cream Victoria sponges. Come in for the cakes and you never know what you might pick up.

Or drop off. More than you'd expect of that, the dropping off, discreet sales of never to be worn again – or never worn – occasion-wear. Freeing up wardrobe space, they said. It was never because they needed or wanted the money. I played along. Although I was fussy about what I took in. People expected you to buy every kind of rubbish. They learned.

I told himself, everyone, really, that the shop was a hobby, but it was more. It was a life-saver. For me it was, and I do think it's best not to dwell, don't you? In a long life, there's rough and there's smooth and plenty of could-do-better moments to look back on.

Which isn't to say that a person might not have a regret or two.

39

MY SECOND VISIT TO THE MORTUARY AT CORK
University Hospital. This time it's sanctioned. Bugsy McKeown
driving. Sadie in the passenger seat. Me in the back. We pull
into a spot at the end of the warren of slip roads, entrance
barriers, bollards, car parks and annexes. The morgue is low-
slung brown brick, with a few random slanting pitched roofs.

The post-mortem is being carried out by Assistant State
Pathologist Davina Manning. I haven't met her before. Sadie
introduces us. Manning smiles, shows no adverse reaction on
hearing my name. 'Welcome to Funderland,' she says.

She's small and bright-eyed, her movements quick and curious
as a mouse. I warm to her immediately, and keep chatting to
her longer than necessary because she's the one ray of light in
this horror movie. And because I can hardly bear to look at the
reason we're here.

Garry McCarthy. Lying naked and lifeless on the autopsy
table.

He's got a graze on his forehead and down his right cheek
that he didn't have yesterday and marks on his neck I don't
recall, though his coat was zipped up when I saw him so I may
have missed them. Along his arms, there are old track marks,

and there's a fresh-looking injection site surrounded by several small round bruises near the crook of his right elbow.

Davina Manning is talking again: 'As you know, the deceased man was found apparently unconscious by an early-morning jogger at approximately five forty-five a.m. lying on his back in front of a bench at the western end of the Lee Fields. The civilian concluded on the basis of seeing the hypodermic protruding from the right arm that this was an overdose. Ambulance and uniformed gardaí were called and, as no life signs were discovered, and as there appeared to be no suspicious circumstances, the remains were conveyed here by hearse.'

Manning beckons us closer. 'On initial examination earlier, I observed bruising to the neck. On closer examination, I spotted a pinprick puncture wound to the rear of the neck, in addition to the right arm. It's another injection site, and it's in an unusual location. That, taken together with the other injuries, was enough to raise questions as to the cause of death, which is why I notified Coughlan's Quay.'

Sadie asks, 'What's your working hypothesis?'

'Too soon to say anything for sure. We'll need full histology and toxicology. But it looks to me like the injection to the neck may have been administered first, maybe even without the deceased's knowledge.' She points. 'See the bruises here, here, here and here, and at the back of the neck too . . .' She lifts the head slightly and replaces it. 'The marks are consistent with the neck being held or grabbed forcefully from behind by a third party and with an injection being administered by that third party.'

She takes a step back. 'The deceased may have passed out and slumped to the ground at that point, or been assisted to the ground somewhat roughly. That could account for the grazing to the right cheek and the forehead. Impossible to say for sure when those injuries occurred but either just before death, perhaps there was a struggle, or just after death. And at some time following what appears to have been the first injection, the second and possibly fatal dose was administered by the third party. There's bruising around the second injection site, from the arm being held unnecessarily tightly. Also, the indications are that he died where he was found. That he wasn't moved after death.'

'Do you think it was murder?' Sadie asks.

Manning says, 'It's questionable. That's all I can say.'

I ask, 'Could the bruising to the neck have been self-inflicted? And could he have done the neck injection himself, as a test shot?'

'Yes, to both questions,' Manning says. 'In support of the test theory, it's hard to see, but look, there are two injection marks on the right arm, one that looks like a tentative first attempt, then the second.'

Sadie asks, 'Wouldn't the two injection marks in the arm be consistent with a third party as well, though?'

'Could be,' Manning says.

I ask, 'Stomach contents?'

'Oats with nuts and seeds, mainly. He hadn't eaten since what seems to have been a late breakfast.'

We talk through the rest of Manning's findings for a while. Then Bugsy clears his throat and asks an obvious question, but one I hadn't thought of because I was so engaged in the possible scenarios conjured by Manning's working hypothesis.

He asks, 'Have you an approximate time of death?'

'Rigor mortis commences within two hours of death. To the face initially. It was five degrees last night, on the cool side for October, and the deceased was found with his coat half off and on. Rigor was well advanced. Taking everything into account, I estimate that the body was discovered between six and eight hours after death. I can't be more precise than that.'

Bugsy says, 'So we're talking time of death nine thirty or ten to midnight?'

'That's right,' Manning says, 'probably later in that time frame than earlier, or he might have been found by an evening dog-walker. But I can't say for sure.'

'And you can't confirm causation without the test results?' Sadie asks.

'No,' Manning says, 'but we've done a rapid reactive test on the residue in the syringe, which confirmed the presence of diamorphine, so it's reasonable to assume that we *are* dealing with a heroin overdose, or at least that heroin is a contributing factor.'

'He told me he was on a programme,' I say, 'methadone, presumably, but I haven't had a chance to confirm that yet.'

Manning asks, 'You knew him?'

'I arrested him for burglary a while ago. He was adamant that he was clean.'

'Wouldn't be the first time someone mixed the good stuff with the free stuff,' Bugsy says.

Sadie asks, 'If a third party was involved, was it with or without consent?'

Manning says, 'The dose is important. The higher the level, the more likely it's a deliberate act. The question is did *he* do it or did someone do it for him?'

Patricia

I want to clear up one thing in case you got the wrong impression when I said that it was more than a hobby to me. The shop was never about the money. It never needed to be. Jeremy was always generous. I always had my own cheque book and there was never any shortage. Compared to a lot of other families in the 1980s, we had a lovely time. Cork was on the floor back then. The Ford and Dunlop factories closed around 1983, '84. It was seismic for the city, really, dreadful, and there was massive unemployment.

But people will always need cardiologists – even more so in the eighties when everyone smoked. Jeremy had an extremely healthy private practice in the Bons alongside his public post at the Regional.

So we had two foreign holidays every year. Theatre weekends in London. Tennis. Sailing. And there were the children. But once they went to secondary school they didn't need me as much – it's not like now with the helicopter parenting that goes on, and probably has to because of the eating disorders and the revenge porn and so forth. I think it's horrendous, having to compare yourself to the whole world every day on social media and always coming up short. There's no doubt about it, it's hard to be young now. Probably it always was to some extent, but wasn't it something to be celebrated too?

In our day, of course, women got old faster than they do now. I had no career to speak of. Nothing to fall back on. Nothing to distract from the crêpy neck and the wrinkles spreading like cracks in a badly plastered wall. I married young

– the year Jeremy finished medical school at UCC – and became a housewife at the ripe old age of twenty-two. Started popping out babies. All well and good, if it's what you want.

The GP said I had low mood, offered me happy pills. Half my friends were on them but they weren't for me. I knew what was wrong. I had to get out. Couldn't face the wait for O'Connor's undertakers to come and carry me out the front door in a wooden box. Though I'd prefer a wicker one, I've told the kids. They're much nicer than the wood and brass.

That's what the shop was. An escape from the long, slow slide into the grave. And there it is again. It keeps working its way back into my mind. Try as I might, I can't forget. I can't stop thinking that there's something I could have done. Should have.

40

IN THE CAR ON THE WAY TO THE SCENE, SADIE ASKS me again to tell her about my encounter with Garry McCarthy the day before. It's the third time she's asked. I feel weird recounting the story in front of Bugsy, but I'm telling the truth so it comes easily.

'Okay,' Sadie says, when I've finished, same as the previous two times. Then she asks, 'Why didn't you inform Garry McCarthy that the burglary charges against him were being dropped?'

Now I twig what she's doing. It's a rehearsal for when the superintendent asks me later. And she's asking in front of a neutral witness so that word gets around the station, and beyond, that I'm in the clear procedurally. So that the rumour mill is stalled before it starts.

'Because it's not my role to decide if charges are to be dropped. Or Martin Campbell's, the complainant, either. That's a decision for the DPP, on the recommendation of a senior officer. As to that aspect, I completed the necessary paperwork in under twenty-four hours and dropped it on Inspector Feeney's desk. I also notified you in person and asked for your advice. If charges *are* to be dropped, the right way to do it is by sending a letter or an email to the accused's solicitor, and after that, by applying to the court. A chat about it with the accused on the side of the street would have been the wrong thing to do.'

'That's absolutely correct,' Sadie says, 'and extremely clear.'

I watch Bugsy. He seems impressed by Sadie's certainty.

There's silence for the rest of the journey. We're inching towards the lights at Dennehy's Cross. Some cars dodge into the bus lane, jumping the queue. We stay put. The turn-off for Model Farm Road, the area where Garry McCarthy grew up, is ahead on the left. Before that, on the corner, there's the church. It was probably in there that he made his first communion.

I may have stuck to the letter of the law, but I could have been nicer to him yesterday. I could have given him some hope. But I didn't. We may never find out the full truth of what led Garry McCarthy to an overdose, accidental or deliberate, self-inflicted or otherwise. What I do know is that I was too caught up in the puzzle of what Martin Campbell was trying to hide to care about the vulnerable person standing in front of me.

And Garry McCarthy's is another of the faces I'll see when I close my eyes at night. Because I may not get criticised for it this time, but I know in my heart and soul that I've made another mistake. Small acts or omissions can change the course of a day. Or a life.

Patricia

I never opened on a Sunday. I never minded missing the odd Monday if we were away, though Mondays could be surprisingly busy. I wasn't the only middle-aged woman in need of escape. I'd usually close for the holidays – put a notice in the window and off I'd go to Marbs or Quinta or wherever we were going that year. I loved being my own boss. That was the joy of it. I kept my expenses low. The rent was for nothing – down a side street off the South Mall, in a semi-derelict shop-cum-office premises that had been vacant for years. Not exactly prime retail. The owners were friends of Jeremy – who was never less than 110 per cent supportive of me, I want to make that clear – and they nearly paid me to take it on. All that mattered to himself was that I broke even, and I made sure that I did.

There's always a but, and there's one here too. I became something of a destination. A victim of my own success. The shop got busy, and the café. I couldn't manage on my own any more. I needed help and there was no bother getting it, at the beginning especially, a time of sky-high unemployment, like I said. I took on numerous girls down the years, boys every now and again, although they never worked out. It was better having someone who could move between the café and the clothes side. That was the hard part. Most were better at one than the other. Most didn't stay. Saw me as a stop-gap. Fair enough. I was happy to see them go up in the world, when it happened. I had a few excellent girls, who've gone on to great things. The overwhelming majority of them have done well for them-selves.

I should focus on the big picture, but it's not easy and it's getting harder.

41

THE TARMACADAMED PATH IS WIDE AND SMOOTH at the start but, the further along we go, the narrower and more puddle-strewn it becomes. To our right, the Lee runs, high and deep and fast-flowing, a single channel before it divides into two around the back of the Kingsley, a hotel inexplicably built on a cast-iron guaranteed flood plain, where a public swimming-pool used to be. To our left, the fields lie, an open watery expanse of green with wild vegetation, scattered trees and rushes in the marshier parts.

Across the river, to the north, at the brow of the hill, the old grey asylum presides, reputedly the longest building in Ireland. In times past, if I'd had the misfortune to be admitted, I might never have got out. It's been converted into apartments. I hear they did a good job, but this side of the river is as close to it as I plan to get.

Two thirds of the way up the footpath, we meet Noel Tobin. He's white-suited. We're not. We stay outside the tape. The exclusion zone is horseshoe-shaped, centring on the bench where the body was found, the nearby path, and the surrounding grass and riverbank. The bench is situated inside a pronounced curve in the path, like an oxbow lake, or the Thames in the opening credits of *EastEnders*. There's a little pitched roof over it, slated and, in front of it, an inlet. There's a small beach here when the river is lower. Along much of the riverbank, gnarled spreading trees and bushes block direct access to the water. Not in this spot.

Sadie asks, 'What's the story, Noel?'

'Ah, it's stable-door stuff,' he says. 'The scene wasn't preserved. By the time we got here, it was just too late. There's nothing that hasn't been contaminated by every power walker and their pooch. Found the remnants of some blood on the ground in front of the bench, more than likely the dead man's – he had cuts to his face, I hear – but we won't know until we test and it doesn't help you anyway. Nothing pointing to anyone else being here with him. No paper cups, no lipstick-marked cigarette butts. We're running on fumes, more or less done.'

Sadie asks, 'No sign of a phone? There was none with the body.'

'Nope. Nothing of any importance. We got a few prints off the bench – it's made of a plastic composite material – for all the good they'll do. In the nature of a fishing expedition, if you'll excuse the location-related joke.'

Bugsy is the only one to laugh. He says, 'Loads of benches here. I suppose he picked this one because it had shelter.'

Sadie says, 'And it's distinctive. The only one like this. If you were arranging to meet someone, it'd be a good place to pick.' She runs with the idea: 'There's no CCTV out this far. If you came down the path from the other direction, off the road, say, no one would see.'

Bugsy says, 'There might be dashcam footage. We could put out an appeal.'

Sadie says, 'We could. We *will*, obviously, but we'd be mighty lucky to . . .' She looks at me. 'You're quiet. Any thoughts?'

'Maybe one,' I say, 'and it's not much of a one.'

'Say it, for fuck's sake. There's enough fuck-ups at this scene already and we haven't all day . . . I mean, sorry. Jesus. Just say it.'

Sadie's frustrated by the belated scramble to cordon off the scene after the pathologist identified Garry's death as suspicious.

I take a beat. Try to express my unease as coherently as I can. 'It's just that it's over-complicated. If it's murder. The two injection sites on the body. One on the neck to subdue, the second on the arm to kill. We're two metres from the river. If Garry's unconscious but still breathing after the first shot, why didn't the murderer just slide him into the water and let him wash up somewhere? Heroin in the system. Water in the lungs. Next to impossible to say where he went in. Chances are, no one would've looked twice at it if he was found drowned.'

'You're thinking it's not murder, just a straightforward over-dose?'

'No, it's not straightforward. It's like Dr Manning says, it's . . .'

Sadie finishes the sentence. 'I agree. It's questionable.'

Patricia

It's been a wonderful life but I might as well tell you, Cork city centre isn't what it was. Between the dereliction and the never-ending road works, people prefer to stay in the suburbs. And then Covid came along and put the tin hat on it all.

I shut up shop. Had one final everything-must-go sale, turned the key in the lock and posted it back through the letterbox. To everything there is a season and all good things must come to an end.

That's what I told myself then, too. I was too accepting. It's the way I was brought up. We learned to look the other way, no questions asked. I'm not making excuses: it's how Ireland was. How *I* was. Respectability was important to me.

I was stupid. I had my priorities all wrong.

42

THE NEXT MORNING, I TAKE A MIDDLE SEAT IN THE incident room, beside rookie Siobhan O'Sullivan. I'm surprised she's still here after her poor performance on the door-to-door. Then again, I'm not surprised at all. We're so short-staffed that, after requesting extra help from Divisional, Feeney's not going to throw it back in their faces. Besides, she's boots on the ground, and she might be a fast learner. She looks considerably less bouncy than she did, though.

'How are you getting on?' I ask.

'Good. What doesn't kill us makes us stronger.'

I remember that she's some kind of athlete. 'What is it you play?'

'Camogie. We won the county final last year and this.'

Women's hurling, but called a different name because historically the pitches the women played on used to be smaller and the rules were adapted for 'ladies'. Not any more. And hurling is one of the fastest, toughest sports in the world.

'Which grade? Senior, junior or intermediate?'

'Senior.'

I laugh. 'This is a cakewalk so.'

'Yeah,' she says, 'it is. Some people don't know who they're dealing with.'

Her eyes are fixed on Feeney, talking with Sadie at the front of the room. He bangs the desk. 'I'll make it quick,' he says. 'DNA results in the Barrack Street Jane Doe. No match with anyone on the system and no joy from the missing-persons database either. We'll do a trawl further afield. And when I say *we*, I mean you, McKeown. I want formal requests for Interpol et cetera done by the end of the day. I'll check them before they go out. I don't want any cock-ups,' his gaze lands on me as he says that, 'but I'm not holding my breath we're going to get anywhere. She's young, female, may not have had a record, and even if she did, if the murder happened during the time window we're looking most closely at, the late nineties to early 2000s, databases weren't as sophisticated as they are these days. That said, this is *not* a box-ticking exercise. It's something we have to do, and if we do something around here, we do it right. Do you hear me, McKeown?'

Bugsy straightens himself. 'Yes, sir.'

Feeney takes a breath. 'The reason I'm not holding out too much hope of results from our colleagues in Europe and across the water is that the other thing the results show is that she's Irish. A bit of English, a little bit of Viking, a dollop of Scots, some Spanish, but ninety-two per cent of her DNA is consistent with being bog Irish. The problem we have is that no one matching her description has ever been reported missing in this jurisdiction. DS O'Riordan?'

Sadie walks to the display board, taps it. 'This is what we now know about her. She's a hundred and seventy-two centimetres or five foot eight inches in height. Size five shoes, but wearing a size six. So she wasn't small, and remember, she would've looked taller in the platforms she was wearing. Slim build, size eight to ten, based on the jacket size and what they got from the clothing remnants. We're talking shreds and threads so bear that in mind. We have nothing definite apart from the jacket and the shoes. But light brown hair dyed blonde, worn in a nineties style. Deborah Winters in Forensics has provided us with this computer-generated image of what she may have looked like.'

She holds up a laminated A3 printout, gives us a chance to take it in. There are front, side and rear views. The blonde hair. The two high bunches at the side. The blue and white Adidas jacket. The blue boots. The white T-shirt dress. Hoop earrings. Only one thing is missing.

Sadie goes on, 'Obviously, she has no face yet and we're looking at a long wait on budgetary approval for going any further with the reconstruction.' She turns around, pins the picture at the top and centre of the board. 'We're not going large with this. To repeat, I don't want the image showing up in the *Echo* tomorrow, or anywhere, until we get the all-clear. We don't want the investigation skewed too early in one direction. We're still covering *all* bases.'

Feeney speaks again: 'We now also have the Garry McCarthy case. We're behind the curve on that one but we'll catch up. Don't know what we're dealing with so far, but we're ruling nothing in or out. We're multi-tasking, ladies and gentlemen. You as well, Fogarty . . .'

The room erupts in laughter as Feeney departs.

Sadie takes over: 'I wouldn't be laughing, if I were ye. There's a lot to be done and no sign of any overtime going so listen up.'

She runs through the room, acknowledging updates and

doling out jobs. There's nothing for me until her final words. 'Get a set of keys for something decent and meet me in the car park. Two minutes.'

Patricia

The other problem with Covid was that, overnight, people stopped using cash. I would have had to get a card machine and that wasn't a runner for me. As far as the Revenue is concerned, I never had anyone working in the shop except myself, and I never made a profit, none I declared. I was a cash-in-and-cash-out woman mainly, and that went for the employees too. Decent hourly rate, commensurate with experience and ability, but no tax, no PRSI, and if some of the girls happened to be signing on the dole at the same time, it was none of my beeswax.

How I saw it, I was effectively running a training scheme. Rendering unto Caesar the things that are Caesar's never kept me awake at night.

I suppose that last bit isn't true, now that I think of it. Indirectly, it did bother me, because of what happened. Because of what it meant.

43

I TURN LEFT ONTO A NARROW ROADWAY THAT
leads to The Crescent, a small 1960s estate. It's a solidly middle-
class but unshowy address. The semi-detached houses are
arranged in an arc along the right-hand side, with a well-kept
green, a few ornamental trees and shrubs in front. The look of
the place says 'active residents' association, keen gardeners'. An
occasional petty row about a rota is about the height of the
problems you'd expect to find in The Crescent.

You'd be wrong. Garry McCarthy grew up here, but his
privilege couldn't save him. I park a few houses down.

Sadie says, 'Like I said, our main duty today is to let them
know we're on it, that whatever happened to Garry, we're going
to get to the truth. The part I didn't tell you until now because
I want no discussion on it is that I'm appointing you family
liaison officer, so that if they have any questions, you're their
point of contact. It's not the most complicated FLO job but, as
you know, you have to keep your eyes and ears open. However
unlikely it is that any of the family staged an overdose in the
middle of the night in effectively the middle of nowhere.'

'Not so far from here, mind you, if you take the shortcut
down through the woods.'

Sadie gives me the side-eye. 'True, but keep that to yourself, for God's sake. We're going for a non-controversial informal meeting with the family. No drama, please.'

'I was just saying the Lee Fields aren't that far away if you go cross-country.'

'Come on,' Sadie says, 'before I decide I've made a terrible mistake.'

She rings the bell. A cheerful ding-dong sounds, then silence, then running steps. The door is opened by an exhausted-looking blonde woman in her fifties, wearing leggings and a Gym + Coffee sweatshirt.

'Sorry,' she says. 'Mum isn't feeling too well. It's been . . .'

We step into the hallway – spotlessly clean parquet flooring, a good wool carpet on the stairs, recently vacuumed, a dried-flower arrangement on a console table that I'd bet anything came from Casey's, the posh furniture shop on Oliver Plunkett Street. We follow her to the back of the house. The kitchen is ahead of us but she takes us instead to a side room on the right. What might once have been a dining room is now a bedroom-cum-sitting room with a single bed in the rear left-hand corner, two armchairs at either side of a gas-flame fireplace, three kitchen chairs in a semicircle. The air is stiflingly hot. There are no photographs.

Deirdre McCarthy, Garry's mother, is in one of the armchairs. At a guess, she's over eighty. A walking stick leans against one of the chair arms. She's thin and frail and her pearls look too heavy for her neck. She's wearing a grey and pink patterned gilet over a pink blouse and navy trousers.

She says, 'I'm not as bad as I look. I got my knee done and

they set this up for me down here, but I'm going back up to my own room as soon as I can. Sit. Bernie will make tea.'

Garry McCarthy had two sisters, but it looks like only one is here.

'Imelda's late,' Deirdre says, 'but she's on the way. A problem with one of the kids. Bernie has children too. Garry is the only one who never . . .' She brings a paper-thin blue-veined hand to her mouth.

From behind me, Bernie says, 'Don't upset yourself, Mum.'

She's back with a tray of tea things and a plate of individually wrapped chocolate Kimberleys.

I say, 'I'll take care of this.'

'Okay,' Bernie says.

She selects one of the kitchen chairs and pulls it as close as she can to her mother's armchair. Deirdre reaches out her hand. Bernie holds it in her lap.

Sadie takes the other armchair, and the lead, as I pour. She introduces us, explaining the process and my role. The McCarthys listen. The only questions they ask are about the body being released. Sadie can't answer that except with general 'As soon as ever possible' and 'We'll be in touch the minute we know' comments. After I've run out of things to do with the tea tray, I sit on one of the kitchen chairs.

Sadie asks, 'Was it a while since you last saw Garry?'

Bernie responds, 'What do you mean?'

'Was it days or weeks or might it have been even longer?'

'But sure I saw him that morning, the day before he was found,' Deirdre says. 'He's been living here. Occasionally he goes away for a night, and he's out walking during the day, but mostly he's here. Did the uniformed gardaí not tell you? I was sure I said it. Maybe I didn't.'

Sadie looks at me. 'No, we didn't realise that. We had a different understanding of the situation.'

'Oh, yes,' Deirdre says. 'Garry's been very steady the last year or so. Better than he's been for a long time. That's why I can't understand it.'

'None of us can,' Bernie says. 'We really thought he'd turned the corner at last. We thought we had him back.'

'He seemed well when I met him,' I say, 'the afternoon before he died.'

Deirdre looks up suddenly. 'You met him that day? You knew him?'

There's no immediate need to go into the *reason* I know him. 'I just met him two or three times, but the most recent was on Cornmarket Street that day.'

'He was sober? Clean?' Bernie asks.

'He certainly seemed it,' I say. 'Yes, I believe he was. He told me he was.'

Deirdre says, 'He had his breakfast here that last morning, about noon. He wasn't an early riser. He'd stay up late watching Netflix in the front room. No wonder he couldn't get up. Then when he did get up, he'd be faffing around for ages tidying things and doing little jobs for me before he'd finally sit down. I used to say to him to go to bed earlier so he'd get a head start on the day, but Garry always ploughed his own furrow. He had muesli, I think, and a cup of coffee. He had it on that chair you're sitting on, Sergeant, opposite me here. Made me a coffee too. Then he left and said he'd be back late and not to worry. I take a sleeping tablet at night. I didn't even realise he wasn't home until the knock came to the door to tell me what had happened. I can't bear to think of him down there by the river on his own.'

She starts to cry, great heaving sobs.

Bernie says, 'I think we're done for today.'

'Of course,' Sadie says. 'I wonder could we, maybe, have a look at Garry's room before we go?'

'It's the box room,' Bernie says, 'his childhood room. It's the only one he'd take. There's nothing there. Clothes. A few books. No drugs, if that's what you think you'll find.'

'We don't expect that,' I say. 'We can do it another time, if you'd prefer.'

'Do it now,' Deirdre says. 'Get it over with and leave us in peace. You weren't able to tell me the one thing I wanted to know. When are you going to give me my son? When can I bury him beside his father?' She curls into a ball, her shoulders quivering.

Garry McCarthy's room is as Spartan as a monk's cell. No drugs. No phone. A few changes of clothes, all casual, and a couple of spare pairs of shoes. There are four books, two on the top shelf of the small wardrobe: the Bible and a well-worn paper-back copy of *The Da Vinci Code*, a light film of dust on both. On the locker beside his bed, there are City Library copies of *Man's Search for Meaning* by Viktor Frankl and *The Alchemist* by Paulo Coelho.

I say, 'The Viktor Frankl seems to be the one he was reading. He used his membership card as a bookmark.'

I snap the card with my phone, then follow Sadie downstairs. In the hall, she mouths, 'I'll say goodbye.'

While I wait, I push open the door to the sitting room. I find a coffee-table with a selection of school and baby photographs of Garry scattered on it. There's only one recent picture. I snap it with my phone even though there's no need: it's the same one the family used in the death notice on rip.ie ('Funeral details to follow'). In it, he's wearing the khaki jacket he had on the day I met him. The one he was wearing when he died. Garry's smiling in the photo but he looks so sad. He looks like he's suffering.

44

BACK AT THE STATION, I CHECK THE BIRTHS,
marriages and deaths register for Garry's father. He died in 1996,
when Garry was twenty-five. The occupation on the death
certificate is 'retired civil servant' but, as he was sixty-seven
when he died, he wasn't retired for long before his death from
a heart attack, the cause given on the certificate. It might have
been sudden, sent shockwaves through the family.

I look at Garry's record again. In 1996, he was found in
possession of Ecstasy for the first time. Section 3 of the Misuse
of Drugs Act, own use. Probation Act applied so no conviction
was recorded. It's unlikely that he started taking E only after
his dad's death, but maybe the grief complicated things and he
got messier, drew attention to himself. There was a gap but, at
the end of the nineties, the pattern restarted with several more
MDMA possessions mixed with public order and drunkenness.

In 2000, at the age of twenty-nine, Garry had his first conviction for heroin possession. And again, unlikely that he only
started taking it then. That first conviction was followed by a
string of others, along with shoplifting and the usual, over
ensuing years. Then, nothing for a long time, not because he'd
stopped taking drugs but because he was in England.

He returned in 2020, around the time of the first lockdown. After a brief burst of activity, he went quiet. Presumably it was around then that he started taking methadone.

Something that my brother Billy said sparks in my brain. I check Garry's MDMA record again. But none of the arrests took place anywhere near Henry's. Which doesn't mean he wasn't there. He could have been part of the scene. Unfortunately, he's no longer around to ask.

I flick the switch in my head and start thinking about the girl again, about Bertie Allen's pub. From my drawer, I dig out a copy of the memo I did on the 1996 licensing prosecution. This is one of the jobs that Feeney allocated to Olly Fogarty. He reported it as a dead end at one of the morning briefings.

It looks like Fogarty's right. Running my finger down the list of names, I realise it's far worse than I'd originally thought. Nearly all the names look false. Robert Marley (Bob?), Karl Cox (DJ Carl?), Candy Staunton (singer Candi Staton?).

And then the Murphys. Murphy is the most common surname in Ireland but Edward Murphy, John Murphy and James Murphy all out together? And there must be hundreds of Mary and Maura McCarthys in Cork city alone, but both of them in the same pub on the same night?

The only promising-looking name is Terry McAuliffe, listed as 'staff member' on the file, but not convicted in the licensing case, according to the District Court record, and with no later record on PULSE either. I make a half-hearted note to look deeper into McAuliffe and throw the memo back into my drawer.

Minutes later, I take out the memo again. Ignoring the names, I examine the dates of birth. With the exception of the pub owner Maurice Bolger, who was also in the pub on the night of the offence, all of the persons found on the premises gave birth dates – whether genuine or made-up – from the early to mid-1970s, which proves nothing.

Except that they must have looked around that age or the guard taking the names wouldn't have accepted them. And that, in 1996, they were all in their twenties. The right age for Sir Henry's, the nightclub a few minutes' walk down the hill.

I check the name of the investigating garda. Find out fast that he's retired. A frustrating series of phone calls to pensions' administration and a data-protection argument later, I hear he died two years ago.

I return to my notes. Go through what I've found. It's tenuous, but it's something. It's an indication that, back in the nineties, Bertie Allen's wasn't an old-man's spit-and-sawdust pub, like Ray Grant said, or it wasn't *only* that. It was also a place where young people – possibly even young people who went to Sir Henry's – hung out on a regular enough basis to be permitted the privilege of a lock-in by the owner himself. I write it up and take it to Sadie.

Patricia

The reason the shop kept going so long is that I learned to adapt. As the nineties went on and the country slowly grew into affluence, my ladies still wanted the china cups and the Barry's tea and the mini-cafetières of Maher's French roast and the carrot cakes with cream-cheese frosting, but they weren't interested in 'nearly new' any more. They were outlet shopping in America by then and who'd want someone else's cast-offs when you could fly to NY with an empty suitcase and return with it bulging? Those Big Brown Bags from Bloomingdale's were everywhere.

I struggled with the change at first. But *Friends* was on at the time – it's always on now too, but it was new then – and it gave me the idea. I picked up some slouchy armchairs and a big couch from an auction at Woodward's and covered them with throws and changed the look of the place. Started to attract a younger crowd. Dropping in flyers for nightclubs and music gigs, asking if they could put up posters on the inside of the glass door. They didn't interfere with my ladies, who were morning people for the most part. The young ones were afternooners, I can tell you.

But I liked the young ones so much. They gave me a new lease of life. Reminded me of my youth, the one I never had because I was too busy changing nappies. I noticed what they were wearing and I began to look for vintage sports gear. I remembered it from first time around, of course. I sold plenty, but I couldn't get much of it, never more than a single rack at a time, unfortunately.

The café was booming, and that was super, but it was never my first love. I visited a few places in Dublin and London and realised where I was going wrong. I became more exclusive – designer only on the newer clothes – and diversified into real vintage. I went eclectic, focused on unique items. I put the word out that I was interested in estate sales, in Great Aunt Maud's costume jewellery and Gran's gown that she wore to the hunt ball and the like. It worked out well. Later, after *Sex and the City* became a big thing, vintage exploded.

Even more importantly, it kept my mind occupied. Kept me from thinking about the could-haves and should-haves which, as I said before, I don't do if I can help it.

It's truer to say that I *used* not to. Lately, with himself gone two years and the nights longer and darker without him, the could-haves and should-haves are *all* I think about.

45

I'M WALKING IN THE DOOR OF DUNNES SUPERMARKET
in Ballyvolane after visiting my parents' house, doing light-
switch and plant duty, when it comes to me that things are
going well at work. I squash the thought immediately, not
wanting to push my luck. Grabbing a big trolley, I retrieve my
scribbled list from my jacket pocket, concentrating on what I
have to get. There's no food back at the flat. No cleaning products. No coffee. No Tampax. No fruit. I need to restock.

In the fresh area, I select apples, oranges and green bananas,
and carrots, onions, a turnip and a cabbage. Nothing too perish-
able because, in this job, you can't predict from day to day, and
there's nothing more soul-destroying than binning lettuce that's
turned to green sludge and hairy strawberries.

I glide through the aisles. The shop's way bigger now than
it was when I was a child. They did a massive renovation and
extension at some point. I still can't get used to it.

I'm in the women's hygiene section when I hear her voice,
like a cold hand on my throat.

'Alice? Alice, is it you?'

It's at times like this that I wish I was a member of the Armed
Support Unit.

46

I THINK ABOUT DUMPING THE TROLLEY AND RUNNING from the shop, but I turn instead. She's smaller and older than she used to be. In her basket, there's caster sugar and icing sugar, a half-dozen eggs, Stork margarine, and a bag of self-raising flour. Making queen cakes for one of the neighbours' kids' birthday parties, probably.

'Hello, Peggy.'

'Alice, it *is* you.'

The comment doesn't warrant a response but I give a one-shouldered shrug by way of acknowledgement.

She asks, 'How *are* you?'

'I'm fine,' I say. I don't ask how she is, because I couldn't care less.

'You're down here now,' she says. 'It must be nice to be home.'

Despite myself, I respond, 'The reason I'm down here isn't so great.'

'I know. I wanted to get in touch with you afterwards . . . your parents too but I didn't think they'd welcome my . . . Or you . . .'

'You did the right thing not making contact. Now I'm going to have to run.'

I turn away and stare sightlessly at the shelves, trying to remember what I'm looking for. When I turn back, she's still standing there.

I ask, 'Peggy, what do you want?'

She says, 'Nothing at all. Only to say that Ralph and I were very sorry about what happened. You were always a lovely girl and we were terribly fond of you, you know.'

I feel a wave of nausea, a squeezing tightness in my head. I put out a hand to steady myself against the shelf but the Tampax boxes slide inwards. I cling to the edge.

She's still talking. 'He's a grown man and he makes his own decisions, but maybe he rushes into things sometimes and I think he might regret a few things as well.'

She's waiting for me to respond.

I say, 'I have to get going. I've loads to do.'

'Of course,' she says, 'I'll tell him I met you. He thinks so much of you.'

I don't know if she's talking about her husband Ralph or her son Calum, my ex-fiancé, but I don't ask. I throw two boxes of green and one box of red Tampax into the trolley and make for the checkout.

I may not have mentioned that Calum was a neighbour. It wasn't quite a boy-next-door story. It was more complicated than that.

He was older than me. Didn't look at me really until after his first marriage broke up. His only, I mean, because he didn't marry me. I've known him my whole life. And, after I finished school, I was interested in joining the guards. Partly because of him. I can say that now. Seeing the pictures on his mother's sideboard of him in uniform at his passing-out parade. Never in uniform in real life. He wasn't in uniform long and he wasn't based down here. He was always in Dublin. Glimpses, though, of him going in and out of his parents' place when he was visiting them. Hearing stories. Seeing him on television at a crime scene or a courthouse. It all had an effect.

He helped me with my application. Told me about some courses. Gave me advice on the interview. Became my sort of mentor. That was what it was, more or less. Except he probably always knew that I adored him . . .

Anyway, after I became a member, he was my colleague, and, after I made detective, my boss, eventually, at the GNBCI. It grew from there.

My parents weren't too happy. Or my sister and brothers. The age difference, of course. And his kids. Two. Who were lovely, by the way. Though, because of the divorce, he didn't see as much of them as he'd have liked.

Although it wasn't just Calum's 'history', as my family insisted on calling it. It was him. The kind of person he was. He was great in so many ways. Clever. Gorgeous. Sexy. But he could be hard going. Could start an argument with himself. And he was never wrong about anything. I know that that's why my error with the warrant hit him so hard.

All through the time we were together, I told myself that my parents, sister and brothers were hopelessly old-fashioned. I told them as well – again and again – that they were wrong about Calum. But they were right. I can see it at last. I just need to keep remembering it.

Patricia

She started out as a customer. She didn't buy anything. She looked, and such an eye she turned out to have for someone so young. She came in with a group one Saturday afternoon. They took over the couch, and you'll think I'm exaggerating, but of all the people who came into the shop she stood out. Partly because the boys she was with were older than she was. I wondered if she was a cousin or a sister, but you don't look at your sister the way those boys looked at her.

I say boys, but they were men, devouring her with their eyes, like she was a meringue roulade. She didn't seem to be with any one of them. She was with all of them, as if they'd adopted her. Even later on, after I got to know her, I noticed that she didn't seem to have any other friends either, no proper girl friends, just those three.

That first day, she came up to the counter asking for more milk and then she said, 'Okay if I take a look at the stuff? I don't have any money, sorry, but it's lovely here.'

You couldn't miss the accent. North of England. Manchester, she told me, when I got to know her better.

And I can't say that I saw from the beginning that trouble lay ahead for the poor girl but, by the time it came, I can't say I was surprised either.

47

THE NEXT FEW DAYS PASS IN A BLUR. I'M NOT sleeping at night so I'm missing things, having to redo whatever I start. People are noticing. Sadie's resumed her 'Are you okay?' questions, which I bat away with a fixed grin and an 'I'm grand' or similar.

The truth is, I may not be okay. I may be on a downward spiral again. I've been late a couple of mornings, not leaving home early enough, then stuck in traffic. I'd be faster walking but I don't want to walk: being in my car feels like a continuation of being in my flat, and my flat is the only place I want to be.

I've been failing in my family-liaison duties with the McCarthys too. Doing an impression of the job, but going through the motions. I've been checking in with Deirdre and Bernie and I got to meet Imelda, though only once in passing. Whenever I visit, the house is busy with grief and neighbours, and the family don't want to hear anything from me until I'm able to tell them that Garry's body is to be released.

When I finally can, it makes little difference. I can't connect with them. I feel far away from other people. From myself as well. From the person I want to be.

Who isn't the person at home every night scoffing pizza, or suddenly Hassan's best customer for chocolate-bar multi-packs. The person doing everything guaranteed to send me back into the pit.

Garry McCarthy is the one who saves me. Less him, more the book he was reading, *Man's Search for Meaning* by Viktor Frankl. I'm on the sofa in my pyjamas and a hoodie. I don't even have the energy to tear up the empty pizza box and put it in the compost bin.

From somewhere, I remember Garry's bedside book. I google it. Turns out it's about completing tasks and caring for others and finding meaning in painful experiences. Which resonates, even after I close the Wikipedia page. Even through the carbohydrate fog.

I start to think about what the book might have meant to him, that and the other one on his locker, *The Alchemist*. Going into my photos, I bring up the picture of his library card. I wonder what other books he might have borrowed. I wonder what his hopes and dreams might have been. I swipe to the photograph of him in the khaki jacket. That sad smile.

Garry's funeral mass is tomorrow at eleven in Dennehy's Cross church, with burial afterwards in St Finbarr's Cemetery on Glasheen Road.

I get up from the sofa and take the pizza box, the small compost bin and the bag from the other bin down to the big bins in the backyard. On my return, I load the dishwasher, switch it on and wipe down the countertop. The floor needs a sweep, and it's almost beyond me to do it, but I manage.

I go into the bedroom. I set the alarm for seven and put it on the floor across the far side of the room near the door. I get into bed. It's only 8.25 p.m. but I sleep.

Patricia

She came back on her own, a weekday, a Tuesday or a Wednesday, I'd say.

'So nice to see you again,' I remember she said. 'I love this shop, I do.'

Nahce, for nice, *loov*, for love: her accent was hilarious, not that Cork people can point the finger in that department, but I hardly noticed it after a while. She talked and talked. She cared about the history of every piece, from a silk scarf to a handbag, you name it. She was always asking questions.

'Oh, I *love* this one, Patricia, where did it come from?'

She had a great sense of style. Modern. Of her time. We were different as could be to look at, and not just in age, but we were peas in a pod underneath.

She told me she'd been working in Ibiza – Eye-beetha, she called it – but that she was here now and was looking for work, and the words were hardly out of her mouth when I said, 'What about here?'

'Seriously, Patricia,' she said, 'I'd only love it.'

I did need her because one of my part-timers was leaving, but even if I didn't, I know I'd have found something for her. This trade teaches you not to hesitate. You have to grab the bargain when you see it.

That's come out all wrong. What I mean is, she was too good to let go. That was her problem.

48

IN THE MORNING, I MAKE THE BED BEFORE GOING across the room to switch off the alarm. It's an old trick and it usually works for me: the visual cue, maybe, or the automatic action. I shower, letting the water run cold on my head for the final half-minute. I dress in a newish black trouser suit and wear black loafers with it instead of trainers. I put on foundation and a little blusher. I even think about putting on lipstick, though thinking about it is as far as it goes. I throw back a coffee and a pint of water, and leave the house without sitting down and scrolling through my phone for half an hour.

On the street outside, I get a hop when I see a D-reg black Volvo SUV on the other side of the road. But it's newer than Calum's, and he'd never dream of parking his car around here. Also, he's in Dublin, and he's nothing to me any more.

Arriving at the station, I badly need another coffee, but I make do with a teabag in a mug and I'm at my desk by eight fifteen. I do what I always do when I'm feeling lost. I flip through my black notebook and start making a list. Forty minutes to the 9 a.m. briefing. Then thirty. Then, Oh, shit, I'm going to be late if I don't hurry. Time flies when you're doing something that might end up being useful.

'McCann, I want to talk to you,' Feeney says, at the end of the briefing, catching me off guard.

I figure he's noticed my deterioration in recent days and I expect the worst. I move to the front, stand by the noticeboard.

Feeney's in his favourite position by the wall. He waits for everyone else to leave the incident room. 'You're going to the Garry McCarthy funeral.'

'Yes, Cig. I'm FLO on the case.'

'That wasn't a question. It was a statement. I'm perfectly aware of what your duties are and how well – or otherwise – you're performing them. Understood?'

'Yes, Cig.'

'I've another statement for you. You're driving me to the funeral. Any problem with that?'

'None whatsoever. Will I call by your office when I'm ready to go?'

He laughs. 'When we depart is my decision, not yours.'

❖

Feeney's a stickler for punctuality so we leave earlier than necessary. Thinking about it, I reckon he's going for PR reasons, on the slim chance there could be blowback on the withdrawal of the burglary charges against Garry. Feeney's was the last desk the file was on, and there really is no problem with him not progressing it that very day, but you never know how a well-connected family like the McCarthys might view it in the cold grey light of the winter to come.

Also, it's a golden opportunity for him to carry out an informal assessment of me ahead of the upcoming review, rolling ever closer. He's reading news sites on his phone but I know he's watching me. I drive smoothly and indicate assiduously. We arrive at the church and find a spot around the side.

The ceremony is straight from the difficult-Irish-funeral handbook: low key, no frills, generic less-said-the-better homily.

Afterwards, in the churchyard, Feeney chats to a few officers who've shown up from other stations and tries to figure out what they're doing here. At the same time, I scan the congregation. I find an unexpected but familiar face. I make my way to him through the crowd.

49

RAY GRANT IS SURPRISED TO SEE ME. HE DOESN'T
even try to look pleased. He's standing between a woman and
a man, both in their fifties, his daughter and son, presumably.
He introduces me first to the man. 'This is my son, Conor.
Didn't you meet him that night on Barrack Street when he came
to pick me up after our little talk?'

He's like his father, but taller, with softer edges, and better
teeth.

I say, 'No, nice to meet you now, though. Alice McCann.'

'I remember seeing you,' he says. 'Good to get to say hello
this time.'

'And this is my lovely wife. Mrs Grant to you.'

It's the second time he's used that variety of joke. Makes me
think some part of him really does want people to call him
Mister, and his wife Missus. Or maybe Grant is nervous. Which
is interesting. As is the fact that she's his wife, clearly not his
first, and not his daughter.

'Ah, Ray, stop, he'd make a show of you. Pleased to meet
you, Alice. I'm Tania.'

I smile and shake her hand. Blonde and discreetly Botoxed,
she's wearing a rock of an engagement ring and an equally shiny

tennis bracelet. I have zero doubt about the quality of the diamonds. 'Did ye know Garry?' I ask.

'I was in school with him in Christian's,' Conor says.

Christian Brothers College is a private boys' school.

'Really? You knew him well so?'

'Same class all the way up through secondary. We lost touch, because of the way things went for him, but he was a nice guy. Oh, and he worked for Dad, of course.'

'Did he? For long?' I'm looking at Ray Grant.

Conor is the one who replies: 'A while on and off, till he went to England. He was over there for years.'

'How did he come to work for you?'

Conor says, 'Dad, you might remember better than me.'

Ray Grant says, 'As far as I remember, he just asked if I had anything going. I knew him through Conor – he was in the house a few times. I gave him a bit here and there during the summer holidays. More than this lad ever did, by the way. Conor never carried a hod, I can assure you. When he wasn't down in Oysterhaven giving lessons to the local sailing brats, he was spending his summers in Cape Cod and Newport, Rhode Island, doing the same thing.'

Conor says, 'I did okay in the end, Alice. My engineering degree came in handy, didn't it, Dad, and the good old MBA?'

Ray Grant: 'A small bit, anyway.'

I ask, 'And Garry? He started during the summer holidays?'

'That's right. He was in college at that time, studying in UCC. But he dropped out and then he was more regular with us. Solid enough for a few years, in fairness.'

'And what did he do for you?'

'Jaysus, twenty questions, or what? The poor fella started

off as a gofer, go for this and go for that, and graduated into labouring. He wasn't the worst by any manner of means. But sure after a while he got into the bad stuff and he wasn't worth tuppence after that. I found him in his car down the back of a site we were working on, smoking it off tinfoil. Fired him on the spot. I called to see him at his mother's house afterwards, to see if there was some way to get him to go to, I don't know, Tabor Lodge or Coolmine. He told me he was clean and that he was doing well. All lies. Terrible to see how he went down. It's a curse, that thing, and the government are doing fuck-all as far as I can see, though what *would* you do? I don't know.'

'Legalise it, maybe,' Tania says.

'Ah, stop,' Grant says. 'What do *you* think, Conor?'

He says, 'I'm on the fence.'

I came over here for one thing, and it's turned into something else, but I can't forget my original purpose, one of the items on the list I made this morning.

I focus on Ray Grant. 'Did you get a chance to look for those photos?'

He slaps the base of his palm against his forehead. 'They went out of my head completely.'

Conor asks, 'What photos?'

'Interior photographs of Bertie Allen's pub before it was demolished. I was hoping the site engineers or the architects might have—'

'Of *course* we have photographs,' Conor says. 'Dad, don't you remember?'

'I don't, son. My memory isn't what it was.'

Conor and Tania laugh.

Conor says, 'Give me your email address, Alice, and I'll forward them on to you later in the day. Tomorrow at the latest.'

A flash of something crosses Ray Grant's face but it's gone before I can figure out what it is.

50

FEENEY ISN'T COMING TO THE BURIAL SO I HAVE
to drop him back to Coughlan's Quay.

On the way, he asks, 'Was that Ray Grant you were talking to?'

'It was. Him, his wife and his son. Grant owns the site, as you know.'

'Do you know them personally?'

'No – I mean, I've met Ray on site in Barrack Street. I was looking for photos from him, of the pub and flat upstairs before it was knocked down. It's a line I've been pursuing, trying to get them voluntarily from him without having to go through a rigmarole.'

'Is he going to give them to you?'

'The son said he would. I don't know was Grant himself all that keen.'

'Why do you say that?'

'Just a feeling he mightn't be.'

'What was he doing there anyway, at the funeral?'

I turn towards him. I'm smiling even though I try not to. I say, 'Garry McCarthy used to work for him. In construction. Ray fired him when he caught him smoking heroin. And Garry went to Christian's with the son. Same class.'

'That's interesting,' Feeney says coolly.

'I thought so too.'

He checks the time. 'You can let me out here,' he says. 'You'd better get to the graveyard. If you're asked, make sure you go to lunch. If there *is* a lunch. If there isn't, you come straight back. No dawdling or diversions. It's a garda vehicle you're driving, using garda fuel.'

'Yes, sir.'

When he gets out, he slaps the roof of the car twice. I don't know if I'm right, but I think I might have managed to please him.

At the cemetery, the crowd has thinned to family, close friends and neighbours. As I arrive, the graveside prayers are under way and I can hear the low hum as I walk down the path to the back. Garry is being laid to rest in a family plot, near the tree-lined boundary. Keeping a respectful distance, I observe the groupings. Bernie McCarthy standing beside her mother Deirdre and, close behind, Bernie's three teenagers and her husband. On Deirdre's other side is Imelda with two kids, a boy and a girl of ten or eleven, possibly twins, though the girl is slightly taller. There are a few men, but at a distance and the wrong age. There's no sign of anyone who looks like he might be Imelda's husband. Maybe she's separated.

At the conclusion of the ceremony, no invitation is extended by the priest or the undertaker to join the family for refreshments at any of the usual post-funeral locations. I wait by the gate. As the family walks by, I step forward and shake

Garry's mother's hand. 'I'm here for you if you need anything at all.'

She looks at me and says, 'Thank you.' I'm not sure she knows who I am.

Bernie says, 'We'll be in touch at some stage – or Imelda will, she's going to take over as your contact – but today we just want to go home and shut the door on the world.'

After they've gone, I walk to the rear of the cemetery and stand by Garry's grave, my right hand gripping my left wrist. The falling leaves are being blown sideways by the wind. Any second, it's going to rain again. The gravediggers must be on a break. The dug-up earth is piled at the side, cloaked in plastic sheeting, held down by stones. A weighted rectangle of fake grass covers the open grave, a single arrangement of white flowers on top.

I whisper, 'I'm sorry.'

Feeling the first drops, I head towards the car. Halfway up the path, I turn and face south-west. I push down my hood. The rain strikes my face. It feels like I'm being pelted with pea gravel. I turn again and break into a run, moving faster than I have in ages. In the car, I find myself crying, but crying is okay. It's when I can't cry that I start to worry.

Patricia

I told her it was cash only and she looked at me as if I had two heads.

'I should hope it's cash. I'm not working for nothing.'

She made me laugh. 'It's off the books,' I said.

She shrugged. 'No skin off mine, Patricia. When do I start?'

The very next day was when. I wondered if she'd show but there she was, bang on time, outside the door, waiting for me to open up.

'The others are at work, and now I am too, thanks to you.'

'The others?'

'The lads I live with,' she said. She didn't hold back. I got the full run-down. Where the house was. How they'd met in Eye-beetha when she'd been working over there and they were on their holidays. How kind they'd been to her.

'I'll bet they were kind,' I said. 'I can only imagine.'

She laughed, I remember, a big round chuckle. 'You've got a dirty mind, Patricia. It's not like that any more. We're friends. They're like my brothers. They take care of me. Everything's more open than it used to be. It's different.'

I thought about that. There *was* a softness to young men, those days. They hugged each other, they were affectionate. I thought she might be right. I thought, What do *I* know?

We grew close. She told me a little about her upbringing. How her mum had been addicted to heroin. How she was sure there had been good times with her at the start, even though she was too young to remember the details.

'It's a warmth I feel sometimes,' she said. 'I think it's Mum when she was well.'

She didn't talk much about the bad times. Didn't like to, she said. She left me to fill in the gaps. Whatever I was able to imagine, I'll bet it was ten times worse.

She did tell me about being taken into care, about being

pushed and pulled from pillar to post. And yet she emerged, as if out of a cocoon, like a butterfly. Or is it moths who come out of cocoons?

'You're always in good humour,' I said to her one day, as we were sorting through a box I'd taken in, contents sight unseen, not my style, but I'd had a hunch and gone with it. I'll never forget her answer, the simplicity of it.

'I'm not. Honestly I'm not. I cry, sometimes, when I'm on my own. It's why I prefer having other people around. I'm always looking for a family. Silly, isn't it?'

'It's not at all silly,' I said, 'it makes perfect sense.'

She hugged me then, and I remember feeling so protective of her.

But that's all it was. A feeling. I didn't *do* enough.

Not enough to make a difference to the result.

51

BACK AT THE STATION, I WORK THROUGH THE REST
of my list from this morning. Achieve little. Make a few phone
calls. Fail to connect with the people I'm looking for.

But coming up to five o'clock, the photographs appear in my
inbox, sent from Conor Grant's Ray Grant Properties email
address rather than a firm of architects or engineers. Either RGP
had them on their system all along and Ray Grant conveniently
– or genuinely – forgot, or Conor requested them and sent
them on to me at top speed.

I scroll down to the end of the email. There's no sign it's
been forwarded from anywhere else. It proves nothing, but it
adds to my sense that, for some reason, Grant Senior is uneasy
with the investigation looking too closely into the recent history
of Bertie Allen's pub. I remember how keen he was to persuade
me that the murder and burial had to have taken place after the
pub was no longer trading. Shelving my questions, I click into
the photo attachments.

It's like Artur Lewandowski said. The pub was a museum
piece, unchanged for decades. The photographs are a treasure
trove, the likely location of the murder and the certain location
where the body was buried brought to life in full colour.

I forward the pictures to Sadie, Feeney and the rest of the team, give it a minute, then cross the room to stand on one side of her open doorway.

She says, 'Get a set of those photos printed for the nine a.m. briefing.'

Olly Fogarty slithers up beside me, the other side of the doorway. He says, 'We're gonna need a bigger board.'

I say, 'I'd better get moving.'

Returning to my desk, I organise the printing from the colour photocopier. Two sets. The first I drop into Sadie's office, the duplicates I place in a folder for my own use. Not permitted under Feeney's penny-pinching disguised as climate-action rules but, hey, I'm celebrating.

I sit down again, intending to go through the photographs on my computer, zooming in on the details, but Fogarty's shouting at me from the other side of the room.

'McCann, what do *Michael Collins*, *The Usual Suspects*, *Heat*, *Leaving Las Vegas* and *Casino* have in common?'

'I have no idea what you're talking about, and I'm busy so . . .'

He asks, 'Do you want me to tell you?'

'Not particularly.'

'That's grand. I won't disturb you.'

'Okay, what is it? And I don't have time for any bullshit.'

'I'm hurt now.'

'Just tell me, Fogarty.'

He gets to his feet, starts walking towards me. 'They're movies from the mid-1990s. They're also the titles of some of the tapes lined up on the shelf underneath the television and video player in the flat over Bertie Allen's. Looks like someone was spending time up there watching TV. If we can find out who, we might be a few steps closer to a solve on our Jane Doe.'

I click back into the photographs and zoom in on the television area. 'I see the videotapes,' I say. I move the focus to the coffee-table. 'There's a phone directory. The *Golden Pages*. For business numbers. Is that a date on the front?'

'It says 95/96,' Fogarty says, 'could be the year of the murder.'

Sadie's come up behind us. 'Nah. People used to keep telephone books for years. We're going to need more than that. I want you two to prepare a request for the photo-analysis section to do a deep dive on the pics. There's a chance that their specialist equipment might find something we can't see. I'll take a look at the request in the morning and send it out first thing.'

We work on for an hour or so at my desk, scrutinising the photographs together, formulating the questions we need the experts in Dublin to answer, making the queries open enough to allow them to spot things we haven't thought of. We've spotted the movies and the phone book, items linked to the 1990s but the pub was trading as late as 2007. We have to be seen to be keeping an open mind. Everything on a file can be disclosed to the defence team so you're always thinking about the others who'll see what you've done. You have to avoid anything that might be used to create doubt in the minds of the jury.

Around six thirty, Fogarty says, 'I think we have it.'

'Yeah,' I say. 'You go, I'll follow in a few minutes.'

'Alice, I . . . ah, I'll talk to you again. It's late. Good working with you there.'

I squeeze out a reply, 'You too,' and I mean it, because he's quick and he's clever. But I feel like a fool for trusting him so easily and it's not a mistake I'll make again.

I'm on my way out the door when I get one of the call-backs I've been waiting for. She says she's happy to talk to me this evening at home, if it suits. When I hear the address, I think I've misheard and ask her to repeat it, but I heard right the first time. I still have the car keys on me since earlier on at the funeral. I say, 'I'll be there by seven.'

There's a black D-reg SUV parked in front of the Centra as I exit the car park, no one in the driver's seat. It's not Calum's, but my high alert kicks in anyway. Which leads me on to thoughts of when the texts from him will start again. I grip the steering wheel so hard it feels like I might break it but I keep driving.

52

GARRY MCCARTHY'S SOLICITOR LIVES NEAR THE building site, on a narrow lane off Barrack Street, a wheelie-bin and pot-plant obstacle course. I stretch out my arms. My finger-tips almost brush the edges. On the left side of the lane, there's a terrace of higgledy-piggledy cottages, a single door and window to the front of each, two skylights or a dormer in the roof of most. Multi-generational families of eight or ten used to live in these houses.

On the other side of the lane, there's a rough high wall, above head height, built of limestone and red sandstone. Cut into the end wall there's a small grey wooden door. I ring the bell and get buzzed into the yard.

The house isn't a house, it's a round tower, but it's not old. It's made of concrete, with ivy and wisteria clinging to it. And, unlike the ancient towers you come across all over the country, the door is at ground level. It opens and a woman steps out.

'Sorry I've been so hard to track down,' Finn Fitzpatrick says. 'I've been on my holidays.'

'Anywhere nice?'

'Spain. Gone for three weeks. Badly needed. The last few years have been . . . challenging.'

'Great to be back, I'd say.'

She laughs. 'Come in. We have to go up three flights to the living room, I'm afraid. Seemed like a good idea at the time.'

It's still a good idea. The top floor is made of glass, encircled on the outside by a perforated steel balcony. Inside, as well as a sofa and an armchair, colourful rugs and cushions, there's a large curved island containing under-counter cupboards and appliances, and a dining table with folding doors behind it that I imagine her pulling back on fine evenings. There are city and sky views from every part of the room, but the roof is solid so it doesn't feel like a greenhouse.

For the first time in a while, I feel the loss of my old apartment in Phibsboro. It wasn't half or even a tenth as beautiful as this, but it was mine. Technically, it was ours. Now it's Calum's and the newer younger blonder version of who I used to be.

'Do you want tea or coffee?'

'No, thanks,' I say. 'I'm trying to avoid having caffeine too late in the day.'

'I have mint or camomile?'

'Mint would be lovely.'

I sit at the dining table and take out my notebook. There's an empty fruit bowl on the table and, at the far end, a child's toy digger, still in its box, with Spanish writing on it.

'Someone's getting a present from Spain,' I say. 'Your nephew, or . . . ?'

'I don't have a nephew.' She brings a teapot and two mugs

to the table. 'Tell me about Garry. I only heard when I got into Cork airport this afternoon. Been avoiding the news while I was away. I rang my secretary, Tina, while I was waiting for my luggage. She told me.'

I give her the short version. She gives me the third degree. I end up revealing more than I'd intended, though thankfully not the entire post-mortem report. Not quite.

'So, yes,' I say, 'confidentially, the circumstances of Garry McCarthy's death are somewhat ambiguous. Test results will hopefully clarify the situation but for now we're just trying to build up a picture.'

'Are we talking weeks or months for the results?'

'Your guess is as good as mine.'

'Okay,' she says. 'What is it you wanted to ask me?'

'First, how did you come to represent Garry? MLC is a commercial practice.'

'That's right, but I inherited him from one of the partners who's a friend of the McCarthy family. When Garry first started getting into trouble, he became a client of the office. Then he went to live in England. Soon after he came home to Cork, he had a couple of section four public orders for intoxication. He dealt with those charges by himself on a guilty plea. Didn't contact MLC, or any other solicitor. He wasn't in trouble for a couple of years until, out of the blue, this. A burglary charge. He asked me to appear for him in court and to enter a not-guilty plea. Which I did. The adjourned date is coming up soon but sadly he won't be there.'

She goes on, 'There was something nice about him. A genuineness. It affected me. *He* did. I was really sad this afternoon when I heard he'd died. And that I missed his funeral. I hardly knew him, but I liked him.' She gets up from the table.

'I have a few more questions.'

She looks surprised but sits down again. 'Sure.'

'His address. He gave it as "care of Anderson's Quay". I took it as Cork Simon.'

'That's right. That's what he told me too. I applied for a legal-aid certificate.'

'Except that he didn't live there. He'd moved back in with his mother. Appears to have been residing there at the time of the offence.'

'He didn't tell me *that*. Maybe he didn't want to give out the home address in case it appeared in the media.'

I say, 'That *could* be the reason. Also, everyone including himself said he was on a methadone programme but we found a small quantity of heroin on his person.'

'When I took instructions from him about the charges, he said he was on a methadone programme. He said he hadn't used in a long time. He said the heroin was in his winter jacket, that he hadn't worn it in months. He hadn't realised the baggie was in the sleeve pocket. He said it was a minuscule amount and that you found no drug paraphernalia on him. No hypodermic et cetera.'

'It was small, all right, and there was no needle but . . .'

'You charged him anyway.'

She's starting to annoy me. 'Yeah.' I pause. 'We didn't find a phone with the body on the Lee Fields. Did he give you a phone number?'

'Just a sec.'

She gets up from the table and logs into a laptop on the

kitchen island. She writes a phone number and the email address on a piece of paper and hands it to me.

'Thank you. One more thing. You said he was going to plead to the drug possession but not to the burglary. What was that about?'

She sits again. She's fully engaged now. 'He wouldn't say what the story was. He said he would, nearer the time, if it went as far as a trial. I told him there was every chance it *would* go to trial. That he was charged with section twelve of the 2001 Act. Entering as a trespasser with the intent to commit an arrestable offence. That you'd found an iPad belonging to the house owner on him and so on.'

'What did he say to that?'

She gets up, goes to her laptop and logs in again.

'I scanned my handwritten note. Let me see. His exact words were "I want my day in court and I want to go into the witness box and give my evidence." As a defence strategy, it was ludicrous, but I didn't bother arguing. I reckoned he'd change his mind once he'd had a look at the statements. I thought, Well, he's been on the straight and narrow. He's finding it hard to admit to himself that he's fallen back into old ways. It fits with what you said about him living at his mother's and providing the false address. It looks like he was trying to save face.'

'The family don't seem to know about the burglary,' I say. 'I haven't explored it with them. I let it go until I could talk to you. Until after the funeral as well. But you're right, it fits. If his family found out he was in court, he'd be able to tell them he's pleading not guilty.'

Finn sits back in her chair. 'Fits with deliberate overdose too, though, doesn't it? Dying before he has to admit to his family, even to himself, he's using again? If that's what happened, it's awful. It would mean that he died of shame. There are no *good* reasons to die, but shame is a really bad one.'

53

SHE ACCOMPANIES ME DOWNSTAIRS. 'THE GARDEN gate can be tricky,' she says.

On the way, I steal a look at the rest of the house. There's a bedroom on the middle floor, presumably en-suite, and on the ground floor, a small spare bedroom, a home office and a shower room with a washing-machine, the door open, a partly unpacked suitcase on the floor in front of it. I'm so taken with the house and with what Finn said about Garry McCarthy that I nearly forget to ask about her – the girl found buried two minutes' walk away – even though she's been at the back of my mind all along.

I steady myself, then ask, 'How long has your house been here?'

'Bought the site in 2006, at the top of the market, then went through a long planning process. Finally moved in for Christmas 2010, after the first crash, before the second killer blow in 2012. It's been a rollercoaster financially, but at the end of the day, I love it here.'

'Did you have to engage an archaeologist?'

'They didn't make it a condition but, after what's been found recently, it's a wonder. I don't think my builders discovered anything, or if they did, they didn't say.'

'Do you remember the pub when it was open? Who the customers were? Or any locals who went there?'

'Off the top of my head, no, but I'll have a think. And if I hear anything, I'll let you or Sadie know.'

'Sadie?'

'DS O'Riordan. She's my friend. We were in the same law class at UCC.'

'Cork is small,' I say, the standard response in these kinds of situations.

Finn laughs. '*Too* small sometimes.'

All the way down the lane and in the car, I nag myself, trying to recall what I said and what she said. Analysing if I did anything wrong, or if I was noticeably incompetent. I dump the car in the station car park and walk home. By the time I get there, I've forced myself to start thinking about the content of my conversation with Finn Fitzpatrick instead of the stupid me-me-me stuff. I transcribe a few bullet points of our conversation from my flip-top to my home notebook. Bad policing practice, but the act of writing calms me down and stops my thoughts spiralling.

Not for long. It's after 9 p.m. and I've barely finished when my phone rings. I don't recognise the number so I make the mistake of answering, thinking it might be something work-related.

It isn't. I recognise Calum's voice immediately.

'Don't hang up,' he says, 'please.'

But I do. My heart racing, I turn off the phone and put it into the knife drawer. I flick on the telly. After half an hour I realise I haven't heard a word of the nine o'clock news or the weather forecast and that *Prime Time* has started without me noticing. I retrieve the phone from the drawer and turn it on. Three missed calls and a voicemail. I delete the message without listening and turn off the phone. I make sure the door is Chubb-locked.

In the morning, when I turn the phone on again at 7 a.m., there are four more missed calls and a text message saying, *Just want to talk.*

I block the new number again. He has to be using burners. Whatever his renewed contact with me was when it began, it's organised now. It's a definite escalation.

As I drive to Coughlan's Quay, I check my mirrors every five seconds. There's no sign of Calum and no black Volvo SUV.

His absence means nothing. Because I can feel him. He's coming for me again.

54

I RATIONALISE MY WAY OUT OF A FULL-BLOWN
crisis on the basis that Calum lives 258 kilometres away and that
the only reason he's been calling is because his mother told him
she met me in Dunnes Stores the other night. She probably told
him I didn't look well. He probably wants my forgiveness. Well,
he can take a long walk off a short plank so he can.

I pick up a large milky coffee from Hassan in the Centra.

'No chocolate this morning?'

'No chocolate ever again. If you see me buying it, stop me.'

'That's not how capitalism works,' he says. 'The financial
health of this business relies on your weakness. Also, KitKats
are reduced. Just saying.'

'You're not a good person.'

'Doing my job.'

'Thanks a million.'

He laughs. 'You'll be back. You know you will.'

'Not today. *Definitely* not this morning. Not before eleven
anyway.'

He's still laughing as I exit the shop.

I'm walking past Sadie's open door when she calls. 'I hear you met a buddy of mine last night.'

I play it cool. 'Yeah. Got a bit more information on Garry McCarthy from her. I think it's worth looking harder at the burglary case. Reckon I should re-interview the house owner, Martin Campbell.'

'Sure. But I want you on the Jane Doe today. Like the inspector said, we have to keep the two cases running simultaneously, but right now, with the helpline so busy, we're just swamped. We're missing stuff, we must be. For now, all the press and public attention is on the Jane Doe and she's what matters to the top brass.'

'So Garry's still in the car, but he's taking a back seat. Not fair, is it?'

'Sometime you can show me something that *is* fair,' Sadie says. 'Meanwhile, you have a job to do. That Technical Bureau request you and Fogarty did last night was good, by the way. I've sent it off. We'll see what comes of it but I don't want to wait for the photo analysis. I want to follow up on the pub. Who was living and working there after the mid-1990s. Whatever you think of that doesn't cost megabucks. We have to keep the budget in mind at all times. You know what Ebenezer Feeney is like. Any ideas on where to start? Cheap but effective ideas?'

'We should go back to the source. The pub owner. Maurice Bolger, the man who owned it during the nineties and the early noughties, died of cancer and it was inherited by his wife, Sheila. Ray Grant told me she went to him and asked him to buy it. He says he bought it as a favour to her so we need to check that out. I know that Fogarty's spoken to her before, but the photos give us an excuse to return.'

'Talk to Olly. He said she didn't know much about the running of the pub. But the two of you should go and see her again together.'

'I don't need him. I can do this myself.'

By way of reply, she raises her eyebrows. She doesn't say a word. She doesn't need to.

I say, 'Message received and understood, skipper.'

55

FOGARTY INSISTS ON DRIVING HIS OWN CAR. 'I'LL pick up a couple of things in Douglas that Mia asked me to get for her. It'll save me doing it later.'

'Whatever you like,' I say.

To annoy him, I flick on Lyric FM. He doesn't change the station.

'Are you into the classical?'

'Did music in school.'

'Do you play?'

'Piano. Not any more.'

'You should take it up again. They say it's good for the brain.'

'Thanks.'

'Ah, shit, I didn't mean it like that. Just something I'm thinking of for herself. The small one. That we should get her music lessons.'

'She's a bit young, I'd say.'

'I don't mean now.'

'Good.'

There's no talking for a while. A jaunty tango piece by Astor Piazzolla comes on. Fogarty seems to like it. I switch over to Raidio na Gaeltachta.

After a couple of minutes he says, 'For fucksake.'

'Do you not *like* Irish traditional music?'

'I like it if I'm in a pub with five pints under my belt and there's a few lads playing tunes in a corner. I don't want to listen to it in the fucking car.'

I flick back. Beethoven now. The start of the Ninth Symphony, the tentative opening phrases before the sudden loud blast of the full orchestra. When the fortissimo comes, Fogarty turns down the volume but leaves the station on Lyric.

He asks, 'Have I done something to you?'

'I don't know. Have you?'

'No. Nothing. I actually thought we were halfway to being . . . And we have to work together, you know.'

'I have zero problem with the work,' I say, which isn't the whole truth.

He makes no reply. We're on the south link, heading to permanently traffic-clogged Douglas. There are three possible exits for the suburb.

I ask, 'Which one do you reckon is best this time of day?'

'West is the obvious choice,' he says. He waits a beat, then adds, 'Sheila said nothing to me when I went to see her the first time. We could be luckier today, I'd say. She's a bit of a wagon. I reckon you and her will get on like a house on fire.'

Maryborough Manor is the name of the estate, a gated and tastefully landscaped development about twenty years old. Sheila Bolger lives in a ground-floor flat, her entrance door beneath the steps of a two-storey townhouse. She's out the front, small and round with flushed cheeks and a smooth grey bob with a fringe. Wearing flower-print gardening gloves, she's carrying secateurs in one hand and a green plastic tub in another. The tub is overflowing with withered clippings.

'I've been cutting back. I'll be with you in a sec. Just need to empty this.'

'I'll do it,' I say. 'Just point me in the right direction.'

'No,' she says. 'I need to keep up my step count.'

We follow her to a fenced area around the back of one of the apartment blocks. When Fogarty tries to help her lift the lid of the communal brown bin, she barks at him. 'Stop. Use it or lose it. I'm seventy-five. When I'm *ninety*-five, maybe I'll need someone but I'll keep going as long as I can.'

Back at her apartment, she peels off the gloves and wipes her feet on the mat, dipping her eyes to our shoes as she steps backwards into the hallway, moving further only when she's satisfied we're clean enough.

Fogarty throws me a pained look that translates as 'You do this, *please.*'

'This is lovely,' I say. 'You have beautiful things, such pretty china, and I really like the little paved area out the back. It's a suntrap, is it?'

'Thank you. They call it downsizing but it's really a come-down. I've done the best I can with it. I didn't need the bigger house – a semi-detached off the Skehard Road, not Buckingham Palace or anything – but I had a kitchen where it was bright from morning till night, and the attic converted. And my lovely garden. I miss it. I don't miss the cleaning and the grass-cutting, of course.'

'I suppose after Maurice died, the garden especially must have been—'

'Is it *joking* me you are? He never did a hand's turn, inside *or* out.'

'Typical,' I say.

'He was forever in the pub. Bertie's. Not at the end, of course. It's the reason you're here, but I can't understand why. I already told Detective Fogarty the last time he was here that I wasn't in Bertie's for years and that I don't know any poor girl who might have been buried underneath it. It's unbelievable, so upsetting to think of her, *when*ever and *how*ever she was put there. Someone's daughter. And somebody *must* know who she is, but I don't. If I did, I'd tell you. I'd be glad to.'

'We're not here about that exactly, Sheila. We have some photographs. Just got them yesterday. We'd like you to take a look at them.'

She frowns. 'Who are they of, the pictures?'

'Sorry, I should've explained. It's not people, it's the place, Bertie Allen's, before it was knocked down.'

'Oh,' she says softly, 'that's . . . Take a seat at the table there and I'll put on the kettle.'

'I can do it, sure,' Fogarty says.

She waits a beat, glances at the folder under my arm. 'Tea and sugar in the press over the toaster, biscuits in the cylinder tin beside the chopping board. The mugs—'

'He'll find them,' I say. 'He's not as thick as he looks.'

She smiles vacantly and eases herself into the chair.

'Memory Lane,' Sheila Bolger says, 'for better or worse.'

I slide the closed folder across the table.

She says, 'My glasses, I can't remember where I—'

Fogarty moves fast. 'Is this them? They were on the mantel-piece.'

She stretches her hand towards him. 'Thank you.'

She opens the folder. One by one, she holds each photograph in her hand, puts it down and moves to the next. Fogarty pours the tea and sets down a plate of biscuits. He looks at me quizzically but has the brains to say quiet. She goes back through the pile again and lays out the pictures in a grid, like a game of patience. Then she starts talking.

56

SHE LOOKS AT FOGARTY. 'I GAVE YOU SHORT
shrift the last time you were here. No excuse except I didn't
want to think or talk about it. Because for a few years, quite a
few, Maurice was his own best customer. He was never a nasty
drunk, but he *was* a drunk. I'm not betraying him. It was well
known. Still is, if you were to ask the right questions in the
right places. Anyway, he'd tell you himself. The drink is what
did for him. Cirrhosis first, then liver cancer that spread to the
bowel. The sad thing is, he'd stopped a few years before he was
diagnosed, was going to AA once or twice a week, but it was
too late. Poor Maurice. The trouble was, he could drink Lough
Erne dry and for years he could hold it. He had hollow legs,
as they say. But it's a poison.'

She takes in a breath and goes on, 'You asked me before if
the upstairs flat was ever let out. I told you it was never rented
in our time running Bertie's and that's the truth. In the old days,
everyone lived above the shop. Maurice grew up over Bertie
Allen's. But I didn't want that. We bought the house off Skehard
Road because I wanted a quiet family home, away from the
noise. And the drink. But the photos make it look like someone
was living there, don't they?'

I say, 'The site manager had a look around before the demo-
lition. He said there were clothes in the wardrobe. He said it
looked like someone had been living there but not for some
time. If it wasn't rented out, was someone staying in it unoffi-
cially?'

She waits a while before replying. 'Maurice. He lived up there
while we were separated for a few years. Five years. Five and a
half.'

'When was that, Sheila? Can you remember?'

'I can't forget, can I? It was 1996 – he went to the dogs alto-
gether and after Patrick's Day that year I told him it was the
drink or me and he made his choice. He never left me short of
money. He was good that way. But he was gone till 2001.
September the eleventh, to be exact. He didn't open on the
Tuesday afternoon when the Twin Towers came down. Drove
out to see me in the old Skehard Road house instead. The world
changed forever that day and the kids were living abroad by
then. Still are. I only see my grandchildren every now and again.

'Anyway, Maurice said he didn't want me to be on my own
that night. And he didn't want to be on his own any more either.
So it was Osama bin Laden who brought us back together, could
you credit it? Maurice never touched a drop after that day. He
told me he'd been making a go of giving it up even before then.
He said it wasn't September the eleventh that finished him with
the booze. It only gave him the courage to come home. But it
was too late for his health. We had a few good years before he
got sick. I'd never stopped loving him. It was the drink I hated.'

She continues, 'I can't tell you what went on in the pub
because I wasn't going in there a long time before the separation.' She looks at Fogarty again. 'I told you the truth about

that. I used to work there in the early days of our marriage. A real community place it was up to the end of the 1980s, start of the 1990s. Ages ago now. But the more Maurice drank, the less I wanted to be in Bertie's. The kids wanted nothing to do with it either. They left the country as soon as they could. Voted with their feet. Didn't want to be press-ganged into being a fourth-generation publican.'

She takes a deep breath. 'There are a few things I *do* know. That I heard. On the Cork bush telegraph. Maurice was prosecuted for serving late. Ten or eleven people found on the premises. I think that was '96 or '97. I might have the date wrong. I suppose you have the record.'

'We do,' I say, 'but we haven't been able to track down the customers.'

She says, 'I'd say they could be anywhere now. The pub changed in the course of the nineties. Turned into a party place. My kids told me it was known as somewhere to go after the Sir Henry's nightclub. A special knock on the side door in the alley, and you were in. Playing "chill-out" records, would you believe, Sunday afternoons even, and Maurice in the middle of them, the oldest swinger in town. Drinking the money as fast as he made it.'

She pauses. 'Have you thought about *when* the burial happened?'

'Yes,' I say. 'It's a very important part of the picture we're trying to build up. Do you have any thoughts on that yourself?'

'Bertie Allen's was a busy place, open almost every day of the year until it closed for ever in 2007. If the murder happened before 2007, there could only have been two days in the year when they'd have been able to do it.'

I ask, 'They?'

'They or he. The murderer or murderers. Whenever or wherever the poor girl was killed, if she died while the pub was trading, she must have been buried on Christmas Day or Good Friday, the only two days the pub was closed. The only two days in the year there would have been time to bury her.'

'We've considered that,' I say, 'but is there anything you might be able to tell us about those two days in Bertie Allen's? What used to happen usually?'

She says, 'Even when we were separated, Maurice was here at Christmas. We were always a family that day. Anyone working in the bar, any regular customers would have known that. It could have happened then.'

I ask, 'What about Good Friday? I think that in some pubs it was the day all the maintenance work was done. Repainting, plumbing, that kind of thing.'

'Maurice had a habit of closing early on Holy Thursday. Before things got messy. A family tradition. He was religious, in his way. Took Good Friday seriously. Always made sure he had the day off. He wouldn't have been repainting. He would have been away from the pub. He sometimes went abroad for the Easter weekend during the bad years. The years when we were apart. He liked going down around the south of Spain with a few pals. Benalmádena, I think. Golf was the excuse, but there was a feed of drink as well, no doubt. I can't imagine what the staff got up to while he was gone. I wouldn't have a clue about that.'

I take that in.

She continues, 'When he was in the pub during those years, he was in a bad way. A pure pity. Passed out regularly, I heard.

Slumped over a table. Having to be helped up the stairs and who knows what going on downstairs. Drugs. Pills, I believe, and a load of free drink being given out by the bar staff. New staff. All the old reliables gone. I couldn't stand the set-up, or the new crowd. Rough, or so I heard. A lot of tracksuits and baseball caps. In the old days, people would dress up for a Saturday night out. I don't understand it.'

Fogarty says, 'That was just what people wore, though, wasn't it? The nineties' look was very laid back for everyone as far as—'

I shoot him a look. He shuts up and I say, 'There was a Terry McAuliffe working in Bertie's around the time of the prosecution, according to the District Court record.'

She shakes her head. 'After my time. Like I told you, I didn't know any of the newer staff. Honestly.'

I look across at Fogarty. We're both thinking, She's omitted information before, she might be doing it again. I decide to ask the same question in a different way. 'What about tax and PRSI payments for the employees?'

'The accountant we used is dead but I'm sure his practice was taken over by someone else. I have the details of the new firm somewhere but I don't think they'd have kept records on employees from that long ago.'

I ask, 'We can contact the Revenue Commissioners if need be.'

She looks away. There's silence for a while. Then she looks back. 'Can I say something off the record?'

'Of course,' I say. I don't add that, if it's important, we'll find some way of getting what she tells us into evidence.

'You're sure?'

'Yes,' I say.

'Okay,' she says, 'and I suppose the pub is long gone and so is Maurice . . . but the thing is, he usually paid the casual bar staff in cash. I know it's not right but it was the way it was done. It was *all* cash at that time, or a lot, at least. The black economy, it was called. Half the pubs in Cork were doing it. Declaring less to Revenue than they took in. Now the taxman counts barrels and checks invoices and it's direct debits to the brewery and people paying for drink with their phone, so everything's changed. But you won't find much of a record with Revenue about casual staff back then. That's my guess.'

I ask, 'What about your children? Would they know anything about the staff? Or might they have known anyone who used to go to Bertie's for the lock-ins?'

'They kept their distance. Too embarrassed to go anywhere near Bertie's because of their dad's carry-on. But I'll give you their contact details and tell them to expect a call. They *may* be able to help, though I doubt it. They were gone even before the separation. Anna went to England in 1991. She's living in Brighton. Married with two children. Both nearly finished school. And Paul has been in Melbourne in Australia since 1993. He has a son. They're always asking me to come out to visit but . . .'

She says nothing for a while, but there's more Sheila Bolger wants to get off her chest. I can feel it. I look at Fogarty. He meets my eyes. He feels it too. We sit quietly. Outside, it's 2023. In here, it's the 1990s. We wait.

She starts talking again. 'I do happen to know *one* of the customers. Because Maurice had a drinking buddy. "My little cousin", Maurice used to call him. Not that little. Four or five years younger. Not an every-night drinker, like Maurice was, too clever for that. And he had a business to run. But anytime he wanted to blow off steam, or entertain one of his bits on the side, he'd stroll into Bertie Allen's and that fool of a Maurice would roll out the red carpet for him. Lock-in on demand.'

A tingle runs through me, the feeling that this could be the break we've needed. I look at Fogarty. He feels it too. I savour the moment before I ask the question.

'What's his name, the little cousin?'

She looks me straight in the eye. 'I don't know how his wife put up with his drinking and his infidelities for so long. The poor creature was lucky to die when she did. He robbed me on the sale price of the pub, too, but it was the pit of the recession and I had a pile of debts and no way of paying them. I was left with no choice. I sold to the only buyer I could find. To Maurice's little cousin. The famous Ray Grant.'

57

WE MANAGE TO ASK A FEW MORE QUESTIONS and hold it together until we're out through the gates of Maryborough Manor, Fogarty driving, radio off. We're heading down Maryborough Hill too fast to the Fingerpost roundabout when he starts with an imaginary interview.

'Mr Grant, isn't it true that you used to drink in Bertie Allen's during the 1990s, and that you were a *cousin* of the owner, yet you failed to mention both of those facts when questioned? *After* a dead young woman was found buried under the floor of the *same* pub that you used to drink in and that you *own*. Why didn't you tell us, Ray? Is it because you've got something to hide, Ray? Might that be it?'

He goes on, 'I just want to get Mister fucking Big Fish in a Small Pond Grant into a room and make him fucking sweat.'

I don't join in the unbridled glee. I'm trying to think through what the new information means. Not easy with Fogarty in celebration mode.

He says, 'When I heard Sheila Bolger say Ray Grant's name, it was only fucking brilliant. I wanted to hear her say it again. One more time.'

He starts singing 'Baby One More Time' by Britney Spears.

I give up listening to him and I give up trying to think. I search for the video of the song on YouTube, watch it on my phone, with the sound down. I don't need to hear it. I know every word of it, every beat. It starts with Britney in a classroom. She's wearing a school uniform and her hair is in two plaits.

But after the action moves outside – the part where Britney's dancing while wearing a tight cropped pink vest and looser white tracksuit bottoms – it strikes me. It's obvious, but I couldn't see it till now.

'Shut up, Fogarty, and stop the car. As soon as you can. I've got something to show you.'

He gives me a funny look but does as I say. Pulling into the car park of the Douglas Court shopping centre, he stops on a clearway, red lights flashing.

'The "Baby One More Time" video,' I say, 'Britney's hair. The high bunches at the side, the rest of it loose. The blonde. It's . . .'

'It's like our Jane Doe,' he says. 'Do you think she was copying Britney?'

'I – I don't know. It's just when I saw it. I feel a bit stupid now. I doubt if our Jane Doe was a Britney fan. But maybe she was. And the video was everywhere, remember? The hairstyle was, too, I think. In our school everyone had it for a while.'

He asks, 'What year was that song out?'

'I checked the release date. The single came out in October 1998. The album of the same name came out in January 1999.'

'It was huge for months, wasn't it?'

I say, 'It was huge the whole year. It's *still* massive. There's probably no one alive who doesn't know that song.'

Fogarty replies, 'Or dead.'

58

IF I'D THOUGHT IT THROUGH PROPERLY, I WOULD
have realised, might've prepared better, but going down the
Britney rabbit hole distracts me. Fogarty too. The one good
thing is, some instinct compels me to close the door before we
start to tell Sadie about the Ray Grant connection to Bertie
Allen's pub. About the family link. That Grant used to drink
there. That he could have told me about it, but didn't.

Reminding Sadie, too, that Grant hadn't seemed to want to
give me the pub photographs. That he'd been extra sensitive
being questioned, about being connected to the Barrack Street
Jane Doe in any way. That we know it's a stretch. That it might
be nothing more than a coincidence.

In response, Sadie says, 'Sit there and stay quiet. That name
doesn't leave this room or go anywhere near a file or a computer
until I say otherwise.'

She picks up her desk phone and we hear one side of a
conversation.

'Something's come in requiring absolute . . . Yeah . . . Yes . . .
Fogarty and McCann . . . They're here in front of me . . .
Yeah . . . Okay.'

She hangs up. Fogarty starts to talk but she brings her left index finger to her lips. We wait in silence. Feeney arrives within a minute. He drags a chair from the side wall to behind Sadie's desk. She moves over to accommodate him. He says nothing.

'Tell him,' Sadie says.

We repeat what we've learned. He listens without comment. When we've finished, he looks at Sadie, then back at us. 'Do either of you have any connection with Ray Grant or his company or any of his employees?'

'No,' I say.

'I don't think so,' Fogarty says.

'Okay,' Feeney says, 'but you can be sure that someone out there does,' he points at the door, 'and that the minute we start looking into him Grant will find out. It was one thing that Grant and his son might have had some past connection to a dead heroin addict who might or might not have been helped to overdose. This is bigger. It's worse.

'If Ray Grant is guilty of something to do with our female victim, he's had twenty-odd years to cover his tracks. We might as well be trying to pin the tail on a fuckin' flea as trying to get him for it. But if he's *not* guilty and his name gets dragged in where it shouldn't, *that*'s when the shit hits the fan. And *that*'s why we need this information like a fuckin' hole in the head. But we have it, and we have to keep a lid on it, and we have to do something about it, ideally without destroying our careers in the process. Career isn't something you have to worry about, McCann, obviously, but the rest of us do.'

Sadie says, 'Shane, that's—'

Feeney says, 'I'm not saying anything we don't all know. Right, McCann?'

I shrug. Stay silent.

Feeney gets to his feet. 'Here's what we do for the moment. Sweet fuck-all until I've had time to think about it. Ye've plenty of work to do. Go and do it and shut the fuck up. If this gets out, both your skipper and myself will know where it came from.'

He tilts his chin in the direction of the door. We leave as fast as we can.

'I was ball-watching,' Fogarty says. 'I was so blown away by the big name that I didn't see the implications. In this job, it's always shoot the messenger.'

He takes a bite from his hot breaded chicken roll (with onions, mayo, potato salad and a double helping of coleslaw) and washes it down with a slug of Coke Zero. We're on high stools at the narrow greasy counter in the Centra window, staring across at the station. Fogarty looks traumatised, like there's been a death in the family, and he's making slow progress with the chicken roll. I ordered a brown ham sandwich with wholegrain mustard and wolfed it down ten minutes ago no bother. Because Feeney's right. I have nothing to lose.

'Man up,' I say, speaking barely above a whisper. 'Okay, like, we're not allowed to do anything for now, but if we *could* do something, what would that *be*? We need to plan. Be ready. Big name or not, if Grant did it, we're taking him down.'

59

I BUY AN A4 REFILL PAD, TWO AMERICANOS AND, as Hassan's off-duty and won't catch me, one of the reduced KitKat multi-packs. I sit back at the counter.

Fogarty says, 'When the brakes are taken off, our first priority is finding Terry McAuliffe, the only Bertie Allen's employee we can be sure of. Social-media searches. Electoral register. Births, marriages and deaths register.

I say, 'Also, where else Terry McAuliffe might have worked – most likely off the books at Bertie Allen's, according to Sheila Bolger, but not everywhere, surely. And we need to look properly into Ray Grant's family and business. His marriage. His kids.'

'What if it's not himself that Grant is protecting? What if it's his son? You met him. What if the son knew the Jane Doe? Went to Sir Henry's?'

'The son's a yachtie,' I say. 'Doesn't seem like a Henry's head.'

'Maybe Grant has other kids?'

'He probably does. It's a good idea.'

As I write it down, Fogarty gets a call. He takes the phone from his pocket. Looks at it. Kills it. Seconds later, a text pings. He checks it but doesn't reply. Puts it on silent.

'What are you doing that for? Feeney might be looking for us. Or Sadie.'

'Yeah, you're right.' He turns the sound back on.

A few minutes later, the phone rings again. He kills it again.

'Take the call,' I say.

'I don't want to.'

'Why not?'

'I just don't, okay?'

When the phone rings a third time, I say, 'Take the call, or speak to her at least and tell her you're busy.'

He walks out onto the street and stands with his back to the shop. He talks for a minute or two before returning and retaking his seat by the counter.

'Are you up to your old tricks again? Who is she?'

'It's not a she, it's a he,' Fogarty says.

'I don't think the gender matters,' I say.

'Fuck off,' he says.

'Just friends, is it?'

'For your information, not that it's any of your business,' he says, 'I'm a hundred per cent faithful to Mia. I actually want to be. This has nothing to do with me. Look, if I tell you something, do you promise not to lose it?'

'I don't promise anything. What are you talking about?'

'The man who keeps phoning. It's your ex. Checking up on you.'

My hands clenched into fists, it takes me a time to reply. 'Since when?'

'I don't know. I wasn't keeping track. A good while. Weeks. Months. Yeah, months. He's, well, he's worried. He was worried before, when you were hiding in the interview room. But since the Barrack Street body, he's worse. He's afraid you'll—'

'What? Crack up?'

'Yeah.'

I blow out a breath. 'Did you tell him about my visit to the autopsy room on the morning of the Jane Doe post-mortem?'

'How did you—'

'Did you?'

'Em, yeah, I did. He happened to phone when you were inside. He asked me where I was and if I could talk and . . .'

'He must have been the one who told Feeney. Nearly got me suspended. I thought it was you.'

'Jesus, no, I *swear* I didn't tell Feeney. It must've been Calum did that. I didn't know, honestly.'

'Block Calum,' I say.

'He's a senior officer in the GNBCI. He was in my class in Templemore back in the day. He's a mate. Not exactly a mate. I never really got on with him, to be honest. But I *can't* block him. And he's only looking out for you. I'd say he still—'

'Fine,' I say.

I pluck the refill pad off the counter, my coat and bag off the high stool, and cross the road to the station. No need to check in, sit with my feelings and analyse them like I learned in therapy. Because what I'm feeling is pure and cold and hard. It's rage.

Making straight for the disused interview room, I fling my stuff on the table. Then I pace, phone in hand, composing phone calls and messages in my head in which I tell Calum in a multitude of ways to back off or else.

Until it dawns that re-establishing contact with me is precisely what he wants. What he's wanted all along. I sit at the table and try to catch my breath.

Later, I'm in the bathroom, splashing cold water on my face, when a text comes through from Imelda, Garry McCarthy's sister, asking if I have any update on the investigation. I call her back and arrange to meet her at her home. I tell her I want to talk about Garry, to learn about him. Texting Sadie to let her know where I'm going, I get a thumbs-up emoji in reply.

I grab a set of keys from the desk sergeant. As I'm passing the Centra, I spot Fogarty, still sitting at the counter, staring out the window, looking as miserable as an abandoned eleven-year-old black Lab with greying fur and arthritis. I keep driving but, a few minutes further on, I do a U-turn and return to the Centra. I pull in. Fogarty sees me, looks confused. I phone him from the car.

'Do you want to go for a spin? Two conditions – no talking about Calum and no reporting to him either. Ever again. You don't have to block him, but you have to fob him off. You have to tell him nothing except that I'm grand. If he's getting no info from you, he might get bored, not bother with you any more. Do you accept my conditions?'

'I do,' he says.

'I'll know if you're lying to me,' I say. 'I'll do time for you if you are.'

'I know you will.' After a pause, he says, 'Where are we off to?'

'Magical mystery tour,' I say.

He ends the call. For a moment I think he won't come. But he does. He gets into the car. 'There's one more thing I have to tell you,' he says.

'What *now*?' I ask.

'I ate the rest of the KitKats.'

I laugh to muffle the doubts shouting at me from every corner of my brain. But I'm tired of being alone and Fogarty's not who I hate. I restart the car, indicate left and ease into the afternoon traffic.

60

ON THE WAY, I TELL FOGARTY WHERE WE'RE HEADED. He's underwhelmed. 'What are we going to say to her? We've no updates on the forensics. We still don't know if the guy was murdered or not.'

'That's what we're going to say. And hopefully we're going to learn a bit more about Garry. Who, by the way, worked on building sites for Ray Grant back in the day and was an old schoolmate of Ray's son. Which I discovered when I met Ray at Garry's funeral.'

'*Now* I'm interested,' Fogarty says.

'Thought you might be.' I glance across at him. 'It's a line worth pursuing. I'd be interested to see if there's any connection between Garry and Ray Grant in more recent times. I put in the request for Garry's phone records but I haven't got them yet and I haven't had time to chase them.'

Fogarty gets out his phone and starts scrolling.

'What are you doing?'

'I'm looking for that young one Siobhan O'Sullivan's number. She can follow up on the phone records. And we'll be able to tell Imelda that we have staff working on the case back at the station right now. The fact that Siobhan couldn't find her own front door if she was standing looking at it is beside the point. It's all about making people happy.'

'I don't agree that it's all about making people happy. Happy is the least of what it's about.'

'Ah, yeah, if you want to go all philosophical. Needless to say, it's about finding the truth and putting scumbags in jail. But what I'm talking about is closure. In my experience, closure makes people happy. Even thinking they *might* get closure makes them a small bit happy and stops them complaining to the likes of GSOC, not to mention the press.'

He finds the contact and makes the call, putting it on speaker so that we can both talk to O'Sullivan.

She listens and says, 'I'm on it. This minute.'

'Good gi– woman,' Fogarty says. He ends the call. 'See, it's all about making people happy.'

❖

Imelda McCarthy lives in St Finbarr's Park, near the Lough Nature Reserve. The street is a cul-de-sac so I dump the car a few minutes from the house, on Hartland's Avenue, facing the direction of the station in case we need a quick getaway. If we're recalled and permitted to start officially pursuing the Grant angle, I don't want to be boxed in.

We walk around the corner and down the slope to the right. Ahead of us, at the end of the street and past the grass and the trees, the lough lies glinting in a surprise burst of afternoon sunshine. Taking in a deep breath, I feel myself relax. 'We should go down and take a look at the ducks afterwards.'

'Good idea,' Fogarty says, 'always liked it around here.

Peaceful. Mostly. During lockdown it was packed, even at night. Mental,' he catches himself, 'no offence.'

I say, 'Stop talking or I'm dropping you back to the corner shop.'

Imelda's is a 1940s or '50s semi-detached, part-pebble-dashed, with a pretty bay window and Virginia creeper still wearing its autumn red. Watching from the front room, she has the door open before we knock. 'I've made a pot of tea. I'll get another cup.'

She shows us where she wants us to go, while she nips down the back of the house through a glass door into what looks like an extended kitchen-dining-living room. Painted a blue grey, with a mix of paintings and photographs adding colour, the sitting room has been left at its original size and not knocked through. It has a solid oak floor, an antique mirror over an open fireplace with an abstract patterned wool rug on the floor in front, a vintage-looking fringed standard lamp and a large corner sofa. A tray with a teapot and two mugs sits on a square wood table at one end of the sofa.

Imelda returns and we sit cradling a mug of tea each.

'No television,' Fogarty says.

Imelda laughs. 'Every man says that the second they walk in the door, but women seem to like it.'

'I definitely do,' I say. 'It feels so calm, and cosy as well.'

'That's what I was aiming for,' Imelda says, 'even if I'm only in here on my own for half an hour or an hour after the kids are gone to bed before I crawl up the stairs, it feels like a mini-holiday.'

'Where are they now?' I ask.

'They're with their dad. He picks them up from school some days.'

'Handy he's able to do that,' I say.

'He works from home a lot of the time,' she says. 'So do I. During Covid we saw too much of each other. We broke up. It's for the best, I think, we know that now. We had a big house, the so-called dream home. Nearly a nightmare by the end. So we sold it and bought two smaller ones. It was fairly amicable. No regrets.' She wells up. 'It's just with Garry, being on my own, it's been hard. The way he died. Not knowing if it was an accident or something worse. Is there any news on that?'

'Not yet,' I say. 'We're working on it, but it takes time. We were hoping you could tell us some more about him, the kind of man he was, if that would be okay?'

She nods, takes a sip of tea. 'How far back do you want to go?'

61

FOGARTY GETS HIS QUESTION IN BEFORE ME. 'TELL us about the time he was working in construction. For Ray Grant, wasn't it?'

'RGP was definitely one of the companies he was employed by, but he worked on various sites around the city and county. I didn't take too much notice, to be honest. He was living out of home by then. For years. A house-share on John Redmond Street over by Shandon. He was the eldest, then Bernie, then me. The thing I remember most was when he dropped out of college. *That* was a big deal. My mum and dad were *so* upset.'

Fogarty persists: 'Could he have been working for the same company but on different building sites?'

'Is who Garry worked for twenty-five years ago important to how he died? I don't understand how it could be.'

I say, 'I think Detective Fogarty was impressed that Ray Grant came to the funeral. It was decent of him, after all this time.'

'I see,' Imelda says, 'yes, him and his son. Conor was an old school friend of Garry's. I think that might have been how Garry got his first construction job, through Conor. It was nice of them to come but I suppose, of all people, the Grants know what it's like to lose someone.'

Fogarty asks, 'What do you mean?'

'Conor's older brother, Tom. He died young. A crash. Single vehicle. High speed late at night. The car went out of control. The poor guy lived for a few days but the doctors couldn't save him.'

'Did Garry know him? Tom? Work with him, maybe?'

'They were in school together so he knew him as an older boy and as his classmate's brother. Apart from that I don't know. What's this about? *Who's* it about?'

'It's about Garry,' I say, 'we're trying to get to know him, what he was like. Just that.'

'He was a lot of different people but mostly he was good. Kind. Soft. Growing up, he was obsessed with music and the sad thing was that when the drugs took hold he lost interest in that too. His life got smaller and narrower until it was all about heroin. He went to London then and we didn't see him for the best part of twenty years. It was as if he'd dropped off the face of the earth. He sent postcards every now and again so we knew he was alive. That was it. But the truth is, by the time he left Cork, he was lost to us. We knew we had to let him go.'

She sighs. 'My dad's death in 1996 hit him hard. It hit all of us but just as he seemed to be coming out of it, seemed to be happy, he got bad again. Got into heroin and there was no getting him out of it. He was on a methadone programme in recent times and it was working for him, we thought. Till we found out in the worst possible way that it wasn't.'

There's silence while I think about bringing up the Deerpark burglary, although it's been clear all along that the family knows nothing about it.

Opting instead for a more general question, I ask, 'You said Garry was obsessed with music? What kind?'

'House. Sweat. Sir Henry's. His first addiction. Started going there when he was in college, or maybe before then. The early nineties is when I remember the scene really kicking off. I was a lot younger than him so we never socialised together. I was never part of the Henry's scene.'

Fogarty is stony-faced, expressionless, but he side-eyes me. He's heard what she's said and he's caught its significance. It's another potential link between Garry's death and the Barrack Street murder investigation, even though we still don't know for sure that Bertie Allen's pub was connected to the Sir Henry's house-music scene.

She continues, 'At one stage he was talking about going back to college, you know, doing music, something artistic. He wanted out of construction. He'd met a girl. He even asked Mum if she'd help with money and she said she'd meet him halfway. But that relationship ended and he went completely off the rails. Into a hole, you know? Refused to talk about what was going on. Lost his job, and the stealing and the arrests began. It got worse and worse until there was no way to reach him.'

I ask, 'Did he ever go anywhere apart from Henry's?'

She opens her mouth to say something, but it's as if a shadow crosses her face and she closes it again. After a time, she shakes her head slowly. 'Haven't a clue. It's like I told you. He was older than me. I didn't know where he went except for Henry's on a Saturday night.'

I look across at Fogarty. He holds my glance, then says, 'You mentioned a girl. Might be good to talk to her. Do you have any contact with her still? A name even?'

'I never met her. He didn't talk about her. He was a closed book.'

I say, 'Maybe his friends would know her. Are any of them still around?'

She asks, 'What do *you* think?'

'I think they could be,' I say, 'yes.'

'It's 2023,' Imelda says, 'and all *you* want to talk about is Henry's in the nineties. Everyone over forty in Cork was in Sir Henry's at some time in their lives. What my family and I want to know is how and why my brother *died*, not what he was doing thirty years ago. Now my kids are due back so—'

'Sure, Imelda,' Fogarty says, 'we'll get out of your way. We're looking through links and connections, is all. We have someone following up on his phone records at the moment too, by the way. It could be the thing that gives us the break we need.'

'That sounds more like what you *should* be doing,' she says.

We stand up from the sofa. She walks to the front door and opens it.

'Our sympathies again,' I say.

'Thanks,' Imelda says. She shuts the door.

Outside on the street, I glance back through the bay window. Imelda's inside, looking out. I give a little wave. She turns away.

Fogarty asks, 'What was *that* about? Didn't like us asking about his past or his friends at all.'

'*Really* didn't like us asking where he used to go apart from Henry's.' I hesitate, then go on, 'I can't help thinking that one of those places was Bertie Allen's.'

'I can't help thinking that too. But even if she does know that he used to go to Bertie's, there could be an innocent explanation of why she doesn't want to tell us. She might not want her dead brother associated with the Barrack Street murder. We could be talking about a coincidence here.'

I take that in. Try it on for size. Don't like the fit. 'No way, Olly. It's not just one, it's a whole series of coincidences. The cases are connected. I know they are. I've felt it since the day I met Ray Grant at Garry's funeral and found out that Garry used to work for him. Then we interviewed Sheila Bolger, and heard that Ray Grant – Garry's former employer – was a customer of the pub during the nineties and also a cousin of the owner. Which he *hid* from us. And now there's Imelda's reaction when we asked her if Garry went anywhere apart from Henry's. She is *definitely* hiding something.'

Fogarty says, 'Devil's advocate, Imelda made a fair point. Everyone over forty in Cork was in Henry's at least once. Our Jane Doe and Garry might have gone there, they might even have both gone to Bertie Allen's, but that doesn't mean they knew each other.'

'Okay, okay,' I say. 'Even so, we need to keep an eye on Imelda. See what she does next. If she goes or stays. Although there's a risk she'll see us if we do. Or the ex might when he's bringing back the kids.'

Fogarty has his phone in his hand already. 'Bugsy, I've a little job for you over here by the lough.'

62

OUT OF DIRECT LINE OF SIGHT OF THE HOUSE,
and nerves jangling, I wait at the corner of the side road into St
Finbarr's Park from Hartland's Avenue, while Fogarty runs back
to the car. It takes much too long for McKeown to arrive and
I'm stressing that one of the neighbours will see me loitering.
I pretend to play with my phone and scroll through photos
and take a call from Fogarty during which I ask him quietly
where the *fuck* Bugsy is. I tie my shoelaces a few times and try
to make it look like there's nothing to see. Having the lough
down the hill is a help. The locals must be used to dog-walkers
and randomers out for a stroll.

When McKeown finally arrives, as instructed, he makes his
approach from the Glasheen Road entrance to St Finbarr's Park.
He drives slowly past Imelda's house and takes up a position on
the right near the bollards separating the end of the street from
the green space with the lough beyond. Satisfied that even Bugsy
should be able to see the comings and goings from Imelda's in
his rear and side mirrors, and that anyone who notices him will
think he's here for the view, if they think anything at all, I
return to Hartland's Avenue and get into the car.

'All good with Bugsy?' Fogarty asks.

'We'll see,' I say.

'Remember what I said about not going overboard with your theory about the two cases being connected. You go overboard, you drown.'

'*My* theory? I thought you agreed with me?'

'I agree that it's worth a close look, I just haven't bought into it hook, line and sinker the way you have. Not yet.'

'You don't want to take the risk of being wrong. You want to hang it on me.'

'That's not what I meant,' Fogarty says, 'but if that's what you heard, it says a lot more about you than it does about me.'

We drive back to the station in silence.

63

AT COUGHLAN'S QUAY, SADIE'S NOT IN HER ROOM
and there's no sign of Feeney either. The general office is quiet
but I spot Siobhan O'Sullivan and make straight for her, Fogarty
behind me.

'Any luck with the phone records?' I ask.

'Not yet,' she says. 'I've sent loads of emails and I've been
on hold trying to get the records released since you rang me.
They keep telling me my call is important to them, but you'd
never think it. I haven't spoken to a single human so far.'

'You might as well give up and start again in the morning,'
Fogarty says.

My head swivels in his direction like an elastic band snapping.
'Why?'

'It's twenty to six,' he says. 'She's not going to get talking to
anyone with the authority to release the records at this stage.
It's outside business hours.'

He's right. He's probably right about taking the possible links
between the two cases more slowly too. I spoke to him too
harshly earlier.

'I didn't realise it was so late. Sorry. And your shift must be
over too, is it?'

'It is, but that doesn't matter,' she says.

'Go home,' Fogarty says, 'and well done for giving it a lash.'

After she's gone, I say, 'I overreacted back there in the car. I do take your point. We should talk it all through properly, shouldn't we? Tease it out. See where to go next.'

'We should and we will,' Fogarty says, 'but in the morning. I've to go home. I forgot to get the stuff I intended to buy in Douglas earlier so I'll have to do it now. And Mia's on a night out with the girls later. She'll probably be asleep by half eight but she's been looking forward to it for ages.'

'Where's she off to?'

'She's not leaving Ballincollig. Going to a place down the main street. Five minutes from the house in case of emergency. I'm useful but not fully trusted to cater for our little angel's every whim, so Mia has to be in easy reach. Which is totally fine by me.'

'What are we going to do about Bugsy?'

'Nothing. He's been decorative since he moved here. Let him get a taste of the donkey work and see how he copes. I told him he wasn't to stir until at least an hour after the kids get dropped back to see if anyone else shows up or if Imelda leaves.'

'It's after six on a school night. You'd think the kids'd be home by now.'

'Maybe Daddy gives them their tea,' Fogarty says. 'Speaking of which . . .'

'You go,' I say. 'I'll wait for Bugsy. And I wouldn't mind a word with Sadie, as well, to let her know what's happened ahead of the briefing tomorrow.'

'How do you know she's not gone home?'

'Her Asics are still under her desk but her Birkenstocks aren't.

Either she's driven home in her Birkies, which is highly unlikely, or she's somewhere in the building.'

He looks pensive. 'I had the exact same thought. What's wrong with us? Normal people aren't like this, are they?'

I say, 'I'm in the job too long. Can't remember what normal is.'

He laughs. Walking away, he's singing 'Baby One More Time'. Still thinking about the Ray Grant lead. And they say men can't multitask.

Fifteen minutes later, a text comes from Bugsy saying, *Daddy's home*.

Although I'm impressed that Bugsy managed to get the apostrophe in the correct place, I reply simply, *Keep me informed*, and resume what I was doing: researching the Grant family on my phone. Ray and Conor are all over it but there's little on Tom, the dead son. There'll be more on the PULSE, but if I go near that, I'll leave a trail, and we're banned from investigating Ray Grant for now. On telly, dodgy cops log in to their workmates' accounts. I figure if you start doing things like that there's no knowing where you'll stop. Plus, sooner or later, you'll get found out.

A while later another text comes in from Bugsy saying he's on the way back to base. I text back two thumbs-up. After a while, too wired to stay sitting, I head for the kitchen to boil the kettle and make a cup of tea. In the corridor, I bump into Sadie. 'Any change?' I ask, meaning the Ray Grant embargo.

'Could be. And I'm moving forward tomorrow's briefing to

eight. I'll be sending the WhatsApps shortly. Going to be all hands on deck so if I were you I'd get some rest.'

'I'm waiting for Bugsy. He's been—'

'I met him two seconds ago. Sent him home.'

'He was supposed to talk to me first.'

'Didn't say anything to me about that,' Sadie says, walking on.

Grabbing my jacket and keys, I run down the stairs to the car park but he's gone already. I phone him, but it rings out. I send him a *Where u? Call me pls* text.

I'm at my desk again when he gets back to me. From the background noise, I deduce that he's in the pub.

'The skipper sent me home. In fairness, like, what was I supposed to do? Tell her no?'

He's half right. I almost tell him we can leave it till the morning. But I remember what Sadie said before. That they'll keep on telling the same story about me until I give them a different one.

I say, 'You had a job, and you're not finished till you report to me. Like we agreed. Tonight.' I wait. The old me wouldn't have let this go. The new me won't either.

64

FORTY MINUTES LATER, I'M ABOUT TO GIVE UP
and go home but Bugsy's conscience must be at him because he
pings me: *Sorry but nothing happened. Honest. Look!*

He sends me through photographs of his notebook pages.
His writing is big and easy to read. On the top of the first page
he writes the make, colour and number of a car.

Below that, and continuing over the following two and a
half pages, he writes:

*18.55 2 kids dropped home by Dad – white male slim build
brown hair average ht. Imelda McC comes out to car. Sends
kids inside. Gets into car. Passngr seat. I McC stays in car
15 mins approx. Exits car when kids come out of hse and
knock on car window. I McC gets out. Crying? Dad gets out
of car too. Hugs her and 2 kids. Departs St Finbarr's Pk @
19.23 by Glasheen Rd.*

Something had registered with me the second I saw the car
model and colour. I send Bugsy another message: *Any pics?
Videos? Pls send asap.*

No reply. I type the car number into the system. It gives me

Catherine Kirwan

the result I expected when I saw the make and model but it's so bizarre that I can't compute it.

I shelve my questions and copy-type Bugsy's notes into a document with an addendum stating the name of the car owner. I need more solid information to prove the identity of the driver. Drumming the fingers of my left hand on the desk, I phone Bugsy. No reply.

I text him: *Photo????????*

Moments later, the picture arrives. It confirms that the man who dropped Imelda McCarthy's kids off this evening, her ex-husband, is the owner of a two-year-old black 3 Series BMW, the same man whose home her dead brother Garry was accused of burgling.

It confirms that Imelda's ex-husband is Martin Campbell.

Which means that Martin Campbell and Garry McCarthy were brothers-in-law. They knew one another before the burglary, reasonably well, presumably, yet neither mentioned it. The family connection has to mean something. But what?

65

I CROSS THE ROOM, INTENDING TO TELL SADIE
what we've learned, talk it through with her, but I hear a yelp
so I hang back. Five minutes later, she's coming out of her
office, coat on, bag in hand.

Surprised to see me, she says, 'Didn't know you were still
here.'

'Some developments in the Garry McCarthy case. Garry already
knew the guy whose house he burgled. They were related.'

As I say it, the connection between Garry and Martin
Campbell loses power, like a blown light bulb. Sadie looks
unimpressed too. 'We'll talk in the morning. I'm mad late
already. Date night.'

She walks past me, leaving her door open. Her desk surface
is unusually clear. Whatever she's been working on, she's filed
away or placed – maybe locked – in a desk drawer. Also, I can
see from where I'm standing that her computer is switched off,
or in sleep mode.

Something's happened. Something big. Maybe to do with the
girl.

I run after her, catch her up as she's getting into her car. I
ask, 'Did you find a name? Do we know who she is?'

'No comment,' she says.

'That's not a no.'

She smiles. 'Interesting observation, McCann, but I've said zip. And Feeney wants no advance rumours or leaks. I'll be watching you at the briefing tomorrow. Make sure you look surprised when he makes his big announcement.'

Patricia

They all went to Sir Henry's, that place on South Main Street, on a Saturday night. She'd go to the pub often during the week as well. Tell me all about it the next morning. At that age you can do whatever you like and bounce back. She never missed a day. She was a great little grafter, and I started taking her with me to auctions and house clearances. You could always rely on her to find something worth squirrelling away. She knew what we had to do – buy cheap, sell dear. A girl after my own heart.

I told her she had a gift for fashion. That she should think about doing a night class. I got her a brochure from the College of Commerce, and she was all for it.

But by then the romance had started and she only had eyes for him. A recipe for disaster to pick one of those lads over the other.

Mind you, she did choose the one who seemed like the sweetest of the three, an artistic Bob Dylan type. Sensitive. And, Cork being Cork, I knew his parents. His mother was – is – one of the Harnetts of Sunday's Well. Lives quite near me now, off the Model Farm Road. Her two girls went to Mount Mercy, where my girls went, different years from mine.

One of the other boys, clever-looking, a steady fellow, was better husband material than Bob Dylan. I tried to steer her towards him. I said, 'When poverty comes in the door, love goes out the window.' She laughed and laughed at that.

The third lad was the leader. Not the leader, the boss. Good-looking, but something about him I didn't like.

Truth be told, they were an odd mixture. Became friends when they were labouring on the same building site, she told me. I said, 'Looking at them, you wouldn't have put them together.' What I meant was, they were from different areas, didn't seem to have much in common apart from the nightclub, which they were all obsessed with, her included.

'I keep telling you, Patricia, it's different now. It's not like the old days.'

Young people always think that, don't they?

66

SADIE REVERSES OUT OF HER PARKING SPACE AT speed and takes off. I stay rooted to the spot, coping with a surge of adrenaline so strong my heart nearly explodes. I walk home and spend the night bouncing off the walls, thinking about the girl, what her real name might be, where she might be from; forgetting for now about Martin Campbell and Ray Grant, and pursuing Terry McAuliffe's employment history and Garry McCarthy's phone records and the rest of the drudgery.

The thing is, though, drudgery is what solves cases. The 99 per cent perspiration thing. Feeney might be the one hogging the final announcement, but it's Sadie who deserves the credit. She's the one who's been combing through missing-persons databases and websites on this island and across the water. It's partly control-freakery, not trusting anyone else to do the job, especially the boring job, right. It's mostly because that's who she is, a workhorse who'd never ask anyone else to do something she wouldn't do herself.

She's talking us through her report and standing at the front of the incident room, looking paler than usual, taking a slug every now and again from a bottle of fizzy water. Hung-over, I reckon.

Fogarty agrees. 'I'd say she horsed into the Pinot Grigio yesterday evening.'

'Prosecco, maybe, a few bubbles for the celebration.'

'Could be,' Fogarty says, 'or something pink. She *does* like the pink stuff.'

Sadie finishes and sits down.

Feeney takes over. 'As a result of DS O'Riordan's sterling work, dental records received last night have confirmed that our Jane Doe is Donna Hannigan.'

He opens a folder and takes out an A4 colour printout. He holds it up. 'This is Donna.'

He gives us time to take her in. Donna's not who she was at the time of the murder. She's two or three years too young. The blurry school photo, cropped from a group shot and enlarged, shows her with hair the original brown, before she bleached it. She's open-faced, looking straight at the camera, unsmiling, eyebrows slightly raised, as if asking a question. She's striking. She'd have grown up to be beautiful, if she'd been given the chance. No, forget that. She'd have grown up full stop.

'Donna was last seen in Manchester in autumn 1998 after her return from Ibiza where she'd spent the summer working, handing out flyers for clubs and bars. She told people she was going to Ireland for a few weeks and was seen taking the bus to Liverpool but there's no record of her boarding the ferry. After she got off the bus, she dropped off the radar too.

'Donna grew up in Manchester. Both parents appear to have

been Irish or Irish origin, based on the DNA results, but there's no father named and Donna lived her first seven years with her mother, Annie Hannigan, Manchester born, a heroin user with convictions for soliciting. Donna was taken into care and lived in a succession of foster and group homes. Thirteen when her mother overdosed and died, so when Donna disappeared, no one was looking for her, except a former social worker, who died of cancer in late 1999, and a couple of school friends. They reported her missing but there was no evidence of foul play so the investigation was over before it started. Some enquiries were made in Dublin, but everyone stopped looking after a while. The view they took was that she was a person trying to escape her past. That she didn't want to be found.'

Feeney goes on, talking more loudly: 'They gave up on Donna, but *we* won't. We're going to leave no stone unturned and ask the questions they didn't. How did Donna end up in Cork? What was she doing here? Who remembers her? Who killed her?'

He opens the folder again, takes out another A4 page, and pins it to the board.

Sadie stands again. She says, 'It's the one you're all familiar with – the blonde hair, white dress, Adidas zip-up jacket, blue boots – only now she has a face and a name. Donna Hannigan. We merged the school photo with the generated image of how she looked. Use it.'

She holds up her phone and presses send. Pings sound all over the room. 'You've all got it now, and there's a press briefing in a couple of hours. We need to hit the ground running. Soon the whole city will have the pics. The helpline is going to come under even more pressure. We'll get a load of false leads. We're also going to get some *good* leads and all we need is one so be prepared.'

I whip out my phone, keen to see her up close, properly, for the first time. I open the WhatsApp message.

There she is. Donna.

Computer-generated blue eyes, dyed blonde hair in the Britney bunches, a hint of a tan. Too young to die, to have her life taken away from her.

I never met her, and never will, but that's not how it feels. It feels like I know her. My breathing slows and around me people are talking but it's as if the volume's been turned down and I can't hear them.

Then Fogarty's waving his hand in front of my face. 'Hey,' he says, 'where did you go? Are you okay?'

'I *am* okay,' I say, too loudly, 'and you can take it from me that unless I say otherwise I'm *always* okay. That question is banned. I will swing for whoever asks it again.'

I stand, holding onto the chair in front. Everyone's cleared out of the room except Fogarty and, up the front, Sadie, looking as if she's had a vitamin-C booster shot because she's bright-eyed and no longer hung-over.

She says, 'My office in five.'

67

WHICH IS HOW I END UP TAKING AN ENFORCED
break from the Hannigan case, as it's now known, and being
put full time on the Garry McCarthy case. Officially, they're
still being seen as separate, but I'm determined to prove they're
connected. In the whirlwind after the discovery of Donna's
identity, the significance of the link we've found between the
cases has waned. Fogarty didn't mention it at the briefing and
neither did I. There wasn't time. And even though I managed
to tell Fogarty about Campbell and Imelda McCarthy having
been married, we didn't get a chance to talk through what it
might mean for the investigation.

Sadie says, 'Someone has to keep a focus on Garry. You're
the obvious choice.'

She might be right, but it's not what I want, and what she's
saying isn't the real reason. The real reason is that she's protecting
me. Because she's afraid I'm losing it again.

'I'm the obvious choice for the Donna Hannigan case too,' I
say. 'I found her. I was there when they found her, I mean. I
can do both.'

'I've made up my mind. Anyway, you were excited about the
McCarthy case last night. What was that about?'

'Garry McCarthy's sister's ex-husband. He's—'

'Follow it up. That's the job, Alice. We sift evidence. Rule things in or out. Now why are you still here?'

I haul myself out of the chair. At the door, I think of something. I stop, turn around, slap the wood.

'It's good she has a name. Donna. *You*'re the one who found her, not me.'

'Yeah,' Sadie says, 'and you're still on the McCarthy case.'

'I wasn't arse-licking,' I say.

'I know,' Sadie says, 'and you might need help. Take Siobhan O'Sullivan. What do you think of her?'

Looks like I'm getting a minder too. I say, 'She's nice. Enthusiastic and a hard worker. But I don't need—'

'Let me know how you get on.'

Dismissed, I return to my desk, but it's impossible to concentrate because the Donna Hannigan case is cranking into high gear, and the station is at fever pitch: groups of people in huddles, nodding furiously, talking out of the sides of their mouths, saying, 'The way I see it is'; more of them, hunched over the same computer, and shouts of, 'Hey, look at this.'

I'm outside the circle again so I retreat to the kitchen, staring into space, boiling the kettle, reboiling it. I remind myself, although I shouldn't have to, that the Garry McCarthy case is every bit as worthy of my best efforts as the Donna Hannigan case. And I remind myself of the connections between them. I remind myself that, if I can move Garry's case forward, maybe I can move Donna's forward too.

I emerge from the kitchen with a freshly brewed mug of tea and a plan.

68

SIOBHAN O'SULLIVAN IS DRIVING, AND SHE'S IN uniform, so that's my excuse for taking a marked garda vehicle to Deerpark. In reality, I want to put the frighteners on Martin Campbell. I don't have a good enough reason to arrest him, but I want him to feel he's under suspicion for something as yet unspecified to see what happens as a result. I tell Siobhan to put on the blue light, but to keep the siren off. We park outside Campbell's house and take our time getting out of the car. This time, there's no wait. I press the bell and Campbell opens up after barely a beat.

'What's this about?' he asks.

'It's about your brother-in-law,' I say, 'your deceased brother-in-law.'

He steps back from the door, waves towards the sitting room on the right. 'Come in.'

I walk past him into the kitchen and take a seat at the counter. 'We never had that coffee. Badger and Dodo, right? I've been telling Siobhan about it.'

Campbell follows. 'Coffee machine's on the blink. What do you want?'

'Can you confirm that the late Garry McCarthy was your wife's brother?'

'She's my ex-wife but, yeah, he was.'

'Any reason you didn't tell us?'

'Didn't think it was important.'

'Were you and Garry close?'

'Barely knew the guy,' Campbell says. 'He was nice, but you couldn't exactly go for a few pints with him and watch the Champions League. He was a recovering heroin addict. Also, he only moved back to Cork in 2020 so, with lockdown and all, I didn't see much of him. By then, anyway, the marriage was on the rocks. Like I said, Imelda is my *ex*-wife, and he's – he *was* my ex-brother-in-law. We weren't bosom buddies.'

'What about when you were younger, before Garry went to London? Did you and Imelda hang out with him sometimes?'

'He'd already been in London for years when I met Imelda. I didn't even know she *had* a brother until later. She didn't talk about him. It was, well, it was painful for her.'

I decide to change tack. 'Why did he pick your house to burgle? Don't tell me it was random.'

'No, it wasn't. He knew where I lived. My guess is, he saw the car was missing and he figured I was out so he thought he'd chance his arm. He would've known there'd be tech equipment around the place, something he could sell. But it's irrelevant. The man is dead. Also, if you recall, I dropped the charges. I didn't want him to go through a prosecution. He'd been through enough.'

'Why call us?'

'No idea.' He looks impassive, blank.

'No idea? You called us directly at Coughlan's Quay, the

Regional Detective Unit, and not 999, not even your local station, and you can't say why?'

He looks uncertain for a second or two before his face settles back into the same blankness. 'This is a waste of time. If I said any more, I'd be repeating myself. I've answered your questions and I told you everything I have to say. I don't know what you're doing other than trying to embarrass me in front of my neighbours. Thank God my kids aren't here. If ye've nothing else to ask me, ye should go.'

I say, 'Just one more question, Martin. Where were you the night your brother-in-law Garry McCarthy died?'

'What business is it of yours where I was that night? Last I heard, Garry overdosed. Not what you'd call a *massive* surprise. But, seeing as you've asked, and not that it's in any way relevant, I was at the Conrad Hotel in Dublin. At a conference. There must've been, oh, three, four hundred people in the same room as me. Tables of twelve. One person didn't show up, mind you, so I only had ten witnesses to me eating my four-course dinner. The event finished about eleven, and a few of us went to the bar, and had a nightcap. I went to bed around twelve fifteen. Drove down the following morning after breakfast. I'm sure it's all on CCTV but I can send you the names and contact details of everyone if you like.' He slides a notepad across the counter to me. 'Write down your email address there. I'll have the names for you later today.'

Siobhan asks, 'Why the delay? And don't say data protection because that's bullshit and you know it. A man is *dead*.'

Campbell raises one eyebrow, smiles benignly. 'Easy, Tiger.'

I ask, '*What* did you call her? You're comparing a decorated garda officer to a wild animal?'

'Oh, for God's sake,' Campbell says, 'I didn't mean anything by it.' He takes out his phone, checks names and contact details and copies them one after another onto the page. I remember how anxious he was at the front door earlier. He's not anxious now. He's cool, relaxed. Doesn't falter once.

Over his head, Siobhan mouths at me, 'Decorated?'

I mouth back, 'Senior county final medal.'

She turns away, coughing to hide her laughter.

But as I'm watching Campbell, I'm remembering the last time I was in this house. I'm remembering the feeling I had that he was hiding something.

I still have it, that same feeling. Because I reckon there's something else. Something he thought we knew, and that he's relieved we don't.

Something he doesn't want us to find out. Something we've missed.

69

BACK AT COUGHLAN'S QUAY, WE RUN INTO
Fogarty in the corridor. He says nothing but tilts his head to
one side. I tell Siobhan I'll catch up with her, then do an about-
turn and go after him. He looks back to check that I'm following
and steps into the disused interview room I used to live in,
leaves the door ajar. When I reach him, he's got the light on.
He's already swept the detritus off the table and pulled it closer
to the end wall, near a plug socket. I stand to one side, watching
as he sets a laptop on the table and drags two chairs towards it.

'You're grand,' Fogarty says. 'No need to help, I can manage
myself.'

'I'd help if I knew what you wanted me to do. What's going on?'

He's sitting at the table now, logging into the laptop, checking
the settings. He looks up at me. 'You know how long we've
been looking for Terry McAuliffe.'

'The barman from Bertie Allen's? The one who was there at
the time of the District Court prosecution? Did we find him?'

'We did. Income tax records from His Majesty's Revenue and
Customs eventually tracked down our Terry. Except he's a she.
Teresa. Married. Living in Highbury in London. Hope she's not
a Tottenham fan. Anyway, she's now called Levy, not McAuliffe,

which is why she was so hard to locate. But in fairness she's agreed to a video interview. I know you're full time on the McCarthy case but you found her name in the court licensing records. Maurice Bolger, who's dead now, was the only one convicted in the licensing prosecution and no one else with any connection to Bertie Allen's in the nineties has been willing to come forward so far but she *is* willing, and she might be useful. That's down to you.'

'Thanks for letting me know. Also, why are you being so nice?'

'I'm supposed to be doing the interview, and I will be, but I want you to sit in. Not directly on screen, if you don't want, but in the room at least. You and I talked to Maurice Bolger's widow. She's the one who mentioned the Ray Grant link but we haven't got any more on the fucker. Nothing to justify us taking the connection further. Terry might be the one to give it to us and two heads are better than one. That's the help I want.'

'You didn't think to ask Bugsy?'

'Ah, no, I did not. Correction. Two heads aren't always better than one especially if one of the two heads is Bugsy's. He was in the Black Dog last night till closing time. So what do you say, partner?'

'I'm not even going to dignify that with a response.'

He smiles as I take a seat on the chair beside him.

Terry's an expertly loose-curled long-haired redhead with discreet black-eyeliner flicks, a mask of pale foundation and brown matt lipstick.

Fogarty asks, 'What part of Cork are you from originally, Terry?'

She gives an address on Doyle Road in Turner's Cross.

'And when did you go to London?'

'I'm here since 1998.'

'And what are you working at over there?'

She looks impatient. 'I thought you knew all this. You tracked me through my income tax records, didn't you? Very CIA, I must say. Can't do much, can you?'

'We have to check,' Fogarty says.

'Okay. I'm part-owner and full-time manager of Stoked. It's a gastro-pub on Stoke Newington Church Street, the Clissold Park end.' She pauses. 'I'm happy to talk to you, like I said, but I only have twenty minutes before the lunch rush. I hope it's enough because it's all I've got. I'm run off my feet as it is and one of my waiting staff hasn't shown up.'

'We're interested in your time working in Bertie Allen's,' I say, 'what it was like, who the regulars were and all that.'

'We're interested in one regular in particular,' Fogarty says.

He starts into the Ray Grant questions and there's no reason to stop him because we're on the clock and we're both interested in Ray Grant. I see him as a potential link between the Garry McCarthy and the Donna Hannigan cases. I'm still vague about what the link might be. Garry used to work for Grant, maybe he drank with him sometimes too.

But Fogarty's laser-focused on the Donna Hannigan case, thinking ahead to the impact of taking down a big scalp, with more than half an eye on career progression now that he's a father. And it looks like Fogarty's right.

Because Terry says, 'However bad it felt back in the day,

getting fired from Bertie Allen's was the best thing for me because everything happens for a reason.'

'Hang on,' I say, 'you got fired? Why *was* that?'

'I got fired because of Ray Grant.'

70

GARRY MCCARTHY'S PHONE RECORDS ARE IN, BUT I've delegated the preliminary analysis to Siobhan O'Sullivan because I'm in Rochestown, parked directly across the road from Ray Grant's palatial residence. I'm driving, tagging along for the big moment only because of my earlier involvement with Ray Grant. Fogarty's the one in charge. I'll be reassigned to Garry's case after this.

It's a bright, fresh morning, and Ray's returning from a stroll to Douglas Village with the *Financial Times* and the *Examiner* tucked under his arm, happily unaware that his reading is about to be interrupted. He's left the electronic gates open, permitting us unfettered access to the 1.2 acres of lush gardens. He traverses the lawn via a stepping-stone path, glancing around at his domain, and skywards, as he walks.

After waiting for Grant to go inside the house, I take the car slowly up the gently curving driveway and stop outside the front door. I stand by the shrubbery at the end of the steps. Fogarty trots up and raps twice on the polished woodwork.

Grant answers, cheeks still flushed after his exertions.

Fogarty introduces himself, gets to the purpose of our visit without waiting for Grant to respond. 'I wonder if you'd like to accompany us to Coughlan's Quay garda station voluntarily in connection with the death of Donna Hannigan.'

'Who?'

'The body found beneath the floor of Bertie Allen's,' Fogarty says. 'She's been identified. I'm surprised you haven't heard about it.'

'Fuck off,' Grant says, and slams the door.

Fogarty retreats, grinning broadly. He calls Feeney, updates him, then ascends the steps again. This time, he rings the door-bell.

On reopening, Grant's on the phone to his solicitor.

'This is obscene. I told you I'm not coming. My solicitor says I don't have to. Let me have my breakfast or arrest me.'

Fogarty replies with a back-slapping, high-fiving zinger. 'If arrest is what you want, Mr Grant, I'd be delighted to oblige at some point in the future. But if you'd consider coming with us now, it might never get to that. We have a job to do. We talk to people. Ask them to cooperate. In my experience, inno-cent people are usually happy to help.'

Grant grunts. He turns away, walking back into the hallway, leaving the door ajar as he talks to his solicitor. Five minutes later, he emerges, still on the phone. 'Right so. Meet you at Coughlan's Quay. Half an hour.' He ends the call, looks down at me. 'Was this your idea? Or Garda Gobshite's here? Doesn't matter, I suppose. I'll get my jacket. Tell my poor wife where I'm off to.'

He's silent during the car journey but he consents to finger-printing and DNA tests and to having his voluntary interview video-recorded. His patience has worn thin by the time the questioning starts. I should be back working the McCarthy case. Instead, I'm watching the Ray Grant show.

At a table in Room Two, beside his solicitor, he looks like a prize bull denied the winning rosette. Poured into an emerald green and blue trim Dromoland Castle-branded half-zip, Grant is fuming, bellowing incessantly at Fogarty at the top of his voice, ignoring Sadie for now.

'Fair enough, I own the place,' Grant says, 'but I know nothing about the dead girl. If I've said it once, I've said it a thousand times: why the *fuck* would I have bought the site and gone through years and years of planning bullshit if I knew she was there? I could've bought a hundred other sites. Is *this* the level of police work in Cork, these days? Is *this* how far stand-ards have fallen? Or are ye just fuckin' thick the whole lot o' ye?'

Fogarty appears rattled, doubt creeping into his face however much he tries to hide it. He's gone out on a limb with Feeney about the Grant connection to the Barrack Street murder and it's not working out the way he'd hoped.

Sadie's not looking at Fogarty but she has to have sensed his uneasiness because she takes over. 'Mr Grant—'

He turns his attention to her. 'You violated my home, at least your dim-witted office boy did, no doubt with your full approval, and you have the *gall* to—'

'Get off the stage, Ray,' she says. 'We all know why you're here so the sooner you address the elephant in the room the better.'

'Enlighten me,' Grant says, 'because I assure you I'm in the dark.'

'We're here partly because of your son.'

'Conor? What's he got to do with it?'

'Not Conor,' Sadie says.

Grant makes no response but his nostrils flare and he takes in an audible breath.

Sadie goes on, 'I'm talking about your late son, Tom.'

Grant's looking at her like he's never hated anyone more.

'Tom worked in Bertie Allen's during the late 1990s, didn't he?'

No reply.

'He was a replacement for Terry McAuliffe, wasn't he? Terry told us that Maurice Bolger, the late owner of Bertie Allen's public house, fired her – at *your* request Ray, that's what she says – to free up a job for Tom.'

Grant's head dips almost imperceptibly.

'Why *was* that, Ray? Why did you want your Trinity-educated son to work in a pub on Barrack Street?'

He speaks in a low, controlled voice: 'Don't you *dare* try to blacken Tom's name when he's not here to defend himself. My son had *nothing* to do with that poor girl, whoever she was. He wanted to give the pub business a try. Maurice needed someone he could trust. That's all it was. Ask anyone.'

After a beat, Sadie goes on: 'We're *also* here because you yourself were a frequent visitor to Bertie's during those years, the late 1990s and early 2000s. We have it on good authority that you were a regular at lock-ins on the premises, lock-ins facilitated by the then owner of Bertie Allen's, Maurice Bolger. He was your cousin, I believe. Sadly, Maurice is dead, as you know, and tragically, Tom is too. In a way, you're the last man standing.'

'Nothing incriminating in any of that,' Grant says.

Fogarty asks, 'Why didn't you tell us about it so?'

'I didn't try to hide it, as you well know, and I don't respond well to bullying. Never have. I'm not going to start now.' Grant turns to his solicitor and nods.

His solicitor says, 'My client has said everything he wishes to say. You might note that he will, in due course, be filing a comprehensive complaint with GSOC.'

Grant can stop talking when he likes because he's here voluntarily. He gets up from the chair and, folding his arms over his paunch, stares back and forth between Sadie and Fogarty as if he's committing their faces to memory. Then, bouncing out of the station like he's on springs, he takes every last shred of hope with him.

Because going heavy on Grant and bringing him into the station was a mistake. He knows now that we have nothing on him. He could be guilty of Donna's murder – or of covering up for his son Tom, or his cousin Maurice Bolger – or he could be innocent. At the end of the morning, the only thing we know for sure is that we may never find out who killed and buried Donna. And we've known that since day one.

Back in the gloom of the general office, Siobhan O'Sullivan crosses the room to my desk. 'I've been through Garry's phone records,' she says. 'Mostly he was in touch with family members and his NA sponsor but I've highlighted some numbers I haven't been able to identify yet.'

I take the folder from her, glance at it, stand up and hand it back to her. I put on my jacket. Siobhan looks at me doubtfully. 'I have an urgent personal appointment,' I say. 'We'll talk first thing.'

I have no appointment, urgent or otherwise. I need air. To get out of here. The investigations, both of them, have run into the sand. And I keep thinking that it's my fault again. That there's something I'm not seeing.

71

AFTER THE BURNING OF CORK BY RAMPAGING
Crown forces on a night in December 1920, as well as being
generally decimated and in rag order for years afterwards, the
city was left without a library, the previous one and its entire
contents having gone up in smoke. It's almost December again,
the daylight and the year fading, when I cross the threshold of
its replacement: the City Library on the Grand Parade. I'd almost
come here while I was still working on Donna's case, but didn't.
Now that I'm deep in grasping-at-straws territory, I'm back.
This time I'm here for Garry McCarthy.

And I'm here for me. The library is too small for all it contains,
and all it needs to contain, and it's a hotchpotch of two
twentieth-century buildings spliced together, but it's a haven
to me: my childhood before place, unsullied by everything that
happened after.

I say, 'Hiya,' to the security guard in the lobby and enter the
bright main room, the high ceilings providing welcome vertical
space, because every other square centimetre is in use. I breathe
in the goodness and the warmth, and scan the notices and flyers
for groups I'll never join and events I won't go to. I lost my
old card years ago and I haven't replaced it since I moved home

to Cork, but I should. I should go to an author reading, too. Maybe, when this case is over, I will. Other guards have lives outside work, but I never have. Living with Calum, it was the job twenty-four/seven. Since my breakdown, it's been job-sofa-telly for me. It's not enough.

I go up to the desk and show my garda ID. I tell the library assistant I'm here to check Garry McCarthy's borrowing record in the weeks and months before his death.

A little later I take a seat in the research area upstairs. They've given me a printout of Garry's books and I've noted down the relevant library rules. When someone borrows a book, they can keep it for three and a half weeks and renew it five times.

When he died, Garry was on his fourth renewal of *Man's Search for Meaning* by Viktor Frankl, a book about finding purpose in every experience, no matter how horrific. He'd borrowed it five times, so it was either important to him, or he found it hard to finish. I reserve judgement for now and consider the list as a whole.

I figure that Garry's recent choices divide into three main types. The first is broadly motivation and finding a way to do difficult things (*Man's Search for Meaning*, *Feel the Fear and Do It Anyway*). The second covers moving on and redemption (*Getting Past Your Past*, *On Repentance and Repair*, *Falling Upward*, *The Power of Letting Go*). The third category is prison memoir (*A Bit of a Stretch: The Diaries of a Prisoner*, *Writing my Wrongs: Life, Death and Redemption in an American Prison*).

It strikes me that the Frankl book combines all three topics – motivation, redemption *and* prison memoir – which might be significant, and might be why he kept renewing it. It's also notable that there's no fiction on the list except *Rita Hayworth and Shawshank Redemption*, the novella by Stephen King on which the hit movie was based, which slots equally well into the prison category, and *The Alchemist* by Paulo Coelho, the other book beside his bed.

I google *The Alchemist*. It's a fantasy quest novel about a shepherd going on a journey and overcoming obstacles. It fits with the list.

As, arguably, does *The Da Vinci Code*, the dusty paperback in Garry's wardrobe, a book about hidden codes and completing impossible tasks in extreme circumstances.

The book choices tell me that, in the months before his death, Garry was thinking deeply about life, about finding meaning in his past as an addict and in a future of overcoming it and moving on. It makes sense, based on what I know of him.

The only slightly surprising aspect is his interest in jail auto-biographies, because I've checked his record. He had a string of possession and theft convictions but only served short sentences and didn't spend long inside. Nevertheless, his time in prison must have had an effect. Maybe he wanted to remind himself that, if he slipped, he'd end up back there. I write up some notes and reckon I'm done.

I stay where I am, sit for a while longer, remembering when I thought about coming here before, intending to research Cork in the nineties. Hanging my jacket over the chair, I go up to the window and ask the assistant for help in accessing the newspaper archive. I say that I'm especially interested in Sweat, the famous house-music club at Sir Henry's nightclub.

72

I CONCENTRATE ON THURSDAY EDITIONS OF THE
Echo's 'Downtown' entertainment supplement. I'm expecting
to find information on Henry's but there's surprisingly little for
such an influential venue. No photos of patrons, or pieces on
upcoming events. No ads. As an underground place, it might
have been a case of if you know you know; if you don't, it's
not for you. The advertising must have been more ephemeral
– posters, flyers, word of mouth.

I abandon the entertainment-guide angle and do a general
search. Henry's crops up frequently in den-of-iniquity mode.
City councillors complaining at Monday-night meetings about
crowd control and drug use. The odd court report.

It's handbag stuff – halcyon days compared to how the city
is now, awash with heroin and cocaine and a smorgasbord of
pills and powders and industrial strength weed and criminality
and debt and broken families and sick people needing help.

Which brings me back to Garry McCarthy and the progress
he was making in his life before he died. I feel like I know him
better after my time here, but I'm struggling to see how anything
I've learned helps the case. My head in my hands, I massage my
temples with my thumbs, try to think. It might be worth putting

out a call asking ex-clubbers for photos from Sir Henry's in the late nineties on the remote chance that Donna might be in one. I make a note.

I'm on my way down the stairs when it comes to me that it's not Henry's photographs we need to seek out, it's ones from the pub, the place where Donna was buried.

I stand in the doorway, page through my notebook and find the number for Terry Levy née McAuliffe, the former Bertie Allen's barmaid, in London. When she answers, I tell her what I'm looking for.

'Sorry,' she says. 'If it was now, there'd be a million photos, but people didn't record every second of their lives back then. I'm not sure I even owned a camera. I used to use disposables for special occasions like weddings and holidays. You might be wasting your time.'

'Thanks anyway, Terry. We'll be in touch.'

The only other patrons or employees of Bertie Allen's that we have definite knowledge of, apart from Terry, are Ray Grant and his dead son Tom. But after today's debacle, the chances of getting any information out of the Grant family are precisely nil.

I walk. North on Grand Parade and down Patrick Street as far as Academy Street, then zigzag past the Crawford Gallery and the opera house and over the bridge. Water nearly all the way, an invisible presence in the culverts beneath my feet or rushing openly, beside and behind me, till I clear Blackpool and the road rises and widens out, swerving east by the Glen boxing club and the flats, climbing past the turn-off for Dublin Hill and further up, as far as my parents' place. It's been years since I've done the journey from the centre of town to Ballyvolane on foot.

It brings little in the way of clarity. Preoccupied, when I get to the house, I do the usual. Flick a few switches. Go from room to room checking the plants. The pots feel heavy so I hold off on the cool-boiled water, and the kettle's still full when I get back to the kitchen. The door's open, as I left it. I walk straight in, expecting nothing and no one, with no sixth sense, and my evolutionary protection mechanisms on snooze because, in my head, I'm still back at the City Library. It takes me a while to process what I'm seeing live.

A middle-aged man. Tall. Fit. Muscular. Faded blond curly hair, cut tight to his skull. Black waterproof jacket, sweatshirt, jeans and new-looking black trainers.

It's Calum.

73

DELAYED SHOCK SLAMS INTO ME, LIKE AN articulated truck in a cycle lane. A crash when the base of the kettle hits the floor so I must have dropped it. The lid flies open and water explodes over the terracotta-coloured tiles. Stepping backwards out of the kitchen into the hall, I keep on backing, making for the front door. Calum leaps over the puddle and catches up with me by the coat stand. He's standing as close as he can be without touching. His breath is on me, though. Minty fresh. And the overpowering stench of the Lynx Africa shower gel he always used no matter how many times I asked him – nicely – to change brands. My stomach lurches. The urge to vomit. I swallow. Manage to keep the acid down.

'Have you nothing to say?'

I shake my head.

'I used my back-door key to get in. I'm surprised they didn't change the locks. Nice of them not to.'

I find my voice. 'Please go. You shouldn't be here.'

'I wouldn't *have* to be here if you hadn't blocked me when I phoned. I just wanted to talk. I shouldn't have had to do this but you made me.'

He fixes me with a look. I meet it, stare straight into his eyes. Barely blink.

'Well, well,' he says. 'Someone's got brave.'

'Why are you here?'

'Visiting my mother. She hasn't been feeling great.'

'Looked fine when I saw her. Same as ever. Older, obviously.'

'Ha! I'll tell her you said that. Women love hearing they look old. You look old yourself. Your time in the loony bin took a lot out of you. I don't like your hair that way either. Too short. Too brown. It looks better with highlights. I've told you that before. And you've put on weight. You're letting yourself go.'

It's almost a relief to hear him put me down. The banality of it. The normality.

'You said you wanted to talk. What about?'

His expression softens into the familiar kindness that fooled me for so long. 'Does it have to be *about* something, Alice? Can't we just talk?'

He's smiling but guarded. Tense. His body rock hard, every muscle braced. It's never flight with Calum. It's always fight.

He goes on, 'Hey, how's work going for you? People tell me you're doing well.'

He's watching me, waiting on my response. We're millimetres apart and I can hardly breathe. It's as if he's hoovering up all the air in the room, sucking it in, hoarding it.

I ask, 'People?'

'Yeah, people. I keep an eye on you. Want to make sure you're safe.'

'No need to. I'm fine.' I turn my face away, but I stand my ground.

His breath on the left side of my neck now. Warm. Moist. The bile rising in my throat again. Another swallow.

'So I hear. You've turned a corner, I believe. Working that Barrack Street thing. Not getting the results yet, mind you. Putting in the hours all the same. Time is what counts. It pays off in the end.' He pauses. 'We could talk about the case, if you want. Like in the old days. The *good* old days. What do you say?'

I look up at him again. He's eager, eyebrows raised, eyes open wide. He tugs my hair across my face, blocking my mouth, presses his thumb into my chin, hard enough so that it almost hurts, but not quite. 'A jaw-length bob, eh? I could get used to it, I suppose.'

That's when I know that I'm not just a hobby to him, a left-over, a nostalgia trip, an occasional distraction. That's when I know for sure that he wants me back.

And that I need to do whatever it takes to get him out of the house.

74

'I ASKED YOU A QUESTION,' CALUM SAYS. 'THE least you can do is reply.'

I feign confusion, 'Sorry, what question?'

'I *asked* if you want to talk about the Barrack Street case.'

I could tell him that I'm no longer on the case but I change the subject instead. Diversion was always the thing that worked best.

'Thanks, but it's the last thing I want. I need a break. Maybe a permanent one. You were right in what you said. That I look old. I *feel* old. After St Pat's, the breakdown, all that, I don't think I'm able any more. The pressure is . . .'

His face visibly relaxes. His body too. 'The job's not for everyone. I can have a word with Shane Feeney for you. Explain how things are.'

'No,' I say, 'not yet. I want to be sure of what I'm doing next before I say anything. I – I was, well, I was thinking of going back to education.'

It's not a lie. I *was* thinking about it. I'm not any more.

He's smiling broadly now. 'Oh, yeah?'

'Veterinary nursing. UCD.'

'Dublin? That's good.'

'I'd have to do an animal-care course first, to get some experience and show that I'm interested, but I can do that in Cork. I've missed the one that started in September but there's another one starting in January. I want to talk to my folks about it when they get back from holidays. I might move home here again for a while.'

'Good idea about moving home here. A flat on Wellington Road is grand in your twenties but—' He stops suddenly. Remembers that I've never told him where I live. I pretend not to have noticed. 'Where are they anyway? My old dear said they're away.'

'They *were* cruising the Norwegian fjords. Supposed to be home by now but they signed up on board for the Icelandic extension. The last time I talked to them they were in Reykjavik. They were going to some glacier, I think, or the hot springs. Maybe both.'

His eyes are glazing over.

'Sorry,' I say. 'I need to get past you. I have to mop up the kettle water.'

He steps aside. Walking by him, I take out my phone.

He clamps a hand on my shoulder. 'What are you doing?'

'Ordering a taxi. I'm late for dinner with my brother.'

'Put the phone away. I'll drop you.'

'I can't,' I say. 'It's Billy. You're not his favourite person any more.'

He lets go of my shoulder. 'Never was.'

'Do you want to go out the front door? Less messy?'

He waits before replying. 'Sure.'

I open the door and he steps through. I follow him out onto the tarmac. He walks towards the gate.

'You should probably return my parents' key,' I say.

'Probably should,' he says. Keeps walking. Turns right in the direction of his mother's house. Looks back, eyes still on me till he heads through his mother's gate.

I stay outside and press the number for Taxi Co-op. Make sure Calum hears me giving my name and location and ordering a car for Lover's Walk.

When he's gone, I run back inside and shut the front door, grabbing a bath towel from the hot press in the hall. I pick up the kettle, put it on the draining-board. It might be broken but I don't have time to check. I swipe the towel over the floor until it's mostly dry. I turn off the downstairs lights except the sensor outside the back door. I dump the wet towel in the laundry basket, and collect my handbag from underneath my coat hanging on the hook inside the back door. The bag looks untouched. He must have missed it because if he'd seen it he'd have poked through it.

I put the strap of the bag on, cross-body, my coat over it. I bolt the back door from the inside and double back through the house. I wait in the front hall in the dark, my stomach in knots, my guts liquid.

A text message comes through to say that my taxi's out front. As I'm easing open the front door, I hear the sensor light click on in the yard and a thump at the back door. It could be a fox or a cat but it's probably Calum. After rethinking our chat. Deciding he might have gone too easy on me. I slam the front door behind me and run to the taxi.

The car takes off, heading east. The driver asks, 'Lover's Walk, yeah?'

'One sec.'

I phone Billy. 'Are your gates open? I'm coming by. Make sure all the outside lights are on. I'll explain when I see you.'

'What's this about? There's no one home. We're in Dublin. Bronagh's in that thing at the Helix so we're all here. I told you about it. Asked if you wanted to come.'

His daughter. The speech and drama competition. 'Sorry, I forgot. I've been pretty tied up.'

'Is everything okay?'

'Everything's great,' I say. 'Nothing to worry about. Enjoy the show.'

I end the call. Look out the window. We're still on Ballyhooley Road.

'Right at St Luke's Cross, please, and down Wellington Road.'

I get out of the cab but I don't go into the flat. Instead, I head for the only place I know for certain Calum won't follow because there are too many cameras and too few reasons for him to be there. I drive to Coughlan's Quay.

75

DON'T TRY TO LABEL MY RELATIONSHIP WITH CALUM.
It's not what you think. That's not how it was. He wrapped
me in cotton wool. Kept me safe. For so long, I *wanted* to be
with him. He was good for me. Amazing for my career. No
special favours, despite what some people may have thought.
He was my guide. To the job. To life. While he and I were
together, I was a fit, skinny, stylish, but never tarty, quietly
efficient supergirl.

Which took a huge amount of effort because I'm a Doritos-
eating all-day pyjama-wearer whenever I get a chance. That's
not *all* I am, but I'm not a supergirl either. I'm a woman. The
common ordinary variety. The reality, shall we say, annoyed
him some of the time and I don't want to say any more than
that because I'm a private person and this isn't about me.

And, no, Calum never laid a finger on me. He put me down
and he built me back up. He called it tough love. Yeah, I know
how it sounds, but he was my best friend too, and I was his,
and in the end, he wore me out. Exhausted me. In the end, it's
a miracle I didn't fuck up at work even more than I did.

At the station, I enter via the public office and head up the main stairs. Snap on the big lights. All of them. None of this working in the dark by the light of one small desk lamp like you see on the telly. Who *are* these people? What kind of idiot would *do* that?

The main room is empty, as I'd known it would be. As I said before, we're day-job cops, apart from overtime when it's going and the odd bit of shift work for the allowance.

On reaching my desk, I let out an enormous sigh. I angle the keyboard and chair slightly to give me a view of the door as I type. The window is to my back and there's no blind or curtain. I feel exposed, like someone's watching but no one is. It's just the night.

Sitting, I start two Word documents – one to type up my handwritten notes of the information gleaned at the City Library, the other for general ideas.

This is how I roll. Deaden myself to stop myself thinking unhelpful thoughts. Like what the *fuck* was Calum doing at my parents' house earlier and what the *fuck* is he doing in Cork midweek? To see his mother, he said, and maybe that's true. Maybe he saw me going in and followed me on impulse. Maybe I've overreacted. Maybe it wasn't planned. Realistically, how could it have been? There's no pattern to my Ballyvolane visits. I start to breathe more easily.

I finish typing my notes on the books Garry borrowed and my idea about searching for photos of patrons of both Sir Henry's and Bertie Allen's in the late nineties, and move on to the 'General Ideas' document. Stare at the blank page for a while.

Something's at the edge of my consciousness but I can't quite reach it. Then I remember Garry McCarthy's phone records, the ones Siobhan's been working on. She said Garry was mostly in touch with family and his NA sponsor and a few other numbers she couldn't yet identify.

I cross to Siobhan's desk and find the folder next to her keyboard. I sit in her chair and go through the printout line by line. She's colour-coded the numbers. Pink highlighter for family (with a separate page listing each name and number), yellow for NA sponsor, blue for contacts with garda station and solicitor (again with a separate page listing name and number) and, the one I'm interested in, green highlighter for the unknowns.

Siobhan's done a great job. I need to tell her that but the morning will be soon enough. I flick back through her notes and that's when I see it.

The Coughlan's Quay station landline, and the date and time of the call. It's the day of the Deerpark burglary, etched in my brain because I've been back through the file so often.

I return to my desk, open my VARIOUS folder, find the audio file, click on it, listen properly to the call report of the burglary for the first time. After hearing it, I have to sit down.

I play it again. Incredible as it seems, there's no doubt.

It's Garry McCarthy's voice I hear, not Martin Campbell's.

That's what Campbell was hiding earlier today. That was why he looked blank at first, then shut down when I asked him about phoning Coughlan's Quay station directly instead of 999. Garry must have been faking sleep that day when we found him on Campbell's sofa.

Because it was *Garry* who phoned in the burglary, not Martin Campbell.

Garry McCarthy grassed on himself.

76

WHY WOULD A BURGLAR CALL THE COPS? WHY would anyone do that? No, forget about anyone. It has to be about him. Why would *Garry* do that?

I take to the floor, pacing up and down between the desks, running through scenarios in my mind. That he was blackmailing Campbell. Or that his recovery from addiction was the key, that he did the burglary and regretted it. Something to do with the Twelve Steps?

Which appears to make sense until I remember that Garry was contesting the burglary case. So it couldn't have been that.

I remind myself of what I know about Garry.

I know that he worked in construction for Ray Grant. That he went to school with Conor Grant. That he and Conor were friendly because Ray Grant told me that Garry went to the Grant home sometimes. Which means Garry had to have known Tom, Ray's older son, who used to work in the bar at Bertie Allen's.

I know, too, that Garry went to Sir Henry's all the time, was so into going there that his sister Imelda called it 'his first addiction'.

She also said that he'd met a girl.

What if that girl was Donna Hannigan?

Imelda said that the relationship broke up and that afterwards Garry went into what she called 'a hole'.

But I also know that Garry had found stability before his death and, based on his reading list, that he had regrets.

What if one of Garry's regrets was murder?

The murder of Donna Hannigan?

77

I TAKE A FEW SHEETS OF WHITE PAPER AND BRAIN storm, spreading the pages in front, crossing out ideas, adding more. In the end, I figure it stacks up like this.

When the excavation work started on Barrack Street, Garry knew that it was only a matter of time before Donna's body would be found. Clean and sober for the first time in decades, he must have wanted to confess to his part in the death of Donna Hannigan. To take his punishment. It explains his strange reading list. Books on meaning and motivation, redemption and imprisonment. Once he'd confessed to murder, he knew he'd be going to jail for a long time.

But maybe he didn't want to do it alone. Because maybe he wasn't the only one responsible for Donna's death. It fits with what Eileen O'Hara, the forensic archaeologist, said. That possibly – or probably – more than one person dug the grave.

So if Garry was one of the gravediggers, might Martin Campbell have been the other?

It's a leap, but it could be why Garry engineered the burglary arrest. To pile pressure on Campbell, his accomplice, to confess with him.

On the day we were called to his house in Deerpark, Campbell played along with Garry. Allowed us to think there had been a real burglary.

Then, sometime before or after the arrest, maybe even the same day, Campbell must have told Garry that if he wanted to confess he was on his own. That no one would believe him. That Garry could confess all he liked, but Campbell wouldn't go down with him.

When pressurising Campbell didn't work, Garry decided to contest the burglary. To take advantage of the opportunity to give evidence in the witness box that he wouldn't get on a guilty plea.

Because the witness box was the only place that the authorities would *have* to listen to him, a former addict with a rake of convictions. The judge, the guards, the usual court journalists, anyone sitting in the gallery, and the DAR – the automatic Digital Audio Recording system – would be guaranteed to hear him make uncorroborated serious allegations in a way that couldn't immediately be ignored or dismissed.

Garry's solicitor Finn Fitzpatrick had told me that Garry wanted his day in court: justice in public. He did. But not for himself. He wanted it for Donna Hannigan.

And maybe it got him killed.

Patricia

Years ago, himself and myself went for a break down at the Great Southern Hotel in Killarney. We went for a walk in the national park. There were signs up, warnings not to approach the deer. We saw two stags fighting. Even from a distance, they were a magnificent sight to behold, the clash of the antlers, the roaring out of them, like they were in the worst kind of pain, emotional as well as physical. For a while, I couldn't get them out of my mind. Their power. Their strength. It upset me, seeing their life-or-death struggle for the top spot. I told her about it one of the days.

'Sounds amazing,' she said. 'I'd have *loved* to see that.'

We got on with our work, but later on, I said what I'd been thinking. 'How did the other two boys take the news about the romance?'

'One's been *so* good about it,' she said. 'The other doesn't know.'

'How could he *not* know? If you're all sharing a house?'

'He's away during the week for work. We've not told him. When he's out of the house, the two of us sleep in my room. When he's home at the weekend, we don't.'

'Why is that?'

'We think he mightn't like us being together. He's got a little thing for me. He'll go ballistic. We're going to wait. Tell him when the time is right.'

'And when will that be?'

'We're saving for a deposit on a place of our own. We'll have our bags packed and we'll tell him and move out so there'll be no awkwardness. It'll be fine.'

That's one of my could-have should-haves. I could have given her the money for the deposit there and then. I should have. Or she could have moved in with me for a while, till after it all calmed down. I could have paid for a flight for her to go somewhere, Ibiza, Manchester, anywhere. So many things I should have done. I talked instead, and talk is cheap.

I said, 'You need to get out of that house.'

'I know that,' she said. 'It's why we're saving. I feel guilty about breaking up our friendship, as if it's my fault. I'd love it if we could still be friends after this but . . .' she shook her head, tears in her lovely blue eyes '. . . it's not likely.'

I didn't leave it there. Kept talking and listening, advising, you know. I told her that if she needed anything, all she had to do was phone and I'd give her whatever help she needed. And I made sure to tell her that none of it was her fault. I told her she was so young, had years ahead of her. Love 'em and leave 'em, I said. You'd be better off if you were like that.

She said, 'I'm not, though, am I?'

No. That's why I never believed them when they said that Donna had gone away. She loved that boy. And when Donna loved things, she loved them. She never would have walked away without a word.

Not from me. Not from the shop. And not from that boy.

78

I SPEND THE NIGHT WRITING IT UP. IT'S RICE-PAPER thin. It's only a theory. There's not a scintilla of hard evidence against either Garry McCarthy or Martin Campbell. And there's the inconvenient fact of Campbell's cast-iron alibi for the night of Garry's death.

It's after 2 a.m. and no amount of caffeine can stop my eyes closing. I think about going down to one of the cells and having a kip, but I can't face the confinement. I think about going home, but it's not an option with Calum possibly still in town. Plus, I need to keep up the momentum. To rest, but keep my brain active.

I stay where I am, use a second chair for my feet and doze, my jacket over me, like a blanket, till my phone alarm goes off at 6 a.m. I have a quick all-over rinse in the manky showers here – best avoided normally – but I don't wash my hair. There's no clean towel so I have to drip and air-dry and use loo roll. I always keep a clean long-sleeved black T-shirt in my desk drawer. I apply tinted moisturiser and deodorant and put on the T-shirt. I don't look too bad.

I make what feels like my nineteenth cup of tea, read back what I've written up, tweak it. I'm not ready to save it to the general office folder, which Sadie and others in the station have access to. Instead, I save the document to a folder on my desktop marked 'Standard Forms', print off two copies, fold them, and put both in my handbag.

Sadie's usually first in, and I want to bring my theory to her. But she's not here yet and I've had nothing to eat since lunchtime yesterday. I'm starving and I'm going to have to eat something substantial or I'm in danger of becoming delirious. It's not yet 7 a.m. I have enough time. I cross the road to the Centra. Hassan's on duty as usual.

'I'm all in this morning,' I say. 'I'll have a breakfast roll with one sausage, two rashers, one black pudding, one white, and Ballymaloe Relish, please.'

Making straight for the coffee machine, I choose the largest paper-cup size, press the button for an Americano. I let out a breath as the machine chugs and gurgles and hisses. I badly need this, and if I never have another cup of tea in my life, it'll be too soon.

I feel Calum behind me, smell him, before he says a single word.

'No wonder you look like shit if that's the kind of rubbish you're eating.'

From the hot counter, Hassan shouts, 'Hey, brown or white roll?'

Somehow, I manage to say, 'Doesn't matter.'

I turn slowly, but Calum is gone.

79

I'VE LOST MY APPETITE, BUT I HAVE TO PAY FOR the food.

At the cash desk, Hassan asks, 'Who was that guy?'

'No one,' I say.

'He came in here about half an hour ago, bought a coffee. He was asking about you. He knew your name and that you'd transferred from Dublin. What you looked like.'

'What did you say?'

'I said I didn't know you. I guess he didn't believe me.'

My eyes blur. 'Thank you.' I swallow. 'How much do I owe you?'

'Nothing,' he says. 'It's on the house.'

'I don't actually want the roll any more. You can keep it. Sorry.'

'Even better,' Hassan says. 'I'll sell it to Fogarty when he comes in.'

I give him a watery smile. 'Don't tell him. Don't tell anyone. Please.'

'I won't,' he says, 'but, Alice, *you* should. Tell someone, I mean.'

'I will,' I say, meaning, 'I won't.'

I leave the coffee on my desk, go to the bathroom and lock myself into a stall. I sit on the lid with my feet up off the floor. Calum can't follow me here, but I didn't think he'd follow me to the shop either. I thought he'd be back in Dublin by now, but he's not. I don't know what he's up to, but I'm starting to rethink those black SUV sightings over the last few weeks. I'm beginning to understand that Calum's been watching me for longer, and more closely, than I'd realised.

A deep chill settles over me, as if I've been engulfed by a snowdrift.

Patricia

I'd closed the shop for the four days of the Easter weekend, but I was back in, bright and breezy, on Tuesday. By then it was her and me, full time, and one Saturday girl for when the café was busiest. Before that, I'd always managed with different part-timers and short-termers, but we had a great partnership going, the two of us. I'd been coming around to the idea that I was wronging her by not having her on the books, building up her stamps, and I was intending to talk to her about getting her properly registered as an employee.

She never came in. Never showed. You must understand, it wasn't like now. People had mobile phones – chunky, solid things, all playing the same annoying tune – but we weren't in touch constantly. I tried ringing her, but no luck. Her phone was off.

At first I hoped she might have got it wrong, mistakenly thought she had Tuesday free, too. I knew that she'd had big plans for Easter. Two nights in the Sir Henry's club for what they called a Weekender. I thought, Maybe she has a bad hangover.

As the morning went on, I got worried she'd broken something, or that it might be something even more serious. That she'd taken a pill and it had made her sick or she was in a coma. I wasn't a fool. I read the *Examiner*. I knew that some of the kids who went to Sir Henry's took Ecstasy tablets, but I never asked her if she did. My policy has always been, don't ask a question if you don't want to know the answer.

I gave it until the afternoon, praying she'd appear. When she didn't, I rang all the hospitals. She wasn't a patient in any of them. I locked up the shop, went straight over to the South Mall and got into a taxi. I told the driver to take me to John Redmond Street, up by Shandon. I wanted to get there as fast as I possibly could. I knocked on every door until I found a woman who told me which house the three boys and the English girl lived in. I knocked and knocked but there was no answer. I felt sure someone was at home, watching, but all was quiet.

'They're at work, I'd say, love,' the next-door-neighbour woman said.

'I'll come back later,' I said, 'but if you see any of them, tell them I need to talk to them.'

I gave her my phone numbers and wrote a note and pushed it through their letterbox. I got the taxi man to drop me to my car. I didn't know what to do so I went back to the shop and waited there, on the off chance that she might ramble in. She didn't.

80

I DECIDE TO HOLD OFF ON TALKING TO SADIE until after the morning briefing. She's not in her office anyway. No doubt she's somewhere in the building. The rest of the team are starting to straggle in, but I'm faced away from them and I don't engage. I try to drag my mind to the job and away from Calum, but I'm at a remove, as if I'm trapped behind a Perspex screen with no idea how I came to be here or what I'm supposed to be doing.

Siobhan O'Sullivan comes over to talk to me. 'How are you today?'

'What? Fine. You?'

'Good, yeah. Did you get a chance to look at Garry's phone records?' She holds out the folder to me.

I take it. 'Right. Great job. I found something interesting actually. Need to talk to the skipper about it. Now that you're here, it'd be a help if us two talked through the records first. In case there's something I've missed.'

'Sure, but not now, like.'

'Why?'

'The briefing's been brought forward to eight thirty. Did you not get the WhatsApp message?'

'Phone must be still on silent since last night. I didn't see it. Didn't check. Why the change?'

'No idea.'

'And what time is it now?'

She laughs. 'Eight twenty-eight. Were you out late or something?'

'Long story,' I say. 'Come on, let's steal Fogarty's seat.'

But when we get to the briefing room Fogarty's already there. He says, 'Where were you? You're not answering your phone.'

'It's on silent,' Siobhan says.

I say, 'What's up?'

He looks in the direction of the door. 'That,' he says.

I turn to see the red-faced well-fed figure of Superintendent Ned O'Brien, followed by a grimly silent Feeney and Sadie, looking inscrutable.

After them, Detective Garda Fintan Deeley and none other than Detective Inspector Calum Pierce, both of the Garda National Bureau of Criminal Investigation.

Calum looks straight down at me, smiles ruefully, mouths, 'Sorry.'

To anyone looking on, he appears genuinely conflicted by the embarrassing situation in which we find ourselves.

Only I know that he had every opportunity to tell me in advance the reason he was in Cork, and that he didn't. He opted to play mind games with me instead.

Under my breath, I say, 'What the *actual* fuck?'

'It's what I was trying to tell you,' Fogarty says. 'I was looking for you all over the station. The car park. Sadie gave me the heads-up. Said to warn you. I didn't want to send a text or a voice note. I wanted to tell you myself. Believe me, it's as much of a shock to me as it is to you. It's a fucking disaster, actually.'

I whisper, 'Why is he here?'

Fogarty keeps his eyes on the front of the room as he says, 'You'll find out. Now shut up and stop drawing attention to us.'

❖

It's Ray Grant's fault. He didn't bother with his threatened complaint to GSOC. He made a call to his friend the superintendent, both of them long-time members of Fota Island Golf Club. Which definitely *isn't* the reason that the GNBCI has been called in, according to the superintendent.

'I've explained to Ray that we have a job to do here and that, in my opinion, Detective Garda Fogarty and DS O'Riordan, not to mention my excellent colleague DI Feeney, all of them behaved properly at all times. I can say that with absolute confidence because I've watched the entire Ray Grant interview video. Not Olly or Sadie's finest hour, perhaps, but there's no question of any issue or concern of *any* kind. In *my* view, at least.'

'Jesus Christ,' Fogarty says, 'I am so fucked.'

Superintendent O'Brien continues: 'Nevertheless, in the interests of transparency, of absolute probity, and so as to draw a line in the sand, to ensure that not only is justice done, it's seen to be done, I thought we could do with some outside perspective. I've told Ray, Mr Grant, and he's happy. He's prepared to let it go at that. A gentleman's agreement permitting us to keep it within the four walls here.'

He pauses, then goes on: 'Right. What I have in mind is a review. A short review, one to three days, something of that order, to look at synergies, connections, the big picture in short, so to speak. And you'll be relieved that it's two of our own that I've asked to come in for a little visit – that's the way I see it. A friendly visit from Detective Garda Deeley, recently of this parish and whom you all know well, of course, and Ballyvolane boy made good himself, DI Calum Pierce. Calum, do you want to say a few words?'

'Not at all,' Calum says, 'I have every confidence in DI Feeney and DS O'Riordan and the rest of the team, most of ye anyway.' He winks. 'Seriously, though, folks, I'm mainly here to observe from close up the good work that's been happening on the ground.'

He glances round the room and his gaze doesn't linger any longer on me than on anyone else because there's no one better than Calum at corner-of-the-eye surveillance. The briefing starts and he takes a seat in the front row, with his back to me. When he can't see me, I can breathe again. I feel Fogarty's eyes on me. I look at him.

He whispers, 'You okay?'

The same old question again.

And then it comes to me that having a fragile reputation might have its occasional advantages. I say, 'Just need some fresh air.'

Stumbling out of the incident room, one hand covering my mouth, I return quickly to my desk, checking to make sure I'm logged out of my computer. I am. Looking around, I grab the Garry McCarthy phone records file and shove it under my arm, concealing it with my jacket. I leave the station, running down the back stairs.

In the car, I send a WhatsApp message to Sadie: *Had to go. Not feeling well. Sorry. Talk later.*

I exit the car park and hit school traffic. Unbelievably, it's only 9 a.m.

Patricia

That evening, I rang himself and told him I'd be late and to get his own dinner – I didn't tell him why because I didn't want him to worry – and I drove over there and nearly broke down the door I hammered so hard on it. The sensible one came out. He looked shook. That gave me an ounce of hope, believe it or not. I thought they'd all been on the razz and didn't know what day it was. He didn't seem to know me, or let on he didn't.

'I'm looking for Donna,' I said. 'Is she in?'

'Why?'

'I'm her boss. She didn't come to work today. I left a note earlier.'

'I knew I knew your face.' He made a show of looking in the hall, on the floor. He picked up the note. 'Sorry, didn't see it until now. Donna's not here.'

'Where is she?'

'She left. Over the weekend. She went back.'

'Back where?'

He hesitated. 'Did she not tell you?'

'No, she didn't. What about her boyfriend? The Bob Dylan lookalike. Is he here?'

'He's in bed. He's not feeling well.'

'I want to see him.'

'Okay, yeah, sure, sorry, come in. Do you want a cup of tea?'

Last thing I expected, the offer of tea. It threw me. And the fact that the house was in reasonable order. Sagging furniture. Dated decor. Old music posters and flyers stuck to the wall with Blu Tack. The whole place in need of a serious dose of TLC but normal for a house rented out long-term. No sign of trouble. No sign that there'd been an argument or fight or that anyone had been taken ill.

He shouted up the stairs for the boyfriend to come down. That threw me too. No opportunity to confer, no whispers. All out in the open, like they had nothing to hide.

Bob Dylan looked shook as well. Garry, his real name was. He had red eyes, like he'd been crying, but why wouldn't he in the circumstances? Donna had dumped him and gone back to Ibiza, apparently.

'She upped and went, just like that?'

He said, 'The season is starting again around now.'

'It's not true,' I said.

'That's how I feel.' He said it with such heaviness.

'What about the third fellow, is he here?'

The sensible one chimed in again. 'He's in Limerick. He's working up there. He's an engineer.'

'She'd never have left without telling me,' I said.

An exchange of looks but Garry was the one to speak. 'I was supposed to let you know but it was a mad weekend. Slipped my mind. Feels like she's been gone forever.'

'When did she leave?'

'Early Friday,' the sensible one said.

That was a shock, hearing she was gone so long. It was Tuesday night. 'Can I see her room?'

'There's nothing left but if you want to, sure,' Garry said.

He took me upstairs, to a box room on the return at the back. 'I've been sleeping here since she left,' he said. 'It's in a small bit of a mess.'

Beer cans and overflowing ashtrays, an empty wardrobe, the sickening stench of cannabis in the air, and not a single trace of her sweetness and brightness left.

He said, 'I don't know how I'll go on after this.' He looked shattered.

I went home to himself and told him that Donna was gone. I didn't say any more that night. I wasn't able. I felt like I'd been run down by the number-eight bus. It took me a few days to gather myself. I was in shock. Because Donna *was* gone. Whatever else those boys were lying about, they weren't lying about that.

81

I RACK MY BRAINS FOR SOMEWHERE TO GO. A strategic retreat only. To think. Calum's not in full control yet, but it's only a matter of time.

I'm confused, though. Of all people, why did Superintendent Ned O'Brien choose *Calum* to carry out the review? Then again, I wonder whose idea the review really was. After Feeney stopped taking his calls, did Calum go up the line to the super? Whispering? Laying the foundations for a takeover of the Donna case by GNBCI? But, again, why?

Unless it's nothing to do with the Donna investigation specifically. Or with me. Maybe he's looking to move south and, with the super nearing retirement, upwards.

But if Calum moved to Coughlan's Quay full time, I'd have to leave. Not because he'd want me to. Because I would.

I'm driving around aimlessly, running through locations beyond Calum's reach in my head. Not my flat. Not my parents' house. My tax consultant brother's office on the South Mall maybe? There's bound to be a spare desk.

No. Too weird. Kieran would immediately want to know why I was asking and I'd have to tell him. Then our parents would find out and I don't have time for any of that.

I think about hotels. Car parks. The library. The railway station. The airport. But it's broad daylight and Calum's down here for work. He's going to be busy at the station all day. As long as I avoid going there, I'll avoid seeing him.

And then I think about where this all started, even though I didn't realise it at the time.

Martin Campbell's BMW is parked in his driveway so it looks like he's home. I park five houses past his, on the same side of the street, behind a big Škoda Estate. If he sticks his head out of the upstairs window, he might notice me. But he's never seen my car, and I'm wearing a smelly old baseball cap that I found in the boot pulled low over my face. Worst-case scenario, he spots me and confronts me. I'll deal with that if it happens.

I picked up a double espresso, a bottle of sparkling water, a tomato, basil and fresh mozzarella focaccia and a bag of those tiny wrapped Italian fruit sweets, from Sicilian Delights on Magazine Road. I throw back the espresso in a single gulp but eat the focaccia more slowly. The water and the sweets are for later when my energy and hydration levels drop.

I've got messages from Sadie, Fogarty and Siobhan O'Sullivan asking how I am. I reply to Siobhan with a double thumbs-up. I reply to Sadie and Fogarty with OK thanks. *Talk later.* I take a small sip of water and get to work.

I find Martin Campbell's mobile-phone number in my notebook. I wrote it down on the day we arrested Garry. I hadn't asked Siobhan O'Sullivan to check for it on Garry's phone records because I hadn't known then that it was Garry who reported the burglary. I didn't know that until last night.

I go through the records, line by line, checking for Campbell's mobile number. It's there, frequently, but it didn't leap out at me earlier because it's registered to his employer rather than to Martin Campbell personally.

The phone records show that Garry phoned Campbell's mobile minimum twice or three times every day. Campbell's number is even there on the night Garry died, when Campbell was in Dublin at the Conrad Hotel. Though Campbell rarely answered, and only then for a few seconds, it's evidence of contact between them. It's mainly evidence that Garry wanted to talk to Martin Campbell – a lot – and that Campbell was less keen on the relationship.

I remind myself that Garry and Martin Campbell were brothers-in-law. That there's nothing inherently suspicious in Garry wanting to talk to Campbell. The frequency of the calls *is* unusual, though, as is Campbell's response. Getting phoned two or three times a day by your ex-wife's brother and rarely taking the call seems noteworthy to me.

Oddly, GNBCI in Dublin, my former workplace, is there as well. Garry made two short calls to the main station number. It makes no sense until I remember that it's also where Fintan Deeley, the former lead detective on the Deerpark burglary, now works. Garry must have wanted to make contact with Deeley for some reason.

Although, as the call durations are so short, he probably didn't get to talk to him. That would be normal. Phoning a garda station landline and expecting a guard to be at his desk? Or to take the call even if they are? Slim to nil chance of that. Also, nine times out of ten, Deeley's not going to take a call from a randomer about a former case of his that he's no longer obliged to deal with.

I look through the green highlighted numbers, the unknowns. Burner phones, probably. To and from drug-dealers?

Maybe not. I'm more and more convinced that Garry was telling the truth – that he *was* clean. Either way, the unknown numbers add up to a brick wall. If Siobhan couldn't identify them yesterday with the full resources of the PULSE system at her fingertips, I'm not going to be able to make any progress sitting in my car. I put the folder on the passenger seat and concentrate on watching Campbell's house. All is quiet.

Too quiet, as they say in the old movies. In minutes, despite the double espresso, I'm fast asleep.

82

MY PHONE WAKES ME. GROGGILY, I HOLD IT IN front of my face. It's the Coughlan's Quay landline number. Could be Sadie. Or Fogarty. I almost swipe to answer it, then remember who else has access to the landline today. I silence the ringtone, let it play out. There's no voicemail. No follow-up *Call me* text. I'd bet a million euros that it's Calum.

Campbell's car hasn't moved. The house looks the same as it did an hour ago. I yawn, stretch, take another tiny sip of water, then a longer slug, because there's no avoiding it: I'm going to need a loo soon. I let out a long sigh. This flight into Deerpark was a stupid idea. I should've hung around the station. Faced Calum. He couldn't have done anything to me.

But he's not the only reason I left the station. I left to think too. *What* am I missing? What am I not seeing?

I'm so absorbed in thought that I don't see Campbell until he's beside me, tapping loudly on my car window. He's unshaven, wearing a loose grey T-shirt and tracksuit bottoms. He looks unwashed, as if he hasn't slept in a while.

'What are you doing?'

I shove open the car door, climb out. 'It's my job to ask the questions, Martin. I was about to call in for a chat.'

'Yeah, well, that doesn't, ah, suit me. I'm just going out,' Campbell says.

I look him up and down. 'You might need shoes. And a shower. Just sayin'.'

'What do you want?' Campbell asks.

'You're grand,' I say, 'it can wait. I wouldn't want to delay you. It's really your wife I should be talking to anyway, I suppose.'

'My *wife*?'

'Sorry, Martin, your *ex*-wife. I keep forgetting. Garry's sister. I'm the family liaison officer in the investigation into his death.'

'She told me. She was upset. She said you were no help. She said that you and the guard with you were only interested in irrelevant stuff from years ago.'

'We might have got off on the wrong foot,' I say. 'I meant to call back to see her. I've been so busy, though. Didn't have a chance the last couple of days.'

His mouth falls open. 'Is there news?'

'News on Garry, is it? Is that what you mean? Or is it something else?'

He hesitates, moistens his lips. 'Of course, that's what I mean. Garry. He's *who* I mean.'

'No news, Martin. But you'll be first to know.'

'*I* will?' Campbell asks, looking astonished. 'Why would *I* be—'

'Your *wife*. Your *ex*-wife. *She*'ll be the first to know. And her family.'

I get back into the car and drive away slowly. I keep my eyes on Campbell in the rear-view mirror. When I indicate left and turn the corner, he still hasn't moved.

I pull into a side road off the green area near the main entrance to the estate. If Campbell's BMW passes this way, I should be able to see it. I wait ninety minutes but there's no sign of the car. It looks like Campbell has nowhere he needs to be after all.

83

I ABANDON MARTIN CAMPBELL FOR NOW AND head towards Turner's Cross, for no reason except that it's in the opposite direction from Coughlan's Quay. From where Calum is.

Driving through, I remember that this was where Terry Levy née McAuliffe, the barmaid fired to make space for Ray Grant's son Tom, grew up. We still know so little about Tom, or the car crash that took his life, and that feels wrong. Maybe he has nothing to do with this. Maybe none of the Grants do. And, whatever my beliefs about Garry's links with Donna's murder, as of now there's still no concrete evidence placing him inside the pub where her body was found. Despite everything, my theory about Garry is still just that. A theory. A fairy story.

In contrast, Tom Grant is the one solid link to Bertie Allen's that we have. We can't stop looking into the Grant family just because Ray plays golf with the superintendent.

I remember something and turn onto Kinsale Road. Further along, I swing the car into a spot in front of a kitchen show-room. I flick through my notebook, but the number I need isn't there. I didn't note it down from the email he sent.

I try the RGP website. Conor Grant is there, in the 'About'

section, as is his mobile number and details of his education and current role. He's listed as chief of operations, whatever that means. Not a whole pile, I reckon, despite his civil-engineering degree from UCC and his MBA from the Smurfit School. His dad Ray, with precisely zero letters after his name, is still CEO, still calling the shots.

'Don't think,' I say, 'just do it.'

I call Conor Grant's number. When he answers, I say my name.

'You've a hard neck,' he says. 'You don't think I'm going to talk to you?'

'Actually, I do,' I say, 'and I'd prefer not to come to your office if I can avoid it. I'm nearby. You could come and meet me.'

'Why would I?'

'Because you know that it's in RGP's interest that this murder is solved. So that the decks are cleared and there's no long-term impact on apartment sale prices. No lingering scandal hanging over the Barrack Street development. Or the company.'

'Nice try, but I'm not talking to you,' he says.

'I think if it was up to you, you'd be talking to me.'

'It *is* up to me, and it's still no.'

'You helped me before. Got me those pre-demolition photos of the pub.'

'And you dragged in my father for questioning, a seventy-four-year-old with a heart condition and high blood pressure.'

'Technically, he attended the station voluntarily, and I wasn't involved in questioning him but, yes, I was there at the house when we took him in. I don't deny it. The thing is, though, your dad's argument about why he would have bought Bertie

Allen's pub and dug up the floor if he'd known there was a body underneath. He was right. So, Conor, I really *don't* think your dad knew about the body. I'm pretty convinced of it, in fact. That's why I don't want to drop by your office. I just want you to give me ten minutes of your time.'

I tell him my location and end the call. I have nowhere else to be except the station and I'm not going there. I figure I can wait an hour to see if he shows.

Conor Grant slips in beside me in less than half that time. He gets out of his burgundy Range Rover and into the front seat of my Renault Clio. He's wearing an expensive-looking blue shirt and navy slim-fit trousers. It's my first time seeing him properly up close. He's fifty, give or take, but he's ripped. He has a Rolex and a wedding ring on his left hand. On his right wrist, he has a woven leather bracelet that's seen better days.

He asks, 'Why are you still bothering us?'

'It's just me. No one knows I'm here. I want to know more about Tom —'

His left hand goes to the leather bracelet. He rubs it. 'No.'

'I want to know about him, not because I have any evidence that he did anything, but because he's the only real lead we have.'

'That's my brother you're talking about. He's not a *lead*.'

'What I mean is, if I can find out more about Tom, who worked in Bertie Allens's, I might be able to find out more about the pub's customers.'

'"Worked" isn't the word I'd use about Tom and Bertie's.

Dad *thought* he worked there, but he didn't. Not much. He was always getting people to sub for him.'

'Who?'

'I can't remember. I don't know if I ever knew. It's a long time ago. But Dad's idea about Tom working there to learn the pub trade? That wasn't Tom. Same way when Tom went to Trinity to study English and history. Dad nearly did his nut. Dad's a business guy. He had a nightmare vision of Tom ending up as a history lecturer with a pipe and an old tweed jacket with patches on the elbows.'

'Is that what Tom wanted?'

'He did a master's and he was talking about doing a PhD but he didn't know what he wanted, really. He died before he found out.'

'What was Tom like?'

'He was gay, for one thing, which Dad knew but never acknowledged. He liked a good time. The crash that killed him, there's no mystery. He was coming back from a weekend at our family summer house in Schull. His boyfriend Kevin was in the passenger seat, and Tom was driving too fast as per usual. Slammed into a tree. Kevin wasn't wearing a seatbelt. He was thrown clear. Had a few broken bones but he was okay. Tom was . . .'

'I'm so sorry,' I say, although I'm thinking of how Kevin Murphy's name appeared in the accident reports, but not the nature of the relationship between him and Tom. What's less clear is why Conor is choosing to tell me about Kevin now.

'Not as sorry as we are.' There's silence for a time. Then he says, 'Tom had nothing to do with this. Let him rest in peace. I mean it, don't contact me again. My father's patience, *my* patience, it's gone. Do you hear me? This bullshit has to stop *now*.'

He gets out of my car and back into his own before I have the chance to ask him anything else. He drives off at speed.

The thought comes to me that Conor is his father's son after all. And that I wouldn't like to cross either of them.

84

I NEED TO FIND TOM GRANT'S BOYFRIEND BUT I'M
in my car and all I've got is my phone and there are hundreds
of Kevin Murphys. I get a call from Sadie.

'Where are you?' she asks. '*How* are you?'

'I'm totally fine,' I say. 'Can you talk?'

'Not for long.'

'Is Calum still there?'

'Oh, yeah. He's in the incident room with his mini-me Fintan
Deeley and the super. They have a table set up, like they're
running an interview panel.'

'Seeing people one by one?'

'That'd be too close to a disciplinary and the super is at pains
to reassure everyone that this is *not* that, so they're seeing
everyone in twos and threes.'

'And people are actually complying with this kangaroo set-
up?'

'It's voluntary. Handing over access to the files isn't – that's
already been done – but no one is being forced to talk to them.
I haven't. Feeney hasn't.'

'Fogarty?'

'I asked him to do it and he did. He and Bugsy went in

together. Bugsy talked to the super about Castlehaven's chances in next year's football championship – they're both from the same parish. Fogarty talked about the Grant arrest and the interview, ran through what happened in microscopic detail. It's all on video, so he wasn't telling them anything they didn't know already. He suggested that all of us should do a course on dealing with bereaved relatives and the super thought it was a great idea. He genuinely seems to think that Calum's only here temporarily for a review. But Feeney is dead sure that Calum's trying to sideline us – that he wants a team from the GNBCI to take over. Apparently, Calum kept trying to steer the conversation back to the meat of the case, but Fogarty stuck firmly to his concern for the Grant family. To keep Calum at a distance from the nitty-gritty as long as we can.'

'What about Siobhan O'Sullivan and the rest?'

'Gone. Feeney transferred them back to their regular duties straight after the morning briefing. So there are four less for the Salem witch trial to grill. Feeney was right to do it. You wouldn't know what they'd say. Where are you?'

'I'm making an appointment with my doctor and I'm thinking about resigning my position but I want to talk to HR first about what benefits I'm entitled to.'

'Jesus. Really?'

'That's what I want you to tell the super. Explain that's why I won't be able to take part in the process. I'm sure he'll pass the news on to Calum.'

'Are you for real? You want me to lie to the superintendent?'

'It's not a lie. I've made up my mind. If I have to deal with Calum ever again, I'm gone. Leaving the guards and that's it. But before I go, I've got a job to do and I want it to be me to solve these cases – this case. I want it to be *us*, our team, not Calum and that fucker Deeley and the rest of those arseholes up in Dublin.'

'Except for the resigning part, I've heard a version of that speech from every other member of the team this morning. And, Alice, I know your history with Calum, some of it, at least, but you have to come back to the station. You can't go AWOL from work.'

I wait a beat before replying. 'I *have* been working. I was planning to talk to you about it this morning.'

'Come back to Coughlan's Quay and we'll talk all you like.'

Sadie hangs up. I take a breath, then call Siobhan O'Sullivan on her mobile.

Siobhan answers: 'Alice, what's wrong? I've been transferred back to Mayfield, did you hear? Is everything—'

I say, 'I need you to find me a man called Kevin Murphy. ASAP.'

Patricia

I went back at the weekend. Saturday morning at around eleven. The sensible one answered the door again. The third lad, the one who was missing when I called around during the week, was inside sitting in an armchair. He was watching television, turned up too loud, and eating bran flakes with a chopped banana on top.

He lowered the volume on the television. 'Long time, Patricia, how are you getting on?'

Cool customer. Fitter and stronger-looking than I remembered.

A show-pony type, wearing a white T-shirt with the sleeves cut off to display his big muscular arms.

'Not great,' I said. 'I'm missing Donna.'

'Like all of us, but thinking about it in the clear light of day, she was never going to stay, was she?'

'I thought she was.'

'She had us all fooled, poor Garry especially.'

'Where is he?'

'In bed.'

'I thought you didn't know he and Donna were together?'

'Of *course* I knew,' he said, 'and I knew it was never going to last.'

'She was too young for him. For you as well.'

'For me? What gives you that idea? We were never an item.'

'She thought you were interested in her.'

He lowered his voice. 'Other way around, if you *must* know.'

'She said you'd go ballistic if you found out about her and Garry.'

A sigh. 'No, but . . .'

'But what?'

'I'm struggling to see how this is *any* of your business.'

'My *business*? She worked for me and we were friends. Good friends.'

'*Were* you, though? She didn't tell you she was leaving, did she? Maybe *you* were the one she thought would go ballistic.'

That was clever, making me question myself, making me reconsider everything. It knocked the stuffing out of me for a while, all right.

85

SIOBHAN O'SULLIVAN ASSURES ME THAT THE KEVIN
Murphy I'm looking for is a dentist with a practice over a shoe
shop on Oliver Plunkett Street.

'Doesn't sound right,' I say.

'Why not?'

'I don't know. It's just not what I imagined.'

'I checked the accident records. Kevin Murphy provided his
parents' home address in Dunmanway and their phone number
at the time. They're still alive and still have the same landline.
I rang and they told me where he is. It was easy.'

'Okay,' I say. 'They've probably told him we're looking for
him too.'

'Probably? More like definitely.'

'You've turned into a right smartypants. I think I preferred
you before.'

She laughs. 'Tell me how you get on?'

'Course. Have to tell Sadie first. Don't mention it to anyone
until then.'

'I'm back on the regular roster,' she says, 'with no one to tell
anything to and no time to tell it even if I could.'

There's a brass plate beside the street door, held open with a rubber wedge that I'm surprised no one has nicked. Inside, in the narrow ground-floor hallway, there's a second door of reinforced glass, the kind with transparent squares. I ring the bell.

A disembodied female voice asks, 'Who are you here to see?'

'Kevin Murphy.'

'Have you an appointment?'

'My name is Alice McCann. I'm a detective garda from—'

She buzzes me in before I can finish the sentence. Siobhan O'Sullivan was right. His parents *have* warned him to expect a visit.

The reception area is to the rear of the first turn of the staircase. I have to go up steps to reach it, then down again into a wide large room with two high windows, a desk and filing area behind a partially glazed partition and a selection of mismatched upright chairs ranged against the walls.

The receptionist is a woman in her forties. 'He could do without this. He's behind already. Sit down. He's with a patient but he knows you're here.'

There are two others waiting, one a miserable-looking teenage boy with a red swollen face, the other an unbothered woman in her twenties playing with her phone, in for a regular check-up and a clean by the look of her.

I take a seat beside a square pine table with a fuchsia-patterned pottery lamp on it, copies of last weekend's newspaper supplements and the *Cork Independent*. RTÉ News Now unspools silently on the television overhead; 96FM, a local radio station, provides audio accompaniment. The disconnect between picture and sound is irritating at first. Half an hour later, I'm losing the will to live. I'm about to ask for an update on when I might be seen when the receptionist takes a call, then addresses me. 'He's free now. Up the next flight of stairs, straight in front of you.'

Kevin Murphy is a man in his late fifties with a soft, comfortable face, a mask around his chin and a pot belly disguised by generously sized scrubs. He stays sitting on his wheeled round stool beside the dentist's chair. His surgery is a white-painted bright room at the front of the building. The open sash window lets in street chatter and the call of the *Echo* boy outside the GPO. In the distance, a busker sings a Snow Patrol song to a backing track.

'He's not bad compared to some of the rest of them,' Murphy says. 'That ballad group on Patrick Street would make your ears bleed.'

'They'd drive you to drink. I'm Alice McCann, by the way.'

'I know who you are and I know why you're here.' He holds up his left hand. He's wearing a wedding band. 'I've moved on, but the memory never fades completely. I don't think about what happened to Tom every single day any more, but for a long time I did. What do you want to know?'

'I want to know about Bertie Allen's, the pub where Tom worked. Whatever you can tell me about who used to go there. The regulars. Anything at all.'

'I wasn't a regular. We used to go to Mór Disco, Loafers, various other places. Then Tom started working at Bertie's and I went in there occasionally when he was doing a shift, which wasn't anything like as often as he was supposed to be working. Tom got out of it every chance he could. His dad hadn't thought to cut off his allowance. If he had, he might have worked more. Because I was there so rarely, I didn't know the regulars.'

'You're saying you didn't know anyone who went to Bertie's except Tom?'

'It'll be faster if I show you.'

He stands and goes to a tall cupboard. Reaching in, he takes out a biscuit tin. He walks to the worktop running perpendicular to the front wall along the left side of the room. He opens the box and turns to me. 'I keep this stuff here because my husband . . .' He pauses, and I notice tears in his eyes. After a beat, he goes on: 'I'm really happy now and this is the past and I didn't want it in *our* house. But I couldn't throw it out, obviously.'

I walk towards him.

He keeps talking: 'Most of what's in here is personal stuff, nothing to do with Bertie's. But after I heard about Garry McCarthy's death, and the pub had been in the news around the same time, I remembered that he used to go there. He actually *was* a regular. Tom and Conor knew him from school and he used to work in construction for Tom's dad. So Garry was one of the people I *did* know in the pub. I'd see him anytime I was in there. Say hi, have a chat. We weren't bosom buddies or anything, just friendly acquaintances, one of many. In the nineties people went to the pub way more than now. I've heard what happened to Garry in the years since. Whatever came later, with the drugs and all that, no one back then thought he had a problem. He was a normal guy. A *nice* guy.

'Anyway, it was a Sunday. I had work the next morning. It was before I opened my own place, I was working in a practice near the lough. I had a film I wanted to get developed and I was going to drop it into the chemist's on that Monday but there were a few shots left and Tom was working and I thought I'd drop in. Take a picture of him.'

He looks down, takes an envelope of photographs out of the box, passes me the top one. He smiles. 'That's Tom, pulling a pint of Beamish. He was criminally bad at it.'

'He's gorgeous,' I say. 'He was.'

'Yeah, he was a stunner. He got away with murder because of it.' I flinch, and he notices, realises what he's said. 'Jesus, what am I like? I don't mean *actual* murder, just that everyone loved him.' He blows out a breath. 'Anyway, the photo that might help you is a group shot. Taken outside.' He holds it up, points at the people in it.

'That's me,' he says, 'that's Tom, that's Garry, and his buddy, can't remember the guy's name, but he was a regular, I think. And in between them that's, well, I'm guessing that's who you're most interested in . . .'

The photograph shows five young people standing on Barrack Street, directly in front of Bertie Allen's pub, leaning against the windowsill. They're all wearing baseball caps, tracksuit bottoms and T-shirts. It's evening, and the sun is shining from the west, hitting them just right so that they look golden and blessed and insanely young. They're smiling these enormous smiles, their arms over each other's shoulders.

A slimmer Kevin Murphy and Tom Grant.

Beside them, a trio made up of Garry McCarthy on one side and Martin Campbell on the other. Martin Campbell, who admitted being Garry's brother-in-law but denied a friendship with him. This picture is proof that he lied about that, and that's huge.

But Campbell's lie almost doesn't matter any more. Because what matters most is the person standing between Garry and Martin. The fifth person in the group.

The youngest.

And the only woman.

Patricia

The more I thought about it, the less I believed what they'd told me. And I kept trying Donna's number but got nothing. I asked the afternooners, my regulars, if they knew anything. I got told all kinds of rubbish. People had heard she was in Ibiza, Thailand, Bali, you name it. A few weeks later, I went back up to the house on John Redmond Street one evening after I'd closed up. Still bright, the long evenings getting into their stride, the summer on its way. I knocked and knocked but got no answer. I went next door and asked the neighbour.

'They're gone,' she said, 'moved out. There's no one living there at the moment. Someone said the landlord might be selling, with house prices going up so high.'

'Do you remember I asked you before about the blonde girl who lived there? English.'

'Yeah, she's gone longer. Moved home maybe. I think I heard that from someone.'

'They told me she was gone to Spain. Ibiza.'

'That could be it,' she said, 'I couldn't tell you, girl. Sorry.'

I left John Redmond Street and went straight to the Bridewell garda station.

86

'I TAKE IT YOU KNOW WHO THIS WOMAN IS?'
I ask.

'I've seen the recent publicity – you couldn't miss it – but I didn't know her name then, or maybe I was introduced that day and forgot. It's around twenty-five years ago.'

'When was the photograph taken?'

'1998, I think. The rest of the photos on the roll are from that year. But it could be early 1999.' He hands me the envelope, Kodak brand, with a pouch at the front for the negatives. 'After I heard about Garry dying, I remembered I had a picture of him. You probably won't believe me if I tell you I didn't look at it then.'

'If you didn't look at it then, when *did* you look at it?'

'One morning last week. A patient didn't turn up and I had some free time. I saw something online on my phone about the garda investigation and Bertie Allen's pub was mentioned. The pub reminded me of the old days with Tom. I took out the biscuit tin and started looking through it and I found the photo. I was looking at Tom, mainly, Garry too. Like I said, I'd heard he'd died. The other two meant nothing to me. It never occurred to me that she might be the body that was found under the pub. After, when ye released the image of what the victim might have looked like, I realised what I had. She was all over. News websites. Socials.'

'Why didn't you contact us at that point?'

'Why didn't *you* contact *me*? You knew Tom worked there, I assume, and you knew about the car crash. What took you so long?'

'Kevin, answer the question. Why didn't you contact us when you realised you had a photograph of the late Donna Hannigan?'

He shakes his head. 'Isn't it obvious? Because I didn't want to get involved. Because I was afraid ye'd all think I had something to do with her death. Or that Tom did. It's complicated. My husband, he says it's hard to compete with a ghost. I've worked so hard to put Tom behind me – we both have – and now this. I know it shouldn't be all about Tom, or me, and it isn't, and I *was* planning to contact the helpline. I actually did phone it, but I hung up, didn't know what to say. That's not true, I did know, but I just couldn't. Over the phone it was too hard. When I heard you were coming here today, I was glad to get it over with at last.'

'I'm going to need to take the envelope of photographs, and you're going to need to come in and make a statement.'

'Now? I've got patients backed up downstairs.'

'Doesn't have to be now but it has to be soon. Either this evening or tomorrow. I can see you anytime, before or after work hours.' I hand him my card. 'Call me on my mobile to arrange an appointment. Otherwise I'll be back here. Or I'll visit you at home.'

'No, no. I'll come to the station. But I've told you everything. I didn't know Donna, honestly. The only person I knew in the photo apart from Tom was Garry.'

'One last question,' I say, 'who took the photograph?'

He hesitates. 'S-some guy. A customer. I didn't catch his name.'

It's the only time in the whole conversation that I'm sure he's lying.

87

WE'RE IN THE COUGHLAN'S QUAY CAR PARK. SADIE
has just climbed into my Clio. She stares straight ahead for a
beat, then turns the stare on me.

'You were supposed to come back to work. Where have you
been?'

'I've found something important.' I send her a message. Her
phone pings. 'Play it. It's a recording of the first report about
the Deerpark case.'

She plays it, shakes her head. 'I don't get it.'

'It's Garry McCarthy's voice. He reported the burglary
himself.'

I run through my theory with her, about Garry's regrets,
what I believe was his plan for redemption and atonement and
justice for Donna.

When I've finished, she says, 'In fairness, it's a good story.
It's so good it might even be true, but it doesn't amount to
anything. Your suspect slash witness is dead of an overdose slash
murder that your other suspect slash accomplice has an unbreak-
able alibi for.'

'There's more,' I say.

I ping her the photograph.

340

She looks at it for a long time, then at me. 'Where did you get this?'

I tell her about Kevin Murphy and my conversation with him. 'He knows more than he's said so far, but I didn't want to push too hard earlier. When he comes in to give his statement, I'll make him sweat.' I pause. 'What do we do now?'

'We talk to Feeney. Well, *I* talk to him.'

'And after that? After we – you – talk to Feeney?'

'We focus on Campbell.'

I take that in. 'You're suggesting we arrest him.'

'On what basis?'

I shrug. 'None as far as I can see.'

'Right. So instead of arresting him, we pull his phone records. His financials. His work history. And we watch him. Hope he fucks up somewhere along the line.'

'How can we do all that when we're no longer in control of the case?'

She smiles. 'We improvise.'

88

SADIE WON'T TAKE THE PHONE-RECORDS FILE
from me. She won't even take the copy I'd made of my theory
document. She photographs everything instead.

'Pity it's not microfilm. Then it'd feel even more like East
Berlin 1962.'

She laughs. 'True, but I came out to the car carrying my phone
and nothing else, not even a jacket. I can't walk back in with a file
under my oxter. I don't want to give the Dublin Mafia anything
they don't have already. Anyway, you know what to do, right?'

'I do.'

'And you promise you'll come back here afterwards?'

'I promise.'

'You have to. He won't stand for you hiding out and doing
your own thing. You have to play by *his* rules.'

She's talking about Feeney. When I get back to the station
later, she'll have spoken to him and either he'll be on board or
he won't.

There's one thing I have to do first. I have to throw a stone
in the water and see what effect the ripples have on our target,
Martin Campbell.

It's 2 p.m. on the dot when I reach Imelda McCarthy's house. I park beside the lough and come to the house from the green area below. I haven't called ahead, but she's working from home.

She takes me into the front room again.

'I'm sorry for visiting unannounced,' I say.

'Has something happened?'

'Not recently, no,' I say, 'but a while ago, yes, something did happen. It's how I got to know Garry. I wanted to tell you. We arrested him. Charged him with burglary.'

'But Garry was clean. He was in recovery. That wasn't him. Not any more. I can't believe he'd break into someone's house. I don't understand.'

'I don't either. But I thought it was right that you should know.'

'Okay. Thank you, I suppose. Whose house was it? Who did he . . . ?'

'That's the slightly weird part.'

I tell her the bare minimum. I don't mention the photograph. The old friendship. The Bertie Allen's connection. I tell her only that her dead brother Garry broke into her ex-husband's house in Deerpark, and that, later, Campbell dropped the charges. It's the first time she's heard any of this.

'I'll kill Martin,' she says.

'Are you going to talk to him about it?'

'I'll be waiting for him when he drops off the kids this evening. I'll talk to him then. Things are going to have to change around here. I can never trust him again.'

'I'm so very sorry,' I say.

And I am. Because there's worse to come for Imelda and her two kids.

I leave the house and walk downhill across the grass to the water's edge. Rain is falling, the drops dimpling the lake. I think about Donna. She feels so close.

I say, 'Hang in there, girl. Not long now.'

Patricia

It was late evening, almost night, when I got to the Bridewell and I thought later that that might have been my first mistake, that if I'd reported it during the day I might have been taken more seriously. We think of garda stations as twenty-four-hour operations, but there was a distinct lack of urgency to the place. I had to ring the bell twice to get someone to open the window.

When he finally did, the wet-behind-the-ears bored-looking child said, 'Passport form, is it?'

'No,' I said.

'Produce car tax and insurance?'

'*What?*'

'Were. You. Stopped. At. A. Garda. Check. Point. And. Asked. To. Pro. Duce. Your. Tax. And. Insurance. Documents?'

I let him finish what he was saying even though of course I got the gist once he said, 'Check. Point.' I felt it would be a mistake to interrupt him. We're like that, the women of my generation, forever taking care not to dent the male ego because you never know what might happen if you do. When he finished, I said, 'I'm here to report a missing person.'

'Now we're getting somewhere,' he said. 'Name?'

'Patricia Linehan.'

'Date of birth?'

'Why do you need my date of birth?'

'Not yours. The missing person. The alleged missing person.'

'Oh. Donna Hannigan. Now that I think of it, I don't actually know her exact date of birth but she's nineteen years of age.'

'Address? The missing person, I mean.'

I gave him the house on John Redmond Street. 'She's not there any more. They were sharing a place – four of them – but they've moved out.'

'So they're *all* missing, is that right?'

'Just her,' I said, 'and she's not originally from Cork. She was living here, but she's from Manchester.'

'Home address in Manchester?'

'I don't know. I'm sorry. I don't even know the area. She didn't have what you might call a *home* address in Manchester as such. She moved around a lot.'

I felt the tide go out inside me as the child garda's expression turned from boredom to pity.

'Gotcha,' he said softly, 'and, tell me, when did you last see her?'

'Holy Thursday.'

'Date and time, please. Holy Thursday isn't really enough.'

I tried to work it out on my fingers but I was getting confused.

'Do you have a calendar?' I asked.

'There's one Sellotaped to the noticeboard behind you.'

I checked it and told him the date and the time.

'What's your connection to her?' He checked his notes. 'How do you know this Donna?'

This Donna. I wanted to call him out on that but I didn't.

'We were friends,' I said.

He gave me a look. 'But you didn't know her birthday?'

'I'm not a birthday person. It wasn't that kind of friendship.'

'How long did you know her, this Donna?'

This Donna again. How *dare* you dismiss her like that, you pipsqueak? was what I wanted to say. 'Less than a year, six or seven months,' was what I said.

'*That* long? *Old* buddies so. And how did you get to know her?'

I was expecting the question. I'd been all set to tell the truth and shame the devil and deal with the taxman, if I had to. Last minute, I changed my mind. The ground felt shaky beneath my feet. That was partly it. That, and how he'd talked about her, how he'd called her 'this Donna'.

'She started out as a customer of mine,' I said, and it wasn't a lie but it wasn't the full story either. It was my Judas moment. I've thought so often since that if I'd told them she was my employee it might have gone differently.

The young guard asked me for a photograph of her but it was the days before camera phones. I didn't have any.

He put down his pen. 'Lookit, I'll be honest with you, she's over eighteen, she's not from Cork, and it doesn't seem like you knew her very well. Ask yourself, would she definitely have told you she was leaving town? Could it have been a sudden decision? If she got word of a job, had a row with the boyfriend? She might have left town. It wouldn't be the first time something like that happened. What you don't realise is, this actually happens the whole time. It's upsetting, but people move on. It's all a waste of time, girl, mine and yours.'

He reached across the counter and patted the back of my hand. I felt beaten and suddenly past it, like I'd been holding onto Donna trying to get back something I'd lost a long time ago. I thought, Maybe she did leave, maybe she followed my advice after all.

I drove home and Jeremy was there. He looked concerned: that lovely big wrinkle he had across the middle of his forehead seemed deeper than usual. He didn't say anything, except 'Would the lady prefer a *little* gin and tonic or a not-so-little one?'

'Not so little,' I said.

In the years afterwards, I kept an eye out for her. Once I got good at the internet, I searched for her online. I even got one of my grandchildren to sign me up for Facebook so that I could look for her there. Like the young guard said, it was all a waste of time.

89

I'M IN THE STATION CAR PARK, INSIDE THE GATE, eyes closed, mustering my reserves for the long walk up the stairs, when my phone pings. It's a text from Fogarty: *Where are you?*

I'm about to reply when the back door of the station flies open and Fintan Deeley emerges, descending the steps quickly. He's followed seconds later by Calum, carrying a bundle of folders and notebooks under his left arm, his suit jacket hooked on one finger over his right shoulder. Calum looks drained. He stalls at the top of the steps, looks around, sees my car.

He sees me, too. I expect him to walk straight over to me, but he doesn't. He throws his stuff into the boot, gets into the passenger seat. Deeley reverses out of the space, and moves in the direction of the gate, then stops. His face expressionless, Calum gets out and walks to my car, stands beside it.

'Put down the window,' he says.

I reply, 'Go away.'

'Don't embarrass yourself,' he says, 'and don't make me shout.'

I press the button, roll down the window by a few centimetres.

'That wasn't hard, was it?'

'What do you want?'

'It was nice to see you. I miss you. I'd like it if we could talk sometime.'

'Is that it?'

'That's it,' he says, 'for the moment.'

'You can fuck off so.'

I roll the window up but I hear him laughing as he walks back to the car.

Before he takes off again, Fintan Deeley raises his eyebrows, gives me a little wave. Clearly, he hasn't a clue what's going on between me and Calum, but he never had much of a clue about anything. I remember that we need to ask about the two short phone calls Garry McCarthy made to him in Dublin at the GNBCI. I reckon I'll leave that task to Fogarty.

I wait a few minutes, just in case Calum tells Deeley to do a U-turn, then go into the station and make straight for Sadie's office. She's at her desk. I pull the door shut behind me, stand inside it.

Speaking quietly, I ask, 'Where are Calum and Deeley gone?'

'Back home to dear old dirty Dublin,' she says.

'How did you manage to get rid of them?'

'I didn't manage anything. Feeney did it.'

'How?'

'He asked Ned, Superintendent O'Brien, to show him the page in the rule book where this kind of ad-hoc internal review was permitted. He said he thought it was a great idea, very helpful et cetera, but that he was a bit worried for Ned. That it might lead to hassle down the line and, with him retiring soon, he didn't need any black marks, or grey ones, to tarnish his otherwise stellar career. So, when it came to it, the super wasn't quite so amenable to Calum's suggestion that he and Deeley stick around for a while.'

She makes a call from her desk phone, 'McCann's here,' then hangs up.

'Feeney?'

'Yup.'

'You told him about my theory?'

'I did.'

'How did he take it?'

'He thinks it's worth a look. Wheels are in motion.'

'Who knows about it?'

'You and me. Feeney. Fogarty. Need-to-know only while the Dubliners were in town. We *have* help. Bugsy's outside Campbell's house now but he doesn't know the full background. He just knows he has to watch. Siobhan O'Sullivan knows she's to dig for every bit of information she can find on Campbell, but she doesn't know the full why of it either.'

I ask, 'Is Siobhan back on the team?'

'Not yet. She'll be here again in the morning.'

I let out a breath, move to sit down.

'Don't get comfortable,' Sadie says. 'Feeney wants to see you.'

He's on the phone to his wife when I poke my head around his door. He points at the chair. I sit.

'I'll be home in an hour max,' he says.

I check the time. It's nearly seven already and I'm so tired I could fall asleep here and now. Feeney ends the call. 'You've been busy,' he says.

'Doing my best,' I say.

'Makes a change. Are you going to keep it up?'

'Yes, sir. That's my intention.'

'Due a review of your work here soon, aren't we?'

'We are. I mean, *I* am. With you.'

'As long as you don't fuck up, or start hiding again, your review *might* go okay for you. Might. I wouldn't have said that a few weeks ago. It was a sink-or-swim situation, and you were heading straight for the bottom. But you seem to have found your sea legs.'

I've heard what he's said but it hasn't gone in.

'Have you nothing to say for yourself?' Feeney asks.

'Sorry, just wasn't expecting you to say any of that. It's a shock.'

'Get over it fast,' Feeney says, 'Campbell knows that we know about the non-burglary by his dead brother-in-law and he has his ex-wife on his back. Even with the photograph, we don't have enough evidence to justify arresting him for murder yet but we've given him rope and this is what we're going to do next . . .'

90

FEENEY'S AUTHORISED A STRICTLY TIME-LIMITED
four-person seventy-two-hour stake-out roster, with rotating
shifts. The team is Sadie, Fogarty, Bugsy and me. I'm rostered
from midnight to eight only because Campbell knows me,
and there's less chance of him spotting me at night. Our
strict instructions from Feeney are 'Surveillance only. No
arrest.'

It's 3.54 a.m. My first midnight-to-eight shift. So far, Campbell
hasn't left his house. He hasn't even been to the shop. According
to Bugsy, he got a Deliveroo around 9 p.m. Other than that,
there's been nothing.

I'm with Fogarty. There are two of us on the overnight in
case one of us falls asleep. He's talking about his memories of
Calum at the garda college in Templemore.

'Looking back, there was always something a bit off about
him. He was older than the rest of us, he'd been to college and
he'd worked for a few years. He never stopped going on about
how he'd be making way more wedge outside, but a lot of guys
were like that and I took no notice of them either. So it wasn't
that. It was as if he was playing a part.'

I ask, 'What do you mean?'

'Hard to put a finger on it. A superior attitude, maybe, the feeling that he was smarter than the rest of us.'

'Which he probably was.'

'Well, yeah. Top of the class but not popular and not because he was a swot. It was just . . . things. One example, he said he was a Bruce Springsteen fan but he never knew any of the words.'

I start to laugh, then stop. A light has gone on in Campbell's downstairs hall. The front door opens. He looks out briefly, then shuts the door again.

Eleven minutes later, a taxi pulls up.

'Shit,' I say. 'He's bailing.'

'Fuck fuck fuck,' Fogarty says.

Campbell emerges with one large wheeled suitcase and a rectangular shoulder bag. He loads the case into the boot, and gets into the taxi, carrying the laptop bag.

The taxi moves off. Fogarty starts the engine and we follow at a discreet distance. Technically, Campbell's not been charged with anything. He's not on bail. He can go wherever he likes.

'Where the fuck is he off to at this hour?' Fogarty says.

'Train or airport. Airport, probably. Fuck. The KLM morning flight to Amsterdam leaves at six fifteen. He can connect to anywhere in the world from there.'

'Feeney warned us. He said it's too soon for an arrest.'

'Look at the size of the suitcase, Olly. Campbell's leaving and he's not coming back. We have *one* chance to question him. We have to take it.'

'What can we charge him with, though? We can't justify murder.'

I rack my brains. 'Shit. I don't know. What about withholding information that might lead to a conviction? He's lied numerous times.'

'Fuck it, yeah, that's good,' Fogarty says.

I put down the window and slap the blue metallic light onto the roof as Fogarty revs the engine. He overtakes the taxi before it exits the estate. Swerving the car into a sideways position, he blocks the onward passage of the cab.

The back door opens and Campbell's out, laptop bag over his shoulder. He's running across the green heading west.

'Fuckin' eejit,' Fogarty says.

We take off after Campbell and he's faster than Fogarty but he's not faster than me. I'll be able to cut him off. I'm gaining on him and, when I catch up, I jump, push him with both hands. He slams face down onto the grass, his head missing the kerb by inches.

I think of Donna as I kneel on his back, cuffing him. She wasn't so lucky.

I say, 'Martin Campbell, I'm arresting you under section four of the Criminal Law Act 1997 on suspicion of withholding information contrary to section nineteen of the Criminal Justice Act 2011. You're not obliged to say anything unless you wish to do so but anything you do say will be taken down in writing and may be given in evidence.'

91

THE TAXI MAN FOLLOWS US TO COUGHLAN'S
Quay. He makes a statement confirming that Campbell was
booked to go to the airport, intending to catch the six-fifteen
flight to Amsterdam.

Meanwhile, Campbell is fingerprinted and DNA-swabbed
and processed by the member-in-charge who contacts his solicitor, Conleth Young, and arranges for him to be seen by a doctor
in relation to his, thankfully minor, arrest-related injuries.

The flight to Amsterdam gives us something to ask Campbell
about, but that's all. It's not illegal. He could have a perfectly
innocent explanation.

But Campbell isn't explaining anything. He sits stoically with
his solicitor, answering, 'No comment,' to everything. He's
running down the clock because that's what he's been advised
to do. What we have on him is a dead witness, a photo and a
few lies. We have zero forensics, zero hard evidence. Nothing.
Unless he talks.

Three of us are tasked with the interview, two inside with
him at any one time. It goes something like this.

'Why were you going to Amsterdam?'

'No comment.'

'You lied about your friendship. You said you barely knew Garry.'

'No comment.'

'You never told us Garry was your brother-in-law. Why did you hide it?'

'No comment.'

'You lied about the burglary. There *was* none, was there?'

'No comment.'

'Garry set up the burglary to put pressure on you to confess to the murder of Donna Hannigan, isn't that right?'

'No comment.'

'You knew Donna Hannigan. What was she like?'

'No comment.'

'You're in a photograph with Donna. Can you confirm at least that you knew her?'

'No comment.'

'Where did you meet Donna, Martin?'

'No comment.'

'Donna was a pretty girl. Were you in love with her?'

'No comment.'

'Did you and Garry fight over her? Did she get caught in the middle? Is that what happened?'

'No comment.'

'Was it an accident, Martin? Were ye after drink?'

'No comment.'

'Did you hit her, Martin? Did you regret it?'

'No comment.'

'Was it Garry who hit her?'

'No comment.'

We keep circling back to the photograph. Asking him about it, about her, to no avail. Martin Campbell shrinks as the morning goes on. Ages visibly before our eyes. Even though his solicitor must have told him that the evidence against him is sketchy.

That all he has to do is stay silent and he'll be out the door.

❖

'If he keeps on like this, photograph or no photograph, we'll have to release him,' Feeney says.

He's right. When Campbell's on his way back to his cell for lunch (a ham and cheese sandwich and a black coffee) I brush past him in the corridor. I take another chance.

'Think of your kids, Martin. If one of them ended up like Donna, you'd want justice for them, wouldn't you?'

His sandwich goes back uneaten and Campbell informs the member-in-charge that he wants to consult privately with his solicitor before the interview resumes.

Afterwards, the solicitor asks to speak to me. My stomach hits the floor. I'm certain it's going to be a complaint about my inappropriate verbal contact with Campbell.

'Off the record?' Conleth Young asks.

'Sure.' Because at this point off the record seems like my best option.

'For some reason, my client wanted me to tell you this, even though I believe you're the one responsible for his facial bruising and cracked ribs?'

'No comment,' I say. 'What is it he wants to say to me?'

The solicitor checks his notebook. 'My client says you shouldn't be asking about the people *in* the photograph. You should be asking who the *photographer* was.'

92

WE'RE IN THE INCIDENT ROOM. FEENEY, SADIE, Fogarty, Bugsy, Siobhan O'Sullivan and me.

'Fucksake,' Fogarty says, 'we *have* asked. There are five people in the picture. Three of them are dead. The two left alive won't say who took it. Kevin Murphy didn't. Martin Campbell won't either.'

I say, 'Murphy said to me he didn't know the person who took the photo. Just that he was a regular customer. I didn't believe him. If only we had some leverage.'

Sadie says, 'Okay, let's wind it back. You went to Murphy because Conor Grant mentioned his name to you. Tell us about that again.'

'I'd been talking to Conor on the phone. Saying it was in the best interests of his company, RGP, that the murder be solved. When he came and sat in my car he was trying to convince me that his dead brother Tom had nothing to do with the murder. That's what his focus was. He was forceful. I *did* believe that he was concerned about his brother's memory. And about his father's health. About the company too. Maybe that most of all. Avoiding scandal and so on.'

'Yet after you met Conor, you ended up going to see Murphy,'

Bugsy says, 'so maybe *that*'s what Conor wanted? He implanted the idea in your brain or something.'

'Like neuro-linguistic programming,' Siobhan O'Sullivan says.

Feeney says, 'Listen to yerselves. I never heard such bullshit. But let's go with the idea for the moment that Conor wanted McCann to go and see Kevin Murphy. That he wanted Murphy involved in the case for some reason. The question is why?'

Sadie says, 'Because Conor knew that Murphy knew something about the murder of Donna Hannigan?'

Feeney says, 'And why might that be?'

Fogarty says, 'Murphy might know who killed her. And whatever he knew would prove that it wasn't Conor's brother Tom?'

'Or?' Feeney asks.

'Conor knew that Murphy was Donna's killer,' Bugsy says.

Feeney says, 'Or?'

I say, '*Conor* might have killed Donna and only mentioned Murphy to distract my attention from himself. I'm just remembering, when he was in the car with me, he was wearing this weird old woven-leather bracelet. The kind of thing you might buy on holidays in Spain.'

'Ibiza, maybe, where Donna worked?' Sadie asks. 'A souvenir?'

'Yeah,' I say.

'Murphy hasn't made his written statement yet,' Feeney says. 'Get him in. Not you, McCann, he's seen too much of you. Fogarty and Bugsy. We need to mix it up.'

The door opens and civilian assistant Dean Hennessy comes into the briefing room. The last time he did that it was to tell Sadie and Feeney about Garry McCarthy being found dead out on the Lee Fields. Now he has less momentous news.

He says, 'There's an old lady here. She wants to see someone from the Hannigan investigation. She says she's called the help-line twice and no one got back to her.'

'You're it, McCann,' Feeney says. 'Go and see what she has to say.'

93

I MEET HER IN THE PUBLIC OFFICE. SHE LOOKS TO be in her seventies. Tall, silver-haired, well-dressed, full make-up. Formidable. Nothing like I imagined when Dean Hennessy called her an old lady. I introduce myself and ask her to follow me upstairs. For old times' sake, and because I'm not expecting much from her, I take her into the disused interview room where there's no recording equipment. I ask her if she'd like a cup of tea.

She says, 'No tea necessary. All I want is for someone to listen to what I have to say. Will *you* listen?'

'Of course I will. Please take a seat. Can you start by telling me your name and address?'

She dusts off the chair and the table with a tissue, then sits down. 'My name is Patricia Linehan. I knew Donna Hannigan.'

We've had lots of people calling the helpline saying they knew Donna. People from Cork and further afield. Patricia looks like the last person Donna would have had contact with. I'll let her down as gently as I can, then get back to my real work. 'Can you be more specific, Patricia?'

'She worked for me in my vintage shop until she disappeared.'

I say, 'And when *was* that? Her disappearance?'

'She started work in late September of 1998. She disappeared at Easter 1999.'

The dates fit, but she could have worked them out from what's been in the news. I put down my pen and look her straight in the eyes.

She looks back. 'Do you believe me?'

I tell her the truth. 'I don't know yet, but I want you to start from the very beginning. You say you knew Donna. I want you to tell me everything about her.'

'I don't *know* everything about her. But I can tell you who killed her.'

94

'THERE'S NOT MUCH LEFT TO SAY AFTER THAT,'
Patricia says. 'I used to see Garry around town. He was in a bad
way. From drugs, it looked like. Then he disappeared. I heard
he went to London. I saw in the paper recently that he died of
an overdose. I didn't go to the funeral. That was a mistake. If
I'd gone, I might have seen the others there. I could have told
you more about them.

'The sensible one, I saw him from a distance a few times over
the years, but I haven't seen him for a while. I'm fairly sure he
got married. I saw him once with a woman and two young
children. I think she was his wife. I don't think I ever knew his
surname, but I can give you his first name. It's Martin. They
used to call him Marty.

'The third lad, the boss I used to call him, disappeared from
Cork.

'Then I saw him on the six o'clock news on the television. I
wasn't sure at first, but I watched again at nine o'clock and it
was definitely him. I wrote his full name down to make sure
I'd remember. It didn't make sense at first, but people change
careers, don't they? I saw him quite often on television after
that.

'When the bones were found on Barrack Street, I phoned the tip line but nobody got back to me. I knew it was her. Donna. I knew immediately it was her.

'And I know they killed her, the three of them, or one or the other of them. In my heart, I've always known that her light was gone from the world.'

I take a beat, a deep breath. 'Patricia, that's all very helpful. We think we know who Marty is. We're pretty sure. The third man, we're less sure about. Can you tell me who you think he is?'

She says a name and I write it down as I hear her say it. After I've written it, I stare at it, scarcely believing my eyes.

Hands shaking, heart pounding, I manage to squeeze out a few words. 'I'm going to get you a cup of tea, Patricia. Milk and sugar?'

'Black,' she says. 'Is everything all right?'

'Back in a minute.'

On autopilot, I ask Dean Hennessy to bring Patricia a cup of black tea. With a Kango hammer in my brain and a sinking in my belly, I tell him I'm going to the loo. In the quiet of the bathroom, I don't even try to analyse what I've learned from Patricia. Hunched over the sink, I have enough trouble breathing. I want to hold this new knowledge inside me. Absorb it.

But, with the clock ticking on how long we can hold Campbell, there's no time for any of that. I need to pass on what I know. I need to move fast.

I look for Sadie. She's in the interview room with Campbell and his solicitor. Rehashing the same old questions. Receiving the same old 'No comment,' for her trouble.

I open the door, 'Skipper, something's come up.'

She pauses the interview, comes out to meet me. 'You look terrible.'

'The woman who called the helpline. You have to hear what she said.'

Patricia is sitting patiently alone, a mug on the table in front of her.

'I see Dean got you your tea,' I say.

'And a Twix,' she says, 'one of his own. He says they're always going missing from the fridge. Dreadful behaviour in a garda station.'

'Can you tell Detective Sergeant O'Riordan what you told me, Patricia, not all of it, just the end part, who the third man is, the man you called the boss?'

She says, 'He was an engineer first. But he's a guard now, one of you lot. I used to see him on the television going in and out of the courthouse up in Dublin, making statements with a load of those coloured microphones held up in front of him. He's well able to talk, that fellow. Always was. I'd know him anywhere. I'll swear it on a stack of Bibles.'

She takes in a breath, releases it slowly.

'His name is Detective Inspector Calum Pierce.'

95

IN THE HALL OUTSIDE, I SAY, 'IT'S THE REASON HE
wanted to do the review. It's why he was pestering Feeney with
phone calls. Calum wasn't checking up on *me*. He was checking
up on the case.

'It's why he was calling Fogarty too. Asking about me *before*
Donna's body was found. Establishing a pattern of concern
because he needed an excuse to have a direct line into the investigation. He knew what was coming. He knew where Donna
was buried. And I think he killed her.'

Sadie says, 'Hang on. That's a big jump. Let's start with the
idea that he was the person who took the photograph. It explains
why Kevin Murphy wouldn't give us the name of the photographer. He said he was afraid to get involved in the investigation.
He must've been doubly afraid to point the finger at a senior
garda.'

'It ties in with the indirect approach that Garry McCarthy
took,' I say. 'He wanted to make amends and he wanted
Campbell to cooperate with him. On confessing their role in
Donna's murder. And implicating the third man. Garry needed
Campbell's help because Calum's too powerful. No one would
listen to Garry on his own. And if Campbell didn't help, he

was going to put it on the public record anyway. In open court where it couldn't be hushed up. That's why he wanted to get charged with burglary and it's why he wanted to give evidence.'

'Campbell has a solid alibi for Garry's murder,' Sadie says.

I reply, 'But maybe Calum hasn't.'

'Go back to the photograph,' Sadie says. 'That's what Campbell wants us to focus on. How do we get him to tell us the name of the photographer without putting words in his mouth?'

I say, 'I have an idea.'

I run to my desk and type a list of initials.

AN. BO. CP. DQ. ER. FS. GT.

Sadie and I go back into the room. I place the list and a red pen on the table in front of Campbell and his solicitor. Campbell looks confused.

The solicitor says, 'What's this?'

I say, 'Martin, you're not on your own any more. Someone else has come forward. Would you be prepared to mark the initials of the man who took the photograph?'

He looks at his solicitor. The solicitor shakes his head.

Despite that, Campbell picks up the list. Scrutinises it.

He puts it back on the desk. Stares at it. The only sound in the room is his breathing. It's laboured and ragged.

Then Campbell picks up the pen and draws the list closer to himself. He holds the sheet steady and draws a circle around the initials 'CP'.

He looks at Sadie. 'CP. That's it. I'm saying no more until you tell me how you're going to protect me and my family.'

96

WHEN KEVIN MURPHY COMES IN WITH FOGARTY
and Bugsy, I print a second list.

Murphy circles CP too. He goes further. He says the name
aloud. 'It's Calum Pierce. He and Garry and Martin Campbell
were joined at the hip. I didn't know the girl. I wasn't lying
about that. I only met her that one time, and I forgot about
her. That is the truth. But I knew the three guys well. They
nearly lived in Sir Henry's, and when they weren't in Henry's,
they were in the pub. Martin used to sub for Tom sometimes
in Bertie's. That day, the Sunday Calum took the photo, they
were together, Calum, Garry, Martin. Donna. Martin's still
around Cork. He lives here. I've seen him. Ask *him* about her.'

We go to Feeney with what we have.

Sadie says, 'We have two people – Patricia Linehan and Kevin
Murphy – naming Calum Pierce as a known associate of Donna
Hannigan. We also have Campbell. He hasn't come out and said
the name fully yet. He's worried about his family. He wants
reassurances.'

Feeney says, 'Tell him he has my word. His family will be safe.' He turns to me. 'McCann, you can't be part of the Campbell interview from now on. For obvious reasons. Your history with Calum Pierce. Have you finished the statement with Patricia Linehan? She signed?'

'Yes. Done. She's left the station and all. I offered to call her a cab but she drove herself home. Insisted on it.'

'You go too. You can't do any more here the way things have turned out.'

I say, 'I understand why I can't be in the room. But I'm going nowhere.'

97

CAMPBELL STARTS AT THE END. 'GARRY ALWAYS thought that if he and Donna hadn't fallen in love that Calum would have moved on and gotten over her. That she'd have moved on too. Wouldn't have stayed as long in Cork. So even though it was Calum who killed Donna, the way Garry saw it her death was his fault. Calum couldn't be bested, you know? Most competitive fucker I've ever met.

'Calum got a new job in Limerick. He was still working as an engineer and construction was taking off around then so he was earning big bucks compared to the rest of us. He kept on his room at our gaff in Shandon – we had a house share in John Redmond Street for years. We'd all met when we were working for the summer on one of Ray Grant's sites. Calum spent week-days in Limerick. Used to come down for Sweat in Henry's at the weekends. Occasionally he couldn't come if he had overtime. But mostly he was there.

'When he was out of the house, it was like a weight was lifted from us. We'd be doing nothing in the evenings. Sitting around watching telly. Going for pints. But Calum used to drive down an odd night and he'd catch us off guard and it was like a black cloud. He was checking up on us. On Donna. We all knew it. He had this passive-aggressive attitude. Big smiles but raging inside. An ice-cold anger.

'Donna had told him she wasn't interested in him. He snogged her that first night in Ibiza. For about five minutes. Well, maybe a bit longer. But it was nothing. Didn't even qualify as a one-night stand. She wasn't interested in him. Friend-zoned him straight away.

'Summer 1998. She was working there. We went over for a week. Did the usual. Café del Mar for the sunset. On to the clubs till dawn. Don't get me wrong. We had a brilliant time. But it felt like the end of an era. The real glory days were gone. And after some of the nights we'd had in Henry's over the years, like, it was hard to impress us.

'We met her at sunrise. On the beach. Loads of people and her. Donna.'

He stops. 'I don't know what to say about her. She was so lovely . . .'

His voice hardens. 'And she was what we needed to keep the party going just that little bit longer. We used her. Do you know the song "I'm Your Toy"? By Gram Parsons? Elvis Costello sings it too. Well, she was *our* toy. I *do* think that. It was like the way couples in danger of breaking up have a saver baby. It was wrong. I didn't think that at the time. I do now.

'The nineties were intense. You'd have these amazing one-night friendships with people you'd never see again. But that sunrise on the beach, she told us where she was working, and we promised we'd go and see her the following night and, lo and behold, we actually did. She was surprised to see us when we showed up. But happy too. We hung out with her for the rest of the holiday. Nothing going on. Nothing sexual. I think she thought we were three granddads. I wouldn't have minded, like, obviously. She was absolutely stunning. It was never going to happen, though. Not with me. With Garry, it was different. I'll get to that.

'Anyway. A few nights later, it's all sorted. She's moving to Cork at the end of the summer. Nuts, when you think of it. But not *so* nuts. Crazy shit like that *did* happen.

'Whose *idea* the move to Cork was? We thought it was all of us, a communal cosmic awakening. But looking back, it was Calum. He steered us in that direction. Organised the whole thing. Ferry timetables to go over and collect her in Liverpool. Everything. He had the serious hots for her. We didn't realise exactly how bad until it was too late. He had hopes. He thought they had a future. He wanted to marry her, I'm sure.

'But soon after arriving here, she made it crystal clear. She wanted to be friends and that was it. Full stop.

'They were wrong for each other. Everyone could see it but Calum couldn't. He was biding his time. Waiting for her to give in. Doing everything he could think of. Flashing the cash. Buying her things she didn't give a shit about. Except when he got her the Buffalo boots. She *loved* them. You couldn't buy them in Cork so he got them posted over from London. They were a size or a half-size too big but she didn't care. Stuffed the toes with tissues and gave him a big hug but that was as far as her gratitude went. It drove him mad. He started suspecting she was seeing someone else. Didn't twig that someone was Garry. Not till Holy Thursday 1999.'

He stops. 'I don't think I can do this. I've changed my mind.'

His solicitor Conleth Young says, 'That's fine. You don't *have* to say anything.' He checks the time on the interview-room clock and scribbles something in his notebook. 'My client has made it clear that he does *not* wish to make a statement.'

Sadie acts as if the solicitor hasn't spoken. Her eyes never leave Campbell. He's rocking his head from side to side, his eyes closed, breathing heavily.

'You don't have to talk, Martin. It's up to you. You're the one in control. But it's never too late to do the right thing. For Donna Hannigan. For Garry McCarthy. For yourself. For your ex-wife, Garry's sister. For your children, Garry's nephew and niece.'

The solicitor speaks again. 'My client is in some degree of distress. As you can see. He needs a break.'

Campbell opens his eyes, twitches them shut a few times. Swipes the back of his hand under his nose. 'I'm okay to go on.'

'Martin . . .' the solicitor says.

'Conleth, thanks, but I *said* I'm okay. Where was I?'

Fogarty says, 'You left us at Holy Thursday 1999. A real cliffhanger. Get on with it. We haven't all day.'

'Fucksake,' Sadie says. 'Don't mind him, Martin. Take your time. Do you want another cup of coffee?'

'No. Thanks.'

'Anytime you do, just let me know. This isn't easy but you're doing great.'

'You're not doing all *that* great,' Fogarty says. 'You've given us precisely fuck-all so far.'

This time Sadie lets Fogarty's words hang. Campbell looks at her.

She shrugs. 'I hate to say it, Martin, but he has a point. He could put it more nicely but if you want to tell us what happened, you have to actually say something.'

Campbell nods. 'I need the toilet. And a bottle of water. Then I'll talk. I swear on my kids.'

98

'I WAS DOING A FEW HOURS CASH IN HAND
behind the bar in Bertie Allen's every now and again, filling in
for Tom.'

Sadie says, 'That's the late Tom Grant, Ray Grant's son.'

'Yeah. He was working there. Slumming it. He was never
going to be a barman long-term but he was helping out. Maurice
Bolger, the owner of Bertie's, was his uncle or something.'

'Bolger was Ray Grant's cousin,' Fogarty says, 'not that it
matters. This isn't an episode of *Who Do You Think You Are?*
Get on with it.'

'Okay, okay. Anyway, Tom had a date or . . . I can't remember,
it's not important, but he didn't want to work the Holy Thursday
so he asked me to step in. It was before I did the master's in
computer science and I was in and out of work so I needed the
money.

'I liked the job in the pub. Maurice had seen what was going
on down the hill at Sir Henry's. He splashed out on an okay
sound system but kept everything else the same so Bertie's still
looked like an old man's pub but it was a chilled place. Good
tunes. Often, we'd just have Radio Friendly on, especially when
it was quiet. Sometimes we'd play the Fish Go Deep mixtapes.

Or someone might have bought something new in Comet and we'd play it. It varied. The main thing is that it was somewhere to meet friends and chat and hang out and not have to put up with shit music.'

Sadie says, 'That Holy Thursday, where was the pub owner, Mr Bolger?'

'Maurice was gone to Spain playing golf for the Easter weekend. He left on either the Wednesday night or the Thursday morning. Tom was off Good Friday. The pub was closed for the day – all the pubs were – and he wasn't due back to work till Saturday at four. So it was just me in charge on Thursday night.

'The guards were on the warpath. There'd been a lot of stuff in the papers about disrespecting the holy day and there was a big garda operation going on for the weekend. Maurice had been warned numerous times about serving late and I think he might have been prosecuted at one stage, too, so Tom had me under strict orders to close on time. It wasn't busy anyway. A lot of people were having their own parties at home. Some people were working the next day. It's a bank holiday, not a public holiday. I always get them mixed up. Used to.

'That's why we didn't expect Calum. We thought he was working on Good Friday. Garry and Donna came into Bertie's for a few, thinking the coast was clear, and they were sitting at the bar keeping me company and having the chats and next minute Calum walks in. He sees the two of them and they weren't all over each other or anything but it was like he just knew. He went as white as a sheet and ordered a double Jameson and he *knocked* it back.

'It settled him. He sat down and laid off the hard stuff, had two or three beers and we thought it was going to be okay. He started joking with the two of them, asking how long they'd been . . . shagging each other, was what he said, and they said a couple of weeks even though it was way more than that. I didn't hear the full conversation. I was serving other people. Dipping in and out. He bought a round of drinks at one stage and went to hand a pint to Garry and he dropped it just as Garry was about to take it. The glass fell and broke all over the floor. It was an accident, he said. I cleaned it up and replaced the drink, no charge.

'I've thought in the years after that him dropping the glass was deliberate. That it was him warning us. That we should've known then that there was going to be trouble. Deep down, I think I *did* know. Garry too. We felt it. From the minute Calum saw Garry and Donna together, the world changed. Everything felt different from that moment. If we'd acted on what we sensed from him – the rage, the danger – Donna might still be alive. But we didn't and, yes, I regret that. With all my heart, I regret it.

'Closing time came. I turned off the music, called it a good few times and everyone left eventually, except my three friends. I told them to head off, that I had to clean up, but Calum said we'd have one more. He said it was a celebration of new love. Poor Donna looked so relieved that I said okay, just the one so. And Calum went over and pulled down the blinds and put the double bolts on the door, top and bottom, and he walked back all quiet and calm. Donna was sitting at the end of the bar, last seat, and Garry was gone to the bog.

'Calum swung his left arm wide, like he was throwing a ball, and he knocked Donna off her high stool and onto the floor. It happened that fast.

'I did nothing for a second or two. Couldn't believe what was happening. When I ran around to the other side of the bar, Donna was alive. She was groaning, I could hear her, she was stunned, but she was definitely alive. I ran to her. Calum was crouched beside her. I thought at first that he was helping her . . .'

Campbell pauses, unscrews the cap from the water bottle and takes a sip.

He goes on: 'Instead of helping her, he smashed her head off the floor. Stone floor. Five or six times. I was trying to pull him off her, I swear, and there was blood everywhere, but she was dead. There was no hope for her.' He shuts his eyes, lets out a long sigh, sniffs short breaths back in.

'It was all over by the time Garry got back from the bog. He was gone a while and he was different. I knew by him that he'd been smoking hash out the window. I could smell it off him. It's one of the reasons he fell apart afterwards. He was relaxing while Donna was getting her brains bashed out. He wasn't there to protect her, like he should've been. That's what he thought. Felt.

'So the three of us were sitting on the floor. Garry was holding her head in his hands and saying her name and it was a mess. We were in shock. Covered with Donna's blood and brains, and that was when Calum said the three of us would be done for it and we needn't think he was going to take the rap. He said if he was going down, we all were. I was serving late when I shouldn't have been. Garry was the one . . . having sex with her – "dipping his wick", that's what Calum said – and if they tested her they'd find traces of Garry all over her. He said it was our fault just as much as his. And we believed him. For twenty-three or twenty-four years we believed him. Because we knew in our hearts that it *was* our fault. She was in danger from Calum that night. And we did nothing to stop him.

'We sat there for ages. It felt like hours. Saying nothing. Garry crying. Calum too, would you believe? I was too dazed to cry. But after a while, Calum stopped crying and started to talk. He said it mightn't be so bad. He said we could hide Donna and no one would ever need to know. He said we could bury her.'

99

CAMPBELL CONTINUES: 'CALUM STOOD UP AND took off his hoodie and his T-shirt. He'd started going to the gym, thinking it'd impress Donna, and I saw how strong he'd become. He wasn't like that before and I was wondering had he started taking steroids or something, was that the reason for the aggression, because he was so built, like. But even if he had, I don't think that was it. It was just him. He's a bad man, and he hid it well, but it came out eventually.

'He wiped the blood off himself with his clothes. Not all of it, but a lot. He went behind the bar and washed his hands in the sink. Came back out and was all business. Like he'd flicked a switch.

'He said, "This is what I think we should do." And we did it. It was a pub with a flat upstairs. There were supplies and some of them were helpful for the clean-up but we found out fairly quickly that the tools in the shed out back weren't going to do. There was a coal shovel but it wasn't strong enough to dig a grave. We needed the right equipment and we had to wait for Atlantic Homecare on Pouladuff Road to open in the morning.

'We spent what was left of the night wiping down surfaces

with newspapers and toilet paper – there was a load of it in the store room – and we put the bloody papers into bin bags. We were going to burn the paper as soon as it dried. We took off our clothes except for our jocks and wiped as much of the blood off ourselves as we could and we taped a few black bin bags to a clean part of the floor and rolled Donna onto the plastic and washed down everywhere so that at least we weren't walking the blood all over the place any more. We knew we'd have to wash it again, and again later, but it was a start.

'We unscrewed the bench seat from the wall in the corner by the fireplace. There was a hammer and chisel in the coal shed so after eight a.m., once the traffic started enough to hide the noise, we took turns chipping away the mortar between the flagstones. It was easy to lift them after that. Calum's engineering training was . . . Put it this way, it came in handy. And the three of us knew how to work hard. We'd spent years on building sites. I told you already, I think, that it was how we became friends. Summer labouring. We all liked going mad at the weekends. Garry was the one who got us into music and going to Henry's. He was always cooler than we were.'

Sadie says, 'You mentioned Atlantic Homecare? Tell us about that.'

Campbell says, 'The three of us went.'

'In your jocks?' Fogarty asks.

'No. Calum had clothes in his car and he was parked just outside. And Maurice Bolger lived in the flat upstairs so we used some of his clothes as well. We bought digging spades – three of them – and Polyfilla and black tile grout and some extra screws and more black plastic sacks and some green garden ones too, made of heavier plastic. Some plywood. And bog roll and J-cloths to replace the stuff we'd used. We went to SuperValu near the lough for that.'

'Did you get anything else there?' Fogarty asks.

'Bleach. Cigarettes.' He looks down. 'Food. Calum said we needed to keep our strength up. That we'd never manage the digging unless we ate something.'

'Did you have something to eat?' Sadie asks.

'I had a cheese sandwich. We bought packets of ham and Easi-singles and sliced pan and cans of Coke and Fanta and had breakfast in the car. We didn't eat in the same room as Donna's body. That would have been—'

'Did Garry eat too?' Sadie asks.

'Yeah, he was starving. He'd been smoking hash, like.'

'That explains it so,' Fogarty says.

Campbell looks doubtful. 'It sounds bad, I know.'

'It does,' Fogarty says.

Fogarty's about to say more when Sadie interjects: 'Tell us about the digging. Who did it?'

'We took turns. Calum was the strongest so he did most of it, and Garry was kind of useless – he was bawling his eyes out a lot of the time – but he did a bit and I did too. We shared the job but Calum was the boss. We didn't go down the full six feet under. It was more like four or five. We were afraid to dig deeper in case we'd undermine the rest of the floor.'

Fogarty asks, 'What did you do with the earth you dug up? How did you take it off site?'

'There was an overgrown wild area out beyond the backyard. We scattered some of the earth there. We moved the coal pile in the shed – it was an earth floor anyway. We put some there under a few empty coal sacks. We made a kind of a shelf of earth. Then we replaced the coal on top. We figured the weight would flatten it and that no one would notice and no one ever did. Tom Grant wouldn't lower himself to haul in coal for the fire. And Maurice was on the sauce big-time back then. He was either pissed or half pissed day in day out.'

'What about the rest of the earth?'

'There wasn't much left after that but what there was we put into the heavy green sacks and put black sacks over them. We had one each. We waited for dark and took them out the side door and walked up the street and put them in the boot of Calum's Ford Focus. He was parked across from Mr Bradley's pub. That's where he'd left it after we got back from the supermarket and Atlantic Homecare. We drove around looking for skips to dump them in. It was the last thing we did. We'd already replaced the flagstones and screwed the bench onto the wall again. We put in extra screws to keep it steady and plywood underneath so that even if the floor sank a little, the bench wouldn't.

'I want you to know that we put a white sheet underneath Donna so that she wouldn't be going straight into the ground. We put her jacket under her too and we covered her in another sheet from upstairs, just laid it on top of her. The three of us lifted her in together. We put her in face down. None of us could look at her.

'We burned the bloody papers in the fire. It took ages but the burning disguised the bleach smell. Not as much as Calum wanted, though, so he spilled beer on the floor and let it sit there for while, and we just washed it down and wiped it with water only, and we lit cigarettes and let them burn down, and after a while it was as okay as it was going to be and we had to get out of there so we did and we dumped the rest of the earth in skips, like I said, and dumped the spades too. Left them in three different places, figuring people would see them and take them home.

'After that, we went back to the house in Shandon and threw all the clothes – every single thing that might have had a trace on it – into the washing machine for a boil wash and tied them in a black sack and binned them the second they came out of the tumble dryer. We cleared out Donna's room too. Which was easy because she had fuck-all. We dumped her stuff in the wheelie bin and put it out to be collected on the Saturday morning – it was usually Monday but because of the bank holiday, it was Saturday instead.

'And that was it. The end of poor Donna and the end of our friendship. We still went to the Weekender in Henry's, though. Both nights, Saturday and Sunday. If we hadn't gone, it would have stood out. If anyone asked where Donna was, we told them she'd left town. People came and went all the time. Emigrating for work. Going to England. Germany. Coming back for the holidays. No one thought anything. But I've an idea that that weekend was the first time Garry tried heroin. That weekend, or soon afterwards. He took to it like a duck to water.

'We gave notice on the house in Shandon. I moved back in with my folks. Calum moved to Limerick full-time. Garry drifted around Cork for a while going downhill. After he went to London, I didn't see him for years.'

Sadie says, 'But you married his sister.'

'His much younger sister. Years later. She knows nothing about any of this. I didn't realise at the start who she was. McCarthy is one of the commonest names in Cork. By the time

I knew, it was too late. I'd fallen for her and then she was pregnant. We got married and it was all too rushed. I never told her the truth. Please believe me. Imelda had zero to do with any of this.'

He pauses. 'Looking back, me and Imelda, we never had a chance. I had a secret and that poisoned the well from the start.

'Then Garry came back from London during Covid and it was a fucking disaster. It was all fine when he was a mess. But after he got clean, he started working through the Twelve Steps. When he got to the making-amends part, that was when the real trouble began. He was hounding us. Me and Calum. Wanted us to confess. That was why he broke into my house. *He* was the one who phoned the guards while I was upstairs. He *wanted* ye to come. He wanted to be charged. I just wanted him to shut up.'

'Are you confessing to a role in the murder of Garry McCarthy?'

'No. God, no. I was horrified when I found out. I was in Dublin at the Conrad Hotel that night. I've told you twenty times already. I had *nothing* to do with Garry's death. He was my brother-in-law. Who do *you* think killed Garry? I can't do any more for you. I want to talk to my solicitor in private again.'

100

WE'RE IN FEENEY'S OFFICE. HE'S BEHIND THE DESK.
Sadie and Fogarty are sitting. I'm standing against the wall
because if I sit I'll fall asleep. I don't know how much longer
I can keep going. Martin Campbell's on a rest period.

Feeney says, 'Secrecy goes only so far.'

What he means is that news of Campbell's arrest has to have
reached Calum by now. The breaking news that Campbell is
talking, and what he's saying, won't be far behind.

Sadie says, 'We might have enough to arrest Calum Pierce.'

Feeney says, 'Not enough for a conviction, though. Not quite
yet.'

Fogarty says, 'We need to get Calum for the Garry McCarthy
murder. That's how we do him. We roll the Donna Hannigan
one in behind that.'

I step forward. 'Yeah,' I say. 'Campbell knows more about
Garry's murder than he's saying. He just doesn't want to tell us
because he was his brother-in-law. He's already in trouble with
his ex. She told me she'd never trust him again.'

'So we *use* that,' Sadie says. She looks at me. 'We use *you*. It's
not ideal, but we have no choice.'

101

'I TOLD HER,' I SAY. 'I'M SORRY, MARTIN, BUT I HAD to. You knew that. It's my job.'

I'm on my own in the interview room with Campbell and his solicitor; Sadie, Feeney, Fogarty and the super are watching and listening.

Campbell's slumped across the table, death-gripping a large takeaway cup of Centra coffee. His Badger and Dodo freshly ground days are behind him and he knows it. He's got the game's-up stare, the future-in-ruins hunch.

He looks at me through closed eyelids. 'Who?' A word spoken so quietly I have to lip-read it.

'Didn't catch that, sorry.'

'Who. Did. You. Tell?'

'Imelda.'

Head in hands. A sudden intake of breath, as if he's thought of something worse. '*What* did you tell her?'

'That you're helping us with our enquiries in connection with the murder of Donna Hannigan.' I pause. 'That Garry and you were involved in the murder.'

'No. *No.* We didn't kill Donna. She can't think that.' He's leaning across the narrow table, centimetres from my face, his eyes wide.

'You didn't wield the fatal blow but you were both present. Accessories after the fact. That's the reality, however you want to dress it up. You know that. Now she knows it too. Not the full details, but she has the gist.'

He collapses again. 'Were the kids there?'

'Not in the same room. They were in the kitchen. Playing a computer game, I think. They're fine. Don't worry. It'll be ages before they'll know anything. They *will* have to find out eventually, of course. Better to manage it. To tell them rather than have them find out by themselves. From friends. Or the internet.'

A whimper. 'I need to talk to Imelda. I need to explain.'

'Explain what, Martin? That you *could* help us to convict her brother Garry's killer but you don't want to? Or you're afraid to? Is that it?'

A shake of the head. 'I want to talk to my wife. To Imelda.'

I stand. 'I'll see what I can do. Though if I were you, I'd . . .'

'You'd what?'

I sit down. 'Look, none of my business but, if I were you, I'd take a close look at what you're planning to say to Imelda and see what you can do to improve on it.'

I'm walking a thin line. I can't be seen to offer any inducements. If we get as far as a murder charge, Calum and his legal team will pore over every word uttered here. If Martin Campbell decides to cooperate with us on Garry's case, it must be on a voluntary basis.

He absorbs what I've said. For almost the first time, he looks to his left, out the window. The view is of a brick wall and the light is fading but the air is fresher out there. He seems to draw strength from it even if he can't inhale or taste it. He turns to face me. 'Garry was trying to make amends, wasn't he?'

'Until he was stopped,' I say, 'he was. Yeah. You told us, remember?' After a beat, I add, 'It's never too late to do the right thing.'

'Do you really believe that?'

'I do.'

It's the answer he wants and, from the way Campbell's solicitor is looking at him, I can tell this is a conversation they've had already. Half a loaf might be better than no bread, but half a confession is nearly worse than none. You've incriminated yourself but you haven't done enough to get the full bounce from whatever benefits might be going.

'Give us a minute,' the solicitor says, with a wry grimace. It's a bittersweet moment for him. His client is taking his advice at last, but he could have taken it sooner and, if he had, the solicitor wouldn't have wasted his whole day here. Plus, with Campbell likely taking a guilty plea on all possible charges, the solicitor's chances of being any more than peripherally involved in what might end up being Cork's trial of the century are disappearing in a cloud of dust over the horizon. I leave the room. Sadie's waiting for me outside.

'What do you reckon?' she asks. It's harder to get a full read on a suspect when you're not right there with him.

'He's desperate for redemption so he's going to tell us all he knows,' I say, 'whatever that is. It may or may not be enough.'

102

FEENEY TELLS ME HE'S PLANNING TO SIT IN ON the next part of the Campbell interview.

I think it's a terrible idea, and that he's only muscling in to steal some of the credit, but my upcoming review hasn't quite gone away. I try to be diplomatic. 'Changing approach at this delicate stage? I'm not so sure about that.'

'This isn't a democracy, McCann. I'm not happy with you in there on your own. Not at this *delicate* stage. If you fuck it up, you could do major damage.'

'I'm not going to fuck it up. Besides, Campbell wants to talk. He knows me best. I – I don't intimidate him.'

'Whereas I would, right?' He waits a beat. 'We're guards, not counsellors. You'll take the lead inside. And, by the way, one slip and you're back on the subs' bench.'

Campbell's solicitor has prepared a short handwritten statement. Campbell reads from it, voice quivering at the start. He hadn't expected to have Feeney across the table.

'"I understand that I am not obliged to say anything and that anything I say may be given in evidence. I make this statement of my own volition and solely from a desire to assist the garda investigation into the death of my ex-brother-in-law Garry McCarthy."'

He clears his throat. "'I had nothing to do with Garry's death. I was up in Dublin at an awards dinner at the Conrad Hotel on the night that Garry died. I bought my ticket several months ago as an examination of my banking records will attest."' He looks up from the sheet. 'I used my Visa Debit. Should I have said that? It's clearer.' He looks at his solicitor.

'It's fine,' I say. 'We can add that in later. You're doing great. Go on.'

He nods, starts reading again: "'Garry told me that he was going to meet Calum Pierce the night he died. I never,"' he looks up from the sheet, "'never in a million years, I *never* thought Calum would kill Garry."'

He sighs. "'Garry told me he thought Calum was having a change of heart. That's why he agreed to meet Garry. That's what Garry said. 'I think he's coming around' were Garry's exact words. He wanted Calum to confess to Donna Hannigan's murder. He was trying to persuade him. I believe that he thought Calum would. I believe that's what Garry meant by 'I think he's coming around.'"'

"'Garry said he was going to meet Calum out the Lee Fields that night. He – Calum – would only meet somewhere quiet. He didn't want anyone to see them together. Garry thought that was understandable."'

Campbell swallows. "'I disagreed with Garry. I thought Calum only agreed to meet Garry to warn him off. I believed that Calum would never confess to the murder. I still believe that. I also believe now that Calum arranged to meet Garry so as to kill him but I can't prove he did.'"

He stops. 'That's it,' he says.

'Thank you, Martin,' I say. 'That's very helpful.'

In my mind, I'm thinking the opposite. All he's given us is an unverifiable reported conversation with a corpse. To make anything of it, we need strong corroboration. I look at Feeney. His face wears a blank expression. He's watching Campbell, hasn't taken his eyes off him the entire time, hasn't scribbled a note, hasn't asked a single question. Campbell looks flustered. He has more to tell, I'm almost sure.

I press on. 'When did Garry tell you about going to meet Calum? Did you meet up with him earlier in the day? Where? Were there any witnesses to your meeting?'

'No,' Campbell says. 'We didn't meet face to face. He rang a few times that day. I didn't take the calls. I didn't call him back either. Which I'm not proud of.'

His voice softens. 'Garry had become a real pest, you know? He had a one-track mind. He was obsessed with us all confessing. That day, after the third or fourth missed call, or maybe more, he sent me a text. It's how I found out about the meeting. I was kind of glad when I got the message first. I thought Calum would soften Garry's cough for him. It never occurred to me that he'd kill Garry. I didn't reply to the message but even if I had I wouldn't have said not to go to the meeting. I didn't think Garry was in any physical danger. I still can't believe it but it's the only thing that makes sense. He *was* off the gear. He didn't OD. I'm nearly sure of it. But, like I say, I don't have proof.'

I say, 'With the best will in the world, that's crap, and so easily disproved I'm disappointed in you.'

His mouth drops open. He looks from me to Feeney. 'What do you mean?'

'We've checked Garry's phone records. The day he died, he didn't text you.'

'Oh, *now* I get you. Garry used to call me from his phone, but I'd never answer on that. It was just a signal for me to phone him back. I wasn't using my *own* phone to talk to Garry. I was using a burner. That's what he texted me on. If you take me to the lough, I'll show you where I put it after I heard Garry was dead. I got the call from Imelda when I was with the kids after school. I smelt a rat. I knew it was too much of a coincidence that Garry had met up with Calum and now he was dead. I had the burner on me and I just wanted rid so, while the kids were feeding lettuce to the geese, I took out the SIM card and slipped the phone into the water, underneath a concrete ledge, across from where the crib is at Christmas.'

I ask, 'So the phone is in the lough? But where's the SIM card? Did you cut it up? Dump it somewhere else?'

'No. I kept it as insurance. I was worried. Just in case Calum—'

Feeney speaks for the first time. 'Tell us where the SIM card is. Now.'

Campbell replies immediately: 'Bottom of the wardrobe in my bedroom. In a box of electrical waste for recycling. Concealed inside an old landline handset. There are two handsets in the box. The SIM is in the one marked Gigaset.'

He goes on, 'The plastic casing. It's glued shut. You're going to need more than a screwdriver to open it but you'll be able to recover the text message. I'll give you the burner number now. The text Garry sent me will be on it. You'll see that I'm telling you the truth. I'll give you a key to the house. Or I'll go with you, if you like. Show you where it is. I want to.

'And you know what? Whatever happens to me from now on, Garry was right. Telling the truth *does* feel good. I'm so fuckin' sorry that he had to die before I followed his advice. He was a good man. He had his problems, for sure, but he was always the best of us.'

Campbell covers his eyes with the palms of his hands and bends his head in shame, or sorrow, or relief, it's hard to tell, and it's hard not to feel sympathy for him.

But he's alive. Garry isn't. Donna isn't. They're the ones I need to focus on.

Outside the door, I say to Feeney, 'You were right to sit in. It helped, I think.'

'Tie this up,' he says. 'Briefing in five.'

I tell the member-in-charge to return Campbell to his cell, then make my way to the incident room.

103

'IF WHAT HE SAID ABOUT THE MOBILE PHONE PANS out, it's more than we had,' Feeney says.

It's typical Feeney understatement. The truth is, the Garry McCarthy case has momentum now. And this work is easier when you know what you're looking for.

Fogarty and Sadie drive Martin Campbell to his house in Deerpark to collect the SIM card – the most important element of the story that Campbell's told us – while I drive to the lough with Bugsy in the passenger seat.

As the last of the daylight disappears in the western sky, I pull up by the place they hold the céilí dances in summer, opposite the blocked-up crib, not yet dressed or lit for the coming Christmas season. We've brought torches and we shine them vertically into the water, both of us doing a slow-moving crouch along the concrete edge in opposite directions.

When I see the ledge, more or less where Campbell said it was, I let out a shout, 'Here.' I add, 'Bugsy, you're it.'

Because of my close connection to Calum, Bugsy has to be the one who retrieves the exhibit. He strips off his jacket, lays it flat on the ground and kneels on it. He rolls up his sleeve, puts on too-short blue nitrile gloves and stretches his arm into the murky water. He feels around, fishes out the phone and gets to his feet. I hold a medium-sized plastic evidence bag open in front of him. He peels off the gloves and drops them and the phone into it.

'Scott Medal for that,' he says. 'It's rotten on the bottom, soft and gunky. Years of bird shit and God knows what else.'

I hand him a towel. 'We'll stop at the SuperValu and get you wet wipes.'

'Should've thought of them on the way here,' Bugsy says.

'You'll be grand,' I say.

'I'm grand already. I just want to get the fucker,' he says.

It's how the whole team feels and it's come as a surprise, even though it shouldn't have. There's an unacknowledged tolerance for garda members straying into grey areas, but what Calum's done is black-and-white. Everyone wants to nail him. Me most of all.

104

WHILE WE WAIT FOR THE EXPERTS TO LOCATE THE text message confirming Garry's meeting with Calum, we concentrate on the other relevant phone numbers.

One of the first things we discover is that Calum's official phone stayed switched on in Dublin – in my old apartment in Phibsboro – on the night Garry died. The night Calum allegedly arranged to meet Garry McCarthy by the Lee Fields.

Fogarty says, 'Either Pierce is in the flat that night, tucked up in bed, or he's left his phone there as cover.'

I ask, 'What about the girlfriend? Is she there with him?'

'Good question,' Sadie says. 'Does Calum have an automatic alibi?'

For these purposes, feel free to imagine that the answer comes as quickly as it does on the telly, even though it doesn't. That said, this case is top priority so it comes real-world fast and, when it does, it's so good it makes us forget all the pain it took to get here.

Social media tells us that, on the night of the murder, Calum's girlfriend wasn't at home. She was at the musical *Hamilton* in London, having flown Dublin–Stansted that morning in the company of a female friend. We don't yet know who bought the tickets, or when, but no one's jaw will drop if it turns out to be her kind boyfriend Calum Pierce, needing to get her out of the way. The question of who bought the tickets and when doesn't matter much.

Because the crucial link in the chain is that, while she was in London, her car, a D-reg Ford Fiesta, showed up on CCTV footage obtained for the Angler's Rest pub at the far end of the Lee Fields on the night of Garry's death. We figure Calum used his girlfriend's car to drive from Dublin, and approached the meeting point from the rural western end, crossing farmland and walking along the river to get there. He was too clever to leave the Fiesta in the well-monitored parking area across from the pub, but it was caught on camera as it went by.

The Fiesta driver's face isn't visible on the CCTV because he's wearing a hood and a baseball cap. I'm certain it's him long before the detailed computer modelling and comparison analysis is completed.

'It's the right height and shape for Calum,' I say. 'It's how he used to look if he ever drove my Clio back in the day. Like he was too big for it.'

Fogarty says, 'There's no report of the Fiesta being stolen while its owner is in London. So if it's not Calum driving, who else could it be?'

'There's something else I've just thought of,' I say. 'Calum's been phoning me. I've blocked him repeatedly but he's kept calling. He's been using burner phones. Maybe he got careless, used one of those numbers to contact Garry.'

I open the menu on my phone and find my blocked numbers. Scam callers, and Calum's mobile and the various burners he's used to get through to me.

Fogarty says, 'He wouldn't have been stupid enough to harass you on the same burner he used to arrange a meeting with Garry McCarthy, would he?'

Except he was.

I find the number Calum used to contact Garry in my phone settings.

Because when you're under pressure, you make mistakes.

And no one knows that better than I do.

'There's one more thing,' I say. 'I've been thinking about Fintan Deeley, his lucky transfer to Dublin. What if *Calum* arranged it after the Deerpark burglary? He must have seen an opportunity when he heard I was involved in Garry's arrest along with Fintan Deeley. He got Deeley transferred to the GNBCI, leaving me in sole charge. He was relying on me to mess up. If that had happened, the case against Garry would have collapsed.

'And there are those two calls Garry made to the GNBCI as well. I thought it was Deeley he was calling to talk to, but maybe it was Calum. Look at the dates. Calum's burner phone calls to Garry only started after Garry phoned the GNBCI number.'

We review the file again and again. Checking dates, times, numbers. Piecing the mosaic together.

Finally, we send everything to the DPP.

Then we wait.

Patricia

After all that, I expected more action, if I'm honest. I expected to see the two of them arrested and charged within hours. But it hasn't happened yet.

I rang Alice McCann, the garda who took my statement. She said that the file was gone to the DPP and that these things take time.

I said there'd been enough delays in this case and that I expected better. She said they'd been promised a quick turn-around on a decision. She said she couldn't say any more to me about it for the moment.

I didn't particularly like the way she spoke to me but maybe she's under stress. She seemed shocked that day when I told her Detective Inspector Calum Pierce's name. I suppose all guards stick together. That might have been it.

Although I don't know. Because when I rang her back again to ask if my written statement would be enough, or if I'd have to go into the witness box, she said she'd come to see me straight away.

She did, too. Herself and Detective Sergeant O'Riordan came to visit me at my home. The sergeant did most of the talking. Explained the procedure, all that. She was very thorough. Very clear. She said that if the DPP approves charges against Campbell and Pierce – she gave neither of them their Christian names and she didn't give Pierce his rank either – my evidence will be vital.

She said that unless they plead guilty, I'll *certainly* have to appear in court. She told me that the guards would help.

They'd collect me and take me in a back door of the court-house if I wanted.

I said there was no need for that: I'd make my own way there and I'd use the front door. She said that was fine. Whatever I'm most comfortable with.

Alice McCann didn't say much but, as she was leaving, she shook my hand, less of a shake, mind you, than a hold. That was it, yes, she held onto my hand. Not for very long. A little. She said, 'Thank you for coming forward, Patricia.'

She seemed emotional and, just for a second, she reminded me of Donna. Only slightly, of course. There's nobody like Donna, really. She was a one-off.

105

SADIE COMES INTO THE GENERAL OFFICE AND makes an announcement: 'Word back from the DPP.'

Fogarty asks, 'What is it?'

'I'll tell you as soon as I know. Meeting in the super's office now.'

Waiting for her to return, someone's ordered pizza, and normally I'd be right in there.

Not tonight. I stare at my screen, clicking in and out of the case documents, hardly able to read them any more, hoping something might leap out at me.

I'm so deep in thought that I miss the moment Sadie walks into the general office, followed by Feeney. What alerts me is the silence, the change in atmosphere. I turn and hear her say the words we've all been waiting for.

'Well done, everyone. We have enough for one count of conspiracy to pervert the course of justice against Martin Campbell.' She pauses for effect. 'And one count of conspiracy to pervert the course of justice and *two* counts of murder against Calum Pierce.'

A roar goes up from the others as I sit in stunned silence. I only realise I'm crying when Siobhan O'Sullivan runs across the room to me holding a box of Kleenex.

106

I'M WATCHING FROM ACROSS THE STREET WHEN, at 6.30 a.m. the next day, Calum Pierce, my double-murderer ex-boyfriend, is arrested at the Phibsboro apartment we used to share.

It's my first time seeing the place since I moved out. It doesn't feel like home any more. In truth, it never did. I was living inside a stage set, acting a role assigned for me by someone else. At the time, it didn't always feel bad to me, but it was bad, and it was fake, and it was all wrong.

Calum is formally arrested by DI Shane Feeney, accompanied by DS Sadie O'Riordan. They don't have to ring the bell, or wait for him to put on clothes because, somehow, he's found out what's coming. He's standing inside the glass door of the four-storey red-brick block, emerging as soon as the car stops. He's carrying a suit bag and a packed O'Neills holdall, signalling that he knows he won't be coming home tonight. That he's prepared.

He makes no reply to the words spoken by Sadie. His mouth is set in a straight line. He glances up at the balcony before getting into the car and I see her leaning over the railing. The girlfriend. Another young woman with straight blonde hair.

Can't say the boy doesn't have a type. He might have made a mistake with this one, though. She's not shedding any tears. She's not giving off 'Stand By Your Man' vibes.

They could take him to a station somewhere in Dublin, but they don't. Despite the limited time available for questioning, because Dublin is home turf for him, the place he's spent his entire professional career, they bring him all the way to Cork. To Coughlan's Quay.

I'm standing near the door between Bugsy and Fogarty as Calum's brought in from the car park. He looks through me as if I'm not there.

But I am.

107

CALUM KILLED GARRY IN COLD BLOOD BY FAKING
a heroin overdose. But he should have put him in the river. He
didn't, and that was a mistake. Sentiment, or something else.
We may never know the reason, because he's saying nothing.

Except once. In reply to the charge of murdering Garry
McCarthy at the Lee Fields in November 2023, he says, 'You'll
never prove it because it's all lies.'

And a second time, after he's charged with the murder of
Donna Hannigan in the early hours of Good Friday 1999, at
the former Bertie Allen's pub, Barrack Street, Cork, he replies,
'I've been set up. I'm an innocent man.'

Conflict of interest doesn't even begin to describe the reason
I've played no part in Calum's interrogation and I'm fine with
that. I don't want to supply arms for his defence.

But I'm there for his charging and his first District Court
appearance. I see it as it happens and I hear what he says.

Calum looks as handsome and as strong as ever, even acknowl-
edges me with one of his big-bad-wolf smiles. He wipes it as
soon as he walks past and replaces it with a look of confusion
and hurt because there are cameras by the station steps.

In a dark blue suit and a gleaming, slightly rumpled white

shirt, although he doesn't open his mouth, visually he's saying, This is a mistake.

He's saying, No way this man is guilty.

If he's convicted, he faces two life sentences and, as a soon-to-be-former garda inspector, he'll serve hard time, much of it in isolation or protective custody. His lawyer makes a statement on his behalf, says his client will fight the charges every step of the way. I expected nothing else.

Martin Campbell could have been charged with Donna's murder – joint enterprise, accessory after the fact – but in unofficial recognition of his cooperation with the prosecution, he gets away lightly. When charged, he replies, 'Guilty.' He goes forward on a signed plea to the Circuit Criminal Court. He'll get jail time, but unlike the woman he helped to bury and allowed to rot beneath the floor of Bertie Allen's pub, he'll have a life afterwards.

She's still in the shadows, Donna, neglected, like she's always been. Some so-called friends have come forward. People she shared the apartment with in Ibiza. Women she went to school with. A long-lost auntie. A few cousins. Where were they when Donna was alive? When she needed them? When she went missing? They make me sick.

Even Patricia – even though she was the crucial witness who gave us Calum – I can't forgive. Even though she tried the hardest. Even though she can't forgive herself.

The cousins insist on getting Donna's body back for a funeral and burial in Manchester. Sadie and Feeney fly over to represent An Garda Síochána at the service.

That same morning, I visit St Fin Barre's Cathedral, the nearest church to Sir Henry's, only a few minutes' walk from Bertie Allen's. I choose it because it's somewhere Donna must have known, from the outside at least. There's an admission charge for tourists but, if you tell the attendant you're a local and that you want to pray, it's free. I pay the fee.

The neo-Gothic cathedral was built in the second half of the nineteenth century, but it's the eleventh church on the site. During the construction, they found thousands of skulls and full skeletons, now reburied under the floor and around the grounds. For fourteen centuries, since St Finbarr's first monastery and school from which the city grew, Corkonians have been interred here. This beautiful place is also a mass grave.

I walk up the aisle to the side chapel on the right of the main altar, the brightest part of the church. Yet, even here, dozens of bodies lie silently beneath the decorative tiles to the front of the choir.

I take a white candle, light it from another, and place it in the top ring of the tiered brass candelabra. I sit for a time in the front pew and watch it burn.

108

IN THE EVENING, I GO TO MY PARENTS' HOUSE
for a family dinner. We're all there, squashed in. Mum and Dad
and the four of us, Billy, Kieran, Marian and me, and spouses,
seven grandchildren and two dogs. It's chaos.

Around nine o'clock my mother produces her legendary
home-made chocolate fudge cake from the press and my name
is written on it in white icing.

'It's not my birthday,' I say.

'No,' she says, 'but it's your cake. To show how proud we
are of you.'

Dad says, 'No harm to remind you every now and again.'

'It's not over till it's over,' I say. 'Calum hasn't been convicted
yet.'

'It's all but over,' my sister Marian says, 'he's guilty as sin.
Enjoy the win.'

Then my ten-year-old nephew Jack asks, 'If it's *her* cake, does
that mean *we* can't have any?' and the conversation moves on
and no one notices that I've stopped talking.

ONE YEAR LATER

109

MY SISTER WAS RIGHT. CALUM WAS CONVICTED.
He's in prison, serving two life sentences. I should be enjoying
the win, like my sister said. But, as it's always been with Calum
and me, it's more complicated than that.

I'm in the cemetery on Glasheen Road, beside Garry's grave.
I didn't bring flowers but there's no need. It's well tended: a
pot of trailing ivy mixed with white cyclamen, a jug of red
carnations. Beneath the gravel, the earth's sunken and hollowed,
but his name's not yet etched on the headstone beneath his
father's. Most people do it before the first anniversary. The
McCarthys probably wanted to wait until after the trial. Until
after the publicity had died down.

Garry didn't kill Donna Hannigan but he was as guilty as
Calum Pierce and Martin Campbell of concealing her death.
He dug the grave with the other two, helped put her in the
earth. He regretted what he'd done. Numbed himself with
drugs. Tried to kill the pain and quench the guilt. When he
was clean, he tried to make amends and paid the ultimate
price.

But I'm not here to talk to Garry about Donna. He knows
that story of old.

I'm here to tell him a story that no one else knows. To tell it to myself too.

No. Wrong. I'm here to admit to myself what really happened to me.

And I'm here with Garry because I think he'd understand how your life can take a turn you didn't expect.

How you can half live for years and years in a kind of twilight.

110

2002. THE SUNDAY OF THE JUNE BANK HOLIDAY.
Fifteen years old. Sixteen in July. I'm grown-up, or that's what
I think. Dad's away – gone to a hurling match in Thurles – and
my older brothers and sister are hanging out with friends so it's
just me and Mum at home in Ballyvolane.

My Junior Cert is starting the week after next and it's baking
hot and sunny this whole weekend. Because that's the rule: the
best days of summer are always before the schools break up and
after they go back in September.

I'm in the garden, lying on a scratchy red and green tartan
rug surrounded by books and folders and highlighter pens in
various colours, which is almost the same as studying. Really,
I'm sunbathing and the heady scent of Ambre Solaire Factor 2
and the little trickle of salty sweat on my upper lip transport
me. I'm not in Ballyvolane. I'm in California. Spain, at the *very*
least. The sun's lightened my hair, helped by lemon juice and
Sun In, and I'm wearing sunglasses and denim cut-off ultra-short
shorts and a white cotton T-shirt that I've tied in a knot so that
my belly gets the sun. I'm more into Kylie now – 'Spinning
Around', 'Can't Get You Out Of My Head' – but I haven't
forgotten Britney and I never will so I'm going retro, wearing

my hair in bunches like her in the 'Baby One More Time' video from three years ago.

It's not Spain, though. It's Cork, and when the sun hides behind a cloud it's cold all of a sudden. It's late afternoon and the heat is gone from the day. I gather up my stuff and ramble into the kitchen.

The very same kitchen I'll meet Calum in twenty-one years later, with some of the same pictures and photos on the walls, but in 2002 the floor is covered with blue and cream vinyl that looks like tiles and the cupboards are still the original maple before Dad went at them in a post-retirement painting project that worked out a lot better than anyone expected.

My mother's by the sink. She could as easily be in the front room correcting a stack of summer tests, and it will be better for me and my future life if she is, but no. She says, 'You haven't done one solitary iota all weekend.'

'I've been working quite hard, if you must know. Even though, like, everyone says the Junior Cert is a complete joke at this stage, but I *have* been working actually.'

'No, you haven't. You're bone idle, Alice. You've got great ability but you have to apply yourself. Look, I don't want to sound like a broken record, I'm just—'

'Literally *no* one plays records. Haven't you heard of CDs? Tapes, even?'

'Oh, for God's sake,' my mother says, 'take these down to Pierces'.'

She thrusts a collection of plastic containers at me. She and Peggy Pierce, Calum's mother, spend their time passing extras and leftovers between them.

'I'm always back and forth with Tupperware. There should be a conveyor-belt.'

'You're it,' Mum says. 'Now get going. I've tons more of these exams to get through. And you can make your own supper. There's loads in the fridge.'

If I stay longer in the garden, Mum misses me coming in and doesn't send me to Pierces' and maybe I study for a while in my room and maybe I end up going to college and becoming a teacher, like I've imagined (for three reasons: June, July and August). Maybe I never join the guards. But that's not what happens.

111

THE PIERCE HOUSE IS ANOTHER BUNGALOW, FIVE
doors down from ours, same layout, with a porch and kitchen
at the back. I've been going there with my mother since I was
a small child. Nescafé and chocolate digestives for the adults,
fun-size Milky Ways and banishment to the TV room for me.

Calum was never at home. Distant and fascinating, he was
funding his way through college – construction engineering –
by working on building sites. He was paying rent – dead money,
according to my dad – and sharing a house with a few other
guys, ne'er-do-wells, Dad said. Then Calum surprised everyone
by joining the guards. He was never *ever* home after that.

He's home today. I come into the kitchen, like always, through
the back door. He's there, by the open fridge, four beer cans
hanging from a finger by those plastic rings that kill seabirds.
He's wearing a loose T-shirt and board shorts. His feet are bare
and he's sunburned. He's been in the back garden for the afternoon too, except he's been drinking beer. His eyes are glassy.
He smiles lazily when he sees me. 'Hello you,' he says, 'Alice,
right? You've grown up, haven't you?'

He's not slurring his words. He's not *that* drunk.

'Em, hi, Calum, is your mum home?'

'She's gone out for the night with the oul' lad. I was supposed to go back to Dublin today but I'm here minding Fifi. She's not been too well so they didn't want to leave her on her own.'

Fifi's the Jack Russell. We're about the same age in human years but in dog years Fifi's ancient. She sleeps a lot of the time and doesn't bark half as much as she used to.

'She's a good dog. I hope she's okay.'

'Me too,' he says. 'She's fine, though, don't worry.' He smiles again.

'I came to give you these. Your mum, I mean. My mum sent me up.'

I've been holding the Tupperware in front of my chest but when I hold it out to him I see him looking down at my breasts and my belly and my thighs. He takes the containers and puts them on the counter.

When he looks at me again, it's as if he's never seen me before, though he's known me since I was a baby. His mouth opens slightly. His teeth are very white.

'You remind me of someone,' he says.

He locks eyes with me and something passes between us and it's like we're playing statues because we don't talk or move for ages.

He breaks the silence. 'Do you want one?' He holds out a can to me.

'Thanks.'

He opens it for me and I think, What a gentleman.

We stand for a while saying nothing but he's looking at me and I'm looking at him. I take a slug from the can. I've had beer before because, like, hello, it's 2002, and I have older brothers, but I don't like it much and this is a tall can. It's huge and I'll never finish it. I start to feel stressed but it doesn't matter. I don't even get down halfway when he touches my arm and it's like an electric shock.

I must be shivering because the next thing he says is, 'Are you cold? Do you want a sweatshirt? A hoodie?'

I say nothing.

'I could give you something to wear. You could pick it. In my bedroom. If you like.'

Every day of every year after this I'll think of a dozen different replies and wonder why I didn't give them. In the here and now what I say is, 'Yeah.'

He takes my left hand with his right and walks ahead of me down the hall.

112

MAN UNITED POSTERS ON THE WALL. A MAN UNITED
duvet cover on the single bed. It's a little boy's room. Except
he's thirty. He shuts the door behind me and doesn't turn on
a light because there's no need. It's still bright. Will be for
hours yet.

'Time warp,' he says, 'I haven't lived here for years.'

He kisses me on the lips – gently – but he's drunker than I
realised because he says something strange, something I only
understand twenty-one years later.

He says, 'I've missed you so much.'

Then his tongue is in my mouth and his hands are in my hair
and up and down my back and on my bottom and I'm kissing
him too and his hands creep up beneath my shorts and that's a
surprise and my buttocks clench and I pull away and he does
too. There's a tiny space between us where there was none. It
feels like the Grand Canyon. He looks down at me for ages and
his hands are back in my hair, rubbing it, smoothing it down.

'You look good blonde,' he says.

'Thanks,' I say.

'Can we lie on the bed?' he asks.

I don't say anything but something in my face must make

him think I've said yes because he says, 'You'd like that, wouldn't you?'

And maybe I would, so I say, 'Yes.'

He pulls his T-shirt over his head and he's standing there, his shorts low on his hips, muscles defined, like a footballer or a movie star, a line of hair running down from his belly button. I reach out and put my hand flat against his chest. He smiles.

'You now,' he says, 'if you want. Only if you want.'

I unknot my T-shirt and pull it over my head. I've got a new white bra on underneath it. He pings one of the bra straps.

'Can I?'

I nod because there's weird stuff happening in my body and I'm not sure if I can talk any more.

He unhooks the bra and slides the straps down over my arms. 'Oh,' he says, 'you're so beautiful.'

He leads me to the bed and we lie on top of the Man United cover looking into each other's eyes and it's romantic and kind of scary and how did we get here so fast but this is probably normal, right?

He says, 'You're so hot,' and he slides off his board shorts so that he's just wearing boxers.

'You next,' he says, 'if you want to.'

I want to but my knickers are old and grey and they don't match my bra. I shake my head.

'That's okay,' he says, and he kisses me again but harder, and if I thought he was passionate before, I was wrong because this is it. His mouth on mine, and him grinding himself against me, touching me all over, through the denim even, and his fingers working their way around the edges and all the way inside. But my shorts stay on the whole time so it's not sex and loads of girls in my class have done way more than this. Anyway, my entire body is melting and aching and I'm totally weak for him.

He's weak for me too. I know it because I feel a wetness against my leg and he says, 'Now look what you made me do,' and he rolls onto his back and he's breathless and for a moment I think he's crying but he mustn't be because he reaches for a towel from the radiator and wipes himself down and dries me too. We lie there for a long time and I'm beside him but it's as if he's somewhere else. I'm looking at him but he's staring at the ceiling. In the distance there's a hum of traffic. A few gardens over, Noel Donnelly is practising the guitar, stop, start, repeat, never finishing a song. It's still bright but there's a radio alarm clock beside the bed and when I look it's nearly seven o'clock.

He sees me looking. 'Do you need to get home?'

'I guess.'

I sit up and he raises himself onto an elbow and turns to face me. 'Is that the first time you've done anything like that?'

'Yes.'

'So now you know what it's like between a man and a woman but other people mightn't see it like that. You mustn't tell anyone. It has to be our secret memory, right?'

'I know that,' I say.

'Of course you do.' He sits up fully and takes my head in his hands, holds it and kisses me softly for a bit until he pulls away again. He looks downcast. 'I'm going back to Dublin tomorrow and I wish I could stay but I can't and there's something I have to tell you and do you promise you won't get mad?'

'I promise.'

'I've got a girlfriend up there. For the last two years. I work with her. And I'm moving jobs. I'm going to be a detective and

I'm planning on stepping up to DS as soon as I can after that. I shouldn't have done this. It was wrong. In fairness, you tempted me. You did, don't deny it, I *saw* the way you were looking at me, and you're beautiful. But I should've been stronger. I'm sorry.'

He starts crying and keeps saying, 'Sorry,' over and over again and I tell him it's okay, really it is, and it's as if I'm the grown-up, smoothing his hair, wiping his tears away.

More kisses after that and more touching but he looks miserable and when he asks again if he can take off my shorts I don't say no. I don't say yes either, but I undo the top button. He undoes the rest and slides the shorts down over my hips, grey knickers at the same time, so I needn't have worried, and then he's by the side of the bed, naked and perfect, rooting in his gear bag. He puts on a condom – so that's how you do it – and I shimmy the shorts as far as my ankles and kick them off, and before I know it he's on top of me and there's pain but it's what I wanted and anyway it's over fast and next thing we're saying goodbye at the back door.

He says, 'We'll always be friends after this, won't we?'

'Always,' I say.

'You're a good girl.'

He gives me a little wave but no goodbye kiss. He goes back inside and shuts the door, slams it almost, but maybe a breeze caught it. I wait on my own for a bit at the back of the house, and it's like a sinkhole has opened up inside me.

I'm hoping he'll run after me and kiss me one more time but he doesn't. I hear the shower. I move slowly, then stand outside the bathroom as the window fogs up. I hear him singing 'I Feel Love' and I think about how he was crying a few minutes ago and how he seems happy again and it must be because of me and what we did. That's good, I suppose. The shower stops and I see the shape of him inside the bubble glass of the window and his hand reaching up to open it but he doesn't see me.

I go straight to my room when I get home. I think about taking off my clothes and putting them in the wash basket but, instead, I lie on the bed. I fall asleep and when I wake up it's fully dark. For a second I think he's in the bedroom with me but it's just his smell.

113

THE MONTHS AND YEARS BLEED INTO EACH OTHER.
I finish school and, because I'm bone idle, I get a crap Leaving
Cert compared to everyone else in the family but not too bad
in real-world terms.

I think about joining the guards, and it's my idea to ask Mum
to talk to Mrs Pierce about it and she's delighted to arrange for
Calum to drop into our house for a chat the next time he's
home. Which is way sooner than I expected. I guess he was
coming down anyway.

It feels weird at first, us together on the sofa in our sitting
room, and the door ajar. We know that my mum and his mum
are listening but they can't see us. It's like we're in a world of
our own as he tells me that, seriously, like, it's a tough job and
he doesn't recommend it, and that he's not being sexist or
anything but, the truth is, it's tougher for girls.

But all the time he's saying that, he's smiling at me and,
just once, he reaches across and traces a line with his index
finger down the centre of my face as far as my lips. He rubs
his finger over them, like a lipstick, and he sticks the finger
in my mouth and, for a second or two, I don't know what
to do so I sort of lick it. He smiles a really big smile then

and he takes the finger out and brings it to his own lips and does the exact same.

And that lets me know that he hasn't forgotten our secret memory, and it should make me happy, and it does and all, but not as happy as I'd thought it would because what good is a memory?

Calum talks and talks about the bad things that happen on the job and I'm not listening because my stomach is doing dough-nuts. After a while he says that if I want to join, I should, and that he'll help me, and that if I ever need advice I should ask his mum Peggy and that she'll make contact with him for me. He'll call me anytime, he says, because we'll always be old friends. He looks at me as he says that and it's like he can see through to my soul.

When he stands up, I stand up too. He puts his arms around me and gives me a squeeze and he puts his nose against my hair and breathes in my shampoo and he nuzzles and kisses me on the top of my head and his hand creeps up and accidentally on purpose grazes the side of my breast and I'm fizzing and melting again and I feel all right for the first time in a long time. Better than all right.

When we go out to the kitchen, Calum says, 'I think her mind's made up. She's a girl who knows what she wants. She definitely does.'

I don't expect him to say that and I feel like my mind wasn't *totally* made up about applying for the guards but he sneaks me a sly glance, and I can tell he's not talking about the guards and that he's trying not to laugh, and then I'm the same, and it's just brilliant because we're the ones who really know what's going on.

But my mum stares at him daggers and my dad's there too and he just seems confused and Peggy Pierce is the only one of the three parents who looks happy because she's so proud. Her Calum's a detective sergeant and he knows what he's talking about and he's married to a lovely girl and her first grandchild is on the way.

You know the rest. I join An Garda Síochána and I like it because there's mile-a-minute stuff going on the whole time and no time to think. I go for detective and, naturally, I end up working with Calum in the GNBCI and soon he's an inspector and I'm his protégée. He's nice to me no matter what, and always strictly professional, as you'd expect. A comforting arm around my shoulders every now and again, a hand in the small of my back, a hug – long and full and close – when there's no one to see us and misinterpret what's going on. Slim pickings compared to what I think I want from him, but enough to keep me sweet.

Absolutely nothing happens until after his wife dumps him without so much as a by-your-leave; and she's a member too and there are rumours about her threatening a barring order for psychological and emotional abuse unless he moves out voluntarily, which he does because it's better for the kids, obviously; and I don't listen to the he-said-she-said because I've known him forever and we're old friends.

He's free and single again except now we're workmates and, after a while, he starts looking at me like he did that sunny June Sunday. And I go towards the danger, because it doesn't feel like danger. It feels like love. Even after he stops being nice.

Because he twisted something inside me that sunny June Sunday, though it takes me a long time to see it, and even longer to come to terms with it.

To forgive myself for being so bored and so stupid and so willing. So fifteen.

114

CALUM'S APPEALING. STILL PLEADING HIS
innocence, using every technical argument he can think of. He's
claiming the convictions are unsafe. That Martin Campbell's
accomplice evidence was given too much weight by the trial
judge in her charge. That Campbell lied through his teeth to
get himself off the hook. That the burner-phone records should
never have been put before the jury. That there was insufficient
proof that the phones were his and, even if they were, there
was a breach of his right to privacy in the way the records were
disclosed.

His good looks and charm are a help. He's gathering quite
the following. A few naive journalists doing jailhouse inter-
views. Legions of dopey female fans active on social media.
There's even a time-wasting we'll-never-really-know ten-
episode podcast in the making. I've heard they're calling it *The
Seventh Body*, that they've interviewed Artur Lewandowski and
Johnny McDonagh, the digger driver, and a few more of the
construction workers. They went to Ray Grant's house as well.
Unsurprisingly, he told them to fuck off.

They talked to the forensic archaeologist Dr Eileen O'Hara
too. She said they called the first six skeletons 'loose ends', and

wanted to know exactly who they were. She told them to look up the excavation report online and never to contact her again.

But she told me that the six men were fighters, young and fit mostly, cut down in their prime, and that scientific tests have carbon-dated them to some time between the 1400s and the 1600s. She says that no one knows their names, or which battle they died in, and it's unlikely that anyone ever will.

Calum's parents, Peggy and Ralph, sold their house in Ballyvolane and moved to Dublin to be nearer to Calum, and to be more anonymous, because there's nowhere to hide in Cork. They're living in Calum's flat in Phibsboro – his girlfriend packed and left the same day he was charged. One of the other neighbours told Mum they'd heard that the Pierces paid off the mortgage on the apartment with the money they got from the sale of Ballyvolane.

I've heard that Peggy attends mass daily in St Peter's Church. She talks regularly to the press about how *some* people in the guards were out to get her son. She never mentions me by name. Ralph has her warned, I reckon. Or Calum.

It's all white noise, as far as I'm concerned, and whether Calum's appeal succeeds or not, I know he did it, and he knows I know. He hasn't reached out to me, and he never will. What he did to me when I was fifteen was a crime. You can't consent to sex if you're under seventeen. I didn't know that at the time, but I've known it for decades, since soon after I joined the guards, even though it took longer for me to truly see it for what it was.

I've thought about making a formal complaint about what he did to me but I've decided against it. He's locked up already and, even if I managed to secure a conviction, he might only get a concurrent sentence, no time added on. I don't want to put myself through a trial because it would be a step back for me into his orbit.

It's enough for me to know that I did right by Donna and Garry. And that I did right by myself. I feel free of Calum now, as free as I'll ever be. I don't know if what people call closure even exists. I just know that, these days, I think less about the past and more about the present and the future.

I leave the graveyard behind and walk into the remainder of the afternoon and tonight and tomorrow and all the days after that.

Author's Note

IN OCTOBER 2021, THE SKELETAL REMAINS OF SIX
men were found under the floorboards of the former 'Nancy
Spain's' pub on Barrack Street in Cork. The pub had been closed
for years and was being redeveloped as part of a Cork City
Council housing scheme. Quickly, the remains were deemed to
be of archaeological interest only.

But not to me. I walk up and down Barrack Street every
day and I badly wanted to know what was going on behind the
hoardings. I also began to imagine another body.

From those idle morning and evening musings, this book
was born, although I've made the site bigger, and increased the
number of apartments. I've also made it a privately run development rather than a council one, and I've swapped around the
order in which the bodies were discovered, made the finds more
recent, and invented an entirely different pub called Bertie
Allen's, which did not and does not exist.

I've taken liberties with the excavation because I made a
decision early on not to talk to anyone directly involved. I
relied instead on publicly available resources, primarily the
Irish Examiner and excavations.ie. Archaeologically, I was

guided by the amazing Niamh McCullough, forensic archae-ologist, and by Mick Monk, who has been giving me ad hoc archaeology tutorials for years. Former state pathologist and superwoman turned author Marie Cassidy was incredibly kind; and I also benefited enormously from the generous assistance of garda consultant and author Casey King. On the legal side, I was aided and abetted by Jane Hyland, Ronan Barnes and Elizabeth O'Connell, but all mistakes are mine, and might even be deliberate.

And now to Sir Henry's nightclub. This is a work of fiction, but Henry's *was* the home of house music in Ireland and there *was* an extraordinary club called Sweat. Its importance to the cultural life of Cork and to the people who went there is hard to overstate. Sweat ended in 2001 and Henry's closed in 2003 and was demolished. Where it stood remains a vacant site. As I say in the book, it's only a five minute walk from where the six bodies were found. And so, as I began thinking about a seventh body on Barrack Street, geography led me to Sir Henry's and I formed an imaginary link between the two places.

As more than one character in *The Seventh Body* says, everyone over forty in Cork has been to Sir Henry's, me included. In truth, I didn't go there much – I was a City Limits and DJ Mike Darcy (now of The Friary) regular, like Alice's brother Billy (sadly, without his big house and money). My Sir Henry's research includes:-

a) Ray Scannell's wonderfully evocative radio play *Deep* (directed by Tom Creed).
b) *Sir Henry's 120 bpm* (documentary, a Vinyl film, by Keith O'Shea).

c) DJ Stevie G's *Stevie Wonder[s]* podcast episode with adored DJs Greg Dowling and Shane Johnson (*Fish Go Deep*) (Stevie G is equally adored, obviously).

d) Chats with event promoter and repository of music lore Joe Kelly of *The Good Room* and *Live at St. Luke's*.

e) More chats with the brilliant Des O'Driscoll of the *Irish Examiner* (and I read Des's excellent 2021 thirtieth anniversary of Sweat piece for the *Irish Examiner*).

f) Hugely enjoyable nineties fashion chats with Joan Hickson, costume designer and textile artist.

g) Thanks also to Cass Darcy-Lane of St Fin Barre's Cathedral – I called in one day to check where Alice would light a candle and he gave me an amazingly helpful and entertaining tour.

h) Like Alice and Garry, I went to the City Library on the Grand Parade. Thanks to all the library staff for their kindness and friendship.

i) And, in 1995, I saw a Corcadorca Theatre Company production of *A Clockwork Orange* by Anthony Burgess in Sir Henry's, directed superbly by Pat Kiernan. Maybe *The Seventh Body* really began that unforgettable night.

Acknowledgements

The Seventh Body would not exist without the encouragement and expertise of my agent Luigi Bonomi, and Alison Bonomi, and Amanda Preston and all at LBA; and my editors Ciara Doorley at Hachette Ireland and Lucy Stewart at Hodder & Stoughton; and Joanna Smyth, Elaine Egan, Ruth Shern, Stephen Riordan, Jim Binchy and all at Hachette Ireland; and Phoebe Morgan, Charlea Charlton and Rachel Southey at Hodder & Stoughton; and David Shelley at Hachette UK. Thanks also to copyeditor Hazel Orme, proofreader Aonghus Meaney, cover designer Lisa Brewster and Plunkett PR.

Thanks to Catherine Ryan Howard for so much (including the Sir Henry's wet walls detail) and to Claire Connolly, Christine Moore, Daniel Snihur, Diarmaid Falvey, Dyane Hanrahan, Eimear O'Herlihy, Fin Flynn, Ger Kenneally, Jean Kearney, John Breen, Kieran O'Connor, Lynn Sheehan, Marguerite Phillips, Mary Jones, Miriam O'Brien, Nick Daly, Paul O'Donovan, Peter Byrne, Rachel O'Toole and Tadhg Coakley who supported, advised and/or amused at critical moments.

Thanks to you dearest reader and seven times the thanks if you take the time to write an online review. Thanks to my friends and colleagues in Finbarr Murphy Solicitors; and thanks also to the legal community in Cork and beyond for your unstinting support.

Thanks to all media folk, and to journalists, editors, reviewers and bloggers, with special thanks to Mairead Hearne; to book club members; to libraries and librarians everywhere especially Cork City and County Libraries, and Kilkenny and Waterford County Libraries; to all event organisers and festivals including Cork World Book Festival, Crosstown Drift and The Good Room, Spike Island Literary Festival (and Michelle Dunne), Kinsale Words by Water, Murder One, UCC Schools of English and Law and Waterstones Cork. Many thanks to all bookshops and booksellers with particular thanks to the people who arrange the window displays. Special thanks to much-loved and much-missed Eibhear Walshe for his kindness to me over the years.

Thanks to the wonderful and inspiring company of authors who have been so good to me. Particular thanks to the ever-growing band of Cork-based writers.

Thanks to my friends for putting up with my writing-related unavailability; thanks to everyone I thanked in my earlier books, because I wouldn't be here without you; and thanks to all those I've forgotten to thank either now or previously.

Finally, my eternal gratitude and love to my mother Breda Kirwan, my late father Michael, to Marcia and Neil; to Michael, Molly and Elizabeth; and to Nicola and Rob to whom this book is dedicated.

And one last reminder that this is a work of fiction and that, except in the case of historical fact, any resemblance to anyone living or dead is entirely coincidental.

Catherine Kirwan